1/2

OPERATION REMISSION

"Jake is angry. He's entitled. The U.S. government has killed him and half a million other Americans, by deliberately exposing them to atomic radiation. . . . Dying of leukemia, but more alive than he has ever been, the hero of Paul Johnson's adventure novel wanders through America's 'hidden places,' saying goodbye and looking for allies, among old lovers and Movement comrades, in a bold scheme to monkey wrench the government's slow-motion conspiracy of genocide. *Operation Remission* is the book Jack Kerouac might have written if he'd had active politics, the story Norman Mailer missed because the murder is social not personal. Paul Johnson's tender, fast-moving story is a radical page turner."   — Clancy Sigal

ALSO BY PAUL JOHNSON
Killing the Blues

OPERATION
REMISSION

PAUL
JOHNSON

NEFYN & SHAW • DELHI, NEW YORK

Published by Nefyn & Shaw, 19 Delaware Avenue, Delhi, New York 13753

Book design by Kip Shaw

Manufactured in the United States of America

The quotations on the part title pages are reprinted from the following
sources: Stephen Jay Gould, "This View of Life," Natural History, page 29,
January 1991, reprinted by permission of Stephen Jay Gould; Per Bak and
Kan Chen, "Self-Organized Criticality," Scientific American, page 46,
January 1991, reprinted by permission of Scientific American, Inc.; Wallace
Stevens, "Extracts from Addresses to the Academy of Fine Ideas," from
The Collected Poems of Wallace Stevens by Wallace Stevens, Copyright
1942 by Wallace Stevens, reprinted by permission of Alfred A. Knopf, Inc.

ISBN 0-9637974-3-3

It would take half these pages to thank all the people
whose help with this tale has been unique and essential.
And any such list would necessarily include nearly everyone
I've ever called a friend. So I won't even try—
but once again, you all know who you are.

If I named three living persons only (I'm going to), they'd have to be
Kip Shaw, Jack Hayward, and Bob Calese, who've stuck
with me on this one from the bleakest of beginnings
until—but as R. Crumb put it, long ago, it's never quite
The End, for These Guys. . . .

Three of the dead demand mention. I can't recall and now
there's no way left of learning if they more than recognized
each other's names, but it's a good bet they were in the same
loud room at the same time at least once during those
whiz-bang years of nonstop emergency dreams and
meetings. If ever found together, I'm sure all three
were on their feet within seconds, each shouting down
the others' rhetoric. But they shared a good deal besides
my admiration, consternation, commiseration, and friendship;
for starters, none suffered fools gladly,
fools in high places least of all.

Sid Hammer: 1926–1969
Gordon Christiansen: 1920–1978
Abbie Hoffman: 1937–1989

There's very little I'd like better than to know
what *they'd* think of what I'm up to here.

But any formal dedication has to be:

*To the millions of victims past and present
and to those many millions more to come
of all our modern madness
and to their executioners
because we are both*

I: CONTINGENCY

(10/12 – 11/5)

"Contingency is rich and fascinating; it embodies an
exquisite tension between the power of individuals
to modify history and the intelligible limits set by
laws of nature. The details of individual and species'
lives are not mere frills, without power to shape the
large-scale course of events, but particulars that
can alter entire futures, profoundly and forever."

—Stephen Jay Gould

1 : INTERSTATE

The morning of the twelfth of October that year dawned cloudless and cool from Bangor to Miami and stayed that way (except for brief showers in the northern Rockies) as sunrise swept across the continental United States. The calm, seasonably crisp day to follow would be a sweet surprise, after a parched but muggy summer.

Among the millions of human beings hurtling along the forty-four thousand miles of divided highway in the U.S. Interstate system that morning was a man whose driver's license gave his name as Wendell Jacobsen—but no one who knew him well enough to say more than hello would ever call him anything but Jake. Other vital statistics noted there included: eyes BL, height 6′2″, and birth date 3/13/37. The only *Restriction* typed in was *B*, meaning "Corrective Lenses," which Jake was duly wearing as he approached the low khaki mesas along I-40 east of San Jon, New Mexico, just as the sun popped over the Texas Panhandle receding to infinity behind him and set his rear-view mirror ablaze, even as the world all around him and up ahead, beyond the windshield, remained a purplish monochrome for what seemed like a full minute longer.

Through his old Ford stationwagon's surprisingly good built-in speakers, he was hearing Artur Schnabel's long-dead but digitally remastered fingers coaxing out the syncopation coiled inside the melody in the *Opus 111*: Beethoven's final work for piano, Jake remembered reading somewhere, not so much because of his failing health as because the composer was convinced he'd taken the instrument as far as it could go, musically.

If that was true, Jake thought, you were prodigiously mistaken, Ludwig: you staked out an awesome chunk of territory, but you never dreamed how far guys like Tatum, Monk, or Powell would ramble in that same direction, from right where you called it quits—and on that instant, as the Dixielandish riff finally strutted free of the staid Viennese format, a razzle-dazzle dawn overtook Jake and that whole murky, monochromatic world around him, suffusing everything with sunlight as improbably intense and orange as the reconstituted juice he'd gulped with his wake-up waffles and sausage back in Amarillo a little over an hour ago.

Soon his mind returned to fragments of discussions of *On the Road* in an American Lit course he'd taught for several years, and how he'd tried but almost certainly failed to convey why the America Kerouac and his buddies bopped back and forth across during the late Forties and early Fifties was in many ways as different from this one today as from all those other, earlier Americas that Bartram, Toqueville, Prescott, or Muir journeyed through: so much slower, so much more parochial, with almost all roads narrow, full of sharp curves, and only a single lane in each direction, inevitably leading you the full length of the main street of every city, town, and village along the route. No beltways around anywhere then, no cloverleaf exits or shield-shaped signs bearing an "I" followed by three digits. This meant, among other things, that you learned to pull over and catch three or four hours' rest if you happened to approach somewhere like Cleveland in the late afternoon. Otherwise you'd spend an equivalent amount of time creeping in first gear, bumper to bumper, from one traffic light to the next. . . .

Then he remembered how those cities, even the biggest, were all so much more distinct from each other, and how the dialect, diet, and what was later called lifestyle—even the morality of the people in them—had all seemed so much more *local*, peculiarly suited to each particular place. Television and these Interstates more than anything else had combined to alter that state of affairs irreversibly. . . .

That other, earlier America was the one Jake himself had experienced on his first trips across, in a maroon '37 Plymouth, a cream-colored driving-service Cadillac convertible, and that ill-fated two tone-gray '49 Ford coupe with the clutch that burned out in the middle of rush-hour Cleveland. It wasn't by car at all the very first time, though: it was being crammed into a beat-up old coal-burner along with hundreds of other crewcut, olive drab sardines, all the way from North Carolina, playing (and consistently losing) varieties of poker he'd never heard of before (or since), swapping giveaway Pall Malls for limp, disintegrating paperbacks, but mostly gaping through the greasy windows at what an incredibly sun-drenched, wide-open world it was out here, west of the Mississippi. California-bound, or so they'd all supposed, from there either to a cushy year's tour of duty in Japan or else to freeze their nuts off, "keeping the peace" along the 38th Parallel in Korea. But those bets were all off, when they'd suddenly been ordered to grab their gear and fall out on a dusty depot platform in Las Vegas, Nevada.

Jake steered his mind back to that endlessly unspooling gray concrete, much patched along this stretch with successive strips of macadam, thumping away hypnotically beneath his tires at seventy-odd miles per hour. These roadways were falling apart: hardly surprising, considering how old they were already, how much traffic they'd borne and continued to bear. The only thing holding them together nowadays was more and more of those asphalt Band-Aids. Everybody moaned about the oil they kept spilling into the oceans, Jake thought, but what about the billions of tons of this gunk criss-crossing every continent today, bubbling in the summer sun, befouling air, soil, and water table? Petroleum residue, that's precisely what it was—and who was ever going to clean up *that* "environmental hazard"?

Strange to remember how impossibly pristine and futuristic they'd once seemed . . . but when Jake focused at random on one of the scraps of recollection flitting around in his mind, he could hear his own voice from at least a quarter-century before, declaring that these Inter-states would probably be the only American artifact still discernible from the surface of the moon after the dust of World War III had settled. That was years, of course, before anyone had heard of Nuclear Winter, but both he and the friend he'd been riding with that faraway afternoon were aware of the direct connection of the Interstate system to the possiblity of nuclear war . . . it had to've been with Simon, Jake was sure, and somewhere in the Midwest . . . and Simon had made a big point of how the whole Interstate system had been funded originally with Defense Department money, with the preposterous stated purpose of swiftly evacuating urban areas in the event of a Soviet first strike.

And here they still were, enormous crumbling relics of classic Cold War mentality, as well as chief American symbol of one of the worst environmental hazards going—but a hazard generally considered unavoidable because, in the blink of a bureacratic eye while Jake was still in high school, the essentially adequate railway system that had been in place from the beginning of the century had been torn up for scrap and its rolling stock sold off to the Third World because it couldn't compete with all those new eighteen-wheelers, since *their* roadbeds were built and maintained for them by taxpayers.

"Costing an estimated *million* dollars per mile!" Jake could still hear Simon yelping indignantly. Surely that was only a fraction of the actual price; Jake had seen figures like fifty million a mile quoted on current expressway projects. But what an awesome figure a mere million had seemed, back then. . . .

❖

Jake may have belonged to a statistically infinitesimal minority, but he was not the only driver at 6:33 a.m. Mountain Daylight Savings Time who was reflecting on original motives for the Interstate system. Slightly more than four hundred miles almost due north, on the section of I-225 slicing south along the eastern edge of Denver to connect I-70 with I-25, a man in a lipstick-red Porsche was just about to add another reason to the one recalled by Jake. The license he had with him this morning said he was Orville Webster, a resident of Boulder, but it was only one of several in his possession, and most of the people who believed they knew him called him Gil, Gilberto, or Bert.

— It never dawned on any of those assholes, but they really built these marvelously accessible, wonderfully anonymous, coast-to-coast escape routes for folks like *me*! This life of mine is a fervid testimonial to these dear old I-Ways. It would've been not merely impossible but utterly inconceivable, without 'em. . . .

"Folks like me," though—all right, there weren't too many of *us* left, but aside from all the transcon truckers, truckstoppers, and Winnebago nomads, there was an entire subspecies who wouldn't otherwise exist: un- or only occasionally employed, technically homeless except for their rattletraps but generally with a little check of some sort appearing at a post office box somewhere to keep oil showing on the dipstick and a few spare gallons sloshing in the tank. They'd all learned to the minute how long you could safely camp in every rest area on the beltways around their favorite cities, and whether you could risk a basin bath or wash out your underwear in the rest rooms, and which local junkyards would let you strip your own parts.

He'd met entire tribes of such people, shared their six-pacs and fried pies and corn chips, spent weeks at a time, driven thousands of miles with some, on gas money cadged from better-heeled hitchhikers to visit the somebodies they always seemed to have, away off somewhere, who'd take them and any companions in for a week or two, no serious questions asked. He'd learned to feel safe in their rusted-out hulks, safer than almost anywhere else. Because hardly anything ever gets stopped on an Interstate, no matter how weird it might look, so long as it keeps moving with traffic and doesn't start passing everything in sight. . . .

But that wasn't Gil's life; it was only one of many possible, convenient ways he had of taking expedient, unscheduled vacations. His life was—like most, he guessed—nothing he'd ever planned on. He'd just lived it as fully as he could as it came galloping straight at him and, whenever given choices, he'd gone with whatever seemed the most interesting alternative. According to conventional wisdom, that was probably his biggest mistake. But for quite a while there, this life of his had certainly zipped right along, was mostly enjoyable, and challenging, and even looked, sometimes, as if it were going somewhere absolutely worth getting to.

Conventional wisdom also said, Crime Does Not Pay, and although that was clearly bullshit on more exalted levels, if you confined your definition to the small-scale, freelance, direct-action varieties, it was by and large the bitter truth. As a career, he'd found crime was a lot like the fine arts: an overcrowded field that paid piss-poorly considering the huge risks and inordinate amounts of initiative, perspicacity, capital, and plain old-fashioned hard work required. That was unless you hit it lucky very early, moved quickly on up to Big Shot status, and outlived your accumulated creditors.

But Gil seldom thought of what he did for a living as either crime or career—another serious mistake, and most likely why he'd remained a sometimes inspired but forever struggling amateur. Well, okay, he hadn't hit it early, but if the idea he'd traveled all the way up here yesterday to check out would only come together, it might more than make up for all of his near misses. He realized, though, that he was pushing things in calling it even as much as an idea at this stage; there were still so many essential pieces missing he couldn't begin to count 'em. . . .

Of course, "crime" wasn't what he'd thought he was getting into— they'd had lots of bigger, brighter words for it back then. Which brought him back around to where he always seemed to wind up: *I'm getting too goddamn old for all this crazy shit!*

But this was no time for introspection, because his life still had its moments, and right now should definitely be one. He'd driven Porsches before, but not in years, maybe decades, and this model was a sweetheart, he loved everything about it so far, including those Pro-Choice, Anti-Handgun, and Greenpeace stickers decorating the rear window, and the white poplin golfer's cap he'd discovered in a plastic bag beneath the driver's seat and immediately yanked down to his eyebrows.

Aside from a little blue Toyota headed in the opposite direction, there was no other traffic anywhere in sight at the moment, and he would've rejoiced in learning just how fast he could send that needle careening around to that smug "150" at the bottom of the dial. But he was getting on for that sort of thing as well; the requisite reflexes certainly weren't what they used to be. Then, too, there was Rafael, who could be rounding that bend back there behind him any minute now, and he didn't want to get the poor *pendejo* too uptight—

Whoa, I don't believe it!

but at the same time yes he did, he'd been waiting all these years for this to happen, and in precisely such a fashion: an entirely empty road all around only a splinter of a second ago—right?—but glance up again *now*, and the rear-view mirror's wall-to-wall cop car, gumballs twirling, siren shrieking. What could he do? Outrun 'em? Sure, no problem in this little mama, but there was also nofuckingwhere to run. He was on a goddamn bowling alley, all they had to do was hit the airwaves and every exit was gonna be sewn up tighter'n a termite's twat before he got anywhere near it. . . .

— So, do I meekly pull over, like they're motioning for me to do? Not only on hot wheels (probably not even reported yet, but no ID to show, either) but here I sit holding, both ways. Jesus, *why* didn't I leave the piece and the snort in the van? Because I never do, that's why. Apparently, I believe I'm Fucking God-Almighty. And why'd I have to swipe this silly toy in the first place? Because I'm a fucking kid playing fucking games! Because I was being just too fucking cute, as usual. We could've run up here in two bona-fides but no-o-o-o, it was more *environmentally responsible* to ride up with Rafael in the van and swipe a second vehicle on the spot. Can't believe I actually, seriously said that to myself, but I did, so help me. Can't believe any of this, including the shit-eating grin on my face—and now what? I'm stopped on the shoulder and so're the smokies, right behind me, and here comes one of 'em, and Christ, he's ten feet tall—and probably half my age.

Okay, viable options: for starters we can scratch the good ol' Jersey Highway Maneuver. There's no discernible advantage in blowing this guy away with his partner sitting back there on the honker already. No consolation, either, in the near-certain assumption that there wouldn't be a dozen people in the whole state of Colorado, outside law enforcement, who'd know what was meant by the phrase "Jersey Highway Maneuver," or recognize names like JoAnne Chesimard, Manning and Williams, the Sam Melville/Jonathan Jackson Unit: ancient fucking history, already. . . .

So what's that leave us? Nothing very brilliant comes immediately to mind, does it? Go limp like Rosenberg and Blunk? Who drew an infuckingcredible fifty-eight years apiece, remember, for nothing more than weapons possession. Well, okay, up-thrust fists and yelling stuff like *Long live the Armed Struggle!* inside the courtroom couldn't've helped much, but that was first-offense for both—while Gil's own record, as he knew very well, could be just as long as they felt like taking the trouble to make it. . . .

❖

There was at least one driver out there on the Interstates that morning to whom alternative means of transportation seemed like an excellent idea. Thirteen hundred miles east of Denver, Suzanne Klein's decrepit Malibu had finally dropped dead on I-475 along the western edge of Toledo, halfway between the Ohio Turnpike and Airport Highway exits. A drag, all right, but not to worry; she'd been through this drill before.

She managed to get it onto the shoulder before it seized up completely, and luckily her mechanic friend Pam had foretold the inevitable and helped her grind off the serial numbers on both body and block several weeks ago. Now Suzanne was down on her knees patiently searching through greasy layers of lint, crumbs, and Kleenex under the seats, then inside the trunk and glove compartment, for strayed envelopes and anything else that might possibly serve to connect her to this heap of superannuated plastic, glass, and rust. She'd neglected to do that the first time this happened to her, and three months later she got a towing and disposal bill from the State of Ohio for $287.39, which she had to pay or have her driver's license suspended.

That search thoroughly accomplished, she got out her Swiss Army knife, removed both plates, stuffed them into her rucksack, scraped the inspection sticker off the windshield, and without a backward glance stepped over the guard rail and slid on her heels and ass for thirty yards or more down the steep rubbish-strewn embankment. Then she had to scramble over monumental trash piles for nearly a block before she found a hole in the hurricane fence, but that let her out right beside a bus stop, and one came wheezing along before she'd even caught her breath.

Luck again, she had the right change in her fanny pack, and several seats near the front were empty.

—Hey, this is okay, she thought, as she slung herself onto the nearest seat and glanced around. Compared to the poor old Malibu, this contraption was clean, quiet, and comfortable. It cost almost twice as much as she remembered paying last time she'd used public transit, but then what didn't nowadays, and besides, she didn't have to drive it, park it, feed it gas and oil, keep up the insurance, or worry about what might wear out on it next. The sexy young Asian woman driver had even smiled at her when she'd requested a transfer—or had she only imagined that? In any case, Suzanne felt . . . disencumbered, that was the word. *De-albatrossed!* Years younger, too, feckless and unfettered.

—Call the cops and report the heap stolen as soon as I get home, she reminded herself, and try not to sound too happy about it. Call those leeches, too, and cancel the insurance—she might even get some money back. Whether she did or not, what a load off! Maybe she wouldn't let Pam or anyone else bestow another clunker on her for a while, try to get through the winter without wheels of her own. She could do it—what did she *really* need a car for? Not much, when you came right down to it. And the few times she really did, with what she'd be saving she could probably afford to take cabs. In any case, she ought to walk more: she could stand to lose a few pounds. . . .

❖

Nearly six hundred miles still farther east, where it was nearly nine o'clock Eastern Daylight Savings Time, John Meacham had taken advantage of the blessed break in the weather (and the presence of his visiting sister-in-law as a baby-sitter) to cycle from his home in the western Catskills to Oneonta, the nearest real town. Not by

Interstate—bikes, horses, pedestrians, and farm vehicles were for-
bidden—but he did have to pass the entrance and exit for I-88. And as
he pedaled along the shoulder between them, a tractor-trailer came
rolling down the off-ramp faster than it should've been going, in order
to make the traffic light at the next corner. When its rear wheels
clipped the turn onto the street, John went flying head first to avoid
being crushed beneath them, landing in a shallow stone-lined culvert
beyond the knee-high guard rail.

He came bounding out again in a matter of seconds on pure indignation, in time to see his oblivious assailant rounding the next bend,
headed for Route 28. A big sign on the dusty tailgate proclaimed self-
righteously: THIS VEHICLE PAID MORE THAN $10,000.00 IN ROAD-
USE TAXES LAST YEAR. Which didn't make John happier: he knew
very well that a five-axle, forty-ton rig like that one causes nearly as
much wear annually as ten thousand cars.

Then he became aware of the fact that both his forearms looked
like minute steaks, and so did his left shin from knee to ankle. Well, at
least he could be glad he'd spent the extra money on the very best
helmet available. His ears were still ringing from the impact, his eyes
streaming tears—but without that fancy fiberglass bonnet, he'd be
knocked unconscious now, if not killed outright.

His main worry, though, was the bike, which had followed its own
trajectory and landed a dozen feet farther along the cut. It wasn't his
bike; this ride had been sort of a test run for the repairs he'd made on
it yesterday. And it was worth a lot of money, more than he'd managed
to earn so far fixing these expensively simple machines. Gingerly, he
climbed down again and retrieved it. There were a couple of bent
spokes and some fresh scratches in the chrome, but none was conspicuous. All working parts seemed to be in perfect order. So no real
harm done, after all—except to John's already precarious sense of his
own inviolability.

❖

Some three hundred miles south-southeast of Oneonta, Jake's old
friend Simon was out on a section of the Interstate this morning, too,
but he wasn't doing 70 MPH. He was creeping along at approximately
three car-lengths per minute on I-395, while cursing himself for
several breeds of jackass to have expected that his errands in downtown Washington would proceed smoothly enough for him to get out

before rush hour could catch him. Two or three times a year, it seemed, he took a vacation from common sense and tried something like this, as if to remind himself of the complete futility and near-total stupidity of the world he lived in. But Simon had been thinking of Jake a few minutes earlier, as he had almost every day recently, wondering where the guy might be by this time, how he was doing, and regretting again that they'd never gotten around to any real goodbyes.

"— Up yours!" Simon suddenly roared, in reflex to the horn blasting behind because he hadn't instantaneously rolled forward yet another four feet when the Lincoln in front of him did so. For good measure, he shoved his left arm out the window and raised his middle finger, waggling it backward. In his mirror he could see two white-haired, red-faced, bull-necked types in a silver Chrysler avidly returning the gesture.

This sort of exchange was all he needed to make his day—or no, maybe not quite all: his beloved Saab didn't like traffic jams any better than he did, and now he noticed the temp needle was well over into the red. The car was nearly as old as Simon was, and he had to admit that the steadily increasing effort required to keep the thing together enough to be almost dependable was getting kind of ridiculous. He took perverse pride in his ability to continue to do so, though, in view of the fact that his fellow Americans had already discarded damned near three-quarters of a *billion* motor-driven vehicles since 1900.

But he had to do something, and pretty damned quick. If a hose should blow, he could be in a lot more trouble than merely missing a few appointments and phone calls. But if he so much as tried to get out and look under the hood, those creeps in the Chrysler could be counted on to do their best to drive right over him. Simon knew for a fact that such a thing had already happened on this beltway, more than once, and he wasn't even sure he'd hold the average commuter fully responsible for such behavior, considering what going through *this* torture twice a day, five days a week, must do to anybody's mental state. . . .

With the stick in neutral and his right foot just reaching the brake pedal, Simon stuck his long left leg out onto the pavement and stood as tall as he could, peering ahead. He spotted a pedestrian overpass a little more than a hundred yards farther along. There ought to be enough space just beyond that, where he could pull over and let her cool down, if the two solid lanes of traffic to his right would only let him.

In the middle of that mesh-encased footbridge up there, backlit by a furry fluorescent disk that was the sun doing its best to burn through the smog, someone was cradling his chin between his fists, elbows splayed on the ledge, gazing down. What was *that* idiot up to? Simon wondered. Couldn't he find anything better to gaze at than a thousand fuming cars and fuming drivers? Or was he breathing all this poison on purpose? A new fashion in suicide, maybe, slow but absolutely certain. . . .

❖

Although he'd never owned a car or even held a driver's license, the man on the footbridge—whose name was Roosevelt Edwards—had a definite opinion of automotive transportation. He thought it was insane. But so was most of modern life, as far as he could see. He didn't listen to the radio much or watch television. He didn't read newspapers, either. But he did spend a lot of his free time at his local public library, and that was where he was headed now.

He'd read or at least looked into everything published about the environment from Rachel Carson onward, and he'd picked up enough basic chemistry to comprehend what chlorofluorocarbons actually did to ozone once they'd risen into the stratosphere. He could also calculate, in pounds, the amount of greenhouse gasses being released down there at this moment. And he'd finally figured out that the expression "ozone layer" was more or less a synonym for stratosphere. He knew the atmosphere was about thirty miles thick, beginning with the troposphere—the land, water, and first half-dozen miles of air—and that all the rest was the stratosphere, and there wasn't much up there *but* ozone.

It's only in the troposphere that life can happen. And all the atmosphere taken together, he'd learned, isn't any thicker in proportion to the planet it surrounds than its skin is to an apple. Roosevelt Edwards really liked that image; it made him smile to himself for weeks after he first came across it. He couldn't see how anybody, once they'd grasped it, could ever forget that one.

What had been bothering him most recently was the fact that the books always gave the figures for pollutants, including greenhouse gases, in pounds, and he couldn't visualize how much space one pound of gas would occupy. It would vary from one compound to another, he supposed, but it seemed reasonable that whatever it was would have to be fairly light, to be a gas at all. So he'd estimated, very roughly, that a pound of assorted greenhouse gases should at least fill a bushel basket.

But it would be nice to know if he was basically right or a mile off here. He was a careful person, and liked to believe that he knew what he was talking about. Not that he talked much to anybody, certainly not about any of these subjects.

In any case, he'd resolved to get up his nerve and ask whoever was at the reference desk this morning if she could suggest any book that might tell him just how big a pound of gas was. He hoped it would be one of the younger ladies. The head librarian had a way of glancing up over her trifocals as if she were doubtful whether he could actually read the sort of books he usually checked out.

He'd stood here daydreaming long enough. A moment ago he'd almost imagined that one of those drivers down there was swinging his door open, half-rising out of his car, and waving up at him. But carbon monoxide sometimes causes hallucinations, he'd learned somewhere in his reading, and maybe he'd just had one.

❖

Jake's stationwagon on I-40 West was passing the Tucumcari exits by this time and Art Tatum was on the tapedeck, instructing him to "Get Happy!" But he wasn't aware of either until he had to switch lanes abruptly for an over-long stainless steel tank truck—with DANGER in yard-high red letters on the back—swinging out in front of him from an on-ramp. He'd slipped off the narrow ledge of his resolve several minutes ago, and fallen deep inside everything he'd been trying hard not to think about:

— *What do you do when you're told it's over, for you?*

He'd wondered what living was all about, that's where he'd begun. He'd told himself, *It really didn't amount to so very much after all, did it?* as reality zoomed down to the dimensions of the cozy pastel room they'd led him into, where the sloe-eyed young person in fuchsia silk and cool white linen made certain he was seated comfortably before she cleared her throat behind her small ivory fist with its slender gold and silver band, picked up his folder, pressed it to where her breasts would've been—there were none that he saw—then laid it down again, precisely in the center of her dove-gray desk blotter, unopened. . . .

He wondered, while she was saying it, whether this is what she did all day, every day, and whether it was just a job or something she'd always wanted to do. Oh, she was doing it well enough—very well, in fact: no question that she'd been thoroughly educated as well as indoc-trinated within her field—but how did anyone spend nine to five passing out death sentences, then go home and fix supper, read to the kids, set the alarm, snuggle up to hubby, get laid, fall sound asleep? That must be what the long years of training were actually about: how to turn it off again, every night, and on again, each morning. . . .

He hadn't caught many words. He didn't need to; he knew by heart now what was coming. There was one phrase, though, he couldn't miss: *six months*, she'd said, enunciating crisply, or he'd heard it that way—as if she were handing him a pass good for precisely one hundred eighty-two and one-half days. At least she had the decency, or the training, not to smile as she said it. At least she didn't add, *Have a nice last half year*, as she saw him to the door. . . .

It was later, alone, that he'd started casting back over this insignificant life of his, with its trivial fits and starts of all sorts of would-be clever schemes and projects—any of which might've become meaningful, or anyhow successful, if he'd only stuck with one or another long enough. That was when he'd begun asking himself why he didn't ever feel a greater sense of urgency, or take more risks, make more noise, care more intensely about being a success at *some*thing? He might've wrung so much more out of everything if he had. He might be wrapping up loose ends now with a sense of, Okay, so I didn't get my regulation three-score-and-ten, but I've still pretty much had, done, and seen my share of what there is to being human.

He'd tried counting the considerable advantages he'd had and didn't use, mostly didn't recognize as such until too late: *Too late*: he'd started drawing up a list of the things it was now too late for. No, actually, he'd only thought about it, he'd never made that list. But very late one night he'd picked up a pen and written *Before-I-Die* at the top of a clean white page in a brand new notebook, and even taken it as far as

>　*#1. Say my other important goodbyes face to face: Elizabeth, Eric, Mom & Sis*
>　*#2. Set aside some clear-headed time for thinking about what (if anything) it has meant to be me, a late-20th-century white male human being*
>　*#3. Put America together in my head somehow*

　　　　　　but never mind anymore about getting any of that down on paper. . . .

And only after all that circling had he begun to acknowledge the self-pity, and the anger: coming up with wise-guy lines, but none, the second time around, were really funny, and by the third they weren't even biting, just kind of sour, whiny, and wistful.

It didn't help to tell himself it wasn't his fault he was born at an unprecedented point in history when the world population doubled, then tripled within his lifetime. Not a lot of comfort, either, in the argument that his coming of age in what was the wealthiest and most powerful nation in history only meant it was just that much easier for anything special he might've had in him to be overlooked. The real trouble was that he hadn't really believed in himself, not consistently, and seldom if ever when it meant some uncomfortable choices.

Then there was the anger. That was the trickiest part to get clear in his mind. Anger at himself was where it always began . . . at being no better a father than he'd been a son . . . at showing many of the same weaknesses with most of the women in his life as with any serious work: tremendous initial enthusiasm but sadly insufficient persistence, and fatal twin tendencies toward either a premature cutting of losses or a putting-off of decisions until events conspired to make them for him.

And it was only when he was tired of berating and belittling himself that Jake had begun to discover that he was truly angry—enraged, furious, pissed off—at those jerks, those incredible assholes supposedly running the show, specifically the idiots who'd done *this* to him, and by their own accounting, to some 458,290 other Americans as well.

It was 7:12 a.m. Mountain Time, and commuter traffic was thickening rapidly but still moving along well in excess of the legal limit as the little red Porsche pulled smoothly onto the tarmac of the first rest area past where I-225 rejoins I-25 south of Denver. It came to a neat stop, squarely positioned in the slot directly facing the battered green door to the men's room.

You switched off the ignition, you thought about another noseful, but you recognized for once that it wouldn't do any good. So you just sat there, deep-breathing, gripping the wheel with both hands, reliving it again, exactly the way you'd already done at least half a dozen times on the way here. You were right about a couple of things: behind those cliché mirror glasses, he *was* only half your age. And if not ten feet tall, at least six-eight. . . .

He said something (you didn't catch it, you were too busy becoming accustomed to the notion of being ordered around by people like him for the rest of your life) and stuck out his hand, palm up, so you reached without hope or plan behind the visor above your head, and *lo!* there was something up there, in an appropriate-sized plastic folder. So you passed it over, but without feeling it was any tremendous stroke of luck because, of course, you had no idea what it said and that's precisely what he was going to ask you.

But instead of doing it the way he should've, he glanced at the first lines, then back at you, and demanded: "So who's this Louisa Joycelyn Holtman ?"

And you said, "My fiancée—oh, wait a sec," reaching into the breast pocket of your folded jacket on the seat beside you in such a state of instant innocence that when your thumb bumped the butt of the .357 concealed there, you couldn't for the life of you imagine what *that* might be. But of course, at the same time another part of your brain was making absolutely certain that whatever it was stayed covered when your hand came back out with your own folder already flipped open to the appropriate window.

Naturally, you've got everything it says on that expensive piece of plastic permanently embossed on your brain. What's more, you're 95 percent positive it'll stand up to at least a run-of-the-mill tour through the computer. So he forgot all about that registration in his other hand and asked your address in Boulder and your birth date and what you did for a living.

Which wasn't on that thing in front of him and was none of his goddamn business, really, but he seemed to think he was being clever, and you were totally willing to let him go on thinking whatever he wanted. You could see he was more than a little confused already because he knew he had to be smarter than you were, since he had a badge, a gun, and a uniform and you didn't. But you apparently had a girlfriend with a Porsche, plus what felt like half a pound of credit cards stuffed in there under that driver's license. So you said, "Systems analyst." Which always sounds impressive and even happened to be true, as far as it went. You didn't need to specify *whose* systems, or what you did with your analyses. . . .

And *he* (extremely tough-guy all of a sudden, stiletto eyes, ferrocement jaw, and mimimal lip movement) snarled: "Better see to it Miss Holtman gets them brake lights checked, Orville. The left one's not working," shoveling both folders back at you, flicking the brim of his stetson, revolving as smoothly on his right boot heel as if it had a ballbearing in it, striding back to his vehicle.

And you very nearly heaved pepper steak and blueberry pie all over his retreating back. But not quite. Nossir. As a matter of fact, you made it all the way to this rest area where, as soon as you're sure your legs will carry you that far, you're going to go lock yourself in a booth and retch until you turn inside out. And when you manage to stop gagging and heaving and feeling totally helpless and hopeless and finally get washed up and stagger outside again, Rafael will be here, dozing in the van, three slots past the Porsche. . . .

There was nothing else in the lot at that slack hour except for an elderly Airflow hitched to an even older Mercedes at the far end, with blinds drawn on every window, so Gil didn't bother to be sneaky as he took out the square of chamois he usually carried in his hip pocket for this purpose and not merely wiped but thoroughly polished everything he could've even so much as thought of touching, inside and out. He began with the reggie folder, and stuffed both the golfer's cap and its plastic bag into his hip pocket for safe disposal elsewhere.

"— We leavin' it here?" Rafael asked him when he sank into the passenger seat in the van. "You don' wanna put it back?"

"Brake lights ain't working right, I'm told—no point in chancing getting stopped again."

That was fine with Rafael, who'd never been keen on Gil's distinctly odd policy of returning the cars he "borrowed" to the same neighborhood, and if possible, the same parking space. "Brake lights, huh? That's all them *chotas* wanted back there?" Then, taking a closer look at him (but nothing like what Claude would be doing by now) asking, "You okay? Don' look so hot."

"Musta caught a bug someplace but reckon I'll live. Had to ditch that *carne asado* you talked me into last night, though. Come t'think of it, that's most likely where I picked up whatever the fuck's making me feel this way."

"Hey, I don' talk you into nothin', man! Never!"

"I know, just kidding, *compadre*."

Which he shouldn't. He knew that, too. He should be glad as hell it was Rafael along with him this time, not Claude, or he'd never hear the frigging end.

2 : JAKE

The unsurfaced road zigzagged mostly north, skirting arroyos as it hugged the western slope of a meandering valley growing ever narrower as it wound up into the Sangre de Cristos, becoming more of a canyon as the road became more a pair of rutted tracks. Crumbling sandstone, glittering quartz, bleached roots of long-gone junipers, and a few silvery clumps of grass studded what was left of the loose red soil. Much-mended strands of rusty barbed wire ran along both sides of the road on crooked gray posts, and every hundred yards or less, other lines shot away at roughly right angles either toward the ridge above or the creek below.

His elderly stationwagon had seen better days and more favorable terrain, but Jake was paying minimal attention as it wallowed ponderously from outcropping to pothole. He was busy studying the jagged skyline, checking its shifting shape against memories not nearly so vivid or accurate as he'd expected. Not so painful either, and he was grateful for that. . . .

The post–rainy season sky was flecked with just enough wispy cloud to demonstrate how impossibly cerulean it actually was. From time to time a small patch scudded across the sun, and every color in the landscape instantly switched from a throbbing pastel to a heavier but no less resonant register for the several seconds it took before the light broke free again. Full-force or filtered, the sunlight was so vibrant that Jake could almost imagine he was hearing as well as seeing it.

It was supposedly post–rainy season, but certainly didn't look it. Maybe he'd just gotten used to the East again, or maybe this was the dry end of one of the traditional seven-year cycles this climate was supposed to go through; or those Greenhouse Effect predictions were right. The scenarios he'd read all foresaw radical changes in prevailing global air/ocean currents that would make a few parts of the world cooler and wetter (northwest Europe, for one), others much hotter and drier. The American Southwest was always cited as one of those others. And it didn't make him any happier, knowing that, to remember it wouldn't matter to him personally if this once-green place was going to look like Death Valley in a few more decades. . . .

Up ahead a big brown hawk reluctantly flapped itself off one of the sturdier fence posts and struggled aloft until it found an obliging air current, then coasted up and away in the direction of the yellow cliffs beyond the creek. And suddenly, there was the old gate. Jake found he'd swung in toward it as automatically as if he'd only been to town for gas and groceries, his absence a matter of hours rather than years.

He shouldered open the door and climbed out on stiff legs to slip off the wire loop that held the gate tight against the post. "Texas gates," they were called around here: simply a section of fence detached at one end, reinforced with a little extra wire and a few sticks woven in, so it could be dragged out of the way without getting too entangled. All actual Texans he'd ever heard of had steel gates that swung back and forth and latched with a touch. Probably in Texas these were called "Mex" or "Okie" gates, if they had them. Nobody wanted credit for the damned things, but in efficiency if not aesthetics, they were a distinct improvement on the "pole gates" Jake recalled from growing up in western Pennsylvania, where each horizontal pole—heavy hardwood saplings usually—had to be dragged out of place separately. He remembered proudly performing that chore at fence lines there, whenever his family went berrying in his grandfather's 1935 Chevrolet.

— Jesus! He wouldn't've believed this driveway could've gotten worse but it obviously had, and once he had started down, there was no help but prayer and clenched teeth. The locally reasonable argument went this way: *Don't want nobody comin' down so fast we can't figure out who the hell it is and how the hell welcome they are before they get here, do we?* He'd probably said it himself a hundred times, and meant it. Most folks up here seemed to feel like that: the xenophobia of mountaineers anywhere, Jake supposed. So when the guy who did the county road each year offered to run his grader down to the house as well, the response was, "*Gracias pero no, gracias,*" until eventually he stopped asking.

Halfway down, something silent, brown, and very large flew by his window and vanished before Jake could even think *jackrabbit!* Eric must not be hunting them as ardently as he used to; never saw any so close to the house after the first year we lived here. For an anxious moment Jake wondered: What if Eric isn't up here anymore? But Eric anywhere else was impossible to imagine. . . .

Finally off the washboard slope, he picked up speed and watched house and barn and all the dead trucks out in front grow shabbier and somehow smaller as he approached, against all known rules of perspective. Not smaller, really—less significant compared to the cliffs and peaks looming above, that was it. He pulled in between a stripped logging truck lying upside-down like a huge helpless June bug and a whole row of disemboweled pickup carcasses. Sallyanne wasn't one of them, or anywhere else in the yard. She must still be a runner, then, and Eric was off somewhere in her now. Certainly he'd never get rid of her, dead or alive. . . .

As soon as Jake unfolded from behind the wheel, a black and tan Doberman bitch with sagging dugs and untrimmed ears growled from a chain sliding along a slack cable slung between house and barn. The chain looked plenty long enough for her to reach the doors to both structures. She was since his time, so he gave her a wide berth while approaching the only window in the old adobe low enough to look in through without climbing up on something.

. . . "Since his time": the phrase had never meant anything much to Jake before. Now it served to remind him that this had been home, for almost a decade, to somebody who'd answered to the same name and worn the same fingerprints. Jake couldn't even picture that somebody at this point in time, couldn't begin to guess what had brought him up here and held him for so long. . . .

Cupping his temples in his hands, he saw a cavelike, once-whitewashed room dominated by a greasy plank table heaped with dirty dishes, tattered magazines, cartridge-reloading equipment, a torn-down chainsaw and small discreet heaps he recognized as the periodic disgorgings of jeans pockets: crumpled wads of change and receipts, nuts, bolts, fence staples, a lot of empty brass in various calibers. Beneath the window there was a stone sink without spigots, filled with more moldering dishes. The shelf above it held a brown lump of homemade soap, a toothbrush shoved into a baking soda box, a straight razor, and a rear-view mirror pried off that inverted logging truck out in the yard.

A mammoth cast-iron woodstove loomed beyond the table, and in the farthest corner, under the crowded gun rack, there was a canvas cot covered by a crumbling strip of naked urethane foam and a torn purple sleeping bag. A curled-over stump of a broom leaned beside the doorway on top of a foot-high pyramid composed mainly of lint and ashes; there were signs of the broom's occasional passage over the brick floors, especially where it had detoured around the furniture. Cobwebs drooped from fly-specked rafter logs—Jake couldn't think for a moment what those things were called, but then the word returned: *vigas*. . . . God, if Elizabeth could see this place now, she'd have three-colored kittens. . . . Wondering next about the many weapons hanging in plain sight on that rack, inviting burglary, Jake gradually became conscious of another Doberman watching him from the shadows behind the stove, iron-ore colored, muscled like a comic-book hero, motionless and invisible until its unnervingly intelligent yellow eyes blinked, twice. Gorgeous beast, fit to star in anybody's nightmare. . . .

Jake stalked back to his car and stood gazing up at those cliffs beyond the creek. It looked from here as though he could pitch a pebble right over them, but he knew that topmost edge up there was a good hour's hike away and a thousand feet higher than the eight thousand above sea level where he stood.

—That's where I'm heading, he suddenly decided. Now. I can make it all right, I'll just take my time. I'm *not* hanging around until Eric gets home, this place is getting to me already. . . .

He dug around in the back of the stationwagon until he found an old canvas knapsack. The sun was hot on his back through his teeshirt, but he knew what the wind could be like on those cliffs this time of year, so he stuffed in both his nylon shell and a woolen sweater, along with two apples, a packet of cookies, and a small flat can of fish filets in red-hot sauce. He tugged off his Tony Lamas and replaced them with Reeboks: pretty Mickey-Mouse for this terrain, but the best he had with him. He thought about a camera and a canteen, but settled for stuffing a bottle of Dos Equis into the sweater instead of either. Plenty to tote as-is, and what good would snapshots do me? Be lucky I got 'em developed in time to glance through 'em once. He crammed his straw stetson down on his forehead against the glare, and was ready.

The path wound past the chicken coop and down across the irrigation ditch—*acequia madre*, he was pleased to recall—to the footbridge over the creek below the beaver dams, where a vastly pregnant Holstein and an all-black heifer placidly stood their ground, completely blocking the path, while a chestnut mare and matching filly melted back cautiously into the jungle of willows.

Jake finally had to claw his way through the bushes to get around the cattle—as déjà-vu shivers shook him: an identical cow in precisely the same spot had once managed to plant a hoof (and what felt like *more* than her full weight) squarely on his ankle as he'd tried to wriggle past. Which forced him to use a cane for weeks, and to wonder if he was any better suited to farming than to teaching or editing—and which also, somehow, evolved into an all-night shouting match that had left him shaken and almost convinced, for once, that he and Elizabeth couldn't keep patching it back together for too much longer . . . he found himself recalling all this as abstractly as if he'd read it in a book somewhere, then wondering why his time here seemed even farther away, the feelings and reasoning behind it even more obscure, now that his time left to be anywhere was only a matter of months. . . .

Eric must've had a bumper blue corn crop this year, judging by the dropped kernels like bright beads come unstrung in the trodden spaces between the truncated rows, so many the ravens hadn't pecked them all up yet. A flock of at least sixty had been working their way down from the far end of the field, but flapped away grumpily when Jake started out across the sharp stubble.

Beyond the field the land rose swiftly, scrub oak and huge lichen-dappled boulders clutching at the near-vertical red raw sides of arroyos thirty feet deep and as many yards wide at their mouths. No gates in the fence along here, and the sharp scent of sage overwhelmed him with memories and nebulous regrets as he rolled in it to get under the bottom wire. He chose an arroyo to start up without considering why, except that it was nearest—until he rounded the first bend and recognized the blasted juniper against the sky at the top of the cut. He scrambled up through the powdery dirt, and there was the stone beside the tree, looking like any other boulder until you walked around to the side facing out across the valley, where it had been split off more or less flat and roughly dressed with hammer and star drill. He'd made the letters deep enough, if not very even:

MIRIAM ELIZABETH JACOBSEN
Gone but with us always
For such as she
there ought to be
a Heaven
Aged 9 years, 3 months, 12 days

. . . and the date. He found himself unable to subtract the years between then and now in his head, it couldn't be so many. And I wasn't even thinking of coming here today, he admitted, fumbling with his eyeglasses and bandanna. I haven't thought of her once since I got here. And I almost wish I didn't have to think about her now.

He blinked and stared at the stone again, and that was all he saw. No pinched little senile mummy of a face, no hospital corridors, no Elizabeth clutching his forearm until a fingernail snapped off in his flesh (and he so drunk and otherwise numb he didn't even know it until he happened to glance down, at drops of blood collecting on the scuffed toe of his boot). No. Just that stone, and the solitary hours he'd spent chiseling away on it while there was so much else he should've been attending to. Mourning. Ignoring the words of Joe Hill, the soundest advice ever offered on the subject: *Don't mourn, organize!* Organize your own life, for starters. But wasn't it too late for that even then? Maybe not. Maybe if he'd known then, if anyone had known, maybe things'd be different. If any of those bastards in the government who *must've* known by then had said anything at all. . . .

—You don't know for a fact that Miriam was a consequence, another casualty of those six weeks in Nevada. You can't, nobody ever could, prove it was connected in any way. *Progeria*: all the word describes is the general condition, "premature aging." They don't know any more now about causes than they did when you dragged her around to all those specialists. You don't even know for a fact about *you*, when it comes down to it, it didn't have to be that, it could've been asbestos, benzene, any or all of the shit you wallowed in so ignorantly over the years, those summer construction jobs back in college . . . no proof, no way, there's nothing but statistics—*but I know what I feel in my bones. . . .*

Deliberately he looked away, back across the cornfield and the willows along the creek to the house and barn roofs floating on a needlework cloud of leafless cottonwood and locust branches. You picked this spot for the view, didn't you? So let's look at it, and quit thinking about causes and if's and maybe's, it all goes nowhere. Nobody *knows* anything anymore—it's all statistics. But what you're looking at is no statistic, it's as real as anything you're ever going to get. Or it was, once upon a lifetime. *Your* lifetime, whether you remember it or not.

Deliberately again, after less than a minute, he turned and stared up at the yellow cliffs where he was headed. It was past four o'clock already by the sun; he'd better get a move on; there couldn't be much more than an hour of direct light left, and then it'd be getting damned cold, damned fast.

One last glance at the stone, as if it mattered to Miriam, any more than the view did. "With us always" was a pretty sentiment, but you didn't really mean it even then, did you? You were just imitating the faint inscriptions in those mossy old Back-East family plots where you used to take rubbings, and the occasional nubile student, elegiac pedant/womanizer that you've always been. Okay, I plead guilty to both charges. But tombstones are only for the living, always, nothing is for the dead, the dead *are* nothing, that's why I don't give a shit what gets put on my own stone, or if there even is one. I carved this for *my* sake because I missed the meaning she'd given to *my* life for a little while. I doubt there's anyone who's going to feel that way about me, but that's the least of my legitimate considerations. . . .

There was waist-high scrub oak to struggle through for a few hundred yards, half of it still green, half winter-brown already. Then the dwindling piñon vanished and ponderosa pine took over, scarcely any taller at first than the piñon had been but quickly towering as he went up. He crossed an overgrown logging road, then another. One of them led to a trail to the top but he couldn't say which was which anymore, and he might easily spend half an hour finding out he'd guessed wrong. Better to head straight up, find the trail in the scree below the ledge, where it was unmistakable.

This was all scree really, from the cornfield up: all of this slope had crumbled away from the cliffs above, in chunks ranging from battleship-sized on down to dust. And was still falling: geology in action, Nature doing her jailbird routine, little ones out of big ones, forever and ever amen. Water from on top seeped steadily out to the exposed face up there, evaporating as soon as the thin dry air touched it, building up salts in the tiniest fissures until another slice was pried loose. At the same time, an unrelenting alternation of extremes: scorching Southwest sunlight and its icy absence. And as soon as each tiny new fault appeared, voracious plantlife leaped in to finish the demolition: the top of every boulder held its own little Japanese garden of moss, weeds, cactus, and stunted evergreens, deformed but determined and always, in the end, triumphant. . . .

—Whoa, there, getting really steep now, can't run your head full-throttle like this and your legs and lungs at the same time. Not any-more you can't, especially at this altitude. And look, there's a seat nobody could resist, a throne no less, a sedan-sized block of sandstone half beneath the trees and half jutting out into the south-facing side of an arroyo. Jake shed his pack, tossed it up on top, and climbed up after it to find himself standing with one foot in Sonoran desert among pincushions and prickly pear, the other in Alpine forest with soft moss, frost-killed ferns, and even some pockets of rotten snow from an early flurry huddled against the end of the rock, where an overhanging fir permanently blocked the sun. Transition Zone was what they called this in the guide books to the region. Juxtaposition Zone would be more like it.

He could see almost the entire length of the valley from up here, corrugated tin roofs and the oxbows and beaver-built ponds in the creek bouncing back pinpricks of sunlight, cattle and horses like slowly shifting micro-dots in the tiny odd-shaped patches that were tilled fields and pastures. He found he could recall hardly any names to go with those neighboring homesteads, other than the few remain-ing old Spanish families. The majority of them probably had different owners by this time, anyhow. Or stood empty. A lot more people had liked the idea of living like this, far from the herd, in some functional harmony with the rhythms and revolutions of the natural world sur-rounding them, than could handle the everyday realities of such an existence. As thousands of would-be back-to-the-landers across America had discovered to their sorrow over the past several decades, Jake among them. Most had lacked the inner wherewithal, or what-ever, to welcome the isolation and never-ended chores as unmixed blessings and to find themselves at truce, if not at peace, with the out-side world so long as it left them alone, never mind whatever current craziness it might be up to. Elizabeth hadn't lacked what it took, though. And neither had Eric. . . .

Down in the valley now, a vehicle too tiny to identify as either car or truck crept along the county road in the direction of the post office with the picayune persistence of an ant. Above everything else, but well below where Jake perched, a solitary buzzard cruised the ther-mals patiently in meticulous search of immobilized protein.

—I'm one hungry sonofabitch too, Jake realized. He'd had nothing all day but water and coffee, since his pre-dawn breakfast in Amarillo. He dumped the contents of the knapsack, rolled back the top of the fish filets with the key so thoughtfully provided, gobbled them down with half a gingersnap for a spoon, and wished he'd brought along another can. The beer was drinkably cool and very tempting, but he was light-headed enough from the altitude and all his exertions, so he slaked his thirst with an apple, peeled, sliced, and mumblegummed. He'd left his broken bridgework in his shirt pocket again, and that shirt was down in the car.

— Why in hell won't you go see a dentist, are you afraid there won't be time enough left to get your money's worth out of his handiwork? Penny-pinching at this point is pretty silly, don't you think? The money's not going to do you any good either, you know, where you're going . . . well right now where I'm going is to the top of those cliffs. And no farther. Not even that far, if I don't get up and moving. He tugged his jacket on first: sharp-edged sundown winds were already rising.

Spruce and fir became as common as ponderosa as he continued upwards, but all vegetation was thinning out rapidly, opting for one quality—toughness—over quantity, as the limits of what could be endured by any living thing came steadily closer. Life at the Edge, where there's no room for surplus or sympathy. The oaks were still hanging in there but scarcely knee-high, gnarled, awkward, half dead, and increasingly beaten out of the damper niches by better-adapted species like deer browse and apache plume. Wherever there was pro-tection from sun and wind, the crystalized snow was deep and at least as slippery as the loose gravel. Jake found himself wishing passion-ately for a decent pair of hiking boots.

The clifftop was suddenly less than a hundred yards away, but that distance was purely vertical. Somewhere along this narrow ledge where he now lay sobbing for breath there was a pass, a track wide enough to lead a horse up, if both horse and leader were cautious enough about it.

But Jake recognized he wasn't going to look for that path, he'd pushed himself too far and too hard already. It seemed to take forever for his heartbeat to stop booming in his ears like kettledrums. While he waited for the return of sufficient strength to begin the slide and lurch and scramble back down from there, he lay flat and stared up at the rock-face, where nothing could live but lichen: ancient scaly empires of it, in all the sickly-beautiful hues of corroding metals, seizing and munching the bare stone directly, no cracks required, no luxuries like stems or leaves or roots allowable in this howling environment.

God, but life on this planet is truly amazing, he told himself. It never gives up, does it?

But I do. And I'd damned well better get moving. It'll be difficult enough to get back down there by daylight.

First tell it all goodbye, Jake. You won't see this again.

Somehow, he didn't believe that. Somewhere deep inside his head, he could hear his own voice protesting:

— *Hell, yes, I will!*

3 : ERIC

The dogs began barking as soon as Jake started back across the corn-field, but he didn't realize they were loose until they confronted him at the foot bridge. He froze. They circled on stiff legs, sniffing him thoroughly, twitching their tail-less behinds. Then he heard the *whack!* of a splitting axe up in the woodyard and hollered, "Hello! Eric?"

Three more fast whacks and the loud sigh of seasoned fibers sur-rendering to the wedge. ". . . Yeah?"

"Can you call off these monsters?"

"No need to, c'mon up."

"You're sure?"

"They wouldn't bite *any*body, goddamnit." For good measure, though, he whistled feebly a couple of times.

Jake took a few tentative steps. Both dogs crowded his shins but made no attempt to halt his progress. It was deeply dark along the creek by now and the sky directly overhead was filling up with stars, but there were still a few smears of cobalt and salmon above the western ridge, and at the top of the path a figure stood outlined against them, beside a wheelbarrow heaped with split oak. An inch or two taller and a noticeable number of pounds lighter, but to Jake it was like approaching a darkened mirror, stepping straight through that mirror, and touching—cautiously—the man he'd been a quarter-century ago.

His first impulse was a bear-hug, but all that felt possible within the event was reaching out across three feet of air and kneading each other's shoulders briefly. Then Eric stooped to grab the barrow handles again and began pushing it toward the house while Jake stumbled along beside him, wishing for something more profound to say than, "Hey, you're looking great. The place looks good, too. Christ, it's been a while. . . ."

"Figured it had to be you," Eric said, dumping the wood into the box at the end of the porch. "Couldn't think of anybody else showing up with New York plates."

"Sent you a postcard from Tennessee, you didn't get it?"

"I dunno. Haven't got over to the post office in, Christ, a couple weeks, anyhow. Hardly ever worth the trip."

"Well, I also brought you a souvenir of Tennessee. I'll get it out of the car." There was something Jake needed from there, too, but his main reason for wanting to go now was to find out what Eric had been driving that day—and as soon as he rounded the corner of the house he could see that he'd guessed right. There she loomed beyond his Ford, caked with mud, cowshit, and sawdust, windows cracked and bulbous fenders full of rusty dents, but still beautiful to his eyes, and obviously still a runner: Sallyanne, his 1953 Chevrolet half-ton pickup.

When Jake entered the kitchen minutes later, bridgework in place and a quart of clear sourmash gripped firmly by the neck, the stove was roaring, scorched butter perfumed the air, the kerosene lamps were lit, and Eric—cuffs of his grease-streaked coveralls rolled back, hands scrubbed fairly clean as far as the wrists—was slicing spuds and onions into a skillet with a bowie knife. "Homefries, steak and eggs and green chiles, okay?"

"Sounds beautiful. Want a hit of this now?"

"Hmm . . ." Eric eyed the unlabeled bottle warily, pulled the cork with his teeth, sniffed, up-ended it for a good one, coughed, shuddered, wiped his mouth on the back of his hand, and returned to slicing without comment. "It wouldn't, if you ate it every night. Sound so beautiful, I mean."

Jake took a swallow of the unaged bourbon himself and felt it explode in his head and stomach simultaneously, a velvet fragmentation bomb. "Anything I can do?"

"See if you can find a couple plates that ain't too damned crusted, I reckon, and clear us a little more space on the table. Otherwise everything's under control. I did the chores while I was waiting on you."

"How long you been a bachelor this time?"

"Huh? I dunno. Seems like forever folded over. Guess it must look like that around here, too. Just shove that stuff over the far edge if you want. I'll sort through it one of these years."

"Last I heard there was a lady named Laura?"

"Lorna. That was a long time ago. She finally decided her folks were right, she did belong in college after all. Rare? Here it comes, then."

Thick and bloody venison, overdone eggs, chilis so hot one bite was as much as Jake could handle, mostly raw potatoes, huge leathery flour tortillas dripping fresh butter, all washed down with the morning's milk, strong black tea, and bourbon. Between rapturous mouthfuls, Jake asked, "Anyone since Lorna?"

"... A couple. Make that three. I dunno, they all seem to find it pretty hard and lonesome up here after a while. I guess I'm not the greatest company sometimes." Clearly Eric didn't care for this subject. "Where'd you take off to this afternoon, up on the mesa?"

"Not quite, only made it as far as the base of the cliffs."

"Any fresh deer sign up there?"

"Didn't notice any. I was thinking about deer, though, one in particular, on my way back down. Remember the night you and I took turns carrying that three-point buck all the way down the trail on our shoulders? New moon as I recall it, we left the mare on top—we didn't want to risk breaking one of *her* legs in the pitch-dark—and you ran back up after her in the morning? One of the first deer we got, maybe *the* first. We hung him to butcher right out on the porch, with his liver sizzling on the stove."

"I remember," Eric said.

"You remember telling me the whole story of *The Man Who Killed The Deer* on the way down, another couple chapters every time we stopped to catch our breath?"

"I remember that, too, kinda."

"That's the only Frank Waters novel I've still never read, did you know that? I've always been afraid I'd lose the way you told it, if I ever did."

"How'd I tell it?"

"I couldn't even begin to repeat it, but I remember very clearly how I felt, listening. And I can still see you perched on a boulder, living every minute of it as you told it. You must've been—what, fifteen, sixteen? One of those years when jeans instead of a breechclout was the utmost concession you'd make to civilization, hair halfway down your back tied out of your eyes with a strip of rawhide, that gutted buck's blood all over you—me too, I guess—no shoes, no shirt—"

"— No service," Eric put in, stretching for the bourbon. "But your little boy's no blond Indian anymore, is he?"

Jake looked at him now, at his ragged walrus mustache and almost muttonchop sideburns, his sun-bleached hair that was only neglected, not deliberately long in defiance of anything anymore, under a cap proclaiming MACK trucks. Then at the rest of him, from his holey blue undershirt to his huge steel-toed high-tops. As if to complete the mountain redneck image, Eric produced a can of Copenhagen from his pocket and dragged the ash bucket nearer for somewhere to spit.

". . . I just noticed something," Jake said after allowing the moment to pass when he always had the urge to reach for a Lucky (what was he saving his lungs for *now*, anyway?), "neither of us has said the other's name even once since I got here, and you just made the very first reference to how we happen to be related. I guess we never did call each other anything more than 'you' or 'him' if we could help it. You ever notice that?"

"Well, I just never knew *what* to call you. 'Dad'?"

"No, thanks. I used to break out all over in guilt bumps at that one, I'm sure I still would."

"'Wendell?' 'Jake' happens to be *my* handle, too, you know."

"Huh. I guess it would be. It used to be *my* father's as well, come to think of it. Nobody's called me 'Wendell,' though, since parents and teachers and that whole generation."

"Well, nobody but you and Elizabeth calls me 'Eric' anymore. Everybody around here just knows me as plain old Jake."

"What're we going to do about that while I'm here?"

"How long you figure that'll be?" Once asked, it was plainly a question that had been waiting for an opening.

"I'm not sure. Not long, in any case."

Bluntly this time: "What'd you come back *for*, anyhow?"

"To see you, and the place again . . . and to borrow Sallyanne for a while, if I can."

Eric made no attempt to hide his quick displeasure. "She *was* your truck, I know. But *I*'ve kept her running ever since we rebuilt her together, and right now she's all that *is* running on the place."

"I'll leave you that wagon I came in. It's a pig, but it'll get you to town and back without too much trouble."

"It's not worth a good goddamn for what I mainly need wheels for, firewood and hauling hay and stuff like that."

Here it came: Jake hadn't meant to blurt it flat-out like this, but it was too late now to approach the subject obliquely. "I'm dying, Eric. They figure I've got six months. I want to spend as much as I can of it on the road, saying some goodbyes to people and places that've been important to me. Elizabeth, for one, wherever she is. My mother in Arizona, for another. And I'd really like to do it in Sallyanne—you must remember my daydreams while we had her all torn down, about touring the Rockies when and if we ever managed to put her back together again. And I'll absolutely see to it, somehow, that she gets back here to you when . . . when I'm done. I've got some money, if that's all it'll take to get one of those other clunkers out there functioning."

In the subsequent silence, both of them could hear the cheap plastic alarm clock clucking away on the gun rack, and oak splits shifting in the firebox as coals dropped through the stove grate. Neither looked at the other's shadowed face across the table, beyond the small circle of lamplight. Eric studied the backs of his hands. Jake studied them, too: much darker brown, yeah, but give or take a few scars, swollen veins, and split nails, they could've been his own.

". . . Who told you that? Six months?"

"Most recently, a young woman, speaking for a bunch of doctors. For all the frigging doctors."

"Cancer?"

"Yep. Leukemia. Old Buddy Luke. In the bones, you know, where your white blood cells grow—"

Fast and loud: "I know. I've read about it. And Lorna had a brother who . . . went out with it, in his teens."

"Gotten to be a real popular guy, old Luke has."

There was a large knothole in the tabletop between Eric's thumbs; suddenly he jammed both of them down through it. It was a gesture Jake had seen a thousand times at that table, especially when Eric was being told something he didn't want to hear. Once there'd been room for index fingers as well and a good deal of rebellious twiddling down below, out of sight. Now his thumbs filled the hole completely. Next he'd begin gnawing on his lower lip, Jake knew. Jesus Christ, and I'll bust out bawling, if we don't get through this soon—

"When'd you find out?"

"The first I heard it was the end of July. But it wasn't any great surprise even then. They just made it unanimous in Maryland a few weeks ago." Keep talking, Jake told himself, say anything, it's easier than sitting here listening to what's going on in his mind: nobody ever completely buys the inevitability of his own death until one of his own parents bites it; I know I didn't. . . . "That was at NIH, National Institute of Health, so-called, in Bethesda. Took 'em a little while to decide whether it was A-M-L or A-L-L, Acute Myeloblastic or Acute Lymphoblastic Leukemia, but they agreed right away it's Acute, all right, and finally decided it's 'a subtype of A-M-L with an indolent course,' whatever the hell that's supposed to mean. I stayed with Simon Blake while I was there, d'you rememb—"

"— This is from what they did to you in the Army, isn't it?"

"There's no way of proving that."

"But it *is*, isn't it?"

"I believe it is, yeah. And A-M-L is the leukemia type most often associated with radiation exposure. Since I found out about myself, I've been trying to locate some of the other guys in my outfit. Turns out there's nobody left that I knew personally. Not many others either, that I could trace. This moonshine's a gift from the widow of a guy I went through Basic with, and on into the Signal Corps. He died of a brain tumor seven years ago. She runs the still by herself now. They had one kid, almost your age, I figured. He was born without arms, just two little stumps. He's her lookout. . . . "

Eric wasn't listening. "— Where was that, anyway, where they sent you?"

"Camp Desert Rock. Couple hours north of Las Vegas, Nevada. The actual test site was called Yucca Flat."

"And what'd they do, just march all you guys out there and set it off?"

"That's how it went in the beginning, I guess. They did this sort of thing for a lot of years, you know, to nearly half a million of us. I've heard that some of the first troops out there got orders to stand at attention and salute it. By 'fifty-eight, though, there were trenches we were supposed to lie down in."

"They give you special suits to wear?"

"Nope, just little 'film badges,' they called 'em, that were supposed to record whatever 'dosages' we might receive, to pin on our chests. And full combat gear."

"What was that for?"

"Well, as soon as the dust cleared, they were going to hold maneuvers. That was the whole crazy idea—they were still trying to figure out how to combine a nuclear strike with conventional military operations. Our CO told us they wanted to learn just how soon after a blast they could send in a force to occupy Ground Zero, as they called it. But I didn't have to do that. There was this tremendous wind—rushing in to fill the enormous vacuum created, I suppose—and it scooped me and most of my battalion right out of those trenches and rolled us ass-over-teacup about thirty yards forward, like a bunch of khaki tumbleweeds. So they trucked us all back to base camp, collected our badges—the ones that hadn't fallen off somewhere, like mine—and daubed our cuts and bruises with iodine, and issued weekend passes. I won over two hundred bucks that night, playing the slots in Vegas. My first-and-last gambling spree. Bought a money order for most of it next day and sent it back to Elizabeth in Ohio. . . ."

"What'd it look like?"

"What'd *what* look like?"

"The blast, the mushroom cloud."

"They instructed us *not* to look, to stay down and face the other way. I knew just about enough to obey *that* order. All I remember is glancing at my hands, and being able to see every bone, like in an X-ray. Lots of guys said the same thing later. There were all sorts of dire consequences threatened for discussing anything about it with any-body, even among ourselves, but how could we avoid it? Aside from that little adventure, we were all bored out of our minds. I remember a Georgia stump preacher who claimed he'd stood up and gawked right at it. He said it was like gazing straight into the face of the Lawd Gawd Almighty. One weirdo even confessed to coming in his shorts, it was supposedly so gorgeous. But my guess would be that a lot more of us befouled our britches than ejaculated into 'em. . . .

"But, hey—that climb really did me in, and this corn likker's not helping any. Mind showing me where I can crash? I've got a down bag out in the car."

"Guess the back bedroom's cleanest," Eric said. "There's a side of beef hanging in there now, so I've kept the dogs and cats shut out," he explained apologetically. "I'll get your bag for you. D'you want any-thing else from out there?"

"The brown briefcase and the duffle. Thanks."

Jake fell sideways on the bare mattress in what had once been his and Elizabeth's room, and was asleep before he'd finished extracting his feet from his pant legs. He awoke next morning to find that act accomplished somehow, his down bag unzipped and spread over him. The lamp had been snuffed as well, and his jeans and sweater hung from hooks on the back of the door. Noon light poured down upon him from the high, opened window.

Dressed again, he found the floors swept thoroughly, dishes either gleaming on newly scrubbed shelves or put to soak in the sink, not a single dirty sock or teeshirt in sight, the whole house brighter looking than it had probably been in years. There was bath water oozing steam in a galvanized tub on top of the banked stove, and laid out on the counter for his breakfast were half a loaf of home-baked bread, a mayonnaise jar full of milk, the honey crock, and a smoke-blackened slab of bacon. On the freshly scoured and otherwise empty table-top, a penciled note on a torn-open envelope leaned against the coffee pot:

> Gone to town for some parts we'll
> need to get SA ready. Been meaning
> to replace clutch plate & brake shoes
> anyhow—everything else ok, I hope.
> & I was thinking—maybe I'll go along
> for the ride, if you don't mind.

What brought those stinging tears to Jake's eyes, though, was the block-lettered signature at the bottom:

> —ERIC.

4 : NORA

They both spent most of the next week and a half flat on their backs out in the yard, Eric under the old Chevrolet pickup, Jake handing him tools on occasion but mainly dozing on the folding cot from the kitchen, moving reluctantly around to whichever side of the house wasn't casting shade at that hour, soaking up sunlight and hour after hour of primarily Bach, Haydn, and Mozart by means of headphones and a battery-powered cassette player.

Jake had no way to reach his sister in Phoenix by phone—she was either unlisted or remarried—but he'd written to her before leaving Glen Echo, giving this address and simply asking whether she thought his mother would welcome a visit. He hadn't spoken to either his mother or his sister since his father's death a dozen years before and was sure he was still unforgiven for not going home to Falls Creek, Pennsylvania, for the funeral.

Eric hadn't heard from Elizabeth for more than three months, but figured someone at the health-food store in San Bernardino where she'd worked until then would have a forwarding address. All she'd said on her last card was that she was "most likely heading north soon." So they'd take it from there, and they'd take their time about it, go first by way of the Four Corners and the Grand Canyon, make any side-trips that beckoned when they got to them. In the years he'd lived out west, Jake hadn't done any of that—he'd always been too broke or too busy, generally both, to play tourist.

But as he waited now and tried to rest, Jake found himself thinking less of where they'd soon be headed than of two months ago, an even muggier than usual mid-August in Maryland—thinking very little that he could've put into words, even if there were anyone he'd want to say them to, mainly just staring at pictures from his memory of a small neat house on a narrow, graveled back street in Glen Echo, where tall trees merged overhead to form a glowing green tunnel filled with the hottest sound in the world, the sizzle of a billion cicadas. . . .

Meanwhile, Eric skinned his knuckles on frozen bolts, roamed the junkers in the yard for replacement parts, and cursed quietly to himself in Spanglish. Clutch and brake jobs went quickly enough, but the electrical system presented a number of unforeseen problems—and nope, he couldn't use any help. He'd found friends who'd board the dogs, another who was very glad to take the chickens and the single cow now milking, and Jerry down the valley had said it wouldn't be any trouble to look in on the place. There was enough graze, so the four horses and dozen-odd head of cattle could pretty much fend for themselves. . . .

Jake slept eleven or twelve hours every night, ate at least three squares every day, was still perpetually exhausted, and didn't want to guess whether that was just the altitude and so would pass within a couple of weeks once his system grew accustomed again to being a mile and a half above sea-level . . . or was it his leukemia coming back full-force? As he knew very well by now, it could and would, eventually. . . .

He'd undergone a short but horrific course of chemotherapy at Sloan-Kettering after they'd given him their verdict, and for several weeks it seemed as though remission of sorts might've been induced. But "maintenance" proved problematic, and when they said they wanted to hospitalize him indefinitely, he decided to go down to Bethesda for a second opinion, having heard that the NIH was free for cancer patients—and being neither very well insured nor a millionaire.

The prognosis there was the same, when he could finally pry one out of them, unless (but much more likely, even if) he'd stay around so they could do frequent blood counts, bone marrows, and biopsies, and transfuse hemoglobin and platelets as required. "Bone marrows"—a needle the size of a sixteen-penny nail driven into the iliac crest at the base of your spine in order to suck out a sample of marrow—were the closest thing to Hieronymus Bosch–style torture Jake could imagine occurring in such an antiseptic setting. The four he'd already had by that time were plenty, thanks, unless they could definitely promise him significantly lengthened life thereby. But no, of course they couldn't, they wouldn't even if they could because that would break the paramount rule against ever telling a patient anything definite about anything.

He'd also had a series of transfusions in Bethesda, which did make him briefly feel dramatically better. But the idea of living on like that somehow, hoping fondly that a specific cure for his well-nigh-unique type of leukemia would happen along one of these fine days, was not attractive—as he'd told Simon, it made him feel like Count Dracula.

It was when his three primary specialists at NIH next urged him to submit to a "consolidation course" of chemo (much more, much stronger, much longer than he'd endured in New York)—even though they admitted they were "only trying to learn something" from his predicament—that Jake decided he wasn't going to spend whatever time he might have left groaning and puking along those hushed corridors full of people, virtually all of them at least as unlucky as he was: turning yellow-green and bloated, watching his hair fall out by the fistful, semi-delirious quite possibly, and otherwise with very little to do but feel sorry for himself and keep count of the various side-effects. Nope. Not his style.

Simon had seen the point of his argument: "Hell, Jake, do what you *wanna* do. You always have, haven't you? I mean, except for those two years when the government had you in its clammy grip. Why let 'em experiment on you again? When I think of what those sonsofbitches did to all you poor ignorant slobs, it makes me feel like napalming the Pentagon!"

Simon Blake seemed to spend a big share of his waking hours fuming on behalf of one or another group of victims, human or otherwise, of what passed for civilization in the late twentieth century. He also bestowed time and money upon many causes he considered deserving, from Amnesty International, Greenpeace, and Earth First! to totally obscure organizations with long ungainly acronyms, some still using smeary mimeograph machines for their appeals and probably operating six or eight per storefront, sharing a single unpaid-up phone line and a total staff of two. For the most part he gave money now, since that was in better supply with his business humming so merrily along these days, and generally more welcome than any amount of volunteered hours.

Simon lived in a shabbily comfortable Victorian bungalow of almost baronial proportions, tucked away in its own two-acre jungle in a secluded corner of Glen Echo, a few minutes' walk from the Potomac. Ten years younger than Jake, he'd been a student in the first course Jake ever taught, Freshman English Composition at Columbia. Simon had dropped out at the end of that year and gradually worked his way completely around the world over the next decade, but he'd always stayed in touch, either through annual six- or eight-page, single-spaced letters or hour-long phone calls on impulse, in the middle of the night from places like Istanbul or Bangkok. He'd never gone back to get a degree anywhere so far as Jake knew, but he was an extremely clever guy and had seldom wanted for interesting opportunities to prove it. Somewhere along the line he'd begun writing for scientific, especially electronic, research journals and using letterheads which listed him prominently as one or another sort of "consultant." He'd visited the Jacobsens in New Mexico soon after they'd moved there, and had lived in the Washington area since the early Reagan years.

It was during those long late-night talks with Simon that Jake first really began to accept the fact of his imminent ceasing-to-be, and made up his mind to make as many amends and say as many mean-ingful goodbyes as he could manage before it came, and to go out, when it did come, with as much composure if not serenity (to hell with dignity) as possible. Afterward, alone, he'd lie looking up at the ceiling and tell himself: If I'd *lived* that way, there wouldn't be so goddamned many of those amends to make now, or such painful ones, either. . . .

Inextricably entangled in these decisions, from Jake's first evening in Maryland, there was Nora:

"NIH by all accounts is a damned easy place to get lost in the cracks of," Simon had said. "You oughta talk to a neighbor of mine before you go over there tomorrow. She knows it inside out and can probably save you a week's worth of run-arounds."

Nora Sherman lived a quarter-mile away in a tiny, brown-shingled cottage trimmed with creamy white, at the end of that cicada-filled green tunnel. She was more than neighbor to Simon, or had been in the not-too-distant past, Jake guessed, while they waited side by side for her to answer the bell.

She seemed to take a very long time, and then she was simply there, smiling from behind the screen for what seemed to him like a generous slice of eternity, with what he took at first to be a self-deprecating shrug of her shoulders: tall, luminously ivory-blonde, with the sort of face that can leave a lasting imprint, like a cameo, on the retina. It left an indelible one on Jake's, anyhow. But her shoulders stayed up there far too long—until he noticed the metal bands en-circling her forearms and the crutch poles behind and below them sup-porting her.

"— Come in!" she'd commanded, beaming that smile straight at him, swinging aside to let both men slip by into a narrow hallway. Simon thrust him ahead and Jake found himself feeling ungainly, liable to crash into her fragile-looking furniture. The grin not quite hidden by Simon's beard for the short time before he left (pleading a suddenly remembered obligation) showed Jake that this effect—Nora's effect on *him*—wasn't only in his mind.

Nora knew NIH well because she was, or had been, a cancer patient, too. No recurrence for seven whole years now, but a series of malignant tumors and consequent surgery beginning in her late twenties had left her permanently disabled. On those aluminum crutches, though—or in the light-weight folding wheelchair she resorted to only when exhaustion demanded it—she led a life that most healthy, two-legged people couldn't keep up with: composer, violist, and chief administrator of an understaffed, perennially stuggling performing arts association.

Jake learned all this about her that first evening, and had seen proof enough of her determination even before Nora's alarm clock went off beside his ear at six o'clock the following morning, when she arose and hobbled into the living room for an hour's practice.

"Good morning, Mr. Jake. Coffee's in the freezer. Filters, cone, and grinder are all above the sink," she'd said on her way, "I'll take a cup, too—black—if you're getting up to do it."

Jake spent other nights in that little iced-gingerbread cottage, but strictly at her convenience, and he never heard that alarm go off again. The invitation had extended through breakfast that first time only because she meant to take him to NIH on her way to work and get him "started out right." Which she'd done with characteristic dispatch, brushing by receptionists, introducing him to two of her best friends on staff there, and leaving him in the company of a trusted third.

She'd never inquired about his disease, then or later, or about anything else of a personal nature, and Jake never told her of the sentence handed down. She had to be aware that he was very much in love with her, but he'd done his best to keep her from guessing quite how much that really was. The last thing she—or any woman—needed, he figured, was a declaration of serious feelings from a dying, practically impecunious, middle-aged lover. Simon also asked no questions, either that next day or thereafter, and offered no advice.

A late dinner, preferably cheap because preferably dutch, once or at very most twice a week, entirely as it fit (mostly it didn't) her always "full-to-ridiculous" schedule; a single bottle of a decent wine between them, or a brandy afterward, with their coffee; intelligently amusing talk of books and music both then and later, during friendly, leisurely, eventually all-engulfing sex: clearly unstated, these were her terms, and Jake knew himself in no position to argue for anything beyond them.

"I *like* sex," she'd told him, during that first long night. "Enormously. As I know you can tell already, you leering lout. I probably could but definitely wouldn't want to live without it. What I *can* do without is commitment either way—there's as much on my plate already as I can possibly handle. I've got no time for jealousy, mine or anyone else's, or for the total allegiance that committed love requires, or for grief, whenever it fails. . . ."

No commitment necessary in my case, Lady, he'd thought at first, but very soon he'd found what he was attempting—to keep all his depression, hopelessness, and anger out of the few hours she chose to share with him—goddamned near unbearable. At the same time, Nora's resolute example had probably helped him a great deal toward deciding that he wasn't going to go on dying until his death; he'd go on living as long and as much as possible, tying up as many of his loose ends as he could, trying to leave all the sites of his living as uncluttered as he'd found them. As any good camper should do, after all. . . .

He hadn't said *that* goodbye, it was obviously not the one to begin on. From Nashville, though, he'd sent her a postcard with a funny drawing of two mules playing fiddles. In the cramped space provided, after long consideration, he'd written:

My dear Ms. Sherman—

Called away most suddenly
on pressing business.
Thank you for everything &
the very best of luck with
all yr future endeavors,

Yrs compleatly,

Mr. Jake

❖

He'd lost track entirely of what day of the week it was, let alone the date, when Eric tapped his shoulder, signaling for him to lift the 'phones off an ear for a moment. "I'm just gonna run 'er over to the post office and back, see if that regulator cuts in now when it oughta. If it does, I s'pose we could think about taking off, maybe as soon as day after tomorrow."

"Great," Jake said and dropped back into Schubert's C major quintet. He must've dropped out entirely soon afterward because the tape had clicked off when he was tapped a second time.

"Mail call," Eric announced, and dropped an envelope on his chest. Jake sat up and tore it open, to find one of Hallmark's puppy-dog cards with three scrawled lines inside from his sister, phone numbers and simplified maps to her apartment and their mother's trailer park in pencil on the back:

> —You had to ask? You're still
> family as far as *we're* concerned.
> See ya whenever, Stranger,
>
> —Winona

". . . I opened this one without thinking," Eric said, holding out a refolded mailgram. "Sorry."

"Don't be." That MR. JAKE JACOBSEN on the front, after all, could've meant either of them. The message inside couldn't've been much more succinct:

JAKE: PLEASE CALL ME.—NORA

It was nineteen miles to the nearest payphone, which was also the nearest bar and grocery, and his watch said 4:40 when he reached it. That's twenty to seven back east, he told himself, as if to prove that his brain still functioned. He got both of her machines first try, home and office. So she had to be somewhere on the Beltway between those two places. What a brilliant deduction. . . .

He bought a nearly frozen six-pak of Coors, the only choice, and his first pack of Luckies in two and a half years. He'd bet most ex-smoker terminals turned recidivist immediately upon receipt of the word. And

why the hell not? Any port in *that* storm, surely. Any solace whatsoever would be absolutely justified. He wondered what Kübler-Ross &
Co. would say to that notion. . . . The rush after the first drag reminded
him momentarily of his first smokes ever, at age thirteen. But by the
time it had burned down to the trademark, he felt merely primed for
a second one. Two cigarettes, one beer; he tried her house again. . . .

"Hello, Nora?"

"— *Jake*! I just made up my mind today, I was too late . . . I mean,
you'd already left there. Jake: *why* didn't you tell me?"

"Why did Simon, that's what I'd like to know."

"Because I asked him, why'd you suddenly just disappear, so mys-
teriously? Don't blame Simon. He never could lie to me."

Nobody could, he thought. Not while looking into that face.

"Jake: *You* should've told me."

"For what good reason?"

"Because . . . because I'd come to . . . care for you, quite a lot. I've
missed you, a good deal, since you up and vanished."

"Sorry," he said, popping a second Coors, wanting another Lucky
but unable to strike a match one-handed; almost adding, in his best bad-
guy cackle: *Too bad, lady, I'm gonna miss me, too!* ". . . That's why you
asked me to call? So you could tell me so?"

"Yes, partly. And . . . I'd like to see you again, if I can—if you'd like.
I've got vacation coming to me—overdue, in fact. I could take next
week, it's the lull before the midwinter storm in the 'Serious Music' biz,
I could fly out . . . that is, if you'd like that. . . . Hello? Are you still
there? Jake? Hello?"

". . . Yeah. I'm here. Yes, I'd 'like that.'"

"Good! I've already checked, a friend's even holding a reservation
for me. The schedule's in my purse, just a minute. . . . Okay: I could be
in Albuquerque at one:forty-eight PM—your time, I guess—October
twenty-ninth. Flight six thirty-six, United. Will that be good for you?"

"I'm sure that will be very good for me."

"All right! If you don't get another mailgram, that's the way it'll be,
then. You'll be there—did you write it all down?"

"I've got it, I'll be there. One:forty-eight. Ten-twenty-nine. Six
thirty-six, United."

"How . . . how've you been holding up?"

"Like the Verrazano Bridge."

She laughed. He hadn't needed to hear that liquid-silver miracle on top of all the rest of this, but there it was. "Fine, then. Stay that way until I get there, promise?"

"Absolutely."

He took the remaining Coors back to Eric, but before he left the crossroads he bought all the Lucky Strikes in stock, another five packs, and a fistful of Bic lighters. "L, S / M, F, T," he recited, torching up again: *Life's Sweetest Memories Fade Too* was the best he could do with the acronym on the drive back up through the sunset, into the blood-red mountains. . . .

Eric wasn't happy about the delay caused by this unforeseen development, was in fact pretty confused, disappointed, and upset, Jake guessed. But Eric had certainly done his best not to show any of that, and had even gone out of his way to find the perfect solution when Jake belatedly realized: he couldn't bring Nora up to the valley. Not only would there be no privacy (unless he evicted his son from his own home) but there was nothing like Equal Access there, either. She simply wouldn't be able to cope there physically for a week, with no running water as well as no electricity, and the outhouse a steep and rocky fifty yards downhill from the porch.

". . . Jerry was just saying yesterday," Eric offered, "his and Judith's anniversary's coming up, and they wanted to celebrate it with some 'citified R 'n' R,' so his brother down in Santa Fe lined up a real nice house for them to sit there, beginning this week—but they finally decided they can't, not now, there's just too much they've gotta get done around their place before it snows. Their kids didn't wanna miss the Halloween party up here, either. Anyhow, I'll go see if he's willing to call back and find out what he can work out for you. What were those dates, again?"

"The twenty-ninth through the fourth."

"Huh. That leaves four days hanging loose now, and then a whole week for me to finish battening down the hatches here—what say we take a little shakedown cruise tomorrow, out to the Four Corners and back, just for a couple days? We could go take a look at Chaco Canyon, maybe."

"Sounds very good to me," Jake said. He'd had enough of lying around and thinking.

"Then when we really hit the road, we can shoot straight aross the Interstate to Flagstaff, and on down. That oughta catch us up some."

Eric was counting off weeks and then months in his head, Jake could tell, on up to six, from the end of August. He'd never been told what wild-ass guesses such death warrants usually were, apparently. Jake was a little too superstitious to point that out now, though—he had a hunch the prediction in his own case was probably more accurate than most. "I don't see why it'd matter," he lied smoothly. "Christ, though, that house deal'd be great if it works out. And if it doesn't, there're still plenty of motels strung out along Cerillos Road, aren't there?"

"You wouldn't wanna take her *there*," Eric said, appalled.

"No, I wouldn't."

And as it turned out, he didn't need to. They'd already found someone for the first two weeks, Jerry said, but the last ten days were all Jake's, or as many of them as he wanted.

"Okay, then, partner—Chaco Canyon, here we come!"

5 : GIL

It was one of those crisply cloudless Southwest autumn days when life can't help but seem priceless, and eternal. Their drive west across northern New Mexico began gorgeously enough, with Sallyanne purring through the Sangre de Cristo Range and then across the Jemez Mountains, where armies of aspens still shook their bright gold coins along the higher slopes. West of Cuba the sky became much taller somehow and the naked land turned magnificently desolate, beginning with that tremendous vacant lot mapmakers label the Jicarilla Apache reservation.

A day "rich in shared apperceptions," as Jake quoted to himself at one point from some forgotten source but wouldn't dream of saying aloud, not in present company. He did most of that sharing, while Eric did all the driving. Eric clearly had a great deal going on in there, and plenty of it must have been worth repeating but, living alone all this time, he seemed to have lost whatever urge he might once have had to squeeze his ideas into speech.

So Jake talked, if only as an occasional break from the grand drama of the landscape, and since he was sure the subject currently uppermost in his own mind—Nora—wouldn't be welcome, he talked about what was nearest to those thoughts: Simon Blake's crammed but fascinating life back in Glen Echo. Whether Eric found any of that of interest though was difficult to tell. Eric and Simon had been inseparable for the months when Simon had stayed with them out here, hunting, fishing, exploring the Pecos Wilderness together on horseback, having all sorts of adventures. But that was Simon in his vacationing, naturalist/survivalist mode, and Eric had been in his mid-teens. . . .

Simon made his living nowadays from several discreetly advertised electronic devices of his own conception and design, mainly of an anti-bugging or "personal security" nature. As he'd put it: "There's a god-awful lot of people out there who believe that the government, or their competition, or supposed friends or spouses are out to get 'em—the real pisser of it being, most of 'em are probably right."

Such customers were less concerned with what a product cost than how well it did whatever was claimed for it, and they paid in advance, untraceably if they could manage it. "Except of course for the guys designing the bugs and stuff I'm trying to outsmart," Simon had explained. "They're a sizable chunk of my trade, just as guys like me are a good little steady percentage of theirs. It's a battle of wits supported by quickly forced obsolescence and customers who think they can't afford *not* to have the latest gadgets. The very best kind of Free Enterprise there is, so long as *you're* the Free Entrepreneur."

He'd settled where he was because of the thriving informal community of small independent electronics and other science-related shops and labs that had grown up over the past several decades within the DC Beltway. Originally these enterprises had centered on the NIH because so much medical research requires specially tailored equipment to measure and monitor experiments precisely—but that other great patron of electronic ingenuity, the CIA, lay directly across the Potomac in Langley, Virginia, and all other serious snoops and spooks, public or private, worldwide, did whatever was necessary to keep abreast of the latest products of this protean smart-guy network.

Simon's "gizmos," as he called them, were assembled, tested, and shipped by mostly temporary help—mainly friends who needed to raise grubstakes for their own pet projects and expeditions—in a shop that had overflowed garage and basement and now threatened to take over the entire ground floor of the old house, creating a permanent crisis concerning the safe storage of Simon's other sorts of equipment: flying gear, skis, surfboards, hang-gliders, canoes, kayaks, scuba stuff, mountain bikes, motorcycles, trampolines, body-building devices, and countless salvaged whatnots he considered too potentially useful to throw out. Literally thousands of books, catalogues, and magazines on all those and most other subjects—as well as the overflow of science and electronics literature from downstairs—were stacked clear to the ceiling, wherever there had once been an unoccupied square foot of floor space.

All sorts of intriguing people trooped through Simon's busy life, staying for days, weeks, or months in one of the half-dozen bedrooms upstairs. He had footloose friends from all over the world, met on his excursions to such places as the Galápagos, or Borneo, or anywhere on earth that had a mountaintop still worth scaling. Jake had had a room to himself while he was there, and someone he'd only known as

"Gil" had stayed in the next one down the hall for three or four nights. They'd talked about all sorts of things—this guy was quite a talker—but at greatest length about the horrendous cancer toll among uranium miners in this part of New Mexico, where Gil had said he now lived. . . .

Jake and Eric had gotten a later start today than they'd intended, a lot of the mountain driving had required third gear, and now the sun was already going down. But it seemed to take forever to do it, poised precisely at that point on the ever-receding horizon where the visors over the windshield weren't any help, burning straight through their dark glasses and into the backs of their eyeballs. Eric's eyeballs, anyhow. Jake studied the map—not that there was a lot to study in this section. "Nothing between here and the first turn-off, at Nageezi, which doesn't look like much, either," he said. "Then thirty miles of gravel roads—either route—to Pueblo Bonito, where there does seem to be a campground, but no indication of anything else."

"Should've gotten gas and groceries in Cuba, then," Eric grumbled. "We've only got . . . not quite a quarter-tank."

"Yeah . . . maybe we better drive on. Another ten miles, there's something that's just marked 'Trading Post.'"

They arrived barely in time to persuade the fat, frowning, turquoise-laden proprietress to delay closing for the night. She allowed them to gas up and buy beer, baloney, and corn chips, then shooed them out, flopped into a battered silver Cadillac, and bounced away up an arroyo, as indigo descended on all that wind-whipped emptiness, where the only other sign of life was a naked bulb glowing bravely over the pay phone out beside the road.

"Now what?" Eric asked. Things weren't going as they should, and he was beginning to take that tendency personally.

"Dunno, but I'm not too keen on tackling thirty unfamiliar miles of dirt roads in the dark, are you?"

"Not really. What else is there to do, though?"

"Well, Farmington's another forty miles, but they're paved. Tell you what: I'll try calling Simon. Maybe Gil's ranch isn't too far from here, and he won't mind putting us up."

It was a miserable connection, and Simon seemed more than usually preoccupied—Jake guessed he'd caught him in the sack with one of his collection of more-or-less steady lady friends. Nope, Gil didn't have a phone, but yeah, he should be home now, and Simon had almost stopped by there once himself, which meant he had detailed directions jotted in the margin of his address book: only six miles farther west along Route 44, then left at a big boulder with a splash of orange paint on it, then just follow the wash until you see another paint-splashed boulder, where you turn right. It didn't sound too far or too complicated.

Jake hung up sensing some hesitation in there somewhere, but maybe it was only awkwardness on Simon's part over his broken promise not to say anything to Nora. The end of their exchange, though, was definitely curious:

"— Oh, hey, I almost forgot, what's Gil's last name?"

". . . You never heard *him* say what it was?"

"No—why?"

". . . Well, it's Torres, I think. T-O-R-R-E-S."

"You 'think'?"

"He doesn't use it much. Look, ask *him,* I gotta run. . . ."

It wasn't too much more complicated than Simon's directions suggested, but certainly much farther and more difficult, and took a lot more time. Driving by starlight down what had to be at least ten miles of broadly meandering dry riverbed was a very tricky as well as eerie business, and once begun, there was no turning back. On five or six occasions, Sallyanne's rear wheels slipped off the narrow packed-down tracks and was instantly hub-deep in powdery, phosphorescent-seeming sand. Each time Jake was sure they'd have to dig her out, but Eric always managed to coax her gently back to where she belonged.

So it was ten o'clock before they'd crossed a rocky hogback and narrowly avoided sliding into the same arroyo three different times in rapid succession, and finally arrived at a tumbledown collection of adobe walls squatting at the base of a sandstone bluff, some fifty yards behind a stout, new-looking, ten-foot chain-link fence surmounted by spiraled razor ribbon.

At closer inspection from beside the padlocked gate, some of those walls still had rusty tin roofs over them, and there was definitely a dim light back there somewhere. Jake blinked, and there were two lights now: small windows that, once noticed, conveyed a vivid sensation of being peered out at. After at least a minute, a vertical slice of light came into being between them, was partly blocked, then vanished again. Gradually a vague figure could be guessed at among the shadows, gliding toward them. Eric touched his elbow, and Jake sensed more than saw two others taking up positions at either side. Then a heavy-duty flashlight clicked on, ten feet away, aimed straight at them.

"We're looking for Gil," Jake said, blinded, showing his empty hands and feeling totally vulnerable.

"I'd say you found 'im. Howdy, Jake, c'mon in!" Turning as he snapped the lock open, the still-invisible man called over his shoulder, "¡Ola, amigos!" then said, "Simon told me you were headed west, but I didn't think we'd meet up again. I'm real glad we did, though."

As they walked back toward the adobe walls, Jake explained the Chaco trip and why they were here now, to which Gil responded immediately and sincerely with the formula, "¡Mi casa es su casa!"

Then Jake asked, "When'd you speak last with Simon?"

"I was back there again briefly just a couple weeks ago. Been East, let's see, six, no, seven times so far this year."

"Business?"

Gil nodded.

"I don't think you ever told me just what kind of business you're in."

"Import/export."

Gil was holding his long flashlight pointed down now, like a lantern, so they could see each other fairly well. His beaming face was totally open and friendly, but didn't invite further questions. Jake could also see the heavy revolver riding on his hip. Those two other shadows had fallen into step behind them, both carrying what had to be rifles as unobtrusively as possible, barrels down, close against their outside legs. "Jake Jacobsen—my partners, Claude Phillips and Rafael Madero," with appropriate wags of the flashlight. "— And you're . . . ?"

"Eric," Eric muttered.

"Jacobsen, como no. Gilberto Torres, at your service."

He hadn't had that broad Southwest Chicano accent in Glen Echo, Jake thought. Or the look that went with it, either, or the actual feel of being Latin-American. But now he did.

By this time they'd crossed a sagging porch and entered a long, low-raftered room lit by three Aladdins and looking more camped in than lived in. A two-burner Coleman stove on a ping-pong table held a tall coffee pot and a big kettle half-full of beans and chilis. Hungry as they were again by this time, both looked good to Jake and Eric. So did the whittled-at, home-smoked ham dangling from a beam. Neither one hesitated when Gil pointed to chipped but clean enamel bowls and mugs.

The other two men hung back, but more in shyness than wariness, Jake thought. They'd stashed their longer weapons somewhere, but the one called Claude was wearing a .45 auto, Rafael had on a .357 Colt revolver like Gil's, and all three of those weapons remained prominently displayed on their hips—but quite unselfconsiously, as if they never took them off.

Claude was well over six feet tall, long-limbed, round-shouldered, with a waxed blond handlebar mustache, Harpo curls escaping from a dusty brown derby and, when he got around to saying something aloud (never very loud, or very much), an accent unlike any Jake had ever heard before, somehow combining Red Hook Brooklynese with Southwest cowpoke in equal measures.

Rafael, on the other hand, was small and compact, five-foot-three at most, and managed to be intensely Indian and Spanish at once, with an overlay of big-city barrio swagger, proud, reserved, alert, and almost totally silent . . . even when he and Claude resumed a domino match on a card table near the door, passing a tin of Prince Albert, a packet of rolling papers, and a liter of tequila back and forth. When he noticed Eric glancing his way, Rafael held the bottle up in solemn invitation until Eric shook his head, No thanks. Later, catching Jake's eye, Claude repeated the gesture, receiving the same response.

Gil was a shorter than average man, too, with no more than a couple of inches on Rafael, but his erect, well-muscled body and large, well-shaped head made him seem taller whenever he stood alone. He was probably the eldest, and clearly the leader here—as he would be almost anywhere, Jake thought, by sheer force of personality. But in spite of a receding hairline and more than a few gray hairs in the strip of reddish-black beard tracing his jawline from ears to chin, there was above all a distinctly young quality about him.

His face reminded Jake of a number of different people, most vividly of the slightly sinister, almost sneering handsomeness of Orson Welles as the youthful Charles Foster Kane—until Gil smiled, which happened often and transformed him entirely: the gloriously beaming here-I-am-everybody, I-know-you-love-me sort of smile that's usually described by that worn-out tag "child-like." But Gil's smile came and went as instantaneously as a flashbulb.

His mind seemed as quick and elusive as his face, pursuing several lines of thought at once, switching without segue from dead-serious to irresistibly comic and back again: quizzing Jake feelingly about his fate in one breath, teasing Claude over a miscalculation in the domino game that cost him thirty points in the next, and seconds later drawing Eric out about the land and people in his part of the state. Then gone again, but back in a blink, and really there—then elsewhere, but seeming never to lose track of anywhere. . . .

Eric could only keep his eyes open long enough to finish his supper. Gil showed him to a room where he had his choice of half a dozen bunk beds, then helped Jake move Sallyanne inside the fence for the night, admiring her lines while letting it be known that he was well aware that 1953 had been the last model year for the split windshield. "Goddamn, Detroit could still build trucks forty-odd years ago," he marveled, "before they went into the fucking tin can business."

"She wouldn't've been just as safe out there?" Jake asked, parking where he was directed, behind the outbuildings, at the end of a row of new-looking, heavy-duty trucks and all-terrain vehicles deep in the blue-black shadows cast by the crumbling sandstone bluff—thinking meanwhile how Gil, back in Maryland, had called this a ranch. But you didn't need daylight to know there hadn't been any livestock near this place in years: there wasn't even a ghost of that sort of smell. Import/export what, then? Goods you needed a bunch of expensive off-the-road capability for, and didn't leave traces of lying around. . . .

"Coyotes might steal the hubcaps," Gil answered, grinning. "You wouldn't want to tempt a young coyote into a life of crime, now would you?"

A late last-quarter slice of lemon-custard moon had risen above the bluffs by now, rinsing the yard with an unreal light that glowed on their faces like greasepaint as they sat on the porch steps and Gil produced—*presto!*—a tiny turquoise pipe and a block of nearly black hashish half the size of a paving brick. "You *do* do this on occasion, don't you?" he asked, toking. "Grown and processed in America," he added, gulping air, tapping the block, "and certified organic. . . ."

There was no trace of Chicano accent anymore, and suddenly Jake almost had it, that shred of a memory he'd been reaching for since his arrival here. "We met before, I mean a long time before we met at Simon's. And your name wasn't Torres then."

"Simon said you were a sharp old fucker!" Gil snorted, delighted. "Long, long before. Ancient fucking history. Got it yet? Here's a clue: what were you up to in May of 'sixty-eight?"

Now Jake got it, with his first hit on the pipe, the right name as well, and even a detailed recollection of an out-of-focus news photo to go with it: a lot more hair and no beard of course, a ripped-open tie-dyed teeshirt, skinny arms stretching skyward, a loud-hailer in one hand and an up-thrust middle finger on the other.

"Yeah. I was standing out in front of Columbia's Low Library with a bunch of other sappy liberals, trying to sing 'We Shall Overcome' while having my head beat in by New York's Finest. I believe 'Getting Radicalized' was the current term, maybe you coined it? You were all over the campus—all over the whole country that spring, weren't you? Making more noise than Hoffman, Rudd, Dohrn, and the rest of them put together. 'The Political Peter Pan,' media types called you, 'The Gingerbread Kid.' Just how the hell old were you then, anyway, fifteen?"

"Sixteen," Gil admitted, exploding quietly into another of his sky-rocket smiles. "But I don't think I coined that one—you remember how it went: you're all passing the jay, and suddenly this amazingly acute insight comes out of nowhere, a deathless phrase neatly summing up everything worth knowing on whatever, but you're all so stoned nobody's sure who said it first. And then wherever the action is next day, you discover everyfuckingbody's saying it, and inside of a week, those media types're spouting it, too, and not just in quotes. But by then, naturally, *we*'ve come up with a totally unrelated slogan, equally brilliant and all-encompassing, and equally short-lived."

"Yeah, I remember," Jake said, wondering how those Movement heavies felt, with a wiseass kid capable of such observations horning in on planning sessions. "That particular insight didn't fit me, though. The experience eventually led me out here to tend my own garden, and to hell with your Revolution. How about you?"

"Me? I never got *my* head beat in. Always was pretty fast on my feet."

"So I recall. They never quite caught up with you anywhere, ever, did they? And you were into some heavy shit there at the end, weren't you? But Little Gillie Townsend always vanished somehow, when the indictments were coming down."

Gil shrugged, refilled the pipe, and tapped two knuckles on the nearest porch post. "Haven't had occasion to find out yet, but I'm pretty sure I'm fatally allergic to incarceration."

"So what'd you do, just mumble some magic spell to turn yourself into Gilberto Torres of *Nuevo Mexico*?"

"I've turned into quite a lot of people, most of whom still exist. You're only looking at a couple of 'em now."

This seemed less a boast than a rather wistful appeal for some sort of romantic status: still another reason why he seemed so young. Jake found himself liking this odd little guy more by the minute, and he could tell it was mutual. He could also tell by this time that this was the best hash he'd ever smoked.

". . . 'There at the end,' is that what you said?" Gil asked. "The end of what?"

"Of the Sixties, and everything they stood for. Especially the notion that things *could* be changed, for the better, and that *we* could make that happen."

"You think all that ended back then, huh?"

"For me, for most people, yeah. Maybe it didn't for you?"

Gil bypassed that question for now, asking another: "Then I guess you think it's totally hopeless, they'll just go on poisoning the rest of us and the whole goddamn planet, the way they did you?"

"Christ, I'd like to think otherwise, but I certainly don't see cause for optimism anywhere."

"Nope, there's not a lot of that commodity around anymore, is there, even with those blowdried JFK knockoffs fronting the operation these days and promising wonderful things like a return to the good old 1990 levels of poisoning everybody—as if those levels weren't what got us where we are today. Want some more coffee?" Then, throwaway, over his shoulder, already rising to his feet and heading inside as Jake nodded, "Did you ever consider what could be accomplished," Gil asked, "by someone in your position right now?"

"You mean by someone with only a few months to lose? Yeah, I've given it a little thought. . . ."

Gil didn't wait to inquire further, but as he sat out there alone for the next few minutes, Jake couldn't help but review the only vivid thoughts of that sort he'd had, soon after he'd been told the medical verdict and become convinced the cause of his leukemia was that ionizing radiation he'd been deliberately exposed to thirty-odd years before. They weren't thoughts he would've willingly shared with anyone, but they had amounted to something more than a momentary urge toward revenge: he'd gone as far as to take a look at Simon's charts, after being taken up for a spin around DC in the old Beech Bonanza Simon owned a third of—and it was feasible, so entirely feasible the wonder was that someone hadn't already attempted something like it.

The small craft lanes go right up and down the Potomac. Given, say, a Cessna with a small nuclear device built into it—plus the skill to fly it, and fanatical determination—all that would be necessary would be a swiftly executed ninety-degree turn at the Washington Monument, and within a very few seconds, five or less, you could kamikaze into the White House.

He hadn't gone on the tour, or stood out by the Rose Garden, looking across the Ellipse, to picture what it would be like. But he *had* repeatedly imagined going, standing there, visualizing it, filling in the blank differently (but never satisfactorily) each time: *Take THAT, you* _____! And this nightmarish daydream of his had been undeniably gratifying, a kind of bitter solace somehow in those first days of growing accustomed to the notion that he was going to cease to exist in the very near future, most likely before next spring.

Jake had certainly known, though, all the while he was entertaining that black fantasy, that he could never do anything like it. Even supposing he had the wherewithal, the know-how, the necessary assistance. Not for so questionable a motive as personal vengeance, he couldn't. Not for any collective sort of vengeance, either, considering himself to be acting on behalf of hundreds of thousands of other declared or probable victims of the federal government's criminally careless (to put it very kindly) nuclear policies, or lack of same, over the past half-century. Not, ultimately, for vengeance in any sense: he knew very well, or he used to think he knew, that revenge leads nowhere but into a viciously escalating spiral. And not for any other reason he could think of, either, if it risked the life of a single innocent person. That was the worst thing about the sonsofbitches who usually wind up running the world, in Jake's opinion: a smug assumption that supposedly worthwhile ends will always outweigh not only dubious means, but innocent bystanders and all other "collateral damage" as well.

And you couldn't avoid that risk, whatever your scheme, your weapon, or your target—and who *was* the right target, anyhow? Not, personally, the creeps currently running the show; most of them hadn't even been hatched from under some flat rock of a law school or purloined their first millions from widows and orphans, back in 1958 . . . the Pentagon? the AEC or NRC or whatever they called themselves these days? Even there, anyone directly responsible had to be either dead or retired by now.

—What had Gil said, though? 'What could be accomplished. . . .' That had a different ring—that wasn't just getting even. . . .

But when Gil returned with two brimming mugs of bitter black coffee and a freshly opened bottle of cognac, he seemed to have forgotten all about his parting question.

"I'm sure the end of the world's gonna be a real gas," he declared now, flashing his special grin. "A lotta different gases, actually, but a major component's methane. Y'know what I mean?" As if to demonstrate, he broke wind loudly through his threadbare Levi's as he squatted back down on his boot heels.

"Came across a most impressive figure someplace or other: the contribution of termite farts to this Greenhouse business, all those quadrillions of 'em digesting all that slash from when the Amazon Basin got clear-cut. Then of course there's the getting-on-toward six billion of us, digesting our *frijoles* or lentils or mung beans or whatever. And a single cow, I'm told, vents as much methane as seven hundred humans! But you gotta admit there's a certain aptness in the prospect of this supposedly sapient species of ours waltzing out in an eye-smarting blue haze, with Bronx cheers and whoopie cushions for funeral music. . . ."

That slice of moon had turned deep orange and floated halfway across the sky by this time, Jake noticed, as Gil talked on—amusingly for the most part and clearly enjoying himself in the state of being amusing—about the desperate plight of the species and the planet today and the vanishing possibilities of averting many, if any, of a relentless procession of impending catastrophes. Most of his facts Jake had read or heard elsewhere, but Gil had his own way of stringing different pieces of the sorry tale together:

"— Can you think of any goddamned thing that's turned out the way we were all sure it would, back there at the end of the Sixties? Consider, if you will, the slapstick sequence of events which, if we could've foreseen any of 'em, would've absolutely convinced us the U.S. of A. was down the tubes: beginning just a few years past the Chicago Convention with Watergate, lurching along through the Iran/Contra minstrel show and that yuppie gangbang known as the S&L crisis—all of it leading inevitably to what? Keeping the world safe for oil spills by dumping more explosives on Iraq than fell on all of Europe during World War Two, and the discovery that *Marxism,* not Capitalism, was the paper tiger, swiftly followed by the spectacle of most of Eastern Europe lining up with their trousers around their ankles, eager to get screwed, blued, and tattooed! Now I ask you, is this History, or a Three Stooges script? But through everything, it goes without saying, two themes've never faltered: a steadily accelerating destruction of the global environment, and further impoverishment of the powerless. . . ."

"— What'd you mean? 'Accomplish'?" That was pretty cryptic, even to Jake's own ears. It seemed as if hours had passed, and at least a couple must have, since Gil had said whatever he'd said just before he'd gone inside to get that coffee. Jake understood that he himself must be very stoned, and not a little drunk. But as he registered this reminder, he also accepted the cognac bottle, sloshing another good stiff one into his yet-again empty mug, and then the pipe once more, for another lengthy toke.

But Gil caught his reference without missing a beat: "Before I try to answer that, how's about a stroll up the bluff? Betchyer as stiff as I am. Just take your cup, I've got everything else."

It did feel good to stand up and move around, but that was no stroll, unless you were half mountain goat, as Gil proved to be. Jake's pounding heart was louder in his ears than his gasping breath when they finally flopped down again, on the lip of a saucer-shaped sandstone outcropping overlooking a few million more stars than had been visible from down below, but nothing much else that could be discerned, at least for the time being.

". . . Okay, let me ask a question first," Gil said when Jake had recovered enough to refuse the pipe and light a cigarette. "Simon said something about how you edited a pacifist newsletter once upon a time. You still think of yourself as nonviolent?"

"Never thought of myself as a bona fide Gandhian—though even Gandhi said it's better to resist evil with violence than not to fight it at all. It was *organized* violence, especially the clear and present danger of nuclear war, that I thought we had to put an end to before it put an end to us. But I don't believe any positive good can come of killing people, if that's what you mean."

"Even when they're killing you?"

"I've got no serious misgivings about killing in self-defense, or to save someone else's life. But that's nothing positive, the best it can do is prevent a greater wrong. And in a case like my own, where it wouldn't prevent anything, it can't do more than even up the score. Which gets you exactly nowhere."

"Okay," Gil said, "but you're arguing the sheer morality of it, in the abstract. This, however, is a last-minute, life-and-death situation for the whole frigging show I'm talking about. We're a sick species, friend, sick unto death and obviously hell-bent on taking the rest of life on earth along with us. Y'see, what it really screws down to is this: it's like there's this disease of the *mind,* I think the Greeks called it *hubris,* but it's gotten unimaginably worse since they were bugged about it because there's so goddamn many more of us around, and we're each capable of so goddamn much more damage. We're all infected to some extent, but some of us carry much more deadly forms of the disease, and some are powerful enough to spread it millions of times further: *they're* the ones we've gotta get—and you're bound to zap a few healthy cells in the process of eradicating any cancer, aren't you? What's that, compared to saving the biosphere from these suicidal—homicidal—*every*thing-icidal—assholes?"

"Killing *some* of them wouldn't stop the process," Jake objected. "It'd probably just make the rest of 'em more determined than ever to carry on with business as usual—after they've taken care of *you,* and all your probable associates."

"Okay. So you *don't* kill 'em . . . you just convince 'em that you could've, if you'd wanted to, and still can, whenever you feel like it—because otherwise they won't sit still long enough to listen to Word One of the painful truth. So you scare the living shit right out of 'em, make 'em understand the way it fucking *is,* that they've gotta cut the crap, stop diddling around with all their greedy little schemes and do what-ever's gotta be done, right *now,* to save whatever's left."

"And how d'you propose to accomplish that?" Jake wondered.

"I don't exactly know yet, I'm just thinking out loud—but you ever hear of the MUF rate? Nuclear biz jargon: 'Materials Unaccounted

For.' Well, the official, published MUF rate on plutonium two-thirty-nine—you know what that is, right?"

"I know it's what they exposed me to," Jake said, "and what I'm most likely dying from now. But I'm no physicist, I don't really understand what radioactivity is, how it works."

"Neither do I," Gil hastened to admit. "But I know that old G-man's tale about any bright high-school student being able to build a bomb out of it is total bullshit. I also know something that's not as widely understood: that you don't *need* to build a bomb, or blow anything up, for it to be an awesome weapon. And I know that the MUF rate since the nineteen-fifties—and this is just inside the U.S., you understand—has been upwards of a hundred pounds annually, and climbing steadily. That much simply disappears from inventory, by their own admission, no apologies or explanations offered, every single year."

"So they're not only homicidal assholes, they're extremely careless homicidal assholes. That's not exactly news," Jake said.

"Nope, it's not. But it's not what I'm getting at, either. There's gotta be literally tons of that shit kicking around loose by this time, all over the place, is what I mean. And I happen to know, right this minute, of a couple different ways some of it might fall into *my* lap . . . very possibly quite soon."

"You'd better be wearing a lead apron, then. But I still don't see what you've got in mind—" Jake began.

"No, I know, I'm going a little too fast here. Sorta got lost myself, for a minute. Let's talk a little bit about delivery systems. I said you don't need a bomb—here's why: by weight, unexploded, with no critical mass or chain reactions or anything, they say P-U-two-three-nine is *two hundred and fifty thousand* times more deadly than cyanide. In other words, the amount they so cheerfully confess to losing track of every frigging year is probably enough to give everybody on earth some kind of cancer, if you could only grind it up fine enough and then somehow make sure that each of us breathes in or swallows our own appropriate speck. So your delivery system can be as simple, at least in principle, as a squirt gun, since all you've gotta do is put a few itsy-bitsy, teensy-weensy pieces of that stuff wherever you might want 'em."

"I guess you mean a squirt gun in the hands of what you referred to a while back as 'someone in *my* position right now.' But didn't you also just finish saying, 'you *don't* kill 'em'?"

"Right . . . so how's about this, then: we *minimum-dose* 'em instead, a whole bunch at once, somewhere—using their own current standard, whatever the hell they call it . . . ALE, Allowable Lifetime Exposure, some cutesy little acronym or other. If we can pull *that* off, believe me, they'll listen up good!—Whaddaya think of that notion? Is that an inspiration, or what?"

". . . Remission," Jake said, in scarcely more than a whisper, as he found his mind swiftly captured by a potent metaphor.

"Come again?"

"Operation Remission," Jake overheard himself saying this time: a clunky, military sort of resonance there, recalling the government's recent incursions in the Middle East and Latin America. 'Operation Desert Storm,' and 'Operation . . .'—what was Panama, anyhow, 'Just Cause'? And what in hell had they labeled Grenada?

"Mission Remission." That was even sillier but sounded better in his ears, probably because it reminded him of Forties comic books and the radio serials he'd followed so devotedly as a kid during World War II, where the good guys were forever outnumbered and outgunned, but assumed bizarre disguises and grandiloquent *noms de guerre* like Captain Midnight or the Green Hornet, and by extra-legal ingenuity always neatly foiled the bad guys at the last possible instant.

It was only one slim quiet edge of Jake's mind, though, that could hold on to any traces of irony in the presence of this idea and Gil's radiant enthusiasm. He fired up his next-to-last Lucky, feeling even as he did as if all the nicotine, alcohol, caffeine, and THC in his system had vanished, leaving him calm, alert, more fully in possession of himself than he had been in years, and more truly inspired.

"You're familiar with the concept of remission in classic AMA cancer treatment?" he asked the face regaining its shape and intensity beside him, as the stars faded now in the rapidly paling sky. "There're two kinds: spontaneous and induced. The first is just what it says, and just about as mysterious as Immaculate Conception or the Holy Ghost. The other's not understood a whole helluva lot better, but one way remissions sometimes occur is when the system receives just the right sort of shock somehow, usually incidental to radiation treatments or whatever chemotherapy's being used, and the body starts fighting back and keeping the cancer from growing or spreading elsewhere. A questionable biochemical concept, insofar as I understand it—but it does happen, in some cases. Anyhow, maybe that's what the world needs today: a carefully administered dose of the appropriate poison, to shock the body politic. . . ."

"And maybe the appropriate poison," Gil offered, "is a dose of their own medicine. God, that's gorgeous! I love it! But where's the proper spot to apply this dollop of P-U-two-three-nine, that's the next question on the agenda. . . ."

At their backs, by this time, a bruise-purple dawn had begun to disclose the spiring chimneys of the Four Corners power plant near Shiprock, fouling the desert air some forty miles away. Jake felt his illusion of clarity and well-being abandon him as swiftly and inexplicably as it had come. Heavy-headed, he slumped there doubting whether he had enough energy left to transport himself that vertical distance back to the row of toy trucks he could just make out now, almost straight down between his knees.

Meanwhile, Gil was saying, "This is *not* just stuttering through my stetson, friend, I'm sure this thing is really gonna come together somehow, it just feels so *ripe*. . . ."

6 : CHACO

Chaco Canyon the next afternoon was everything Jake had ever heard or hoped it would be—but he wasn't up to any of it. The weather continued as flawless as it had been the day before, and there were scarcely any other tourists prowling those massive remains of a city whose once-powerful people disappeared into exile nearly a millennium ago. By the time he and Eric finally got there, Jake was so exhausted that he wasn't able to see anything there beyond some pitiful weathered heaps of sun-baked mud in a stripped and wasted landscape, signifying no more than the foregone defeat of all human effort. . . .

He'd wakened abruptly mid-morning after at most three hours' sleep to catch Eric glancing in where he lay on one of the lower bunks, then sat up contritely to the daunting tasks of dragging clothes and boots back on and somehow contriving to roll up his bag. When he staggered onto the porch, Claude and Rafael were sprawled across the steps, sipping coffee and sharing a pungent, fat-to-bursting joint. Eric was out across the yard, elbows on Sallyanne's fender, supporting his chin in his palms beneath her raised hood, silently communing with her oily innards.

"Help yerself t' coffee 'n' yesterday's beans, man," Claude said, grinning when Jake quickly declined a toke, "'n' here, Gil, he told me t' give ya this." The sealed manila envelope held a photocopy of a hand-drawn map with a penciled note on the back:

> Sorry I won't be around when you get up.
> I trust you found our conversation as
> stimulating as I did—but I got so wound
> up I completely forgot to tell you about
> The Party tonight: plenty of great food,
> drink & smoke, decent country music, lots
> of lissome ladies, & a *good* road all the
> way—nothing like what you went thru to

get here last night, I promise! See ya,
I hope. If not, hang in there buddy &
let's keep in touch via S, OK?—g.

What was left in the coffee pot was undrinkably bitter, and just the thought of "yesterday's beans" was nauseating. So they'd waited to make their post-noon breakfast on milk, cheese, and crackers from the trading post after they'd stopped there again to buy groceries for supper and the next day.

By acetylene-bright daylight, the drive back to the highway took less than half an hour. On the way, Eric asked Jake if he'd noticed the guns Claude and Rafael had covered Gil with at the gate last night? No, not really. Were they the same as anything in that sizable arsenal Eric himself had accumulated?

"Nope. What I've got's a civilian version of the original Armalite that became the Colt AR-15 and then adopted as the M16. You used to be able to buy and sell them legally, before the War On Drugs bullshit. Those guys had the real thing, full auto, which you don't and never could get in any gun shop. And straight out of the case—cleaned and maybe fired once or twice, but so new I could still smell the Cosmoline."

That might explain the "export" side of Gil's business, Jake found himself thinking hazily. So Gil may not've been kidding, then, about some of "that shit" falling into his lap. Not that Jake harbored many doubts on that score. Despite a hammering headache due to too little sleep and too much of everything else, phrases from last night, in Gil's voice or his own, kept ringing in his mind with all the weight of prophesy.

While Eric roamed and climbed, exploring the canyon, Jake unrolled his bag again in the shade Sallyanne provided, falling directly into a calm, naturalistic dream about his grandparents' farm in Pennsylvania: no symbolism there, no action, not even any people, nothing beyond a quiet tour through overgrown meadows and orchards and the sun-dappled sepia and dusty-rose rooms of a quiet place that hadn't existed outside his memory for more than thirty years. The last time he'd actually gone there, it had been a sales lot for mobile homes. . . .

A coyote's yip and crazy cackle somewhere close at hand finally roused him enough so he could recognize where he was in actuality, and notice that the sun had just tipped down behind the ridge. A cool breeze had sprung up, and the two other vehicles that had been at the far end of the parking area were gone. He tugged on a sweater over his teeshirt and rolled over to wait for Eric, soon slipping back, away again, to discover himself in another scene from his past, this time from one of the bleakest periods he'd ever known, six winters ago, when he'd finally left a woman he'd tried living with against both their better judgments, and spent a month feeling sorry for himself in a tiny bile-green furnished room in St. George, Staten Island, drinking more beer and watching more TV than in his entire lifetime, otherwise.

Once again, this was more a vivid restaging of a vanished time and place than a dream about it: the hopeless smells, the self-disgust, the aches and stiffness from slumping on the edge of that never-made bed in his underwear, staring at that tube from the morning cartoons and the afternoon soaps straight through to the Star Spangled Banner. . . . But when he heard Eric's boots crunching gravel, Jake opened his eyes to a realization that his mind had never left what he and Gil had discussed the night before. And now he knew the target, and the date, if only he could stay around that long. . . .

"How're you feeling?" Eric asked. "Should I maybe get some supper started? And *you* didn't happen to think to bring along a can opener, did you?"

"Some better, I guess . . . and yeah, sure—but no, sorry . . . how d'you feel about that party we've been invited to tonight?"

"I could live without it. You didn't wanna go, did you?"

"Not really, but I do want to see Gil again."

"Whatever," Eric grunted, assaulting a can of corned beef hash with pliers and a cold chisel.

❖

The party was at a ranch a few well-graveled miles—just as Gil had promised—off the route to Angel Peak, and when Jake and Eric reached the turn-off at eleven o'clock, they could hear it from there, loud and clear. There were more than forty pickups and vans clustered around the log corral, and at least a hundred very wild and western looking people inside, counting dancers, drinkers, and dopers. High-wattage bulbs festooned the corral and the makeshift bandstand, where three Z-Z-Top look-alikes were punishing a good set of drums, an electric bass, an amplified fiddle, and one of Bill Monroe's finest tunes. After two days of wandering through such awesomely empty country, this scene felt like Dylan and the Dead at Madison Square Garden.

Eric parked in the shadows out beyond some sheds, and they elbowed their way back past pigs, goats, and a whole steer on spits above a huge fire pit, cauldrons of *frijoles* and *pozole* bubbling at either end, washtubs full of iced beer or tossed green salad up on sawhorses. The band had moved on from the Texas Playboys to the New Riders of the Purple Sage, with most of the crowd joining in at a bellow on the refrain to "Panama Red."

The corral gate stood open, and people passed in and out freely through the heavy marijuana haze, but Claude was perched beside it on a 55-gallon drum with one hand cupped beneath a giggling young woman's heavy breast inside her red sweatshirt, a bottle of *mescal* gripped in the other, and a Browning automatic twelve-gauge across his knees. He grinned happily, swaying in time to the music, but his deep-set jay-blue eyes were glinting everywhere at once. "Howdy," he said. "Nice party, huh?"

"Yeah. Is Gil in there?" Jake asked.

"Naw, he's in a maroon 'n' silver Ram van down thataway," nodding, "but he said if ya showed he wants t'see ya fer sure."

"Where'll you be," Jake asked Eric, "in there?"

"Guess so," Eric said, and started forward.

"Not carryin', ya won't be," Claude told him. "Nobody, but nobody, goes in there carryin'."

"Who's carrying?"

"*You* are," Claude said, and instantly his hands were around the grip and fore-end of the shotgun while the young woman found herself juggling his bottle. She sloshed some *mescal* down her cantilevered bosom before she managed a wincing drink. "Ya mebbe thought I didn't notice that Peter Lorre Special in the crack of yer ass when you was lovin' up yer truck this mornin'?"

Blushing, Eric yanked out his shirt-tail, produced a tiny nickel-plated .25 auto from the small of his back, removed and pocketed the magazine, and held it out by the barrel. "I'll get it again when we leave, right?"

"Ya betchyer *cojones*," Claude assured him. "Have fun, kid."

Jake tapped at the rear of the black-windowed van, gave his name in response to a muffled "*¿Quien?*" and then had to step back when both doors swung open at a kick, to reveal Gil flat on his back, in nothing but his socks and his grin, with his arms around two good-looking women in nothing but necklaces and earrings. One attempted to cover her modesty with a small mirror, but very carefully, so as not to disturb the half-dozen heavy white lines scored across it. The other merely drew her knees together, shook her wavy red hair out of her green eyes, and smiled wetly.

"— Hey, Jake! Great you could make it! Don't just stand out there, man, get peeled and c'mon in, the water's fine!"

". . . No, thanks. I just came by to tell you something. It won't take long."

"Okay. It takes whatever it takes. Here—" Gil said, placing a film can and a short glass straw carefully in the black-haired woman's free hand, closing her fingers over them, then reaching for his boots, shirt, and Levi's. "Amuse each other until I get back."

". . . I hope you're not getting the wrong impression," he told Jake earnestly, as they stumbled across a pasture toward a windmill and a stock pond. "I mean, I don't fool around like this all the time. God-damned seldom, really. Sure, I like to party. I like to work hard, too— at everything I do. And I do what I say I'm gonna do, or there's some fucking good reason why not. I haven't been shitting you, honest."

"I believe you," Jake said shortly, intent on the message he'd come here to deliver. He did wonder momentarily, though, where all that self-justification was coming from.

"Good." Gil hauled himself up onto the windmill's platform, then snapped his fingers and said, "— Oh, hey, before you start, lemme say something I meant to mention last night: y'know who told me all that stuff about not needing a bomb? Our mutual pal the Wily Whiskered Wizard of Glen Echo, that's who. Just wanted to be sure you knew we'll have Simon's expertise and resources to draw on, with anything we get together. Okay, shoot." Gil leaned back against a strut and looked the soul of patience.

Jake lit another Lucky, sucked hard, but couldn't taste it. No great wonder there: since leaving Eric's valley yesterday around noon, this was pack number five he'd just torn open. "— You ever catch the State of the Union Address on TV? Well, it's the one time every year when you've got all elected and appointed government leaders, plus a bunch of the captains of industry and the media, in a single enclosed space," he said. But even before he'd finished that last sentence, he could see nothing in the notion but delusions of grandeur. Mission Remission? Make that Mission Impossible—

"Jesus God," Gil whispered. "That's beautiful, absolutely beautiful! It's in the House of Reps, right? Any idea when?"

"Late January, I'm pretty sure." Had to be: it was one of the last things Jake could recall watching in that nasty little room in St. George.

"I'll check it out." Gil ticked off months on his fingers, seemed surprised to find there were only three, pulled out a red bandanna, and blew his nose, carefully. "Pretty goddamn close, but lots of times things work out best that way." Glancing up and catching sight of that film of doubt already veiling Jake's eyes, he said, "I bet I know what you're thinking: imfuckingpossible, right? Well, lots of things were 'impossible' until somebody came up with a good enough reason, and then just went ahead and fuckin' *did* 'em. What wouldja say if I told you I've got a guy in mind already—totally dependable, we go back a quarter-century—who knows the whole goddamn Capitol Building as intimately as the inside of his own outhouse door?"

"I'd say that was a remarkable coincidence."

"All right—but I've made a whole career out of coincidences just like it."

"You never pulled together anything like this, though, that I've heard about."

"Maybe not, but maybe I just never had a good enough reason. You could be it, pal. How's late January fit your . . . schedule?"

"Pretty goddamn close there, too—that's just about exactly what they gave me."

"But the docs wouldn't ever tell you more'n you've most likely got, it'd always be a very conservative, very low minimum estimate, I betchya. And anyhow, Jake, you look just as good right now as you did at least a couple months back there, when we met at Simon's."

"That's because I've been in remission," Jake said, evoking the brightest smile yet. "Spontaneous—no telling how long it's good for. And that was only six weeks ago, not a couple months. But yeah: no guarantees, but I think I'll still be around."

"Look, where're you gonna be this coming month?"

Jake said he didn't know yet, but he'd probably be on the road somewhere with Eric, for as long as he could take it.

"Okay. Will you do this? Will you call Simon once a week?"

"Probably would, anyway." No, not that often. But he could.

"Great. That's the safest arrangement," Gil said. "Simon, I guess you know, 's got the cleanest phone in America. So will *I* call him, then, I'll keep you posted right up to the minute on any progress. And there *will be* progress, Jake, believe it."

At this particular moment, Jake couldn't find it within him to believe anything, and didn't care if this state of mind showed clearly on his face. Now that he'd said what he'd come for, for whatever it was worth, he felt bone-weary and anxious to be on his way. Solicitously, Gil accompanied him back to the corral, where Rafael now presided on the oil drum and held out a tall bottle of Spanish brandy. Jake accepted it gratefully, for the single long swallow he was sure would put him right out within five or ten minutes. Eric was nowhere in sight.

"He dance like crazy for a while," Rafael said. "Then that little Margo—you know, Gilberto, *la loca*?—she drag him off, I don' know where."

"Seems like Young Eric's in for a treat," Gil said.

"That's fine," Jake told them, "he needs one. G'night."

Gil still followed, and stood by Sallyanne's fender while Jake yanked off his boots and crawled inside his bag. A few times Gil looked as if he might be about to speak, but then he'd appear to think better of it. At last, as Jake tugged up the zipper, Gil coughed and stuck out his hand. "So okay, so long for now. Won't be here when you wake up, me 'n' my partners, I mean. Business to check out. You'll be okay, though, nobody'll mess with you, I'll leave word. Take your good old time leaving, but . . . it might be a good idea if you never came back out this way."

"Returning anywhere isn't something I have to worry very much about anymore," Jake answered, reaching up for a quick handshake. Gil actually opened his mouth this time and his other hand flew up before he caught himself, converted whatever gesture he'd been about to make into an oddly truncated sort of salute, and stalked away.

Fading rapidly as he was by now, Jake still had to grin, having belatedly guessed what that little charade was most probably about: it nearly killed him to do it, but Gil had been determined to let *him* have the final word there, on the theory that he, Jake, would feel more fully committed that way to this supremely unlikely pipedream they'd cooked up between them.

What a funny little guy he was, Jake thought—funny-strange, as well as funny-funny. . . .

❖

The sun was halfway up the sky the following morning when the maroon and silver Dodge van stopped for gas in Hermosa, Colorado, but nobody else was ready for a real breakfast yet, so Claude contented himself with a derbyful of Reese's peanutbutter cups. Gil had driven that far, but now he'd buried himself in a stack of newsletters and magazines. Rafael had taken over at the wheel, and shoved a Los Lobos album into the tapedeck.

Claude, cross-legged on the wall-to-wall purple shag behind their bucket seats, wished Gil would leave that eccle-logical shit alone, it always put him in a real piss-ass mood. At least he wasn't reading any of them goddamned scare sheets out loud today: some of them stories'd give a billygoat nightmares, the infuckingcredible shit them crazy assholes all around the world could get us into. But Claude wasn't in any mood to count his blessings. He wasn't happy about the reason for this trip, and he didn't care if Gil knew it. In fact, it might be a good idea to make sure Gil knew it: "— Hey, Gil, kin we discuss somethin'?"

"Huh? Just lemme finish this paragraph . . . okay, what?"

"Well . . . I dunno, man, I jist don't see nothin' wrong with th' way things've *been* goin'."

"Claude Phillips, A Portrait in Contentment. Has everything he wants in life. Eager to spend the rest of it playing Butch and Sundance, looking forward to going out just like 'em."

"C'mon, Gil. I jist mean, maybe we ain't millionaires, 'n' sometimes we sure as hell do earn every dollar we git, but on th' other hand, we ain't broke, 'n' we ain't none of us woke up t' find hisself dead or busted lately, neither. We go tryin' on somethin' like *you*'re talkin' up, though, they ain't *never* gonna stop comin' t' git us."

"You've never been busted once since you met me, either of you, since you got out of the Presidio—Am I right, Rafael?"

"*¿Que?*" When Rafael drove, he gave it his full attention. Too damn many *locos* on the roads these days not to, in his opinion. "Yeah, you right, Gil."

Claude could recall more than one occasion where nothing but dumb luck had kept Gil's claim true, when another minute or so either way would've meant a ninety-nine apiece in Leavenworth, but he knew he couldn't get Rafael to admit that. If Gil said, Let's drive to Kentucky and clean out the Mint, Claude thought, that stupid greaser wouldn't even blink. "'N' jist what're we s'posed t' *do* with this shit, if 'n' when we git any?"

"Blow up Washington, DC."

". . . Don't put me on, man. It ain't funny."

"What d'you *think* we're gonna do with it?"

"I dunno. *You* tell *me*."

"Well, for one thing, make enough in one shot to quit this cops-and-robbers bullshit, and grow old and feeble in comfort."

"'N' how're we gonna do that?"

"First we find it, then *you*'re gonna have to say just exactly what it is we're gonna have to do to get it. I'll take care of getting rid of it, as per usual."

"They don't keep that stuff in Nashnul Guard arm'ries, man. All I know about is arm'ries."

"You'd be surprised, Claude, where they do keep it, and how they schlep it all around the country. But hey, hang loose, pal, we're just going up there to look at it this time, okay? And then we'll talk it over. And we'll go real slow and careful, just like we've always done."

"We have, huh? I kin remember some times, man—"

"Claude, I swear to Christ, sometimes I think you should've been a CPA!"

Okay, he'd shut up about it for now, but he still didn't like any part of it. And he'd be god-diddly-damned before he'd ask Gil what the fuck a CPA was. . . .

That same afternoon Jake and Eric drove back to the Sangre de Cristo Mountains, following U.S. 64 through Tierra Amarilla, then across the Taos valley and the Rio Grande Gorge. Jake had wanted to tell Eric everything he'd talked about with Gil; he'd wanted to hear just how crazy it would sound cold-sober, told to a third person, in the light of day. But Eric had apparently had his hopes suddenly raised the night before only to be cast down even more precipitately. Unless getting laid made him as touchy as a broken toe—Jake had no way of knowing about that. In any case, very little was communicated in either direction.

Jake spent that night back in what had once been his and Elizabeth's room, staring by starlight at that hanging side of beef, thinking,
when his mind wasn't engaged in rehashing pieces of the two previous nights' conversations: That's all *I'll* be in a few months, a hundred-
eighty pounds of meat and bone—or less, if I waste away for a while
first. . . .

Then he found himself remembering Simon's words again: "Hell,
Jake, do what you *wanna* do. You always have, haven't you? I mean,
except for those two years when the government. . . ."

No, he always hadn't. Almost never, it seemed like, looking at it
from where he was now. There had always been sufficient reasons why
he shouldn't do what his heart and mind had both told him sometimes
was the right, the important, and the effective thing to do, never mind
the personal consequences. It wasn't as if he'd seen himself as a would-
be hero or martyr, or that he'd ever wanted to take such stands alone:
the whole idea was to set an example everyone else would follow,
eventually, once they understood the issues. He'd never been interested in purely symbolic acts, either; he'd wanted to make a real difference, to put an actual stop to injustice, misery, or the threat of
universal destruction, not just to call attention to them.

Not that he'd known so very many of those noble impulses, or that
any had ever come close to this idea in either audacity or potential. The
first one, he remembered now, had occurred to him during the Cuban
Missile Crisis, soon after they'd moved to New York, his first year of
graduate school, when Elizabeth was pregnant with Eric: and it seemed
as if John Fitzgerald Kennedy, simply to prove he was the tougher
hombre, was double-daring Nikita Khrushchev to push the button first
—but Jake found he could no longer recall exactly what it was he'd
imagined doing, to avert what certainly had felt like the onset of World
War III, only that it hadn't been anything especially audacious, or (he
thought now) at all likely to have accomplished very much. . . .

Later on, he'd taken part in organized protests against the arms
race and the Vietnamese, Nicaraguan, and Iraqi misadventures, had
even gotten himself arrested a few times, pleading *nolo contendere*,
paying his fine when it wasn't suspended. He'd admired the people who
went to jail instead of cooperating in that craven fashion, or to prison
for draft or tax refusal, but he'd never seen his way clear to becoming one of them. His three best reasons why not had been Elizabeth,
Eric, and Miriam—but even when they no longer stood in his way, he'd

always managed to find good enough substitutes to keep him from acting on his principles—if not some woman who said she needed him, there was always work he felt he couldn't delegate.

It wasn't as if he'd run out of worthy causes; there definitely had been no shortage of them during his slice of the twentieth century. So maybe it was only a daydream, maybe he'd just been kidding himself all these years, that there was anything out of the ordinary inside him.

This was a different ballgame now, though. Different in at least two ways, as Jake had just realized: not only did he have very little left to lose, in any sense, but . . . well, to put it in plain English, it's not every-day, or even every lifetime, that you get a shot, however long, at being a literal savior of the planet . . . no, that's not right, Earth herself is in no danger, she'll recover somehow, whatever damage we do . . . it's more a question of saving *our* world, the world as we've known it, or some humanly habitable semblance thereof . . . but anyhow, it was quite some notion to drift off to sleep on. . . .

But Jake woke next morning shaky and depressed, unable to refocus on those thoughts or much of anything else. Eric had already gone off somewhere on an errand, so after he'd fixed his own break-fast Jake wearily piled most of his gear back into the Ford and drove down to Santa Fe. Too much of too many drugs, he knew. He'd have to be a damn sight more careful from here on out. Music helped, though. Bruckner's, and then Mahler's, fourth symphony pulled him up a long way. Now there was a death-driven pair to contemplate—but Christ, just listen, would you, to what wonders each had wrung from his obsession. . . .

The only good thing about the stationwagon was its sound quality. Jake had missed it sorely the past three days, and he knew he'd miss it even more when he and Eric hit the road in earnest. His Walkman was a whole lot better than nothing, but he couldn't stay plugged into it all the time; that wouldn't be very sociable. A pity they couldn't pluck the tapedeck and speakers out of the Ford and transplant them into Sallyanne, but she had a six-volt system, which meant more time and trouble than it was worth, for as long he'd be around to use it: another of *those* things, like that dental work he needed. . . .

The house he was to sit, a *café con leche*-colored three-room adobe in the barrio, was a pleasant surprise. Uncluttered and simply comfortable inside, with a small neat yard made fairly private by a tall peeled-pole fence, it reminded him in its spare quiet taste of Nora's cottage in Glen Echo. The single front step was low, broad, and solid, the oiled brick floors were smooth and even, doorways ample—excellent crutch and wheelchair terrain. He hoped she'd like it, and that he could give her a good week there to remember him by, and that he'd be able to keep his feelings under control while so doing. Yeah. A pretty tall order.

When he'd finished lugging in his stuff, he sprawled on the brightly blanketed couch and tried to call Simon, but whoever answered after a dozen rings said, in a nearly impenetrable accent, that "M'sieu Buh-laike" had gone off camping in the "Suh-mokies" for a few days.

Jake wished he could think of somebody else he could talk over this Remission business with . . . but then again, that whole episode was already beginning to seem like a letter that had slipped down behind a desk drawer . . . and maybe it hadn't been addressed to him, in the first place. . . .

7 : WALSENBURG

The Dodge van bore steadily north and east in a zigzag route across Colorado, passing through Montrose, Gunnison, Leadville, the Eisenhower Memorial Tunnel, and a great amount of spectacular scenery, arriving in Denver in time for a fashionably late prime rib dinner, then a leisurely tour of the dark perimeters of both Rocky Flats and Rocky Mountain Arsenal before the trio separated temporarily, when Rafael and Gil borrowed a black-and-silver Cherokee and a lime green Subaru, respectively, within two blocks of each other near the Arapahoe County fairgrounds and then followed Claude south along I-25 for another couple hours, to a Ramada Inn between Fountain and Piñon, Colorado.

All that driving, a hot shower, a brace of Coors six-pacs, and his choice of *RoboCop IV*, a karate flick, or any of three different soft-porn cable channels should've mellowed Claude out considerably, Gil thought, but the guy was still tugging at his curls, slapping the furniture with his derby, and ranting:

"Man, I can't b'*lieve* I letchya muh-noover me inta this!"

"Just a little dress rehearsal, pal. I only wanna show you what a piece of cake it really is."

"It jist beats the shit outa me, man, why we gotta screw 'roun' with sech a pisser, anyhow! It's fuckin' nuts! Doncha unnerstan' *who* we'd be goin' up aginst?"

"I believe so: the same dudes as always. But swiping their M16s, grenades, and launchers, that's cool, huh?"

"Ya *know* this is diffrint, Gil—they ain't *never* gonna stop lookin' fer *this* shit!"

"So? Taking it away from 'em won't make 'em any smarter, will it? Then they won't catch us, if we do it right."

"Well, whatchya jist said's too fuckin' hard to b'lieve, man—only the driver and one guard with a cargo like *that*?"

"I'm telling you, to *them* it's a milk run—one they've been making nigh-onto thirty years. They schlepp these things around all the time, see. Once a year, every single one's gotta be lugged back to Rocky Flats to be 'rejuvenated.' On a rotating schedule, naturally, so there's never too many warheads out of commission at any base at any given time. When it's a shitload all at once—that'd only be if they're changing models or something—they use those wide-load jobbies, you know, half a house on wheels, rent-a-cop-cars front and back? Otherwise, like I said, it's ordinary-looking intermediary haulers, generally reefers. Whole idea's to maintain a low silhouette, they don't wanna freak the turistas, or have anybody understand that these things get transported on the Interstates at all. Some Pentagon Pinhead came up with this policy in the Seventies to foil the anti-nukers, I guess, and it worked fine, so of course they never changed it."

"But everybody knows about it, huh?"

"No, everybody does *not* know—did you, before I told you? But it's gotta be common knowledge around Rocky Flats, and pretty much so at the various installations as well. After all, it's a routine, a continuous operation."

"'N' they allus stop at that same joint?"

"No, goddamnit, they *don't* always. But this one pair does, or anyhow we know they did, three trips in a row."

"— So just the two guys," Rafael inserted, zeroing in on what he saw as the point of this discussion. It was half past four and he, for one, could use some sleep. "So how we take 'em out?"

"That's the simplest of our problems," Gil said patiently, "especially if your friend Teresa cooperates—"

"She cooperates, that one. I wan' *anything, anytime—chiles rellenos,* blowjob, you name it—I say, she *do,* no back-talk."

"You're a very lucky fella. You should marry that woman as soon as this is over. Okay, Claude: I think what we gotta expect here is not just locks and alarms but fancy homing devices—"

"But how about them two guys?" Rafael insisted.

"Any number of things we can do there," Gil said wearily. Claude wasn't even pretending to be listening anyhow, he was busy with the TV's remote control gadget, flicking back and forth from a screenful of tracer bullets, to several grinning naked young people with a jug of mineral oil on a waterbed, to a Bruce Lee-look-alike's callused heel smashing into someone's adam's apple. "Here . . ." Gil splashed the contents of his dittybag out across the coffee table (hoping incidentally to snare Claude's attention with this small diversion), deftly plucking a tiny brown bottle out of the sprawl of film cans, glass jars, pillboxes, and little foil bundles, "this for instance, courtesy the Army's own fun 'n' games department: a couple drops in anybody's food or drink and they shit themselves blind for a week—Claude! Goddamnit! Would you kindly quit playing with that electronic dildo for a couple seconds and tell me what you know about *homing devices*?"

❖

It was a quarter to six the following afternoon when a dirty white refrigerated produce truck pulled into the potholed gravel lot in front of Serafina's Cocina, a roadside restaurant a few miles south of Pueblo, Colorado. Two young men climbed down from the cab. Both were husky, blond, short-haired and wore wraparound shades, stonewashed jeans and loudly striped doubleknit sport shirts. One slouched around the truck, kicking tires, while the other went inside with a two-quart thermos under his arm.

There were four other customers in the place at the moment. The first two the young man took note of were a silver-haired husband-and-wife owner-driver couple in matching jogging suits quietly eating dinner in the booth farthest from the door, who clearly belonged to the huge new Kenworth out by the highway.

The next was Gil in a pigskin vest and straw stetson with his nose deep in a thick book beside the congealing remains of an enchilada platter, at a table by one of the picture windows.

The last was Rafael, on the stool closest to the kitchen hatch, nearly forehead to forehead across the counter now with the only waitress on duty, a portly woman in tight pink Lady Wranglers, thick pancake makeup, magenta eyeshadow, and a low-cut purple sequined sweater, with beet-red hair in a braid dangling down her bare, mole-speckled back. Rafael glanced at Gil, who ignored him, then winked his right eye—the one neither the young man nor Gil could see—at the waitress, who nodded wisely.

The young man stood tapping his thermos against the side of the cash register until she disengaged herself and sidled over there. "Ten sugars and plenty of milk in it," he told her, "two chiliburgers well done and two Okie burritos to go." She took his thermos and strolled through the swinging kitchen doors.

Tapping his foot now, the young man polished his sunglasses very

carefully, put them away in their case, and surreptitiously appro-
priated a fistful of toothpicks while studying the rococo Madonna and
Child on a calendar hanging crookedly on the wall behind the register.
Gil went on reading. Rafael combed his hair. The owner-driver couple
pushed back their plates simultaneously and fired up matching stogies.

Teresa returned at last with the thermos, a grease-streaked paper
bag, and a cosmetic-deep smile. The young man paid impatiently,
tipped stingily, and let the screen door slam behind him. Rafael moved
down two stools in order to observe him climbing up into the passenger's side of the reefer. The truck rolled slowly back onto I-25 South.

Two minutes later the green Subaru disengaged itself from the
clutter of vehicles behind the restaurant and followed it, Claude at the
wheel in his working costume: denim coveralls and heavy hornrimmed
glasses, with a jaunty sky-blue baseball cap replacing the dusty brown
derby.

Gil had flipped to the back of his book to check something in the
index when he noticed Rafael and Teresa conferring in urgent whispers. Then Rafael jumped up and came running over to his table: "She
don' unnerstan', she went 'n' did it *this* time!"

"She went 'n' did *what* this time?"

Rafael gulped, blinked, and whispered, "You know that bottle you
show me? When you 'n' Claude was yellin' last night, I stuck it in my
pocket, 'n' I show it to her this mornin', so she knows I'm not kiddin',
then . . . I don' know why but I say, Keep this till we're ready, okay? But
I guess she don' hear me right, 'n' now she sees nobody's lookin', so she
dump in the whole damn bottle! *Chinga'o*, man, I'm sorry!"

"Yeah. You're gonna be even sorrier, you're not on the road in that
Cherokee in two minutes. Thanks to you, this ain't just a dress rehearsal anymore, it's our one-and-only, *comprende*? And it's leapfrog,
d'you remember what that means?" Book in hand, Gil was halfway out
the door by that time, headed for the van.

"— Hey, what kinda pie y' got t'day?" the woman in the jogging suit
hollered across the long, low room.

Teresa checked both cake safes. "Apple, peach, 'n' Boston cream,"
she yelled back, adding softly, "Raflito, you wan' pie?" But he was
gone now, too, sprinting out across the parking lot.

❖

The van, the Cherokee, and the Subaru each took a turn at staying a
quarter-mile behind the refrigerator truck, while the other two passed

it at discreet intervals, then took the next exit, waited, and came back onto the highway behind everybody else again. Whenever he passed, Rafael hung alongside in the left lane for as long as he dared, trying to see what the hell was going on up there in that cab: were they drinking any of that coffee already, or waiting to get somewhere and stop? But traffic otherwise was very light, so he couldn't stay out there beside them long enough to tell anything much besides the fact that they were maintaining a steady sixty-five to seventy, except for where the hills forced them down a gear or two.

His third turn in front, just south of Walsenburg, going up a steep one with the reefer momentarily out of sight around a bend up ahead, he suddenly shot past and almost missed it just beyond the crest, nosed into the shallow ditch on the far edge of the shoulder with both doors hanging open. Slamming the Cherokee into reverse, squealing back uphill, he braked and leaped out in a crouch with his M16 at the ready.

He heard their grunting and moaning before he spotted them, a dozen yards up the cut, maybe twenty feet apart, squatting behind clumps of chamisa. His first sweep scythed down the nearer one, the guy who'd come into Serafina's, but the other *cabron* was quicker, or maybe he had his .45 out of the holster already. The rest of the mag put him away, too, but not before he'd gotten off a single round that caught Rafael in the hip.

Then the van was there and Gil was beside it, waiting to flag Claude down. A few other cars whizzed by, a couple heads turned, but they couldn't see anything until they were over the hilltop, and by then the vehicles on the shoulder and the figures sprawled above were already behind them.

"Holy shit on pumpernickel!" was all Claude could say when quickly told the situation. "We gotta haul ass outa here!"

"Are you kidding?" Gil yelled, inches from his face. "This is *it*, pal! We didn't plan it this way but we'll never get this close again, and since we're already in shit up to our eyebrows, *I* say we go for it. Drag those stiffs down outa sight while I see if I can plug up this leaky Rambo here." Dropping to his knees with a wad of gauze and an Ace bandage, he deliberately didn't watch while Claude twitched and sputtered indecisively for several seconds and then went loping up the steep cut.

"Not bleeding too bad—how it missed all the big arteries beats me, hombre. But it mashed your pelvis some, didn't it?"

"Oooh! Hurts like god*damn*, man, gimme morphine, quick!"

"Wait a sec." Gil let Rafael slump to the ground, ran to the reefer, stuck his head in the cab, ran back, and said, "Uh-uh, not yet, *compadre*, gotta hold on awhile, make do with nose candy," shaking a half-gram bottle over Rafael's upraised palm. Rafael inhaled the pulverized crystal in two desperate sniffs and licked up the crumbs.

Claude was back now, huffing, both corpses bumping behind him, each gripped by a wrist. "Jeez, but they stink!"

"Stuff 'em in the back of the Subaru," Gil said, lending a reluctant hand at that task, then, "Go check the rear end of that truck while I put this crate in the culvert right down there—if you're not sure you can make the locks, blow 'em now, otherwise we'll do everything when we get there."

"Whaddaya mean, get *where*?"

But Gil was behind the Subaru's wheel already, and now he got it started and tore away downhill. When he came panting back, Claude was standing with his fists on his hips over Rafael, who was pleading again for morphine. Claude just looked down at him, shaking his head in resentful wonderment. "Stupid fuckin' beaner, shoulda stuck *you* in that Subaru, too."

"Racist remarks do not become you, buddy," Gil said shortly. "What about those locks? Didja look?"

"Yep. Don't need no playdough, I could pick them suckers blind-folded, with my prick. So whudja mean, where we goin'?"

"Gotta get this show on the road, the law could come over that hill any second, and you're gonna need—ten minutes?—to get us inside, and it'll probably take at least as long to shift that cargo. There's a rest area only five miles farther, where we'll be a lot less conspicuous." It was more like fifteen miles, Gil knew, having memorized where every rest area was on I-25, from Boulder to Belen, but this was no moment for strict and discouraging accuracy. Kneeling, he shook out another quick spill of cocaine. Rafael honked it in, but still begged for a shot. "Nope, we'll need both these other buggies, anyhow I'm hoping we will, so you gotta drive that mama for us, and we can't risk you nodding off. C'mon, *jodido*—you got us into this shit, don't forget. Now you gotta help get us out. You can do it, it's not far, it's an automatic, all you're gonna need is one leg, so hang in just a little while longer."

Around the knuckle he was biting down on now to keep from faint-ing, Rafael whimpered, "Okay Gilbertommmmhangin'!"

He couldn't help the tears or the yelping when they hoisted him up onto the seat, he damn near did pass out then, and after Gil strapped him upright with the safety belt and got the motor started for him, he found he couldn't hold it on the road at much more than fifty. A couple times he was sure he'd lost it, he blinked, went onto the shoulder, almost hit the guard rails. And *¡Jesu, Maria!* it was a fuck of a lot farther than any five miles, but finally he did see those beautiful green signs with the magic white words on them, and at last he got there, wallowed to a stop at the emptier end of the truckers' section, and Gil kept his unspoken promise, he was beside him right away with that needle, and then everything faded out fast, as Rafael tried again and again to get those words out, ". . . I'm sorry. . . ."

It wasn't audible but Gil understood him anyhow: "You made up for it, *compadre*! Just keep your fingers crossed now, we're gonna be millionaires before you know it."

There wasn't much Gil could do then but stand around and worry as Claude quickly disabled the two-way radio in the cab and then attacked the rear doors to the box. Both knew there had to be a call-in schedule and devices pinpointing the truck's precise location. Alarms were certainly going off from Boulder to Sandia by this time, maybe even farther away, and others could explode into earsplitting noise right here and now, if Claude should cut the wrong wire. Or maybe much worse than alarms, maybe it was booby-trapped—but that was as far as Gil's imagination took him before Claude snorted in disgust and stepped aside to allow both doors to swing open. "I call *that* Mickey-Mouse," he muttered. "No fucking other word for it."

"Nothing else?" Gil asked.

"Nothin' I kin see . . . jist a buncha big shiny cans strapped against the front wall."

Gil could've wished for a Geiger counter, but faint heart ne'er won fair anything, he told himself, as he leaped up there. The thirty-eight identical, gleaming stainless-steel canisters stood two and a half feet tall and weighed about a hundred pounds apiece, he was sure of that much by the time he'd lugged the first one to the rear of the truckbed, where Claude caught it on his shoulder like a sack of cement and heaved it down on the tailgate of the Cherokee. That was already a little late to be wondering what might happen if these things weren't kept upright. In any case, the answer was, apparently, nothing. . . . Don't get greedy, now: ten per vehicle, Gil decided. Half a ton apiece was plenty, if they wanted to be able to run away from anybody. Which was next on the agenda. "Take your pick," he told Claude.

"Cherokee," Claude answered promptly, as Gil had guessed he would.

"Rafael goes with *you*, then."

"How come?"

"We can strap him on the back seat there, that's why. Those things'll roll, and they'd squash 'im in the van. C'mon, I'll help shift him." The job required both of them, Rafael was as limp as a sack of bran by then. When they'd done it, Gil said, "Drop him off with Marisol in Pecos. She'll patch him up if anybody can."

"Where *you* gonna be?" Claude wanted to know.

"Right behind you I hope, but *quien sabe*? If we do split up, I'll see you back at the ranch—or use the regular times and places to call. But c'mon, let's goddamn *do* it, pal, I can almost hear those choppers already, can't you?"

"Didja wipe down the reefer?"

"Oh, shit, no."

So they did that together, very fast but as thoroughly as ever. The sun was an overripe tomato oozing thick red juice over everything by that time, and everyone else in the rest area had already disappeared inside their trailers or under their snug camper-tops, their little yellow twelve-volt lamps showing ever more brightly now as mauve darkness rose up out of the hollows all around them. No one had shown the slightest interest in all that puffing and lugging and wiping down at this end, at least that Gil had noticed.

"Nighty-night, *turistas*," he told them now. "Sleep tight—while you can."

❖

If it had been anyone else, Claude would've been the first to point out that the jerk should've known better, but he was so rattled by then that he never even looked down at the gas gauge until he'd realized that he hadn't seen the van behind him in a fuck of a while. The needle was swaying between just over and definitely under a quarter-tank: enough to get him across the New Mexico line, to Wagon Mound maybe, not much farther.

Just another good reason why, in Claude's opinion, that soldierboy back there near Walsenburg should've shot a little straighter—it had been Rafael's job to top up this tank today, since he'd swiped this mawdicker, but it looked like he'd been too busy getting his *chiles relleno*'d, or whatever. . . .

So, ain't *that* jist what we fuckin' needed? And the faster Claude pushed this goddamn guzzler, the sooner he'd have to do something about it. But the slower he went, the sooner they'd overtake him. Yeah . . . or the more time they'd have to get their roadblocks ready, up ahead. He was past Trinidad now, it was real mountains again, the big climb up to Raton Pass, which was where they'd probably shut off the Interstate first. That's where *he*'d do it, anyhow, if it was him. Pitch-dark now, too, and no more cross-routes before the border, only little dirt tracks that most likely just went up to the head of each canyon and quit.

— Well, so what the hell we gonna do? He wished there was a damn police-band on this radio, like there was on the van's . . . wish for wings while you're at it, he told himself, ain't no radio gonna getchya over that motherin' pass—

And then he saw answers to the prayer he hadn't even gotten around to yet: a deliberately weathered sign that said "Old Baca House/Pioneer Museum," then the standard green EXIT marker and after it one that said GAS, and way down there on his right, at the base of the deep raw fill he'd begun to climb, dim yellow lights and a single bright one on a hand-painted fuel company logo, some brand he'd never heard of, they probably pumped it out of their own back yard . . . he'd better do it, though. . . .

It was mainly a grocery/dry goods store, Claude saw as he got closer, a real old-timey one with a faded Lebanese-looking name on the cracked and taped front window. The battered gas stand, just one regular hose and one no-lead, was off to the side, under one of those orange yard lights. He drove straight to it and jumped out fast, hoping to pump it himself and avoid curious glances at his strange cargo and that unconscious figure in the back. But immediately this kid about fourteen, who could've been Rafael's baby brother, came trotting out of the store, so Claude just said, "Fill 'er up," and leaned up against the Cherokee between the kid and the windows, keeping his eyes glued right on him all the while, so the kid kept his own eyes aimed downward and just pumped. It came to $24.82.

Claude produced a twenty and a fiver and said, "Keep the change," then climbed back in behind the wheel, slammed the door, and turned the key.

Where the sonofabitch came from he never knew, he never even laid eyes on him, not even at that instant because the guy seemed to be speaking from directly behind Claude's head, almost as if he were on the back seat with Rafael. But Claude could recognize the voice of authority when he heard it, especially when it said:

"Stay where you are!"

Like fuck I will —

❖

Gil had followed the Cherokee out of the rest area and south for a little while on I-25, but hanging back at a moderate sixty-five to seventy until there wasn't anything in sight on a stretch where he could easily do it. Then he cut across the nearly level median to the northbound lanes, flooring the gas now until he found an exit that let him onto the parallel county road.

From that he took the first promising unpaved road headed east, running as fast as he dared without lights, certain that search planes or choppers were out by this time, across a dead-flat nothingness he figured was or soon would be the Comanche National Grasslands. There was a final pale paring of old moon riding low in the sky beside him, shedding just enough illumination for him to make out thin white fenceposts whizzing past. They looked unreal, unearthly, and close enough somehow to reach out and touch on both sides at once.

Claude must've figured the Cherokee was less conspicuous, and it certainly was that—but then, anything at all would be conspicuous where Gil was bouncing along between forty and fifty right now, if anyone else just happened to be out here in the middle of nowhere to see it. Claude had probably also reckoned the Cherokee was better built for loads like this, and there was no question about that, either. Every time the straight (but not flat) as a string roadbed dropped into any fair-sized draw, the van bottomed out with a shrill screech of protest.

Claude had most likely thought Gil was being generous or foolish. Of course, Claude hadn't glanced at either vehicle's gauges. By that point he probably hadn't been taking it all in, let alone adding it all up, having just been shoved by fortuitous circumstances into one of the last things on earth he wanted anything to do with. Anyhow, he hadn't remembered the two extra tanks they'd installed over the wheel-wells (which Gil had looked into that morning and found full) or guessed what was the biggest advantage of all to the van: Gil had real papers for it, papers matching good-enough but disposable ID, so he could turn it into something else if he could just get clear tonight, something else that nobody could possibly be looking for. . . .

Hitting a sunken cattle-guard he hadn't seen until too late to brake, Gil thought for some seconds he'd bought it—the rear bumper banged down deafeningly crossing every single pipe welded in there, sending a shower of sparks out behind that looked like the Fourth of July in the rear-view mirror.

Somebody in a plane could've noticed that from miles away, but apparently nobody did, and the springs and shocks survived, after all. Gil began to relax to the extent of allowing himself to calculate that, at his present rate of progress, he just might make Dodge City by sun-up. But Dodge was too small to risk holing up in for long enough to make the switch to another means of transportation and catch up on his sleep. He'd better push on to Salina, or better still Topeka, where it'd take days for anyone to check out all the car lots and figure out what he might've switched to, if they ever did manage to find out about the van and trace it there. . . .

Then Gil let himself think about the odds against their computers coming up with anything leading to him, supposing they could get as far as the van. Or—Worst Possible Scenario?—if they caught the Cherokee, with either occupant in any shape to talk. It'd spell the end of Gilberto Torres—but being him had been pretty boring now for quite a while. . . .

By this time, Gil was relaxed enough to admit that it was probable that he'd just pulled off the most impetuous act yet in a life of, for the most part, very nicely calculated impetuosity. And from here on, he should be operating in what was basically familiar territory. The stakes were a hundred, maybe a thousand times higher, that's all—and that was counting on only what was right there behind him in the van, never mind the equal number of those doo-hickeys headed south.

The road ran on, due east, straight as a ruler, clear to Kansas, where it turned macadam and eventually led him to U.S. 56. He stopped for black coffee, a thermosful and as much more as he could drink in one sitting, Canadian bacon, blueberry waffles, and the use of an immaculate restroom in a mom-and-pop café beside a reeking feedlot a few miles beyond Spearville.

Two hours later the caffeine abruptly quit working, so he checked into the otherwise empty Claire de Lune Motel near Moonlight, Kansas, in the shimmering afternoon. Not too smart, maybe, but those names were impossible to resist, and he slept until a thousand starlings woke him just before dawn. Then he lay there for another delicious hour, finishing the cold coffee in his thermos, reading around in his thick book. It was *Gödel, Escher, Bach,* and he'd been carrying that tattered copy around the country for at least a dozen years now. He'd never actually read most of Hofstadter's text; he used it more the way some people do the *I Ching,* opening it at random and seeing how the words his eyes first fell on applied to his life at that moment. Nothing fit this time, but that was all right. He loved studying the illustrations, and rereading the dialogues in the manner of Lewis Carroll, and what he considered to be the underlying ideas, especially the 'Strange Loop phenomena,' the notion that "reality is a system of interconnecting 'braids' that are endlessly folding in upon each other. . . ."

By that evening he'd emptied and washed the van, sold it for five hundred bucks more than he had in it, and found a great bargain, a little-old-lady special: a twelve-year-old Plymouth sedan, standard-shift, dove-gray, with only ten thousand miles on it. Into which he'd promptly installed a set of heavy-duty shocks at a working-stiff's motel east of Topeka, where trying to make it *look* different might've aroused suspicion, but nobody'd think twice about a construction worker–looking guy doing practical stuff like that to a car he'd prob-ably just inherited from a maiden aunt.

Then, after dark, he'd test-loaded everything he'd kept from the van, beginning with those canisters, now shrouded as discreetly as possible in green plastic garbage bags. Five just filled the trunk; the remaining five went under the back seat, raising it nearly to window-level; but with all his other stuff piled on top, that wasn't awfully noticeable.

The rear tires bulged, though, in spite of all the pressure he could safely give them. Tomorrow somewhere he'd buy new radials all around, as many ply as they sold in that size: this cargo deserved the very best . . .

After a great catfish and hushpuppy dinner, so-so peach cobbler, several phone calls, a few hours' TV (nary a word of their activities on the news, as he'd expected), and another solid night's sleep, he made a bright and early start on I-70 East.

❖

At the same time—but the clocks here read an hour later—clutching her viola case and crutches, Nora Sherman sat beside a ramp in Dulles International Airport, waiting to be wheeled aboard her flight to Albuquerque. Despite her best resolves, she was furious at being treated like lost luggage and at being poor-thinged by several of the sillier able-bodied passengers.

She couldn't find *any* comfortable position in their klutzy official wheelchair, either. If they'd only let her use her own, she could wheel herself right through there, then they could fold it up and stow it somewhere in the cabin. But oh, no, absolutely not . . . and if she asked why not, she knew she'd only have to wait there that much longer, finally to be told: Because airports, dearie, just like hospitals, have their inflexible rules, and this is one of them. . . .

She was also, she'd finally admitted, experiencing an acute if belated attack of cold feet regarding what she was about to embark upon: it went directly counter to everything she'd long ago decided was necessary to hold her life together and allow her to do the work that made the hardest parts of it worth enduring. What she was up to wasn't so kind, either: she knew very well how strong Jake's feelings were and guessed how mixed his reactions to her visit must be. He'd already cut that connection, the one so quickly established between them; he'd done it so abruptly because it hurt him so much to do it at all, she was sure. And he must have older, maybe even more difficult connections still to be severed—but here she went asking him to reconnect to her for one more week, and then go through it all over again. And just because she found herself unable to abide by the ground rules *she*'d laid down in the beginning, the way she always did. . . .

These were considerations and accusations Nora had subjected herself to before, but not often, and the last times were so long ago she might've read about them in a book for all they meant to her now, emotionally. She'd been very—well, okay, just *pretty*—good, for so long, about keeping her personal life (all right, what she meant was her *sex* life) within fairly discreet, reasonable, endurable bounds. She'd known some bad times, loneliness and worse, because of that, but she'd always been convinced it was the only way, given her options. How had she let herself do something like this, then? Was going to bed with that man really so special? (Don't even try to answer that question, not now!) Why, she hadn't done anything so stupid since—well, since her first tumors came along and made this life of hers as complicated and difficult as it had been for the past dozen years, and always would be from now on . . . whatever "always" meant.

This wasn't like her, this . . . this *dithering* over her own motives. She knew herself well enough, she certainly ought to by this time, to be quite sure she wasn't that irrational, she wasn't so completely governed by such murky things as passions and appetites. Not actually, not normally: what was happening here was that she'd been exaggerating everything just now, and she knew why—but never mind why. Her initial impulse, to see Jake one more time, was a decent, caring, mostly unselfish one, really; and this should be a good week for both of them, bringing no harm to either—oh god don't think of an elephant, but while her metaphorical head was turned, here it came from behind her, at a deafening gallop: that reason why she'd been exaggerating. It always did come charging and trumpeting into her consciousness sooner or later, whenever she *flew* anywhere, obliterating everything else in her mind, at least until takeoff:

Plane Crash. Ah, yes. Planes *do* crash, you *know* they do, they do it all the time. Why not this one? Can you think of one good reason why not? Why it definitely won't? No. Nobody can. This plane is going to crash, I'm sure of it, I've never been more certain of anything. So whatever I might've been going to do to Jake, to myself, it simply won't matter, nothing will. . . .

Oh dear god *please* won't somebody come and put me on that plane, where I can ask a flight attendant for a glass of water and take a Valium—*two* Valiums . . . can that really be the plural? It never sounds right—but you couldn't say *Valia*, either, could you? . . .

Also at that same time (but here the clocks would have read two hours earlier than at Dulles, if there had been any to be seen), a pair of GI's in camo fatigues pushed a gurney into the bay of an olive drab transport at Sandia Air Force Base, barely a mile east of where Nora's plane would touch down half a dozen hours later. The GI with more chevrons on his sleeve handed a clipboard with a sheaf of receipt forms on it to the senior of two military intelligence officers waiting there by the hatch, who smartly returned their nearly nonexistent salutes, then signed where the finger had pointed, tore out his copy carefully, folded it, and put it away in his wallet.

On the gurney, strapped down, heavily sedated and covered with a green sheet as well as signed for and delivered, was a thirty-seven-year-old ex-MP from Brooklyn named Claude Wilbur Phillips—and that was almost the sum-total of what the government knew about him, so far.

They hadn't done any better, yet, with his accomplice: only his naturalization papers and his undistinguished Army file. Then he, too, had vanished from all available records. Of course there were the meager facts that, while Phillips and Madero were never stationed anywhere together, they did share two months' stockade time at the end of their military careers, and that they had been discharged only two days apart (both dishonorable, both cases involving drugs, but apparently unrelated).

— Too bad his partner didn't make it through the crash as well, the junior MI guy thought, we could play 'em off against each other. This way, all we've got is one hand clapping. . . .

The senior MI guy wasn't worried. This creep'll talk, he was thinking, he's going to tell us everything he ever even thought he knew. All you've got to do with somebody in that condition is make sure he knows he's entirely at your mercy, and he'll never walk again, never so much as wiggle his wee-wee, if he doesn't cooperate completely— it seems this poor fucker's never going to anyway, according to the preliminary medical report, but he won't want to believe that. And you always want to be sure you have your little confabs with him when, and only when, he's slightly overdue for his next round of pain-killers. . . .

To the extent that their prisoner could be said to be cognitive, he wasn't worried, either. As far as Claude Phillips was aware of anything at that moment, he still had his left hand cupped inside that young woman's loose red sweatshirt, the *mescal* bottle still clutched firmly in his right, and the band was still belting out "Panama Red."

8 : SANTA FE

Awaiting Nora's flight in the Albuquerque terminal, Jake felt unspecified anxieties climbing steeply, in spite of all his best intentions, plenty of rest, and huge doses of vitamins from a health-food store he'd discovered near Coronado Plaza. Out in the parking garage, he smoked an all-but-forgotten joint laid on him months before, which didn't help. And just before her scheduled arrival, he climbed quickly but as if sleep-walking up the escalator to the airport bar and downed a double bourbon.

That didn't help, either, especially when he discovered immediately thereafter that her flight would be at least three-quarters of an hour late. To keep himself out of the bar, he paced the length of the terminal's lower level until everyone working there seemed to be watching him circumspectly, then hiked out to Yale Boulevard and back, twice. Finally, at 2:39 p.m., the notice up on the monitor declared her plane was landing.

Because of remodeling in progress and the iron exigencies of insurance coverage, they wouldn't let him wheel her in from the jetway; they would instead deliver her at the baggage section. Jake felt like slugging the smug young sonofabitch who told him that, but he could still recognize that this was an impulse to be resisted, so he stood beside the tireless luggage belt until there was nothing riding on it but Nora's folded wheelchair and two bulging navy-blue nylon cases that had to be hers as well.

As he stooped to capture those when they swept by him again, she approached him quietly, from behind, on her crutches. And when he turned to face her, the only words to enter his mind couldn't be spoken: *Jesus God, why do I have to die so soon after I've finally found this woman?*

"Howdy! That *is* what you actually say out here, isn't it? Sorry to sneak up on you—didn't know I could ever do that to anybody, on these sticks, with this fiddle-box on my back. The jerk who was pushing me in that—" she made a comic, little-girl face, searching for suitably ridiculing words "— bawth chair, or whatever, kept running into things. I was afraid I'd lose my *good* leg, the way he banged me around! Hey, Mister Jake! Don't I get a hug, or something?"

He hugged her. He kissed her, too, and said, "Howdy." He opened her chair and then carried her bags out to where he'd parked as she rolled along beside him, smiling up, with her viola in her lap. He couldn't tear his eyes off her face unless it was to watch her hands spinning the wheels along, or to glance at that magnificently disheveled crown of shining hair. He was very nearly run into three different times: twice by cars that fortunately had loud horns and used them, and once by a furious young woman with a dufflebag on her shoulder.

They had late lunch/early dinner somewhere in Old Town, but he couldn't've said two minutes later what either of them ate. He drove along Central Avenue to show her the University, then took her straight up to Santa Fe, straight to that little tan house in the barrio, straight inside, and straight to bed, and they made better love, on into the night, than either could—or for the moment wanted to—remember ever having made before, with anybody else. But he found it very hard to talk, afterwards, lying there nose-to-nose in the dusk on those delicious-smelling sheets. *Like this,* he thought, *right now: I could die this death, this one would be easy.*

"— Can *I* say something?" she asked. "Since you're quite apparently not about to? I was just lying here thinking that it must be our . . . respective physical problems that make the physical side of our being together so astonishingly good. I'm sure it has something to do with both of us understanding—and knowing that the other understands, too—the . . . terrifying fragility and susceptibility of all bodies, our own in particular, but out of that bitter knowledge we somehow create something new, a strange, sweet kind of freedom—d'you know what I'm trying to say?"

"I think so," he muttered into the veil of her hair, like tangible moonlight now in the cool almost-dark. But our 'respective physical problems' are of different orders of magnitude, Lady. Mine's simply that I'm just about due to run fresh out of 'the physical side,' and there goes the ballgame. . . .

Nora would not have accepted this way of thinking, he was sure. Ever since their phone conversation, and almost constantly these past two days, he'd been carrying on a dialogue with her inside his head, or anyhow with his idea of how she'd most likely react if he could bring himself to say any of these things aloud. 'We're all under sentence of death, you know,' this interior Nora would tell him here. 'We get postponements sometimes, but no commutations. I'm in remission, just like you. My tumors came back twice. They could again, any day of the week, and next time can always be somewhere I can't survive having removed.'

It had come as no great surprise to Jake that Santa Fe had grown still bigger, wealthier, and uglier in his absence. He'd observed enough of the process over the past quarter-century to know it was as inexorable as any cancer. The reasons were as obvious as they were beyond solution: too much money, too much power, too little land, and far too little water in one used-to-be-lovely place. So people kept on slapping together new shopping malls and new fake adobe condos, filling the streets with ever more vehicles, which filled the once-pellucid air with petroleum by-products that cast faint ochre haloes around all distant objects. But you could still see the mountains most of the time, Santa Fe Baldy with its glittering snow eagle almost directly above the city, and the Jemez range to the west, rising out of the dusty yellow plain—otherwise, you might guess you were somewhere in Los Angeles. . . .

The worst of the tourist season was over; you could even get a car up Canyon Road if you had sufficient patience, but there were still crowds enough to jam the narrow sidewalks both out there and around the plaza, too densely for anyone on crutches to get around, he thought. From that first afternoon, though, Nora knew otherwise—and people melted from her path as always, as if dissolved by the silvery radiance of her apologetic smile.

Yes, she wanted to visit the Folk Art Museum, and San Juan Pueblo, and Taos, and Bandolier National Monument, and to ride the Sandia Tramway, and definitely, to go up to the valley for Halloween—she wanted to see and do everything he thought of suggesting. She'd never been out to the Southwest before and already found it dazzlingly different from the East, telling Jake excitedly, over green chili burritos at Tia Sofia's after a tour of the crafts shops, that she'd love to move out here. She wondered how expensive it was, and whether she could find work that would support her:

"Surely, with all the music there seems to be around this town, there's some little niche here for me. It's the summer home of the New York Metropolitan Opera Company, as I'm sure you're already aware . . ." and at last she looked up, to see his feelings written all in capitals across his face: she'd meant, of course, a life out here without him. There wouldn't *be* any him very soon, anyhow. ". . . I'm sorry, Jake. But I know you don't want my pity."

Who told you that? Sure I do, if that's all you're offering—I want whatever I can get! But this was something else he knew he couldn't say. . . .

They drove up to the valley the next afternoon. Nora gasped and sighed and even clapped her hands in delight, like a child at a birthday surprise, as they climbed up into the Sangres, where the aspens were fast losing their yellow coins and the snow line was moving down the high slopes so fast that Jake noticed the difference from just three days before.

Bouncing down the driveway hurt her hip, though. He saw the white spots forming on her cheekbones as she swallowed the pain.

Eric was across the creek, up one of the arroyos shooting target when they got there. Jake explained that that was all it was, not a guerrilla war in progress, then waited for the end of a clip, and hollered his loudest. The yard was too rocky and uneven for her chair, so he carried it to the porch while she made her way on her crutches.

If Nora found everything funky, primitive, and cluttered, she didn't say so. Her face shone whenever she looked up at the cliffs and the white-mantled mountains beyond them. It shone still more when she met Eric.

Jake was amazed. Within minutes she'd gotten more words—whole sentences—and smiles—even laughter—out of his son than anyone else had managed in years, he was willing to bet.

The party, Eric told them, was going to be at Jerry and Judith's place, since they had the largest clearable space for dancing. They also had a solar-battery-powered stereo. And yes to Nora's question, it *was* a costume party. "But I usually can't think of anything and just go as I am," Eric said. Rubbing his cheek, he added, "I've got more hair on my face'n usual this year, that's a little disguise." True, he hadn't shaved since Jake had first arrived, probably not for a couple of weeks before then, so by this time his beard was nearly as long as Jake usually kept his.

"You two could go as each other," Nora was inspired to say. "Trim yours to whatever Eric usually looks like, Jake, and just switch clothes." Meekly, unwilling to refuse her anything, they obeyed. Eric exchanged his logging boots, ragged pullover, and MACK cap for Jake's squashed stetson, Tony Lamas, leather vest, and snap-fastened long-sleeved denim shirt, and Jake scissored his facial hair down to a mustache and sideburns.

The switch had all the force of some fun-house optical illusion. Suddenly before her, like movie magic, there stood a ruddy, robust Super-Jake and a shrunken Rip van Winkle of an Eric—the main effect being that Jake showed both his age and his disease much more starkly. Nora covered this perception with applause (no going back on her inspiration) and by moving on quickly to the question of her own costume.

"There aren't too many things you can be, sitting down. Once I went to a masquerade on my crutches. Some woman there assumed they were part of my costume, and immediately proceeded to berate me soundly for my inexcusable insensitivity."

Eric offered to construct something out of cardboard and duct tape around her in her chair, but Nora couldn't decide what, so in the end she went as the Beautiful Blonde Mystery Woman in the Wheelchair. . . .

It was a glorious party, and the twenty-three assorted goblins, nuns, Sixties hippies, knights in aluminum-foil armor, princesses, and witches in attendance were among the luckiest people on earth, to be living in this enchanted place, she thought; and all of them seemed to realize it, at least for this enchanted night. Nora had never wanted to live quite this simply or this far outside contemporary society herself, even when she'd had the physical capability, but she had to admire how resourcefully these folks had done it, if their pastries and homebrew were any indication.

Jake had been right, though; the logistics of daily life here were too rugged for her, and next morning they headed back to civilization—but not before Eric lifted Nora onto his gentlest horse and led her up to the head of the valley, where she could get some sense of the view from top of the mesa. She returned "sore but soaring," as she told Jake. He'd drunk more than he'd meant to, overslept, and missed the excursion.

Even before they'd left the airport parking lot that first day, it had been obvious to Jake that, while Nora was touched by his unbearably intense feelings for her, she couldn't return them with anything but friendship and sympathy—and every night but Halloween for as long as she was there, with more of that truly amazing sex. Nora's love-making, at least with him, had from the beginning been beautifully simple, graceful, and direct. ("Can I safely assume," she'd asked as their clothes were coming off that first night together, back in Mary-land, "there's no chance at all you could have AIDS, or anything else I wouldn't want?") Now she was inspired. And so was Jake, in bed.

The first time he'd kissed her below the waist she'd said quietly, "Just don't describe my scars to me, please—or even mention them, promise?"

"Play me a trio," she'd say now, "I mean, play a trio on *me!*" And he'd comply, with tongue and fingertips and everything else he could think of, on both breasts and that other instrument he wished he could believe no one else had ever played so well, until she drowned out the Mozart, or the Bach, on the tapedeck. "They're the only composers beside Yours Truly I have time for anymore," she'd said on that origi-nal night. He seconded the motion, when it came to music to make love by.

". . . Please don't come in my mouth," she'd always whisper, and stay down there until he'd wonder if his nervous system would short out or melt down, or whatever it was that a nervous system might do from such an overload of sensation. But there were never any prob-lems with what she'd asked him not to do. . . .

The problems all came afterward, lying there beside her, think-ing—or not really thinking anything much, simply *knowing*: in 144 . . . 120 . . . 96 . . . 72 . . . 48 . . . 24 more hours, she'd be gone, back to her bright world, her serious work, her rich, full life. And he'd be back at the dreary little business of dying.

It wasn't envy or anything like it he felt, and he certainly didn't wish a fate like his on anyone, Nora least of all. It was just so hard, so goddamned bitter to taste what his life could've held, if only . . . only what? He couldn't claim he hadn't been endowed with enough time as it was to make his existence as rich, full, bright, and serious as any, ever: he'd already outlasted Shakespeare, for instance, not to mention Mozart, Schubert—he could go on for hours listing high achievers who'd died young, including some like Keats at less than half his present age, but what was the point? He knew too well that having another twenty years ahead of him, guaranteed, wouldn't give him what he wanted most: Nora to share them with. . . .

And then, if he got past all those mental quagmires, there remained the gaping black question of what being alive on this planet in a few more years would be like—the way everything was going, it seemed more than probable that it would be something you wouldn't want to wish on anybody. So maybe he was getting out of it all just in time, and it was the survivors he should be pitying, rather than himself. . . .

But if the nights were bad, mornings were still worse, when Nora practiced for at least an hour before their expeditions, and Jake struggled to haul himself up out of far too little sleep and hangover-magnified depression with too much coffee and too many cigarettes. He kept trying to tell himself he wasn't hurting, he was a tough old bird, but whenever he wasn't at Nora's side, he'd taken to sneaking quick hits from a bottle of bourbon he'd hidden behind a flowerpot out in the yard, where she wouldn't hear any surreptitious clinks.

Aside from the fact that he said so little anymore, beyond what was strictly necessary, there were many things about Jake now that disturbed Nora. He seemed quite different from the man she'd met back east barely two months ago . . . he wasn't so angry then, she realized, or so desperate. Or if he was, he hadn't been showing it so much.

Not that he was showing it so very much now, except for once, on her next-to-last day, when they drove up to Bandelier. But she felt it—the anger—the whole time, excepting only when they made love.

And the desperation: by the third day she'd pleaded, "For god-sakes, Jake, don't keep staring at me all the time like that!" A pause, and a look that tried to tell him: *I know why you do, why you can't help it.* . . . "It's very tiring."

And so he tried his best to keep his eyes from soaking up her image in such a hungry, hopeless way.

The road to Bandelier National Monument wound up past mile after mile of barbed-wire-topped security fence and hundreds of KEEP OUT! signs surrounding Los Alamos. As he drove, Jake found himself unable to refrain from voicing some of his recent reflections on nuclear madness, how the deep secrecy surrounding the acquisition of atomic weapons had insidiously corrupted government at every level to the point where officials not only condoned the routine poisoning of their own people, but maintained a deliberate policy of lying about it afterward, as at Hanford in Washington State; or St. Louis, Missouri; or Rocky Flats, Colorado; or Oak Ridge, Tennessee; or Savannah River, South Carolina; or any of literally dozens of other places around the country—and those were merely the ones where the truth, some of it, at least, had leaked out eventually, like the radioactive waste itself. Who really knew how many more there were?

And once begun, Jake couldn't help going on to tell her about Yucca Flat in Nevada, and how he attributed his leukemia to having been intentionally irradiated out there.

Nora was shocked, and agreed with everything he had to say about all the insanity loose in the world today, up to a point—but not with his fury and despair. Two subjects they'd never more than touched on before were politics and cancer: he knew her own cancer had taught her the pricelessness of time, and work, and enthusiasm—but everything loses value, he was learning, when the clock runs out: like cut and bundled evergreens on city sidewalks, past midnight, on Christmas Eve. . . .

Nora's personal view of her own disease and of cancer in general was diametrically opposed to Jake's. Instead of blaming society for it, instinctively she looked for causes, flaws, in herself. Jake lost his temper over this:

"Jesus Christ, you were raised in northern New Jersey! Don't you know that made you nearly twice as likely to fall prey to some form of cancer as most Americans your age? *They* did it to you, just as undeniably as they did it to me! And believe me, if I had any means, however drastic, of ending such willfully ignorant mass murder, I'd cheerfully give up whatever time I've got left!"

She was relieved when they arrived at Bandelier, and he began to speak instead of how the original Southwesterners had taken refuge in these cliff dwellings during their dark ages, after the abandonment of cities like Chaco, when barbarians and famine stalked their ruined land. . . .

By the time Nora's week was over, Jake found that he was actually more relieved than otherwise to see her go: the strain of seeing, hearing, touching, sleeping with someone he wanted more than he believed he had ever wanted anything in his life before, and knowing it was all just too goddamned late, was increasingly impossible to bear. And the drinking had weakened him, his spleen and liver felt swollen, his joints ached, he often felt weak and dizzy, he was sure his blood counts were dangerously low: all clear indications that his leukemia was back again, in force.

Before she passed beyond the metal detector, Nora told him

quickly, as if she'd rehearsed it (and she had): "I won't say goodbye. I never do. I never—almost never—say this, either: I've loved being loved by you, Mister Jake. I'm very glad and grateful to have known you. It was more than a little special. I join you in wishing it could've been different, somehow. I hope all the goodbyes you do say are good ones. And that you find ways to make your peace with . . . how everything's turned out."

Jake bent down to be kissed, but she drew back and held out her hand instead, sniffing and blinking hard. So he shook hands, gravely, businesslike. Spinning one wheel against the other, she turned and rolled away in one smooth motion and didn't look back. The uniformed man at the metal detector undid a little chain and motioned like a matador, for her to go around it.

After he'd watched her fly away, Jake drove back up to Santa Fe and sat alone in the silent little house, finishing the bottle from out in the yard and contemplating ending it right there. Another quart of bourbon and the painkillers he had left from NIH would certainly do it. But somebody, sooner or later, would have to walk in and find him, and deal with that. And what about Eric and their trip? Nope. That wasn't the way. Gradually he shook off his self-pity and decided to find a doctor.

Out on the street again in too-bright sunlight and early rush-hour traffic, he found himself frightened and disoriented. Making what he thought was—what he was sure used to be—a legal left turn, he was pulled over by a police car. He managed to talk his way out of a drunk-driving charge but not a warning ticket, before the polite young Chicano cops drove him to St. Francis Hospital, where he was held overnight and given a transfusion.

Next morning, the doctor in charge wanted to commit him for tests and therapy, but the fresh hemoglobin in his veins made him feel strong enough to say no, sign himself out, retrieve the stationwagon, pack, straighten up the little house for the last time, and hurry back up to the valley.

Eric looked very relieved to see him again, and Sallyanne looked decades younger—not only washed, but waxed, and the cracked or discolored side windows had been replaced, the worst of the dents pounded out, and the paint retouched around them. Sure, Eric said, no reason they couldn't leave first thing the following day.

"Great," Jake told him. If they got off early enough, they ought to make the Grand Canyon by nightfall, and could reach Phoenix the following day. They'd decide how long to stay there when they saw the lay of the land. Then on to California to hunt for Elizabeth. What happened after that Jake didn't really care, so long as he could keep moving. Traveling meant life to him now, to stay in one place was to die.

Falling asleep that night, gazing into the darkness where the side of beef no longer hung because Eric had traded a piece of it for freezer space somewhere, Jake briefly remembered his promise to Gil, and the fact that he never had reached Simon. But all that seemed like years ago. . . .

II: CRITICALITY

(1 0 / 3 1 – 1 2 / 4)

> ". . . the theory of self-organized criticality: many
> composite systems naturally evolve to a critical
> state in which a minor event starts a chain reaction
> that can affect any number of elements in the
> system. Although composite systems produce more
> minor events than catastrophes, chain reactions of
> all sizes are an integral part of the dynamics.
> According to the theory, the mechanism that leads
> to minor events is the same one that leads to major
> events. Furthermore, composite systems never
> reach equilibrium but instead evolve from
> one metastable state to the next."
>
> — Per Bak and Kan Chen

9: SUZANNE

Halloween again, the same one but some fifteen hundred miles north-east of New Mexico and early evening this time, as a rusted-out old Malibu crept along a shabby, treeless street where a chill mist was aspiring to become a freezing drizzle out there on the other side of a cracked and Scotch-taped window in downtown Toledo, Ohio. For a few seconds Suzanne almost wondered if it could be the Malibu she'd abandoned on the Interstate three weeks before, arisen now from some grim, fog-shrouded junkyard and come back to haunt her—but when it passed beneath the only working streetlight on the block, she could see that this one had once been dark blue, not dark green like hers. . . .

This Malibu was following three thin children in cheap bright drug-store masks and costumes as they trudged doggedly from door to door, poking every bell button. Most houses stayed dark, except for the monotonously eerie flicker of television sets. Most doors didn't open. When someone finally did drop something into their shopping bags, the solemn trio returned immediately to the car, where the woman driver snapped on a flashlight and thoroughly inspected each piece of candy before it was consumed.

They skipped the narrow white and pea-green clapboard house where Suzanne sat watching invisibly from behind a yellowed muslin curtain, even though the porch light downstairs was lit. She could've guessed at why, but she was otherwise occupied at the moment, remembering England . . . Halloween always reminded Suzanne of England because it reminded her of Guy Fawkes Day and of walking along the slick gray streets of East London on that day, thinking that America should have such a holiday—but first someone would have to try to blow up Congress, wouldn't they? Or the White House, that'd do just as well. But not just try, really *do* it. She'd never read any of the history behind his gunpowder plot, and Fawkes had probably been some rightwing asshole, but anyhow, he'd had a good idea there. . . .

That must've been November of '77, when she'd seen those bon-
fires and the tough little brats with burnt cork on their pinched faces,
demanding pennies for the Guy. That was when her grandmother had
staked her to a year in Europe, thinking she could do with a little
civilizing, and clearly, she was never going to be done with college,
or find herself a husband there. But Suzanne hadn't gotten beyond
England, and scarcely anywhere outside London and Liverpool, because she'd met Glor in London through one of the women's groups
Katie had said to look up, followed her to Liverpool, and then hung
around there for nearly eleven months waiting for the stupid bitch to
make up her mind: which was she, anyhow, gay or straight? All right,
Glor wasn't stupid, but she'd certainly been a bitch, and Suzanne
sincerely hoped she was still ass-deep in squalling Cockney bastards,
it'd serve her right.

Liverpool had been the dullest, dreariest, most depressing place
Suzanne had ever seen. Not anymore, though—now she had Toledo to
measure the rest of the world against. Nowhere on earth, she was
sure, could touch Toledo, Ohio, for dull, drear, and depressing. Not
Liverpool, not New York State's Queens or Buffalo, not even Pennsylvania's Scranton. But she'd been here for seven, no *eight* whole
years now, entirely of her own volition. Nobody to blame but herself.
A sobering thought, if there ever was one. . . .

Stabbed a finger at the Heartland of America, she did, with both
eyes shut. To organize working class women, she'd told her parents,
who couldn't *not* approve of that. They couldn't really fuss much about
her name-change, either. And when she'd given her father the new one
on a slip of paper at Grand Central where they'd come to see her off,
all he'd done was nod and say, "It's a good idea, not to have a Jewish
name out there."

It was her mother who'd asked what not to tell "Them" when "They"
came looking for her. Both tacitly assumed it was simply because
she'd known "all those people back then." If there was more to it—
if she'd actually *done* something—they definitely didn't want to know
the details. Suzanne could recall two comments her mother had made
on separate occasions during Susan Rosenberg's trial, and one question she'd asked a short while later: ". . . That girl's absolutely crazy . . .
I pity her family . . . Did you know her at Barnard?" (As a matter of
fact, no.)

But she had to give her parents this much: they understood not wanting to wait around to be questioned by the FBI. Questions was probably all it would've been, in Suzanne's case. She never had *done* anything very serious, but she did know a lot of "those people," and it certainly did seem like they were all being rounded up for one reason or another, the few who were still at large by that time.

Whatever she *said* she was doing it for, though, Suzanne knew that she was really only running away from Lisa. . . .

But anyhow, she'd actually taken that dramatic blind stab at a map, and when she'd opened her eyes, her fingertip was halfway between Toledo and Detroit. Talk about your rock and your hard place. Closer to Toledo, she'd decided. Of course, she could've gone exactly where it landed—Monroe—but she doubted any place that size was quite ready for a karate studio for women only.

But neither was Toledo then, or for bodywork, either. Some days she was sure Toledo still wasn't ready, never would be. Make that most days. Toledo had needed another women's crisis center, though. Badly. As where in this world didn't? Only someplace where there weren't any men . . . no, not true, not even there, she had to admit. Some women can savage others almost as cruelly, and she'd seen plenty of it; she'd been on both ends herself, as a matter of fact. And that was what she missed most about the Seventies: for nearly a decade there, it had been possible to pretend that women really were Better People, just exploited and misled. And that more women in more positions of power would mean a safer, saner, more caring world. By the Eighties, she'd known better—long before then, really, but it was hard to give up such an attractive illusion. . . .

1977. How long ago that seemed. Seemed, hell—how long ago that *was*. And what a different Suzanne: slacks and tailored shirts with button-down collars; she hadn't yet discovered, or required, the lebensraum of overalls. Still a pretty sleek old bod then, still good for the occasional turned head of either persuasion when she chanced to stretch for something or bend over—but my god, she realized, it should've been, I was only twenty-four! And she'd barely even heard of karate, tai-chi, or bodywork. Let alone Toledo. Crisis centers she'd been familiar with, though, since long before the term became part of the language. Sometimes she thought of her whole life as one endless crisis center. Before the bruised housewives who wept on her shoulder, it was boys or men sobbing there, all of them feeling just as battered (all but the first one, anyhow) by life in general, if not by women or each other. That's the great curse of broad shoulders, she thought: forever getting cried on, while the rest of you goes begging. . . .

Speaking of your different Suzannes, how about ten years before that? Miniskirts then—or come to think of it, only a single one that whole autumn, shiny black leather, tight as hell, and *every*body's head turned whenever she bent over. And always with the black boots that went clear to her dimpled knees, and that tight white turtleneck that showed her brand-new, pointy boobs off so nicely, and why the hell not, she'd thought—if ya've got it, flaunt it! Drive 'em up the wall! Such was the consensual wisdom of the Girls' Room at Bronx Science, in 1967.

And at the same time, she was a very shy and studious fourteen-year-old—but still, she was more than flaunting it: she'd already peeled it and offered it, on her parents' Castro (giggle) Convertible, to that sexy sophomore who rode the same "E" train as she did every morning in from Queens, always with his nose stuck in something Very Heavy, until the day when he looked up and stuck his tongue out at her over the top edge of Marcuse, then leaned heavily against her as the doors slid open at Seventh Avenue, and had his arm around her waist before they'd crossed over to the Uptown "D" platform. Then was waiting outside her last class that day. And thrust his cool hand between her bare thighs, and that hot wet tongue in her ear, on both the "D" and the "E," while returning shoppers scowled.

Suzanne remembered calculating, as she put the chain on the door behind them, that they had an hour and forty-seven minutes before her parents could be expected home. It took seventeen from start to finish, leaving an hour and a half for him to quiz her on what her parents had done in the Party in the Thirties and Forties while she bled copiously into the towels she'd had the foresight to spread out underneath them. Pretty precocious, she thought now. She wondered how many fourteen-year-olds, even today, were that practical the first time.

A condom, though, she *didn't* think of. If she were fourteen today, she was sure she would. He'd gotten around to the matter of contraception the following week, escorting her down to a free (but quite efficient and discreet) clinic on the top floor of a Lower East Side walk-up, where she was fitted with her first of the four diaphragms of her brief but fairly busy heterosexual career. By that time, of course, she was already pregnant.

So she had her first abortion during the midwinter break, six weeks before her fifteenth birthday. She thought he'd offer to go there with her, too, but he said he had to be somewhere else that morning. So she went alone, and her parents never knew, nobody ever knew but the sexy sophomore and that drunken wreck of a doctor. And it was every bit as awful as her nightmares had forecast. Next time, she was nearly seventeen and could pass for an adult and the probable guy could afford it, so she went to Puerto Rico. Cleaner, calmer, but just as devastating. The one after that, her last one, she went back to the same place but paid for it herself with money her grandmother had contributed towards "a decent wardrobe"—*that* schmuck never even offered. By the time you could get it done legally, she was as sure as she'd ever been of anything that she'd never need another.

Her parents—that's how she'd always thought of them, her personal pair of parents, like her pair of hands, feet, and everything else you're normally issued two of. They'd looked like a pair, more like fraternal twins than a married couple, and Suzanne hardly ever saw one alone. They were seldom out of each other's sight, and never out of each other's conscious thoughts.

Ten or fifteen years before she was born, when her brother Karl Frederick—that right-wing sonofabitch—was little, they'd traveled around the country together, wherever the Party sent them. But after Hungary, and certainly as far back as Suzanne could recall, they'd run the hardware store on Webster Avenue in the Bronx inherited from her grandfather, leaving their Jackson Hills apartment side by side every morning, six days a week, returning together every night at 5:50.

They'd died together, too, six years ago in a car crash on the Taconic, returning from their cottage in the Berkshires—some communist lifestyle, huh. Goddamn Fred didn't even tell her until weeks after their funeral; he claimed he'd forgotten the name she was using—how could any true-blue American ever forget *Kennedy*?—and couldn't find her number. Eventually she'd pried enough out of him from the estate to buy this skinny little house on this drab little block.

She'd bought it for Lillian really, to give her something to point to and pound her tiny fists against, to prove their life together was solid and would endure. Weepy little Lillian, who ran off to Hawaii a year ago last Hiroshima Day with the biggest, ugliest bull dyke you ever saw. Leaving behind, without so much as *ciao!*, Suzanne and seven Siamese cats in this useless damn shack, that didn't have a single room in it big enough for her to swing her arms around freely, let alone to give classes in, because Lillian had always hated anything *big*. So

Suzanne still had to rent that tacky studio over the hair salon down on the corner, which meant she was working for under five bucks an hour when she taught only six women at a time. And she couldn't even remember the last time she'd had a paying class that large. . . .

What a long way from Northern Boulevard. Yeah. But here she sat now, cross-legged on the edge of her futon, waiting for a gray Plymouth sedan to carry that sexy sophomore back into her life again. How he'd traced her here she hadn't asked him yet, but for the past year or more he'd been calling every few months, always hours-long conversations and always in the middle of the night, just rapping about old times and the fucked-up state of the world. Okay, so she *was* concerned, but would she be willing to *do* something, if an opportunity to make a real difference ever came along? And each time he said anything of the sort, she couldn't help feeling flattered and excited.

He never mentioned where he was calling from or what he was up to, but god, he'd been underground forever, just about. All the Weatherpeople and everybody else had surfaced ages ago and made obeisances to society somehow, but not Gillie Townsend. When she said something to that effect, though, he flipped it around and called *her* 'Wrongway Corrigan' for going under when she did, while all those Sixties types were crawling out of the woodwork.

"Wrongway who?"

"If you don't know already, forget it. Not worth cluttering up your head with. Ancient American folklore, that's all. . . ."

No telling what he was really like anymore, what he might've become. Last night on the phone, he'd given her to understand that something Very Big was happening. As deftly as Jascha Heifetz on a Stradivarius, he'd played on her lifelong left-wing fantasies of an essential personal role in altering the course of history.

The last time she'd seen Gil—until just now, these past two days—was at the Siege of Chicago, only an hour or so before that famous shot was taken, the one with him and two or three other guys (but he was the focus) astride that statue with all the horses rearing, waving an enormous Viet-Cong banner. She and Gil had been separated in the park when tear-gas canisters started popping all around them, and she'd hung back to put on the ill-fitting mask he'd handed her. He hadn't returned that night or the next to any of the pads they'd been using,

so she'd caught a ride back to New York with one of the last stoned car-
loads of Yippies.

Over the next few months she heard he'd turned up at the most
recent DC rally (she went to it, too, but so did over half a million other
people) and that he'd been seen in several places out on the West Coast,
and then in the wings at that SDS conference where Bernardine Dohrn
exhorted everyone to follow the Manson Family's shining revolutionary example ("— Forks! Can—you—*dig*—it?"), and even in Manhattan, right around the time the Whitehall Street Induction Center got
blown up again. And later on that same year, somebody else told her
Gil had been spotted in Europe, hanging out with Danny the Red.

She'd left current safe numbers with everybody he might've
wanted to get in touch with, but never heard another word. After the
Times named him as one of those being sought in connection with the
Dow bombing, she knew she wasn't going to—but she was so desperate for a while there, she might've tried his family, if she'd known how.
He'd never met *her* parents, either, but he'd certainly known who they
were and where to find them. While he, she now realized, had never
mentioned a single relative, or anyplace he'd ever called home. All
right, it *was* an Open Relationship—but the fucker could at least've
said goodbye!

The crash pads he'd introduced her to were too scary on her own,
and those new-style demonstrations, with their "mobile tactics" or
whatever, all seemed pointless as well as dangerous, unless you stuck
with the pacifists, went limp and got busted, or else showed up looking
as if you were there to play pro hockey. Suzanne went back to her
parents' apartment, and they didn't even ask where she'd been for the
past six months. After all, they'd had each other. For lack of better
things to do, she began attending classes again, to find she'd been
passed despite all her incompletes from the previous spring. But high
school was even more boring now, and she took to hanging out around
the Free University, down near Union Square.

There was a very different feeling that year, and very different-
looking young women stood on street corners, passing out leaflets
written and printed by *themselves*: "No More Chicks!" the leaflets
said, "No More Penile Domination Within Or Outside The Movement!"
Suzanne listened with only half an ear for now, and took up with Older
Men, beginning with a beret'd and goatee'd Trotskyist who forcibly
introduced her to the dubious joys of sodomy, then turned out to have

a wife, four little kids, and a big mortgage in western Connecticut. And swiftly concluding with a fifty-year-old beatnik who loved to make casts of her tits in purple Day-Glo plastic, until he shot a little too much speed one fine day and wound up a permanent fixture at Daytop. She was more than ready by that time:

Fuck You All, You Chauvinist Pricks, whatever your politics! Hello, Libby! Greetings, Red Stockings! Welcome to the Lesbian Caucus! And you betchyer sweet ass, kid: Sisterhood IS Powerful!

Funny, how vividly seeing Gil again had brought it all back. Equally so, how little any of it mattered, anymore. And Toledo seemed several times as dreary, since he'd headed east again.

If it hadn't been for that perfectly poised, totally self-assured posture, she wouldn't in a million years've guessed it was him. He'd looked like some guy who'd come by to read the meter, or to fix the washing machine she didn't own. Within a matter of minutes, though, he'd put her entirely at ease and had her laughing fit to bust a gut, meanwhile pulling all her latest political ideas apart and reassembling them in his own way as if they were made of Legos . . . and before they'd made it halfway through the first bottle of that very good champagne he'd brought along, she knew she was In It—whatever It might be.

". . . An international minimum wage, huh? That's what you've been cooking up out here in the Rust Bowl?"

"A worldwide labor bill of rights," she'd amended. "Nothing less'll stop the megacorporations from skipping from one country to the next, as soon as the workers get it together to ask for enough income and job security to live like human beings."

"That's a very pretty notion, but how d'you bring it off?"

"Well, I think first we're gonna have to convince American and European trade unionists of the fact that it's in their best interest to set up education programs throughout the Third World and former Soviet Bloc countries—"

"You're talking *eons*, pardner. And we ain't got that kind of time anymore, if we ever did. To cite just the two most obvious reasons, this greenhouse business and the population boil-over'll have us all dead or wishing to hell we were within another twenty years, unless we can get 'em by the short hairs somehow right *now* and *make* 'em agree to some drastic changes, like what you've just been talking about, and then some."

"And how d'you plan to do that?"

"Aha. That's pre-cisely what I've come all the way to this fair city to invite you to become an indispensable part of. Can't let you in on much about *how* yet, but believe you me, this is the gig we've both been waiting around all our lives for, and just you hang in with me, kid, and I guaranfuckingtee you, we will grab—and twist!—and yank!—on the shortest hairs of all, and believe me, they'll say *Ouch!* and *Uncle!* and anything else we want 'em to."

"They will, huh?"

"Yes, they will. You want 'em singing the *Internationale,* we'll put it in the script."

"Hm," she'd said, and then, pretending to be thinking it over, "So tell me something else—how *did* you find me?"

He'd shrugged and tried hard to look modest. "The way I do 'most everything: a couple of hunches and a lot of blind luck. I s'pose you took the good ol' look-up-a-stiff-and-send-off-for-a-passport route?"

"Anything wrong with that?" No point in denial—she'd thought at the time it was a real stroke of genius. Later on, she'd found her method had been fully described in several novels and at least two Hollywood movies: what's a cliché? any bright idea, encountered more than twice. . . .

"No, if you've got time to burn at both ends, that old chestnut still works just swell—so long as you don't make it a little too easy for whoever might want to look you up, for instance by hanging onto your first name and last initial. I mean like, if you were trying to find a used-to-be Suzanne Klein in the Midwest who just might be teaching martial arts and you discovered there's a Susan Kennedy in the Toledo Yellow Pages doing that, you'd check her out first, right?"

While Suzanne blushed, he'd grinned and added generously, "It's a common and frequently but not necessarily deadly error of the neophyte fugitive—done it more'n once myself, so I know. Very hard to pass up, when something just right like that jumps off the microfilm and hits you between the eyes like Destiny. But in any case, as I was saying, unless you've got months to kill—which we don't—ID is one department you should never shop for bargains in, so for *this* operation, we're gonna buy you the absolute best, pal. . . ."

One of the oddest parts of those two days together, she'd thought, was when Gil brought up the matter of their rendezvous on the East Coast. "What've you got for wheels?" he'd asked, and when she'd answered "Nothing," and suggested she could fly there, he'd stared as if she had two heads.

"People *do*, you know," she told him. "Everyday."

"I've heard tell. You'll never catch *me* doing it, though," he said grimly. "Got as far as the metal detector once—and I was clean as a . . . *kumquat*! But I just couldn't face it, I mean, Christalmighty, strapped into one of those tin cans with all those other sardines, and totally helpless? What if some nut pulls a hijack or plants a bomb, or a piece of the goddamned thing just falls off on its own in midair, those things *do* happen, you know, a lot more often than people tend to remember, and they don't even give you a parachute, do they? Sure you wouldn't rather drive, be your own boss, set your own schedule? Hey, I could probably even pick you up something sporty tomorrow before I leave. No? Okay, then. I sincerely hope not, but it's *your* funeral. . . ."

So, anyhow. She now had twelve days, and she'd probably need them all, to find friends to take over her classes, cats, and work at the center. She also, with the money Gil gave her, had to acquire a wardrobe the likes of which she'd never worn since she'd first begun to choose her own clothes. Overalls and a combed-forward brushcut just wouldn't make it, he'd said.

And she had to set up a safe place to stay in the Washington area for the couple of months he'd figured it might take to pull everything together; there should be no traceable connections between them down there, he'd said. She'd already begun working on this, so far without success . . . she knew it wouldn't be considered sound revolutionary practice to combine important work with personal pleasure, but she hoped to stay with an old friend from Manhattan roommate days whom she hadn't seen in more than a decade, who'd been one of her first and dearest woman lovers.

She hadn't told Gil about this little plan of hers, and didn't intend to unless and until it was actually going to work out, even though she'd decided he was probably one of those rare men who could consider the notion of two women making love without sniggery jokes or open jealousy.

But her plan didn't look very likely to happen. After getting nothing but a screwed-up taped message at her friend's home for two evenings running, Suzanne had tried her office, only to be told she'd gone away on vacation and hadn't left any number where she could be reached, try again next week. . . .

10 : JOHN

Gil had never visited John and Mercy in Meredith, New York, before, but he did have a map John had sent him, on the back of an enthusiastically detailed and labeled sketch of the barn on their property. Meredith lay in the far western reaches of the Catskills, slightly beyond what all but the most driven New York City types considered a feasible commute, so the dairymen still had some of it in their precarious grasp. It was handsome country, Gil thought, if your taste in landscapes ran to gaunt/bleak/majestic. Nowhere else he'd seen on this whole trip across had looked quite as far along into winter yet. . . .

He'd driven straight through from Toledo, stopping only for gas and several phone calls. All but one of those were only attempted phone calls: no luck with Claude or Rafael at any of their regular times and numbers, and Gil decided to quit trying. He doubted there was any way he could be traced without a connection being made (that was something to ask Simon about—who knew what those hotshots might cook up next?), but all his instincts told him, loud and clear, *that chapter is closed.*

He did, however, reach a friend near Wagon Mound, New Mexico, whom he'd called first from Topeka, and no, she hadn't had much luck in turning up much along the lines he'd given her, from newscasters or journalists in the area. "Here's a column-filler from last week, though, the early-edition Pueblo paper, that you just might find of interest: 'Panic at I-25 Rest Area Due to Air Force Night Maneuvers Mix-Up.'"

"Yeah. Read me that."

"Well, the head just about says it all except for the date and the credit, but here goes:

> Vacationers and tourists were rousted from their
> camper shells and mobile homes last Sunday
> evening at a few minutes past eight o'clock,
> when three Air Force helicopters suddenly

landed with searchlights blazing at the south-
bound rest area between Walsenburg and Pryor,
and troops in full battle gear leaped out. Jennifer
Slosson, 15, of Framingham, MA, said she
thought she was 'in a remake of *Close Encoun-
ters of the Other Kind*.' A spokesperson at Sandia
AFB later said the command helicopter had been
given incorrect coordinates. Apologies were
made, and peace was soon restored."

❖

John Meacham first met Gillie Townsend more than a year earlier
than Suzanne Klein did, in the fall of 1966—but not by that name. It was
a golden lazy late-October Saturday afternoon beside the Stop-the-
Draft literature table on Broadway, just outside the Columbia Gate. A
skinny tow-headed eight-year-old in too-big hand-me-down jeans with
a shameful crewcut he'd attempted to hide under an outsized baseball
cap, John was tagging along after his biggest brother, Junior, and
attempting to deal with his hopelessly tangled yo-yo string.

Junior Meacham, eleven years older than John, wasn't doing even
as well as he'd expected to do in college, and he was becoming fairly
worried about getting drafted and sent to Vietnam. As it turned out,
Junior should've been much more worried than he was, and he
should've burned his card the following April along with all those
other guys in Central Park, the way he'd said for a while he planned
to do—because he *did* get called up the following winter, rushed
through Basic, and shipped over, and less than six months later, he was
flown back home in a body bag.

John hadn't paid much attention to whatever counseling poor
Junior got that day by the Columbia Gate: John's eyes and ears were
focused on the real cool big kid with the gloriously unshorn helmet
of curly red hair who was hanging out behind the table, in groovy
sneakers and bellbottoms and a teeshirt that said "Hell Yes I'm A
Marxist!" with Harpo, Chico, Groucho, and Karl all dancing in a row.
(Years later, John spent many hours scanning microfilm but was
unable to find any record of that design having been produced anywhere before the Seventies—but he was positive he'd seen it, on Gil's
chest, that afternoon: just so, time and again, does individual recollection do its utmost to make a liar out of history, even when the mind

in question has been thoroughly trained in that discipline and repeatedly made aware that the human memory is not a camera.)

But back then, John hadn't yet learned enough history to know that Karl wasn't the other Marxes' father, as he'd assumed on the basis of the beard. This kid, though, sure was real smart, and real funny, and everything else John had ever wanted to be; grownups there listened to him; and above all, he was FREE—that's actually what he said his *name* was. Even so, he'd condescended to untangle that yo-yo string, and then taught John how to do Around the World, Walk the Dog, and half a dozen other tricks John couldn't even recall the names of anymore.

He didn't learn his hero's ordinary, real-life name for more than two years, not until the *Times* printed it with a file photo in the spring of 1969, following the Dow action. Within the week after that initial meeting, though, John spotted "Free" on the second page of the *Daily News,* partly obscured by a cop on a horse in hot pursuit, but it *was* him, there was no mistaking that hair, and he was wearing those same bellbottoms (but you couldn't see the front of his teeshirt). And he'd shown up again and again, in the papers and twice on the evening news, over that first winter. If they printed a photo of any local demonstration, chances were that John could pick out his friend. His next-older brother, Robert, began to tease him: "You ain't *sweet* on that funky freak, are ya? Sure it ain't a flat-chested girl?"

By early 1968, with widespread urban riots in the wake of Martin Luther King's assassination, student strikes at Columbia and other campuses, rent strikes and squatters, tent cities, as well as increasingly militant antiwar activities breaking out everywhere, John's friend had become a personage of sorts among reporters, who began to seek him out and to depend on him to lead them to the heart of any action they were assigned to cover. Some would simply ask him where he planned to show up next, and make that their next story. There were even interviews. (Gil spoke at greatest length with Paul Krassner, but John didn't come across the *Realist* piece until many years later, in graduate school, while working on his dissertation.)

Usually Gil just called himself "Free," but he was "Lyndon Bulls--t Johnson" to a writer for *Ramparts,* and "George Metesky, Jr." to publications like *WIN, RAT,* and *EVO* (after the legendary Con Edison bomber—as with "Free," he'd borrowed that one from Abbie Hoffman). He lived in condemned buildings, he said, or in a packing case hidden in the bushes in Morningside Park. And he'd been on his own since "my parents ran away when I was six" (or seven or nine, depending on the source). He also claimed, variously, that his parents had been hoboes, wetbacks, Wobblies, or Gypsies, that he'd never known who or what they were, that his birth was never registered and he'd never set foot inside a school, "so I won't ever have a draft card, either." (Someone once gave John a copy of Paul Goodman's *The Empire City,* but not having gotten around to reading it, John would never know where this particular tale had come from.)

If John had been dazzled before he read any of those articles, it was nothing to the admiration he felt when he considered the wonders of such unlimited liberty. "Gingerbread Boy of the Left," a caption in *Newsweek* called Gil, for the color of his hair as well as for his perfect record at running away just in time. And he was "The Hippies' Huck Finn" to another journalist in the *Nation*—but even Huck hadn't been *that* free, not by a long way, with his pap and the widder to contend with.

And meanwhile there was John, lifelong prisoner in a dismal brownstone on 99th Street just up from the corner of Riverside Drive, the youngest and most picked-on of four brothers, with a father who always wore a tie and jacket at the table and called each and every one of them "Young Man," and a mother who made him brush after every meal and never let him cut school or stay home from church on Sundays.

"The Sixties, so-called," as John wrote later,

> ... occupied nowhere near a whole decade. Depending upon when one first *turned on* to the collection of ideas and feelings generally lumped together under that very broad label, the period was at most five years long, beginning somewhere in 1963 (the year not only of John F. Kennedy's assassination and the Beatles' first American tour, but of Kesey's earliest Acid Tests) and ending in 1968 with any of several convenient markers. My own choice would be the SDS conference where a Lower-East-Side-Up-Against-The-Wall-Motherfucker leaped up beside the podium, swung a tire iron around his head, and proclaimed that space a Free Zone. ...

However long it really was, to his everlasting regret, John Meacham missed out on the Sixties: barely, but a miss *was* as good as a mile in this case. And what was almost worse, he'd been old enough to grasp the extent of what he was missing—and young as he was, a born pessimist, he'd known all the while that it couldn't possibly last until he'd achieved his independence from his family and all the rest of the Straight World. There was so much of *that* to achieve independence *from*. Just how much, he'd seen for himself, when he'd allowed his parents to persuade him to spend his junior year of high school serving as a page in the U.S. Congress. Maybe all that power and endless wheeling and dealing intoxicated some people—it had disgusted John.

During the late Sixties he'd found other heroes to worship from afar, and eventually (always with some disappointment) he met most of those still around ten or fifteen years later. But Gillie Townsend was the only one he'd actually seen and spoken with Back Then. John Lennon's murder caught John in his senior year at Berkeley, where he'd gone because of the Sixties aura clinging to the name if not the place (over his entire family's protests—Meachams *always* went to Princeton), and he very nearly didn't come out of his consequent depression in time to graduate. Abbie Hoffman's suicide, when John was thirty-one, proved nearly as difficult to shake off. He couldn't decide which of those two deaths was the more senselessly tragic. In totally different ways (but both far more than anyone else but Gil), Lennon and Hoffman had seemed to John to contain within themselves the essential spirit of that very special time, when everything necessary to make life truly worth living had appeared to be almost within everybody's grasp.

That essential spirit had seemed long gone when John finally came of age, and the only alternatives he saw were either to attempt to re-create it on his own, as best he was able, or to catch hold of any actual traces left . . . and once he'd learned how and where to look, John discovered that the Sixties hadn't died out everywhere all at once. Tiny pockets still remained, even into his thirties, and some perhaps always would, because no truly beautiful idea, once thought and shared and acted upon, can ever wholly disappear—a Sixties notion if there ever was one, as John fully recognized.

In odd corners all around the continent, he found little enclaves of people who'd tuned in, turned on, and dropped out during those brief magical years before (as many of them put it) "everything Out There turned to shit." And some were still "hangin' in there," still "doin' their thing," spurning money, growing their own, recycling the larger society's castoffs, exchanging goods and services freely among themselves, living out their own personal revolutions.

❖

In several of those enclaves, John heard legends about Gil Townsend, most often of how he'd arrived on the scene at some moment of communal crisis and done something brilliantly outrageous that usually succeeded, and even when it didn't, still made for a great story. John hoped at first to arrange a meeting through people who claimed to be tight with Gil, but all the latest reports had it that he'd gotten very involved in the Peyote Church and had even been adopted by an Arapahoe elder—taking the Gila Monster for his totem, some said—and he didn't have much truck with hippies anymore.

So John began attending every peyote meeting, anywhere, that he was able to learn about beforehand, even though he never developed an ability to keep that horrible stuff down for more than a few minutes, or to contain the amazing volume of gas it always created in his guts; so he was rarely rewarded (either for those agonies or for the many other often intense discomforts inherent in sitting on cold bare earth all night long in an enclosed smoky space full of similarly gaseous people) with any truly psychedelic experiences.

Eventually all his shivering, vomiting, and leg cramps paid off, though, when one night John found himself part of a bleary circle inside of what looked like an old carnival tent on a hilltop near Yah-Tah-Hey, New Mexico, squatting on his haunches beside and bumping knees or elbows from time to time with a wiry brown man in gloriously greasy home-tanned buckskins who knew the words and the drumming to all the sacred songs better than anyone else there, and who told great tales about the "wild old early Seventies" at the goat roast after sun-up next morning, tales of the deserts and mountains that seldom held many clues as to which century he might have meant by that phrase.

John waited until the gathering was breaking up to introduce himself and to remind Gil of how they'd met once before. It seemed to take half a minute for the grin to begin to spread, but then it didn't stop until it was ear-to-ear. "Around The World, huh? Jesus, 'sixty-six. Not just another age, another lifetime! And you remembered. Hey, you doin' anything with the rest of today? There's another meeting I gotta be at this afternoon. You wanna come along?"

They got a lift with two elderly Navajos to an abandoned adobe at the head of a dry canyon about half an hour away, where Gil reverently disassembled his water-drum, a three-legged black cast-iron kettle with a piece of thin rawhide stretched tightly over the top.

"What're those pebbles for?" John asked. He'd only seen such drums in use, during the ceremonies, never close-up before.

"You stick 'em up under the edge of the skin, like this, loop the rope around, then down around the nearest leg and back up to the next pebble, see? This way you can always retune it by tightening up the rope, and you don't tear the leather. Whenever it gets too tight and high-pitched, you just tip it until some of the water inside wets the head again."

Gil peeled off his buckskins and moccasins, stashing them and his drum in a steel ammo box hidden up inside the ruined chimney. Then he put on the jeans, plaid shirt, cowboy boots, and crushed stetson that he'd taken out of the box first, rammed it back up where he'd found it, and led John to a newish Dodge pickup concealed under rabbit brush in the narrow neck of an arroyo.

Their destination was another three hours' hard driving, and it could hardly have been a more different sort of meeting, with a schoolhouse full of very tense and angry Indian-, rancher- and miner-looking people. It was conducted in a mixture of Spanish and Tewa, or so John supposed. He was having a good deal of trouble keeping his eyes open by that time, so he never sorted out the details, but it seemed to have something to do with standing up to the Bureau of Land Management. Gil didn't say very much publicly, but several different men sidled up behind him and whispered things in his ear, and afterward he left John to nap in the truck for nearly an hour while he went into a huddle with half a dozen of the toughest-looking ones. When that at last was over, Gil drove John back to Gallup, where he could catch a bus back to Albuquerque and his plane home. They checked at every general store they passed, but never did find a yo-yo.

Gil had sung the whole night before, and talked nonstop all the time they were together in the truck. Whenever he paused, John would slip in questions that set him going again. But when John got back to Berkeley, he realized he'd learned a great deal about eco-politics and monkeywrenching and alternative energy sources and the steadily lousier shape the Earth was in, but almost nothing about Gil, personally. They had, however, swapped mail drops and, from then on, they exchanged infrequent but lengthy, information-stuffed letters on Gil's part, shy but newsy notes on John's.

They'd met on only one other occasion, two years later, very briefly and by accident rather than prior arrangement, at a Rainbow Tribal Gathering in the Missouri Ozarks. Gil was wearing the same buckskins; that's how John managed to pick him out from a distance in the crowd. But when he'd made his way over there, Gil was deep in a clearly private conversation with four burly, shifty-eyed guys who'd just arrived on Harleys.

"Uh, hey, look," Gil said, "I'll catch ya later, you're gonna be here tomorrow, right?" John made a point of it, and hung around the third day as well until almost everyone else departed, but Gil didn't reappear. Gil's next letter, over a year later, was almost entirely devoted to opposing WIPP, the ill-starred federal plan to store all of the nation's nuclear waste in southern New Mexico, and made no mention of their Missouri encounter, so John didn't refer to it, either, in his prompt reply. . . .

❖

John sought out those hidden places across America for most of his twenties, calling his quest the basic research for his dissertation—until he decided he didn't want any degree in modern history or cultural anthropology, and he certainly didn't want to teach. What he did want, above all else, was to join one of those communities. This was not a simple goal to accomplish, he knew that much already. First he'd need Mercy, or someone very like her: a woman who wanted that kind of life, too, and would work hard for it with him.

He'd found her soon enough, or she'd found him—Mercy's carrel was three aisles farther down the stacks. She'd had *enough, already!* of James Otis and the Stamp Act Congress. And she kept catching herself daydreaming about babies. That silly ponytail of his would have to go, but otherwise, John was pretty nearly what she'd finally decided she was looking for. And she herself was sturdy, in both mind and body, but at the same time a dreamer—true, not nearly as much a one as he was, but enough. She also loved the idea of living somewhere "out in the country," and realized that she looked her best in the sort of clothes sold by New Age firms like Smith & Hawken. It should work.

The real problem was that any really *far-out* settlement, from John's point of view, was by then at least a quarter-century old, set in its ways, and didn't relish newcomers, probably never had, seeking internal stability above all else. He knew this, too, from his travels, but he had a list of five possibilities, where he'd been liked well enough to be invited back. He also had a modest trust fund and some basic manual skills. And during their first (urban) year together, while they were trying for what would eventually be Dierdre, Mercy took social service courses and a class in practical nursing. So they wouldn't be going as completely useless neophytes, or beggars.

Mercy, however, vetoed four of John's candidates out of hand: Iowa, Arizona, the Ozarks, and the Sierra Nevadas. She simply wasn't about to deprive her aging parents in Philadelphia of their long-desired grandchildren. It had to be in the East. John's remaining choice was up in the Blue Ridge Mountains, and they arrived, very pregnant, just in time for one of those fiery waves of evangelical Christianity that sweep that region periodically. John found himself swept along with it, and his soul was briefly saved, not for the first time. But Mercy's wasn't—that far from her urban middle-class upbringing and basic common sense she would not, could not, go.

It proved a difficult first (natural, of course, and at-home) birth, and an even more difficult, cold, and lonely first (and last) winter there, in an ancient warren of a farmhouse John hadn't had time, before The Lord's Call, to make tight. When spring came at last to their rescue, they took a collective deep breath and decided to start over, someplace nearer Philadelphia if possible.

The Catskills looked good, and the farther west they went, the lovelier they found the region, the cheaper, and less crowded. They'd been in the town of Meredith going on six years now, on their own land for three. Dierdre had started school, Sean would go next year, Colin was two, the trust fund was wearing very thin, and Mercy had gone to work in Delhi for the county while John set up his bicycle repair shop and looked after the kids.

John had also replaced his periodic religious binges with an earlier passion: following the Mets devotedly through each season supplied all the ritual he needed, and while Northeast winters still depressed him, arcane baseball lore was the best possible substitute for the doctrinal hairs he'd used to split with other seekers after Meaning—and Cooperstown was under an hour away. It was *not* the Sixties, by any means, but it was a life that he was beginning to find he could be fairly contented with, taking it One Day At A Time—although Three Mile Island wasn't all that far away, either, and the local effects of acid rain were becoming steadily more noticeable. . . .

❖

It *was* a magnificent old barn, and Gil admired it lavishly. ". . . Gonna cost a bundle to reshingle and replace all those rotted timbers, though —but if you don't, no more barn in a year or two. Tell you what, you get into it next summer, I'll try to come lend a hand on that roof. I really hate to see a gorgeous old structure like this get too far gone to rescue. Used to be pretty handy at post-and-beam, in fact I organized about a dozen barn raisings around New England and in the Northwest. 'N' did I ever tell you about how I got tight with some Iroquois once and worked high steel for half a year? . . . Oh, hey, d'you mind if I stash some stuff in here when I go down to the City? Dunno what I was thinking of, but I brought half the homestead along, don't it look like?"

There was a lot else around the Meacham place that Gil could and did praise. And when he wasn't splitting wood or helping John with the carpentry involved in setting up his shop, he was discussing next spring's garden with Mercy, teaching West Texas dominoes to Sean and Dierdre, even changing Colin's diapers once or twice. He was a great cook, too, but if you didn't watch him like a hawk, he'd be out in the kitchen again right after dinner, doing up the dishes as well.

Gil didn't have to help out, John was overjoyed simply to have him there—he hadn't found anyone nearby he could really talk to about anything but baseball, and when Mercy got home from work, she naturally wanted to spend most of her time with the kids. Gil said he wished he could stay around longer, but he had things to attend to in New York, and then he was going down to DC. "Matter of fact, John, I was hoping I could talk you into coming along."

"What's up?"

"Well, I'm afraid I can't tell you unless you *can* come. Not that *I* don't trust you, but I'm sworn to secrecy. It's nothing, you know, heavy, I mean violent, but it's not exactly legal, either—*not* that I'm asking you to do anything that could get you into serious trouble, I know you can't risk jail-time, what with the kids, and Mercy working and all. It's just that you'd be perfect for casing the joint, you've worked there, you know your way around. The rest of us, we're just a bunch of hicks, we'd probably blow it right away, no kiddin'. And it'd be great to just hang out together a couple weeks, probably do your head a lot of good to get away for a while, huh? This is really a lovely scene you've got going here, but ... you must feel sort of, mmm, *closed in* sometimes, donchya?"

John talked it over later that night with Mercy, who had already decided that Gil was the most sensitive friend of John's she'd ever met. He probably would've been the most presentable as well, without that perpetual ten o'clock shadow on his face. Next day she called her younger sister, who proved willing to come up and look after things for a week or two.

Gil said he didn't think it'd even take that long to get everything worked out that they might need John's advice for. After the kids' bedtime, over a few crumbs of that spectacular hash, he unfolded the plot.

John found it brilliant—the Yippies had never concocted anything half so funny. And the point was beautifully clear: serve notice on all those old farts, You're vulnerable, you'd better listen, we could've done something much worse!

"It'd take an awful lot of nitrous oxide, though, wouldn't it?"

"Well, that's one of the things you'll help us find out. We were sorta thinkin', all we've gotta get good is whoever's right around the podium, and then as many as possible near some of the vents. Thing is to get 'em acting as silly as they really are, and who knows, maybe a few'll even blurt out the truth for a change. But if the laughing gas route isn't workable, maybe we'll come up with something else even better, and meanwhile, you 'n' me'll have us some fun down there, okay?"

Next morning, Gil had to leave for Manhattan. "See you in four or five days, then," John called after the Plymouth, noticeably higher now in the rear, as it made rippled tracks down the driveway in the first real snow of the season.

11: THOREAU TO BANNING

Straight down I-25 to Albuquerque and then across on I-40 would be quickest, Eric had decided, so that's what he did, without even asking Jake what he thought best. And whenever he wasn't consciously telling himself not to, Eric pushed the old truck to its limits, keeping up with or passing almost everything else on the road—as if that were a way to recapture lost time, past or future. As if speed would help Jake to stay alive. . . .

While he drove, Eric was rummaging through the crannies of his memory for a word he'd just realized he hadn't heard or read anywhere in years. For no good reason he could see, it finally plopped into his mind's lap as they passed the exit signs for Thoreau, New Mexico . . . *laetrile*. He wondered if people whose cancer was declared incurable by AMA doctors still went to those clinics across the border in Tijuana, or if that treatment had been completely discredited, maybe even replaced by something better. Then he wondered how he could find out—he certainly didn't want to suggest anything until he knew what he was talking about. Next time he saw one of those New Age drugstores he'd just have to get up his nerve and go in and ask somebody, that's all. . . .

Jake sat beside him soaking up Beethoven's last quartets and watching the mesas, buttes, trash heaps, and tourist traps of Navajo Country—Interstate version—roll by. He'd left most of his Mozart and Bach in the stationwagon, knowing he wouldn't be able to hear those tapes again without thinking of Nora. Trouble was, there was really only one other thing for him to be thinking about besides Nora, and that was dying.

Well, Ludwig had clearly done some serious cogitation on that subject, especially from opus 127 on, and by 131 it sounded as if he'd been there already and come back simply to tell us all the cold, sorry truth. He certainly had not gone gentle into that good night, but the resolute optimism and sometimes self-righteous certitude often present in his music before then seemed to have withered away, as if frostbitten by direct contact with that almighty nothingness out there. . . .

They made excellent time, reaching the turn-off to the Grand Canyon at four o'clock and Desert View Point just as the sun slid out of sight behind them, and all the other tourists were buttoning themselves up inside their campers or heading back to their motel rooms. Eric pulled into the first parking area he found, and they scrambled out onto a jutting tongue of stone about twenty feet below, feeling as minuscule as microbes against that incredibly vast majesty, gazing down, down, down, and down, into a quickly darkening void, where night seemed to blossom upward from the bottom like ink poured into deep, clear water.

"Nothing but a big hole in the ground," someone had cracked to Jake once, or maybe he'd read it somewhere. Yeah, okay, it was literally just that—but still an incredibly vast and majestic *something*, a monument to Earthly endurance, not the infinite abyss he'd been staring into all day. And it certainly consigned his personal concerns to a microscopic level of significance, at least for the moment. The rest of humanity's, as well.

"We stopped by here once when you were scarcely knee-high," he said, zipping his down vest against the rising wind and swiftly plummeting temperature. "Before your sister was born."

"I kind of remember," Eric answered, bouncing on his heels, hugging himself, in nothing but jeans and a washed-out teeshirt.

"Did I tell you then about the Box?" Jake asked.

"What box?"

"It was in one of the first books I ever read on my own, I couldn't've been more'n six years old. A kid's geography, by a Dutchman named van Loon, I'm pretty sure. Haven't come across a copy since, but I've never forgotten one particular page in it. He was only trying to convey some sense of the scale of this place, I suppose, but what he said was, if you were to build a box on the edge of the Grand Canyon that was a mile square and a mile high, every human being on Earth would fit inside it. Then one good shove, and that'd be 'all she wrote,' for us."

"Nope, don't remember that. Sounds like a good idea, though. Guess we'd need a bigger box now."

"Yeah, three times as big. That must've been written in the Thirties, we were barely two billion then, and most experts were afraid that world population had peaked and was declining. Now they say it'll go to *fifteen* before it levels off."

"Experts," Eric muttered, shivering. "But it still looks like enough room down there, if we hurry up about it."

They discovered a decent fishfry for their late dinner at a neighborhood tavern on the outskirts of Flagstaff, then spent the night in a fairly inexpensive and clean, if decrepit, motel another hundred yards down the highway, sleeping late the next morning, consuming huge truckstop breakfasts, not reaching Phoenix until mid-afternoon. Jake's mother's trailer court, it turned out, was west of Phoenix proper, halfway between El Mirage and Surprise. The court itself (twenty-odd acres of meandering lanes lined with what looked like out-sized milk cartons in every conceivable pastel lying on their sides as close together as possible) was named ESPERANZA, according to nine spindly, chipped, and faded gilt letters propped against a row of diseased-looking palms outside the corroded metal gate.

The yards in front of the aluminum-clad cartons weren't much larger than bathmats, but each was scrupulously fenced and crammed with cutesy plastic critters, homey mottoes, barbecuing gadgetry, beach chairs, diminutive exotic shrubs, and/or sickeningly pungent oleander. The chartreuse trailer directly across the lane from Mrs. Jacobsen's lavender one bore a neatly woodburned and polyurethaned sign on its porch railing:

> We're NOT Senior Citizens
> We're Recycled Teenagers!

A hunched, wizened caricature of the bustling, big-boned grandmother Eric scarcely remembered, she was so pathetically glad to see them (or anyone at all, they guessed) that she didn't begin to nag about their beards and untrimmed hair until the day they mentioned leaving. Far from senile but unwilling to stay focused on anything for more than moments, she seemed to sense immediately what was uppermost in Jake's mind, and her first remark was: "You don't look good—is somethin' wrong?" Jake wasn't ready to explain about his leukemia, at least not right away like that. But she hadn't waited for an answer, boosting the sound on her quiz show to find out which contestant had just won a round, then spending fifteen minutes describing her bowel and bladder problems in vivid detail, going on from there to debate aloud with herself where they should eat dinner that evening. They wound up going to a Red Lobster, where without preamble, over her deep-fried bay scallops, she demanded: "Eugene, d'you b'lieve in Gawd?"

"I'm Wendell, Mom," Jake said. Eugene had been his father's first name. "But no, I'm afraid not."

"Y'are? Afraid, huh? Me, too, real scared, 'cause neither do I, anymore. Never did really, I guess, not like yer dad did. I jist put off thinkin' much about the whole business, it seemed so far away. Now I gotta, though. No Gawd means nothin' after, far's I kin see. Means it's all been fer nothin', all that pain 'n' sorrow. Oh, lord, I never thought I'd git this old. Sittin' here all alone, thinkin' all day long—no stoppin' that—readin' the obituaries even if I don't know nobody in this town, picturin' how one of these days *my* name'll be in there—you gonna use yer tartar sauce, 'r kin I have it? How 'bout yers, Wendell?"

"I'm Eric, Grandma. Here, it's all yours."

Four days of this, four dinners at either of her favorite restaurants (the other was Pizza Hut), four evenings shoehorned in around the TV while she dozed in her wheelchair and Jake's sister, Winona, struggled grimly but hopelessly for some measure of control over the five perpetually fighting or howling children she and her present (but mostly absent) trucker husband had between them, four nights of Jake trying to sleep on the trailer's diminutive sofa and Eric jackknifed into Sallyanne's cab, were as much as they could take. Jake had suggested the first afternoon that they could stay at a nearby motel, but as he'd expected, his mother found the very idea a nearly unforgivable insult. She seemed quite unaware, or unconcerned, that she no longer lived in her own two-story house: when Family comes to visit, they certainly can't stay at any *mo-tel*!

Winona, ten years younger than Jake, seemed too worn down from her late-starting motherhood and job as a dental technician to show much interest in anything else. There was a young Chicana aide provided by Medicaire who opened the packaged lunch from Meals on Wheels and otherwise read comic books on the porch for four hours every day, but it was Winona who cleaned the trailer on weekends, Winona who came by every morning on her way to work to get Mama bathed, dressed, and seated in her wheelchair, and Winona who fixed Mama's dinner and put her to bed each night, with her fistfuls of pills, glasses of water and juice, her saucerful of Oreos all nicely arranged on her nightstand, and the phone placed within theoretical reach as a charm against all "emergencies."

It had to be more than an overdeveloped sense of duty, there had to be love in there somewhere, otherwise there would've been signs of accumulated resentment, Jake thought, but it was hard to find anything of the sort in how they treated each other. Each evening, Winona addressed almost nothing to her mother between "Hi" upon arrival and "Okay Mama time for bed" two hours later, and received nothing whatsoever in reply. Mrs. Jacobsen never had a word of praise or gratitude for her daughter and viewed her grandchildren with disinterest if not distaste, while mention of Winona's husband always produced a grimace of total contempt.

Winona's conversation with Jake and Eric, the little that kids and TV allowed, was a recital of Mama's medical history and a long litany of deceased or ailing relatives, names that hadn't entered Jake's mind in decades and meant nothing at all to Eric. "Well, there's one thing t'be grateful for," she'd told them the second evening. "Mama 'n' me've been checked out regular twice a year ever since since we moved out here, 'n' there's no signs of any cancer yet, in either of us." When Jake looked blank, she said, "You musta heard about Fernald, that factory where they made the fuel rods for atomic power plants, the one they had to close down 'cause all those tons of radioactive stuff leaked out? That was only twenty-three miles from where we lived there in Ohio all those years—twenty-three miles *upriver.* . . ."

Jake thought about leaving a letter with Winona, to be read to their mother later, when Eric would let them know that he was dead and gone; but as he sat there alone late at night with his notepad, he realized he had nothing of any importance to say to either of them. He didn't have a family, he was forced to admit. A family's something you've got to crave and to work at, and he'd never really wanted any part of his . . . or else your family's the prison cell you never feel strong enough to break out of, and then you're like Winona, it's merely where you happen to be serving out your life sentence. But probably you don't think of it that way—or any other way. You just do your time. . . .

Jake had thought of detouring up to Nevada to try to get another look at Yucca Flat, but he wasn't feeling any better, so they decided to head due west on I-10 towards San Bernardino, where they hoped to learn where Elizabeth was now. As they waved back at the slumped, sobbing figure on the postage-stamp porch, Jake couldn't help saying, more to himself than to Eric: "Maybe I'm lucky—maybe it's growing old that's the ultimate disaster."

The nearly four-hundred-mile drive across the desert into southern California was like having a blowtorch aimed straight at them all afternoon, then heart-stabbingly cold as soon as the sun slid behind the low gray mountains monotonously receding out there beyond the windshield. Eric drove implacably, burrowed somewhere deep inside himself, and Jake, starved for music—in spite of the uncomfortable resemblance to how his sister and mother ignored each other—plugged himself into the first tape he happened to pluck out of the box—Mahler's ninth—and with the first bars he found himself back at exactly the same desolate place he'd been stuck in five days before, receiving more bleak communiqués from that almighty emptiness. . . .

Gustav Mahler: it would be hard to come up with anyone who was more hung up on the inescapable fact of mortality, his own in particular; but he'd struggled heroically to dilate his private little tragedy, to make it matter greatly, somehow. And in his own odd way he'd certainly done that, investing his grief with prophetic import until it seemed to portend all the anguish awaiting us further down the road; so that even though Mahler died three years before the onset of World War I, Camus could write this four decades later: "When I think back over the horrors of the twentieth century, I hear Mahler's music. . . ."

That music plumbed the great abyss, seeking out a ghostly exaltation beyond all loss and sorrow, and it carried Jake on now to a performing version of the tenth as completed by somebody named Derek Cooke, then back through Mahler's darkly stalking adagios from his seventh to his sixth and fifth—and all of it seemed to Jake now to be one continuous, colossal *memento mori*, an exquisite hymn to the chill supremacy of death. . . .

As the hours wore by, it was more and more apparent that he'd caught a bug his weakened immune system couldn't cope with, probably from one of his sister's youngsters' constantly running noses. Wherever it came from, Jake's condition quickly worsened, until he was freezing and soaked with sweat by sudden turns, every ten or fifteen minutes. Then his thigh bones began to ache and throb as if they were about to explode. By flashlight he counted those subcutaneous hemorrhages the doctors at NIH had called *petechiae,* multiplying on his arms and legs as he watched.

By the time they'd reached Banning, California, at half past midnight, Jake was incoherent, huddled into himself against the passenger door inside his sleeping bag. Eric followed the HOSPITAL signs and drove straight up to the Emergency entrance. Fortunately it wasn't very busy that night. A purposeful Chicana intern and two orderlies wheeled Jake straight into Isolation and put him on a crash course of "cidal" antibiotics.

His functioning white blood cells had been almost too few to count, the intern told Eric at 4:45 a.m., before advising him to check into a motel and get some rest. Jake hadn't regained consciousness yet, but his vital signs were fairly steady, and there almost certainly wasn't going to be much change one way or the other for the next several hours. Sure, if Eric would call the desk and leave the motel number, she'd make certain he was summoned if there should be any reason.

Pneumonia was the clearest danger now, they said when Eric returned at 8:30, red-eyed but showered and stuffed with an indigestible breakfast. And it was pneumonia that nearly got Jake that second night, while Eric roamed the hallways, dismally useless.

By the following day, though, Jake's infections had been arrested to the point where the doctors in charge felt it was worth the risk to bring him out of isolation for a platelet transfusion, since Eric's had proven to be a close enough match that he could be a donor.

❖

Diagonally across the continent that morning—while Jake and Eric lay side by side in the hospital in Banning with needles in their arms connected by tubing to a centrifuge somewhere behind their heads, and Jake was mumbling, "Please, go into San Berdoo tomorrow, find out where your mother is"—Gil met Suzanne's flight at LaGuardia Airport.

It was on time for a wonder, but they almost didn't find each other at the gate. Gil finally solved the problem by heading for the most statuesque female figure in sight, bearing in mind that Suzanne had always looked as if she'd stepped out of an R. Crumb cartoon. In that auburn wig, silk blouse, cardigan, and tweed skirt, the effect was statuesque, all right, but more like Marie Dressler. Susanne's own first impression, when she'd glanced into the mirror in the ladies', was of Nick Nolte doing Church Lady on *Saturday Night Live*. She couldn't guess what in the real world Gil was supposed to represent, but he was a different species entirely from the drab little fella who'd knocked timidly on her storm door less than two weeks ago. Like Roy Orbison resurrected, maybe: he'd acquired a wig, too—a wig and a half, in fact. (As her Toledo friends would've said, "They musta seen 'im comin'.") With opaque wrap-around shades concealing what little of his face an actual-enough, short, but thick and glossy black, Sikhish-looking beard didn't obscure. Neither of which went in the least with that Sunday-*Times*-Calvin-Klein-Casual outfit, complete with slightly scuffed topsiders.

"What're *you* trying to be?" she couldn't help asking. She wasn't prepared to admit it yet, even to herself, but she was aware of some twinges of misgiving already.

"Different."

"You're that, all right."

So was New York, even before they got out of Queens. Maybe she'd just been in the Midwest too long, but that tumescent profile of Manhattan looming just before the Midtown Tunnel seemed like something concocted by Steven Spielberg. The sense of unreality was compounded for her when Gil handed over her new ID as they waited in line to pay the toll. Those Photomat closeups he'd made her get before he'd left Toledo were bewigged now, too, but in a completely different style. That wasn't what had her scowling at the moment, though. "Susan Jeannette *Stroehlengutt*? Was that the best you could do?"

"Well, I figure it's not likely to be questioned—who'd ever suspect anybody of *choosing* a handle like that? But you'll notice I let you hang onto Susan, that's a common enough name to be safe. Unlike Gilbert."

"Thanks a lot."

"Oh, you're welcome."

Gil stowed the Plymouth in a parking garage on Lexington Avenue, then took her to one of the few remaining old, dark, sour-smelling Third Avenue taverns, where they nursed flat draft beers in a booth near the door until a tall, redfaced man in a maroon elevator starter's uniform with a huge sagging belly and a lot of marcelled hair all the oily colors of badly tarnished silver hurried in and gulped his midafternoon pick-me-up standing, scowling into the clouded mirror over the bar.

"Study his face," Gil whispered, so Suzanne did that. Once back in the Plymouth, across the George Washington Bridge, and onto the Palisades Parkway, when he realized she wasn't ever going to ask why, he told her anyway:

"You'll maybe hafta meet that guy somewhere, to pick up or deliver something. Most likely both."

"Will I need a name or code-word?"

"I just call him Gorgeous George, I mean, not to his face ordinarily, but if you have to call him anything, say that, and he'll know who sent you, if you look anything like you do today."

Suzanne nodded. When they reached Route 17 and headed west, Gil shed his wig and dark glasses and described the Meachams to her, explaining what he'd told John so far about their plans.

"How long you figure he'll stand still for that laughing-gas routine?"

"Long enough to help us find out whatever we need to know. Then he's gone."

"You're counting on him being quite incredibly dense, it seems to me."

"John's not at all dense. What I'm counting on is his not wanting to believe his old idol could be involved in anything but a merry prank. He pole-vaulted to the conclusion that I cooked this up with a bunch of Native Americans and/or Earth-Firsties, and I didn't disabuse him."

Suzanne shrugged. Minutes passed. Finally Gil asked, "How about you, though, friend? I haven't told you a hell of a lot more than I did John, about what's actually coming down. Aren't you kinda curious?"

"Yeah, I'm curious. But I'm sure you'll tell me what I need to know, as I need to know it. Otherwise I'm better off ignorant, we're all better off, right?"

She didn't have CP parentage for nothing, she thought, and would bet Gil was thinking, too. She didn't have to stop to consider the proper attitudes and responses for this sort of undertaking; she'd absorbed them in her highchair, along with her Pablum and apple juice. Her bedtime stories, those she remembered anyhow, had been about class martyrs like Spartacus, Joe Hill and Joe Little, the Rosenbergs, or young Narodniki who'd tied dynamite around their waists beneath their clothes and blown up Czarist police stations when dragged in for questioning.

"So right. Suzanne, you're beautiful, you know that?"

"Yeah, sure. And you're so full of shit we could be burning methane and conserving gasoline."

❖

People in Eric's valley had always had excellent noses for law-enforcement types and little inclination to pass the time of day with any, even when, like this pair, they looked at first glimpse more like Mormons or Jehovah's Witnesses. So, when asked the following after-noon how long it had been since he'd last seen Eric or Wendell AKA Jake Jacobsen, Jerry struck a thoughtful pose and said he couldn't rightly recall. He just normally looked after Eric's stock whenever he noticed there was nobody there at chore time, and Eric always did the same for him.

When one of the pair suggested that Jake might have been driving a blue 1974 Ford stationwagon, Judith said that's right—knowing Eric had stashed that thing under some hay bales at the back of the barn before he left, so no one would be inclined to mess with any of the stuff Jake had left behind inside it.

— What about a 1953 Chevrolet pickup, registered by Eric?

Oh, didn't he finally dam up an arroyo with that heap last summer? Sorry, nope, no idea what Eric might be driving now. If anything. And as far as anybody knew, Jake left there alone, and he most definitely said he was headed back east. . . .

❖

The rightful owner had just returned to the little *café con leche* house in the barrio, and no, she knew nothing about any Wendell AKA Jake. If such a person told the Santa Fe police that was his address, she had absolutely no idea why. One of her nosier neighbors, however, was con-siderably more helpful:

"Y'mean that middle-aged hippie with the rusty old station wagon? Sure, he was here, stayed, oh, I dunno, about a week. I felt so sorry for that poor blonde girl with him, the one on crutches. She'd be *so* pretty, that one, if she wasn't a cripple—huh? Oh, yeah, it wasn't no broken leg or nothing. She had the permanent kind, y'know, the metal ones that grab yer arms like this, right here—what? No. I *know* she ain't from Santa Fe. How d'I know that? Well, he brought her here with suit-cases, he took her away with suitcases, that's how. . . ."

❖

"— Elizabeth?" the scalded-and-scrubbed-looking young woman at the San Bernardino health food store repeated. "Tall, slender, stands very straight, with long, white, kinda curly hair? Yes, she used to teach an herbalism course here. She lives with an awfully nice young man about your age . . . Timmy, that's his name—is he a friend of yours? I've heard they're up near Mount Shasta now. Mary down at the yoga center should have an address for them. I'm pretty sure she's been forwarding their mail."

And she blushed to confess it, but uh-uh, she'd never heard of laetrile. If he'd like to stop in on his way back down the street, she'd attempt to do some quick research.

At the yoga center, Mary gladly produced the address and also showed Eric a page of directions and a careful map of the last few miles. No phone number, though; she was quite sure they didn't have one.

The young woman at the health food store was still on the phone when he got back there. When she'd said goodbye and thank you, she told him, "Laetrile was legalized in California years ago and there are a few doctors who'll still prescribe it, but everybody else is pretty much agreed it doesn't work." She'd already sorted through all the brochures in the racks behind the counter for him, though, and handed Eric copies of dozens of them describing the more up-to-date alternative cancer treatments.

At the Albuquerque airport, the desk man at the luggage area recalled Nora right away. So did a skycap, who said, "I don't forget anybody that special-looking, not when they're also handicapped—y'see, my kid sister's got MS. . . ."

Came on a Monday, left on one as well, they decided between them. Two weeks ago this coming one, that'd be. Must've been the 1:48 p.m. United, DC to LA, and the 2:25 p.m. return.

The woman at the United counter remembered Nora, too, well enough to confirm that opinion. ". . . Here, see, that little black mark alongside means 'wheelchair required.'—Name and address? Mind if I ask my boss first?"

When Eric returned to Banning early that evening, Jake was sitting up in a chair, noticeably thinner and paler than he'd been three days before, his eyes sunk deeper in their sockets, but well enough already to show both humor and impatience. He'd been listening to Mahler's fourth symphony on his Walkman, and finding hope there.

"That's the leukemia game, or so they tell me," he said now, tugging off his headphones. "Half an hour later getting here the other night, it would've been bye-bye for sure. Now, thanks to your platelets, pardner, they're saying they'll probably let me loose Tuesday, if I can just behave myself that long. . . ."

12 : DC / I-695

Glen Echo, Maryland, a cool and brilliant Monday morning but some-how soft-focus around the edges, almost Indian-Summerish, almost magical enough to pass for what New England must've been a month earlier, Nora thought. Not the right color combinations, though, nowhere near enough red. . . .

She'd just tossed in her bag and crutches and laid her viola case on Plosh's (Poor Little Old Chevette's) back seat behind her collapsed chair, then collapsed herself, down into the driver's bucket, and begun the tedious labor of getting herself situated properly behind the wheel, when a car she didn't recognize appeared at the end of her driveway, blocking it completely. Both doors swung open and two large men in wrinkled suits, crewcuts, and sunglasses unfolded from behind them and came toward her, the one who hadn't been driving saying pleas-antly enough: "Good morning, would you be Miss Nora Sherman, and would you mind coming with us briefly, to answer a few questions?"

"That depends on who you are," she said, knowing full well what they were, if not why they wanted to see her. "I happen to be late for work already."

A quick but graceful flash of ID. No telling what it said, she didn't really look, but she was sure it wasn't phony. "It's regarding your friend Jacobsen. We'd like to know where he is now—and why you flew out there to see him."

Before she could think, Nora heard a choked little voice (could that be her own?) asking, "What has he done?"

Offering a courteous, muscular forearm on which to haul herself up again while his partner retrieved her crutches for her, the man said, almost plaintively, she thought: "We wish we knew, Miss. And we're hoping you can help us find out."

❖

In Sherrill's crowded but homey old restaurant/bakery near Capitol Hill at that moment, Gil, Suzanne, and John were ordering breakfast.

The sausages here were not to be missed, Gil said, requesting waffles, two-over-easy, and a side dish of grits to go with his. But Suzanne glumly opted for half a cantaloupe with cottage cheese, and John could never face much more than tea and toast until lunchtime.

There was a strip of mirror on the wall between the rest room doors, and each time John glanced that way, he wondered who that trio was, especially those two males looking so small and insignificant, with that inscrutable feminine eminence between them. Not that they were so different otherwise from everybody else busily filling their faces and studying their newspapers all around them; more because the two men were oddly, hauntingly familiar, in spite of dress shirts, ties, and tweed jackets. John hadn't seen Gil really clean-shaven before this morning—not since 1966, when of course Gil hadn't yet begun to shave. Nor had he been able to observe the lower half of his own face for three years, since Mercy had learned she was pregnant with Colin.

Aging was a strange process, John thought: some features became more prominent while others receded, and the over-all effect inevitably coarsened, as if painted with an ever-broader brush. That might've been his own father in that mirror over there, the Dr. Meacham of John's earliest memories, before he'd gotten his full professorship. John couldn't put an easy label on what he saw in Gil's appearance; whatever it was hardly ever lasted long enough to classify. Right at that moment, he could've been a business rep in town to press for a particular little loophole in an upcoming trade bill, or an out-of-town lawyer somewhere between struggling and modestly successful hoping to get his pet case before the Supreme Court but not quite sure of how to go about it. . . .

So far, it definitely hadn't been the fun trip John had anticipated. He'd brought his guitar along and had urged Suzanne to sit up front so he could spread out on the back seat and play, but as soon as he was getting really warmed up, she'd swung around and growled, "Don't you know *anything* but that goddamn Dylan or the Beatles?"

No, as a matter of fact, except for some early Stones and Grateful Dead tunes, a couple of the Mamas and the Papas', a few of the Lovin' Spoonful's, and three or four of Joplin's (Janis, not Scott), which she didn't care for, either. For John, any kind of music other than what had come out of the Sixties was just more or less unpleasant noise; but he knew all the verses and guitar chords to everything John Lennon ever wrote and most of Bob Dylan, too, including all of his Christian period. . . .

Last night they'd only driven as far as Baltimore, where Gil had abruptly remembered business he needed to look after and had parked the other two in a dark, dank basement apartment he called "a friend's place" for the whole evening, with nothing better to do than to nibble away at Chinese takeout and watch a snowy little black-and-white TV screen. Finally John had holed up in one of the tiny bedrooms and picked away at his guitar, but that wasn't much fun, playing just for himself; he was too keenly aware now that he was sadly out of practice.

He found Suzanne entirely puzzling. Beyond several snide, cutting one-liners addressed exclusively to Gil, almost the only thing he'd heard her say so far was that she had a place to stay from tonight on, just a few blocks from Simon's, wherever that might be, where Gil and John would be staying. Well, they were probably all a little nervous, John told himself. He knew *he* was nervous, as well as god-awful homesick already. At least he was familiar with where they were headed this morning—he'd once spent ten whole months running around that place—but that was a long while ago; maybe he'd find it totally different now. . . .

At Gil's suggestion they left the restaurant separately, walked the half-dozen blocks to the Capitol Building alone by different routes, and each went to a different Congressman's office to get a visitor's pass to the House Gallery, where they sat apart for an hour or so looking around the place, counting ventilator grills, watching what was less a debate than a sullen wrangle over some point so abstruse that even John (who'd found that nothing so far differed in the slightest aspect from the way it had been when he was seventeen) couldn't guess at the issues behind it.

Then, still separate, they wandered, getting a sense of how improbably vast and baroquely complicated a building it was. Gil even joined one of the tours led by young red-jacketed guides, and came away muttering to himself, *Four hundred thirty-two rooms, five levels, totaling fourteen acres of floor space. . . .*

Back at Sherrill's at 4:30, ravenous, they compared notes over Salisbury steaks and Suzanne's BLT. Gil was euphoric, totally 'blown away!' as he kept saying, by how accessible everything was: "Jesus, they must believe The People *love* 'em!"

"Most of 'em do," Suzanne felt obliged to remind him.

"You really believe that?"

"I wish I could 'really believe' otherwise. Where've you been hiding out all these years, Albania? Sure they love 'em, at least enough to keep voting 'em into office. They know they're all a bunch of crooks and assholes, too, of course. The People are confused, to say the least, and ambivalent, as usual."

"That's why *we*'re here: we're the champions The People're too screwed up to know they need."

"Speak for yourself, bud."

"Okay. That's why *I*'m here. How about *you*, then?"

"I haven't quite figured out why yet."

"I hope you'll let me know when you do. Meanwhile, *my* money says it's gonna be the vent system."

John didn't think so. He remembered being told, after the Weatherpeople planted a small bomb in a Senate washroom back in 1971, that silent alarms had been installed on everything like the ventilator grills and the manhole covers giving access to the steam-pipe tunnels.

Nothing else was as unprotected as it looked either, he cautioned. True enough, dressed respectably, armed with file folders and a purposeful expression, you could pass for some sort of staff and penetrate briefly almost anywhere—but there *was* a multi-million-dollar security system directed from a command center underneath Independence Avenue, where the pictures transmitted by 109 television cameras mounted in the passageways were monitored. There were also quite a few security measures taken since John's time, the most obvious being those metal detectors at all the public entrances, which probably dated from the World Trade Center bombing.

Suzanne, who'd spent much of the afternoon across the way in the Library of Congress, said there was a lot more material to check out there, but she'd learned this much already: they'd never figure out that ventilation system by gawking at it. Begun in 1859, it had proliferated like blackberry brambles ever since.

"And what d'*you* know about blackberry brambles?" Gil asked.

"I'm a Midwesterner now, remember. Land of the Great Unemployed. *They* know from berries, the smarter ones do: freeze or can 'em, if you've got some sugar, and you'll be able to stuff your kids with pies all winter, if you've got some lard and flour, and an oven."

"Yep, so you can." Gil was still elated, and pronounced it 'A Good First Day's Work.' "Now, what say we boogie on out to Glen Echo, where we can relax and put it all together?"

❖

The rush-hour traffic was still heavy, and it was fully dark before they were meandering through the right maze of residential lanes.

". . . Eighty-eight twenty-four . . . eighty-eight thirty-two," Suzanne read aloud, wherever a porch light made that possible. "Okay, this next corner must be it—hey, look, there's my friend now, getting out of that car with those two men—"

Frozen-faced, Gil grabbed Suzanne's wrist before she could wave and drove sedately past the little house, into the turn-around beyond it, and sedately out again. Once they'd rounded the corner, he slammed the Plymouth into second and floored it until they reached a main artery where he could slip back into traffic. Then he raised and dropped his shoulders twice, took three deep breaths, and demanded, but in almost a whisper: "Who *is* this friend? And just what the fuck did you tell her, anyhow?"

"Her name's Nora Sherman. I'm positive she's not involved in anything the law would be interested in. And all I said to her was, I've got a job to try out down here, could she put me up until I decide if I want it and find a place of my own?"

"The law's definitely interested in somebody, and if not her, *who*? Or are you gonna try to tell me those weren't govs, and that they don't have that house staked out?"

"I'm not blind, I saw 'em, too." But not as soon as Gil had, Suzanne admitted to herself. Her freedom hadn't depended on such vigilance for most of her lifetime, as his had, and still did.

"I mean, Jesus Fucking Christ, two more cars parked within a block either way, two more burly dudes in each, and they ain't holding hands—which, I know, I should've spotted going in, but I didn't, did I? So tell me: where d'you know this woman from?"

"New York, years and years ago. Look, it *can't* be anything to do with us."

But Gil knew it had to be. A call to Simon from the first pay phone he spotted made the connection quickly:

"Huh? No, everything's normal here, meaning all fucked up, why? Who? Yeah, sure, I know Nora . . . *what*? Busted? Impossible: she doesn't even smoke dope! What was that again? Well, yeah, as a matter of fact, Jake fell whacky-ass in love with that lady when he was here, and she flew out there to see him a few weeks ago—and no, before you ask, he still hasn't called me."

"Simon? Listen up real good, now: I am about to save your ass, if I still can."

"Just what the hell does *that* mean, 'save my ass'?"

"It means, unless you get it out of there within the next few minutes and take it exactly where I tell you, you're liable to be sitting on that precious tush inside a federal prison for the next twenty-five years, that's what I mean. Are you ready to take down the directions I'm about to give you?"

"*Reasons*, Gil—that's what you're gonna have to give me!"

"When I see you, no time now. No time to argue, either."

". . . This better not be some dumb joke."

"Would I kid around about anything like this? Got a pencil? Well, get one . . . all right, are you familiar with the Wendy's near the Pikesville exit on I-695?"

"No, but I didn't need a pencil for that."

"I'm gonna give you a fancy way to get there."

"And I'll give *you* a dozen fancier ones—I live in this part of the world, remember?"

"Okay. The pencil was mainly so you'd listen better. People always do, holding a pencil, y'know? And I *am* serious, pal: *out* of there in ten minutes. Just grab the clothes and other stuff you'll need for a couple days, whatever cash you've got around, leave your employees a note saying you've been called out of town for some family emergency—"

"You've gotta tell me all this self-evident shit, but you don't have time to tell me *why*?"

"Okay! Do it *your* way! Just get there! I should be there myself within an hour, but if I don't show by eleven—"

"You'd goddamn well *better* show by eleven!"

"I'll do my best," Gil said, and hung up quickly. On the way back to the car he bought a *Post* out of a machine with two quarter slugs like the one he'd used on the phone. John, as he'd expected, looked about to go into shock. Even Suzanne was a trifle thin-lipped. Gil handed her the paper, saying, "Pick out a movie you can both sit through twice, if necessary. Somewhere on this side of the Beltway would be nicest for me. Sorry, but I've got to see somebody again—solo. And then I'm afraid it's back to that Baltimore basement, for tonight, anyhow."

"I've gotta call home," John croaked through parched lips, his first words in half an hour.

Suzanne surprised even herself with a brief, high-pitched giggle: "You and E.T.," she said.

"You even look like E.T. right now, John." Gil said, flashing his most infectious grin. "But, regretfully, no."

". . . No?"

"Yes, *No*. Meaning: No, you'd better not call now. Hey, c'mon, you'd scare Mercy to death now, man. Call her first thing tomorrow, before the rates go up, while she's getting ready for work, when all of this is almost certainly gonna look like the dumb coincidence it almost certainly is. Hey, look, lighten up, it ain't the end of the world, man! Anyhow, I don't *think* so. It's just my life, that's all, it's the rules *I've* gotta play by, if I wanna stay out of their clutches. I'm sorry as hell it screws up my friends' lives, too, sometimes."

This was the right note. John looked calmer already, Gil thought, even slightly sheepish. And when Suzanne proposed a Barbara Stanwyck double bill at a revival house in downtown Washington, John went along with it meekly. Gil agreed as well, with evident relief. The choice added considerably to the miles ahead of him tonight, but he had no intention of reaching Pikesville much before eleven o'clock, anyhow. Simon ought to marinate as long as possible before he turned on the broiler. Bringing Simon into it somehow was absolutely crucial—and until tonight's little crisis, Gil hadn't come up with Idea One about how to make that happen. . . .

❖

By the time (10:52) he saw the gray Plymouth turn into the Wendy's lot and mosey toward him, Simon had spent almost three hours wrestling with the notion that he was suddenly—through no known fault of his own—a fugitive, with nothing to show for all his cleverness, perseverance, and hard work but this ancient Saab, the odds and ends he'd distractedly tossed into it, $655 from petty cash, and the random contents of his pockets, including his now questionably useful credit cards, passport, and roundtrip ticket to Lima, Peru. He'd taken a furiously confused half-hour instead of Gil's proposed ten minutes to leave his beloved bungalow, but in the end he'd scribbled a cryptic note, pinned it to the shop door, and driven up here to this godforsaken stretch of slurbs west of Baltimore.

— Shit, wouldn't you know it, just when his business was finally beginning to give him both enough income and enough free time to really enjoy himself! As, for instance, during three weeks of climbing around in the Andes over the upcoming holidays that he'd been counting off the days to ever since he'd come back from that lovely, but much too short, extended weekend of climbing around in the Smokies. Simon *believed* in enjoying himself—what the hell else are we here for? This was what pissed him off most of all about those corrupt but self-righteous idiots who thought they were running the world today: they were forever fucking up his, and everyone else's, enjoyment of the holy act of living. And meanwhile there were at least three rush orders he'd promised to UPS yesterday and hadn't gotten together yet, stacks of overdues waiting for parts he should be getting first thing tomorrow, and Christ, here he was on the lam, for something he not only didn't do but didn't even know about!

Gil was taking his good old time parking, too, the fucker. Finally, he climbed out, closed the Plymouth's door gently, and ambled over to the passenger side of the Saab.

"This had better be good," Simon growled.

"I'll drink to that!" Gil responded, brightly if inconsequentially. "Still no word from Jake, I guess?"

"Does it look like I've got a cellular phone in this heap? C'mon, what's this all about?"

"D'you remember a little talk we had a couple months ago?"

"Goddamnit, Gil! We've had a lot of 'little talks'!"

"Well, remember rapping down what a crock it was that any 'bright high school student' could assemble a functional nuclear bomb? And then you said, 'But you don't *need* to build a bomb if you've got some of that shit, there're many low-tech means to achieve equivalent effects, more cheaply and controllably'?"

". . . No. Oh, no. NO!"

"Yes! We got some shit now, pal, so this is no longer hypothetical—but neither of us had anything to do with getting hold of it, it just fell out of the sky as far as we were concerned. . . ."

"Wait a minute, who's 'we,' who's 'neither'?"

"Me 'n' Jake, who else?"

"What's Jake got to do with anything?"

"What? Everything, that's what—it's all his idea, and he's gonna do it!"

"Jake's gonna do what?"

". . . I think he'd better tell you."

"Maybe he'd better but *you're* going to. Right now."

"Well, okay, Jake had this brainstorm, see, that's why he called you last month about how to find me, remember? He wants to give the government the same sort of dose they gave him, and he knows where and when to do it—but he's gotta explain that, and exactly why. He's got a whole theory, 'inducing remission,' he calls it—"

"Okay, he can tell me that. Now you go back to where I interrupted you. I wanna know about what fell out of the sky."

"Let's *hope* he can tell you—what must've happened was, the govs got one of the dudes who did pull it off, and the poor jerk must've unloaded everything he knew, including Jake's vitals and my whole Gilberto show. Which went poof! about three weeks ago, luckily while I was elsewhere. That's why I've kept bugging you about Jake—he can't know any of this, unless they've already bagged him. The stake-out on that lady's place is pretty good proof they ain't quite put salt on his tail yet, though."

"So where do *I* come in?"

"Huh? I thought Jake was one of your all-time best friends. I thought you 'n' me were pretty tight, too."

"What's that got to do with it?"

"Well, what're you gonna tell 'em, when they grab you and start squeezing? They're *gonna* squeeze, too, you better believe it. They're gonna tear your sweet little life into itty bitty pieces—and how much of their close scrutiny can it stand? Will your books hold up under an extra-careful audit? How funny are your tax records? How many of those cash deals get buried deep enough? And how about your operating a business in a strictly residential zone, and all the new building and renovating you've been doing without a single permit, and—"

"I get the point. But why should they come after *me*?"

"How'd Ms. Sherman meet Mr. Jacobsen? All she had to do was say your name once today."

"Oh. But Nora wouldn't."

"I find that *very* hard to believe, but you know the lady, I don't. Thing is, you can't go home until we know for sure, she did or she didn't. *You* can't approach her, but *I* can, by means of one hundred and eighty-seven pounds of pure coincidence I just happen to've brought along with me. Suzanne has the perfect reason to pop in and find out, as soon as the dust settles—which I figure to be forty-eight hours, max—since she's already arranged to bunk there temporarily."

"*Forty-eight* hours?"

"Max! And maybe we'll get lucky, maybe you can be back at your drudgery tomorrow afternoon, like none of this ever happened. Until then I extend my hospitality, such as it is at the moment—it *is* one place they wouldn't go looking for you, if they do go looking for you, because it has no connection whatsoever to you, and it's the safest hidey-hole—knock on wood—I've got anywhere east of the Mississippi. Better safe than very, very sorry, right?"

". . . I suppose so. . . ."

All in all, it went down smooth as cold cream, Gil thought. Simon was a very bright guy; you didn't have to drum the obvious into him. It was just as well, though, that he'd never gotten back to what exactly had fallen out of the sky, or why, or anything else that might've required some quick fabrication. There was also no need to burden him further just now with awareness of his own necessary role in coming events. Much better to let Jake soften him up first, with his philosophizing—*Hey, Jake! C'mon, call us!*

"You look beat, man," Gil said. "Look, this place I'm talking about is less'n a quarter-hour from here. I might's well lead you there now, before I go collect my merry crew. Here's the key, just follow me around the Belt, it's near the Perring Parkway exit, I'll lead you to it and point out the door. You brought your down bag with you, I hope, 'cause we're a little short of blankets."

Suddenly extremely weary, nodding, Simon held out his hand for the key.

13: GLEN ECHO / BANNING / BALTIMORE

The following cool, pearly-gray, misty morning, after a stop at the ASPCA in Catonsville, Suzanne walked along the quiet streets, drives, lanes, courts, and avenues of Glen Echo with what she surmised was a terrier/spaniel/dachshund mix who'd outlived an elderly master or mistress. She'd already decided to call him Nebuchadnezzar.

The dog was Gil's brainstorm. No one was ever seen afoot in Glen Echo for any other reason, and "surveying the surveillance," as he called it, would've otherwise required a whole fleet of unobtrusive vehicles. She'd walked past Nora's lane first, as instructed, and while there weren't any pairs of feds in unmarked cars in evidence, there was—just as Gil had prophesied—a van parked illegally in the turn-around at the end, with clear views of both the driveway and the path to the front door. "Loomis & Sons Plumbing & Heating" it said across the rear panels, and she'd bet it'd still be there when she returned after checking out Simon's place. . . .

The only other people Suzanne encountered were dog-walkers, too, and all three turned another way when they saw her coming, rather than let their pedigreed charges fraternize with such an obvious mutt. Nobody ever let their pets run loose in this area, according to Simon, because of the rumored presence of dognappers who supposedly supplied research labs connected with NIH.

She'd picked Nebby out of the yapping throng because he looked easiest to handle, small and middle-aged. She'd guessed right: he was a true little gentleman, stopping at every corner and wagging his silly, feathery little tail as he glanced back over his shoulder to see which direction she wanted to take: *This sure-as-shit beats the Pound,* she guessed he was thinking. . . .

She'd never owned a dog herself, and her live-in lovers had been cat people if they were into pets at all, but this brought back another memory from ancient days with Gil . . . it must've been late winter, sometime before the Columbia Occupation, when she'd waited for him (as usual) on a brownstone stoop somewhere on the Upper East Side, while he'd walked with some old lady (probably early thirties, Suzanne revised—in other words considerably younger than she herself was now) as she'd escorted her poodle around the block. He'd wanted, probably had gotten, something from this woman in cut-off jeans and ankle-length mink, Suzanne never asked what. But anyhow, the two of them had been approaching her stoop again from the other direction when some proto-save-the-animals type drove by and yelled, "Why don't you wear the dog?" and Gil shot right back with: "BECAUSE THE DOG IS FAKE!"

That was the Gil she'd loved, if that word had ever applied; maybe the only right word was *coveted*. It was also the Gil she'd remembered best over the years—god but he could be lightning-quick and razor-sharp and just incredibly funny, sometimes. That side of him was still alive and well, but so were qualities that had always driven her up the wall: not only the way he had to control (and to demonstrate to everyone concerned that he was controlling) every goddamned detail, but his eternal teasing and goading and crass gags and just plain monkey business. And all those tacky little tricks he took such childish pleasure in—for instance, the slugs he always carried for phone calls and highway tolls. . . .

What had Suzanne simmering this morning, especially, was what she'd chanced to overhear when she got up to use that disgusting bathroom somewhere around 2:00 a.m. and found Gil and Simon still smoking dope at the kitchen table. Simon must've just asked about her, what she was doing there, because before a complaining floorboard gave her away, Gil had been saying, "I've always liked 'em monumental—wouldja b'lieve, *that* was the very first 'V' I ever dunked my 'P' in?"

The smirking little prick!

He'd been absolutely all business when he'd wakened her at 7:30, though, and took her out to a Denny's for breakfast: full of military metaphors, how Nora was their "exposed flank," and only Suzanne could "reconnoiter," and how she *had* to stay with Nora now, even if it put her at some risk, because she was the best means they had of knowing whether the feds were growing warmer. And above all, she had to learn as quickly as possible whether Nora had mentioned Simon's connection with Jake. So, as soon as they'd "ascertained the extent" to which Nora was being watched and listened in on, she had to "make contact."

That suited Suzanne fine; the sooner she was out of that basement apartment, the better. But in terms of their objective, wouldn't it make more sense to pull back now just in case those two guys *were* blown and come back in again under some different cover?

"No way," Gil had said. "One's our means—and our motive. The other's gonna create our opportunity. Without those three things, as any prosecutor'll tell you, we ain't got nuttin'."

Well, about Jake she knew nothing yet, but she'd had a look at Simon now, and he didn't seem so special.

"Okay, I'll tell you just how special he is. First off, he's one of seven indisputable geniuses in electronic security in the world today. Second, but even more important to *me,* he's the only dude I've ever met who's actually taken peyote by enema."

"And just what is that supposed to prove?"

"I'm sure you've never messed with any, but you do know what peyote is, right? Anything worse-tasting's beyond imagination. Yet hundreds of thousands, maybe millions of people over the years've suffered not only the taste, but the hours of gas pains and nausea afterward, because they like what it does to their heads. I used to be one of 'em, and I'd heard of taking it that way, but—it was just too bizarre, I guess, or I was too much in awe of the tradition. Simon got there painlessly because he just doesn't give a shit about 'bizarre' or anything else: once he decides to do something, he only sees, or only cares about what works, what achieves the desired results most efficiently. And *that*'s what's gonna get our delivery system to where it's gotta be, by the time it's gotta be there. Nothing else will."

"'Delivery system'?"

"*Special* Delivery, Registered and Certified," Gil had answered, grinning. "And Jake's our ever-lovin' mailman. You'll like Jake—if we can only get him back in time."

Meanwhile, here she stood at the foot of Simon's driveway, where Nebby had conveniently called a halt to squirt his signature on the base of a tree, so she could take her time inspecting the place. If the "govs," as Gil called them, were around, they were more discreet here than at Nora's.

Step two, if it looked good (and she decided it did), was to use the front door key under the third brick to the left of the steps, go into the dining room that now served as an office, and retrieve the back-up box of floppy disks with his customers' addresses that Simon hadn't remembered until he was in Baltimore. First she'd circumnavigated the house, getting good and drenched from the dripping shrubbery in the process, and peeked in through a shop window. A young man in a purple turban was operating some sort of machinery in there, but that was as it should be, according to Gil.

Nobody else in evidence, so she tied Nebby to the porch railing and went inside. The whole place was a god-awful mess, she thought, but the box of disks was exactly where she'd been told it would be. She was just about to leave when the phone rang, twice, at top volume. . . .

❖

In Banning that Tuesday, the hospital administration was playing one of its favorite games. No, there was nothing in writing anywhere that said Jake was due to be released today, and no, the doctor couldn't be reached. When he grew tired of being stonewalled by nurses and office staff, Jake spent two hours and several dollars in change at the pay phone down the hall from his room, trying to reach the sonofabitch himself, without success—then on impulse dialed 1, 202, and Nora's office number . . . it rang three times and he was about to hang up before the recorded current schedule of the performing arts association could come on the line, when he heard her voice say, "Hello?"

"Hello yourself, Ms. Sherman."

"— *Jake*! Is that you?" He knew already: there was something very wrong. "Where are—no, don't tell me. Are you all right? They're looking for you, I was questioned yesterday for six hours, they think you're mixed up in something—something terrible, I don't know what."

Amazing to him, how clear, calm, quick, and practical his mind was suddenly, precisely as if he'd expected something like this all along. "Who's after me? Who questioned you?"

"Some sort of military intelligence. And the FBI. They want you very badly."

"I haven't done anything, Nora. But thanks. We'd better not talk any longer. For what it's worth, I—" *no*, he wasn't going to burden her with that, having avoided such declarations all this while—"Goodbye." He didn't wait for her to respond, hanging up firmly before his hand could begin to shake.

— Gotta talk to Simon. Not this phone, though, he'd better use one in the row at the other end of the hallway . . . 1, 301 . . . god*damn*it! two rings, and he got the fucking machine—well, he had to protest to somebody, somehow, and Simon sometimes turned the sound all the way up if he was busy and waited to hear who it was before going to the trouble of answering: "Hello, it's Jake, and if you're there, please pick up, I need to know just what the hell is going on. . . ."

The big but feminine voice that cut in then was almost as uninflected as a computer's: "Hello Jake, Simon's not here, but you should call . . . "and she reeled off another 301 area number, repeated it once, more slowly, then clicked off. He didn't have anything to write it down—with or on—and he got two digits switched the first time, to be told that number was out of service. But on the next try it was picked up in the middle of the second ring. Not by Simon, though, by Gil:

"Jake! Man, where in hell've you been? If they weren't treating your ladyfriend like the Mona Lisa, we'd've decided they'd already gotchya. And if they getchya, believe me, they ain't gonna letchya go anytime soon—in your position, it might as well be never. You got anywhere safe to get to? Right away?"

Well, Mount Shasta, where he and Eric were already planning to go, was probably as safe a place for now as any. "Yeah, I think so. And I know—I mean, about Nora. That's who I called first, just a minute ago."

"Jesus. On the same phone you're using now?"

"No, but it's in the same building."

"Okay, we'll just hafta hope they aren't any more thorough than usual. Tell me not only every word said by either of you, I want every cough, sneeze, burp, and sniffle."

Jake repeated the brief conversation.

"You're positive neither of you mentioned Simon? Good show! Okay —we've gotta assume they've already traced that call, so wherever you are right now is just about the worst place you could be. Get going, pal! Soon's you're sure you're clear and situated for a few days, call me back—'cause what we talked about is on, pardner, in technicolor, and you're gonna love it!"

"Can you tell me what it is they want me for?"

"Sure. We got the goods! And they think you were in on it!"

"Why should they think that?"

"Well, I guess they also got one or both of my partners. In any case, somebody's naming names, 'n' I'll bet everybody Gilberto Torres had anything to do with lately is getting hauled in by the govs. I know you don't have either time or inclination for that sort of nonsense, so you better amscray, friend. Every second ticking by right now could make a great big awful difference. You didn't write this number anywhere, did you? Good, pretty-please don't, anywhere, just memorize it—s'long!"

Eric was in the waiting room, reading some of the pamphlets from the health food store; they didn't look very encouraging. Jake dropped into the couch beside him, speaking quietly and fast in his ear: "We've gotta get out of here, right now. Gimme that bag"—it had his street clothes in it—"and run Sallyanne around to the emergency entrance."

Eric gulped, but didn't hesitate: it fit his standard view of reality outside his valley. He was up and out the door in one smooth motion, while Jake walked straight into the men's room to change, then briskly down the hall. Nobody even looked once. Within another quarter-hour, Eric was checked out of his motel and they were back on I-10 West. Then I-210 across the foothills of the San Gabriel Mountains to I-5 North, and on up the Central Valley. By midnight they'd reached Kettleman State Recreation Area, where Jake crawled into his bag in the truckbed and Eric curled up in the cab, until dawn and hunger woke them.

All they'd left behind in their hurry (in plain sight on the lid of the motel room toilet tank) was another of those folders extolling the astonishing curative powers of positive ideation, with the San Bernardino co-op address rubber-stamped on the back.

The worst thing about that basement apartment, John thought, was that it always felt like 3:00 a.m. in there. He'd wakened on Tuesday with every intention of calling Mercy immediately, only to find that it was almost eleven o'clock already. He'd slept nine hours straight, somehow, and still felt tired. But not so nervous as last night—nameless disasters no longer seemed to be waiting in the wings to pounce upon them all. A cup of tea was a good idea; there was a boxful of Red Rose bags in the cupboard, and most of a pound of limp but still edible graham crackers. . . .

"Go ahead, call her at work," Gil said expansively, "I was only kidding about the rates last night—this phone bill falls into a Black Hole somewhere, anyhow."

But John didn't want to do that. Mercy never felt free to talk at the office, and it didn't seem so urgent anymore. He'd just as soon put it off now until the kids were ready for bed, he could tell them all nighty-night—and while he was waiting now for his water to boil, he absent-mindedly accepted and took a deep drag off the hash pipe Simon handed him. . . .

Two or three more tokes and a lot of brilliant repartee later, he found to everyone's hilarity, including his own, that the kettle had boiled dry.

By then the topic of conversation was psilocybin, and no, as a matter of fact, that was one psychedelic John had never had the oppor-tunity to try, in all his hippie-hunting. He'd missed what was far and away the best one then, both Gil and Simon agreed. The trip itself usually lasted only two or three hours, they said, but it left you aglow with a sense of well-being for days afterward. That sounded nice, but John had been under the impression that all three of them were going to do it together, when Gil produced his dittybag. . . .

Once he'd washed down his little dose of withered mushrooms, though—with fresh tea nobody remembered brewing—it really didn't matter . . . god, yeah, uh-*huh*, oh yes! John certainly was beginning to see what they'd meant . . . and meanwhile that arsenic-green and sulfur-yellow kitchenette had become the warmest, brightest, coziest, most entertaining place he'd ever been. . . .

His sleeping bag, when he was led back to it, was even nicer . . . and the next thing he knew, a wonderfully sweet little creature with the kindest, wisest eyes in the world and the softest little pink tongue was licking the tip of his nose . . . and Suzanne was back, but she was very different now, wreathed in smiles and talking a mile a minute, intro-ducing him to Nebby, and everyone was chanting: *Get up, John! We're going out to dinner, we've gotta celebrate!*

Suddenly he was in the exact center of a huge, blindingly bright room full of noise (but all of it was jolly) and strange, gesticulating people (but all of them were friendly) and facing an enormous pool (a whole lagoon!) full of linguine in marinara sauce. John didn't know whether he was supposed to eat it or admire the marvelous colors or jump in and swim across it. In the end he devoured it, in three quick slurps, it seemed like. He consumed an entire forest of salad, too, and a tractor-trailer load of bread. Then he gobbled the whole ten cubic yards of spumoni, as soon as they appeared on the table.

By that time John had become as big as Paul Bunyan; even Suzanne was minuscule by comparison. If they didn't leave soon, he wouldn't be able to get out through the doorway, they'd have to chop a hole in the roof. He knew he'd never fit into any car in this condition, let alone inside his sleeping bag when they got back. . . .

But he did, very nicely, thank you all very kindly, and good night, sweet prince. . . .

14 : DC / SHASTA

Another thing about Gil that could always get Suzanne's goat was his way assuming that nobody else ever had a brain in their head. *Yes,* it had occurred to her to back up the tape and erase Jake's message and her response from Simon's answering machine, and *yes,* she'd done exactly that—who but an idiot wouldn't've, in her opinion. But Gil appeared astonished that such a clever move could take place without him at her elbow to inspire it.

Likewise, who but Gil could've realized the safest place to approach Nora would be at her office in downtown Washington, where musicians and all sorts of people breezed in and out all day, and the govs could hardly put a tail on everybody?

"Tell her someone who promised to cover for you in Toledo—I mean Flint—canceled at the last minute, and you couldn't leave until you found a replacement. Take all your luggage, call her at ten-thirty, say you're out at Dulles, you just flew in. Arrange to go out to lunch, and don't ask her any of our questions or tell her about your new name until you're outside her office, just in case they did install a bug there."

—Gee, Gil, that's pure genius. . . .

Nora's office, the first door on the right past the entrance to that old tomato-red-brick townhouse two blocks from Dupont Circle, wasn't quite small enough to be described as a broom closet, but it also wasn't large enough to accommodate her wheelchair as well as herself, her desk, her filing cabinets, and all her beloved plants. Every decent-sized room in the building was needed for lessons and rehearsals, though, so she used a donated Balans chair behind the desk, and *her* chair, as she was fond of saying, had to 'cool its wheels' out in the hallway.

"Suzanne? Well! Here you are, at last! I was beginning to wonder if you weren't coming after all, if maybe that job you mentioned fell through at the last minute."

Suzanne had last seen Nora more than a dozen years ago, before the tumors and consequent operations, at a feminist conference she otherwise no longer remembered. At first glance this was the same beautiful blonde woman—if anything, more luminously so. The shock came seconds later, as the arms outstretched to embrace her dear old friend had to drop again, to press hard against the desktop and so raise herself up from behind it. Then those crutches clattering, close up for a quick kiss. Not quick enough, though, to hide the pain and fear Suzanne could sense behind the delighted sparkle in those cornflower-blue eyes.

Nora *was* glad to see her, Suzanne was sure of that, though she was equally convinced she wouldn't've been recognized, if she'd walked in without being expected.

"Well—we've certainly both changed, haven't we?"

Rueful: that must be what you called that sort of smile. In any case, Suzanne would take it gratefully, and anything else that might offer. But meanwhile she chose to understand what Nora had just said as a reference to her wig and tailored suit, not her thirty-odd additional pounds. "I'm afraid it's that kind of a job—I hope I don't have to dress like this all the time, but I figured the first impression, you know. I said I'd drop by the Library this afternoon to tell 'em I'm here."

"What sort of job is it?"

This was where Suzanne had to acknowledge Gil's acuity. He'd foreseen that such a question would be inevitable, and that any answer might very well need to stand up to scrutiny other than Nora's. She hoped his resources matched his foresight—he'd given her names to use if necessary, New York City numbers that, if called, would substantiate provisional employment, and even some letters of introduction that looked impressively authentic, for having been cooked up late last night.

"For the time being it's mostly just research at the Library of Congress, but if it works out, I'll be first assistant producer for a miniseries based on the attempt to impeach Andrew Johnson." Something sufficiently dim, that nobody knows or cares about, Gil had said. And it's all right if you don't know much about it yet, either—after all, it's a project just getting underway. . . .

"Oh? I didn't know you were interested in history. Or TV."

"Let's say I'm mainly interested in getting out of the Midwest." That was true enough, she realized, as soon as she'd said it. "And right now, lunch."

"Oh, me, too! There's a place just over a block from here that's wheelchair accessible. It saves me the bother of getting in and out of a car, which is considerable. The food's nothing great, but it's bearable. . . ." Rolling out the door and down the specially built ramp, Nora continued, "Speaking of food: tomorrow's Thanksgiving—I hope you're planning on spending it with me? Would you be willing to help prepare a real old-fashioned dinner? You see, I went and invited this wonderful old musician, I couldn't stand the thought of him spending Thanksgiving all alone. And then I got to wondering if I could manage it. I hardly ever cook anymore, it's just too klutzy, in this chair or on my sticks. Ruthellen—she's a student of mine—said she'd join us for dessert, her folks'll drop her off, but I don't expect she'll be a lot of help even then. She's a congressman's daughter, and I doubt she's ever had to boil an egg or wash a dish in her life."

"I'm better at eating than preparing, myself, but sure."

"You will? Oh, great!"

They were almost there before Suzanne managed to squeeze in the information that she had a new name now, and that it was essential that no one be told that she'd ever been anybody but Susan Jeannette Stroehlengutt, from Flint, Michigan. No time then to explain—but Suzanne felt slighted somehow when Nora didn't even appear to wonder why. Nora, in fact, seemed totally caught up in her own concerns and wholly deficient in curiosity, other than about whether Suzanne had kept up contact with any of the old gang. A brief sympathetic smile, apparently at that clunky moniker, a noncommittal chuckle, and a murmured "You always were rather mysterious, weren't you?" or something like that, was all she offered on the subject, then or later.

The restaurant was one of those bare-brick-walled soup-and-salad places where no one could read the menu on the blackboard for all the hanging plants. And as it turned out, almost all Suzanne had to do to learn what they needed to know was to shut up and listen. ". . . You know, it's just as well you didn't get here Monday, I was in no shape to greet anybody," Nora said, and went on to describe her ordeal in some detail.

"What'd you tell them?"

"As little as I could," Nora chuckled, "and even a couple of fibs. Like how I met this person. You see, it was through a neighbor of mine, an ex-boyfriend, really." Quite a blush there; was *she* remembering those

East 83rd Street nights, too? "Silly expression, for people our age—ex-lover, I should say."

Suzanne knew from ex-lovers; she'd made a career out of being one, she sometimes thought. All of Nora's, of both sexes, would probably fill the House of Representatives, she'd bet. The burning questions were: did Nora's lovers still include both sexes, and could any of them ever somehow drop that *ex-*? But these weren't questions Suzanne could be asking now. "Well, this other man's a good friend of his, and—anyhow, I wasn't about to put sweet old Simon through what *I* went through on Monday!"

"What *did* you say, then?"

"A complete fabrication, it just popped into my head. I told them we'd met in the out-patient clinic at NIH. You see, Jake has cancer, too. . . ."

❖

"I hope you've got something encouraging to tell me," Gil said as soon as he'd picked up the receiver, but he didn't stop long enough for her to tell him anything. "Our western friend still hasn't called back and I'm beginning to wonder if he's ever going to, and aside from hovering over this phone all day I haven't accomplished a single godblasted thing, not even returning your nebbish to the ASPCA—"

"Nebby is *not* a nebbish, and if *he* goes back to the pound, *I* go back to Toledo on the very next plane."

"Okay, don't worry, it's not gonna happen! John's in love with that beast, too, and I'd pretty much decided anyhow, what the hell, walking it'll give him something to do. Can't keep him tripping forever."

"*That's* who you should send to the pound."

"Don't be nasty, now."

"I can't see what possible use you expect to put him to. He's strictly a liability. As well as a jerk."

"Look, I grant you, I made a small miscalculation there, we don't really need him, as it's turned out. But I don't wanna take John home until we're ready at this end for me to bring something we're gonna need here back down with me."

"Why not put him on a bus?"

"No. Not only would John be very hurt, but I want a good excuse to go back there, when I go."

Suzanne was damned if she'd ask Gil what he'd meant by any of that. He loved nothing better than dangling little mysteries in front of people's noses, tossing out tidbits of what he was thinking, but never quite enough to follow his logic. From the moment she'd stepped off the plane at LaGuardia, Suzanne had remembered—and had been using—the basic weapon she'd developed all those years ago, when they'd lived together (if you could call sharing a blanket and sometimes a mattress on a crash pad floor, with as many as a dozen other people sleeping or humping all around you, "living together"). That weapon was: *never, ever,* give him the satisfaction of detecting the slightest trace of anything like curiosity.

". . . So what's your news, if any?"

Suzanne told him, as tersely as a telegram, adding, "And now I've gotta run. I told Nora I'd be back at her office by six, to catch a ride out to Glen Echo with her."

"*Je*sus! That's goddamn beautiful! Oh, wow! Simon'll be ecstatic— come *on,* Jake, baby, don't fail us now! . . . But hey, for shit's sake, Suzanne! Why didn't you *say so* right away?"

"Because *you* didn't let me, pal," Suzanne replied sweetly, and she quickly hung up.

❖

He'd told him parts of it the night before, disjointedly. Now, on the interminable drive north through the Central Valley, Jake told it all to Eric again, everything both he and Gil had said on both those nights and as much as he could recall of his own thoughts before and since, including that White House kamikaze notion.

"I've had ideas like those," Eric said quietly. "Never acted on any of 'em, of course, but I know it'd take something like that, something pretty drastic, to turn it around: somebody, or I guess a bunch of somebodies, saying 'It don't matter what happens to us, so long as we can make those bastards do whatever's gotta be done.' But that's supposing enough of it *can* be turned around, and the more I've read and thought about stuff like the ozone layer and that greenhouse effect, the more it seems to me it's just too late and too far gone. I think we're done for. Another thirty years, on the outside."

That was a hell of an attitude for someone Eric's age, Jake thought. But maybe it *was* the only intelligent conclusion: it's all over already, everything but the last hideous death throes of a species that could and most likely was going to take the greater part of all other life on this planet along with it. And it was an attitude it would be hard to argue against in their present surroundings: ironing-board flat, irrigated fields stretching out to those eerie, lunar-like mountain ranges running northward along with them in the peripheral distance on both east and west horizons—vast chocolate-brown expanses, containing mile after mile of straight-as-a-ruler rows of the same damn thing (broccoli or carrots, for the most part), then mile after mile after mile of the same damn something else.

". . . When is this State of the Union thing?" Eric asked, after such a long delay that Jake nearly dozed off.

"Huh? Late January."

"You gonna do it?"

"I don't think—" He'd very nearly said 'I don't think I'll still be around then' but stopped himself, changing it to "I don't think it's possible, not in the time remaining, whatever Gil's got up his sleeve."

"Would you, though, if it was?"

Would he? Jake hadn't formally asked himself that question yet, in any but the most abstract terms. He hadn't really wanted to know the answer, he realized now. A real decision threw open too many other imponderables, such as whether, even if a feasible scheme could be pulled together in time and carried out somehow, it could actually work, psychologically. It would certainly shock the body politic but— as with cancer treatments—you wouldn't know until you'd done it whether or not it was going to induce a remission. And this was necessarily a one-shot deal: you couldn't stand there behind them forever with whatever Gil had gotten hold of. In other words, you couldn't really *coerce* those people with the power to turn it around, you had to *convert* them. And could you ever make them understand how truly desperate the situation is, or how many, sudden, and sweeping the changes—worldwide—would have to be?

Now, though, queried so matter-of-factly, Jake found his answer was there, ready and waiting, as if he'd made up his mind some time before. On that day with Nora, maybe, on the road that wound up past Los Alamos to Bandelier? Or when he'd heard Winona mention Fernald, Ohio? Not that it mattered, because this thing was still—and would always be—totally hypothetical.

"Yes, I would. If it looked even remotely possible, I'd have to try. Because otherwise I think you're right, 'we're done for.'" To himself, Jake couldn't help adding: Because otherwise I'd die wondering if I might've made a difference, and because otherwise there's nothing in my entire life that justifies my ever having existed, and because— but it's *not* going to happen, and nothing is going to change for the better, except that I won't be around too much longer to give a good goddamn. . . .

Eric nodded shortly, eyes front, and drove on at a steady sixty-five, while snarling Ag-Cat biplanes criss-crossed the valley like fat but speedy dragonflies, spraying pesticides ceaselessly. At times the breeze would carry some out over the highway, and the wipers were no use in clearing the sticky white film off Sallyanne's windshield. They had to pull over four times in all, to use soap and water and lots of paper towels. Jake had never thought of monocropping in and of itself as a deadly blight before, but here that view of agribusiness was inescapable—and maddening—until they finally reached the wooded highlands north of Redding.

Elizabeth and Timmy were side by side on their tiny cabin's even tinier porch, cross-legged on straw mats, meditating, when Sallyanne pulled into the yard. Once past her astonishment, Elizabeth was deeply happy to see her son and former husband. Clearly, the spiritual life had been good for her. Jake couldn't remember when he'd last seen her looking so handsome, healthy, and at peace.

Timmy, a slender young man in a Peruvian poncho, muslin draw-string pants, and huaraches, with shoulder-length brown hair and a Jesus beard, was diplomatic, cautiously friendly, and clearly nobody's fool. In half an hour he'd won Eric over to the extent that, on Eliza-beth's suggestion, Eric consented to be shown the path up to the ridge above their little canyon.

"How long has it been since you've thought about . . . our daugh-ter?" Elizabeth asked as soon as both young men were out of earshot— at precisely the same instant, it so happened, that Jake vividly recalled standing beside that rough stone he'd cut on that steep slope back there in northern New Mexico.

"A little more than a month," he said simply.

"Until I looked up to see who it was in that truck," she admitted, "I don't think I'd thought of her for more than moments in . . . six months, at least—and d'you know, I'm not even ashamed? I think I've finally realized, all that mourning wasn't doing *her* any good, and it was doing *me* a great deal of harm. Not to mention those around me. Timmy has been very good for me in this respect. He feels there's entirely too much guilt, sorrow, and anger in the world, or rather in people, and most of it simply blocks the positive feelings we would otherwise be able to share. I think he's very wise for his age."

"Sounds like," Jake said, as noncommittally as he was able. He'd been feeling much the same himself, though, since his arrival here: that none of what once had hurt so much between this woman and himself, none of the many supposedly terrible things they'd done to each other long ago, really mattered anymore—and what a welcome feeling that was. . . .

This evergreen-shaded spot seemed as peaceful as could be found in California, no other humans within the loudest shout. And as beautiful. "Which is claiming a good deal," as Elizabeth said. She and Timmy had come to this area, she explained, to study with a Cheyenne herbalist, healer, and "wise woman" named Sarai Talks-to-Thunder. "But what brings you and Eric?"

"I came to say goodbye. He came along to see you again, I guess, and to keep an eye on both his old man and his truck. I'm very glad he did."

"We said our goodbyes, I thought—but you mean forever, don't you?"

"Yeah." He told her about it simply and directly, not everything, but enough. Not Banning, just what they'd told him at NIH. He was grateful when she didn't fuss or question him further. It was different somehow, telling someone new about it, since Banning. His impending death was gospel now; he believed in it implicitly, deep inside his bones. . . .

Elizabeth was silent for at least a full minute, regarding him with both detachment and affection, Jake felt. At last she said, "There's a Gathering tomorrow we were planning to attend, west of Weed. Sarai's going to be there. You'll come, won't you? I don't claim that she can cure you, but she's saved hundreds of lives the doctors gave up on."

Jake swallowed his cynicism and told Elizabeth he'd be glad to go along.

At dusk he drove back out to the nearest pay phone, clocking it this time—8.7 miles—to call Gil, as promised.

"Terrific, ya made it! Can you hang out wherever you are for a few days? Swell, that'll give me time to work out how to get you back here safe and sound. Hey, now, tell me something: what address did you give 'em at NIH? Your Staten Island one, you're sure, not Simon's?

Fanfuckingtastic, then everything's just gingery-peachy back here, and Simon'll be in Workaholic Heaven, now he can go back home and fill some orders."

"Is Simon there? Can I talk to him?"

"Nope, 'fraid not. Said he was gonna catch a movie, but I'll bet he's shacked up somewhere with one of those ladies of his, in spite of all my good advice about avoiding contact with anybody he could possibly be traced through. Not that it matters, in view of what you've just told me, but *he* doesn't know that yet, so he *should* be keeping his nose clean."

"What exactly did you mean, yesterday, when you said 'We got the goods'?"

"What did I mean? The stuff that goes in the squirt gun."

"Can you tell me about it?"

"What's to tell? I mean, what d'you wanna know?"

"Well, for instance, how and where you got it. And what happened to your partners—was that the guys we met?"

"Uh, yeah. And, sure, I'll tell you everything there is to know—but when I see you, okay? I know this phone's immaculate, Simon's had it all in pieces half a dozen times just to keep in practice, but phones make me nervous, anyhow. This I *can* say now, though: we're making lots of other headway. That guy I mentioned, remember, the one who knows that place up, down, and sideways? Well, he's already on the scene, and we've all been hard at work checking out just how to get you where you gotta be, and I'm expecting an important breakthrough in that department in a matter of days, if not hours. So call me back around this time, or maybe a little earlier, if not tomorrow, make it Sunday, okay? I should have lots more to report by then."

15 : THANKSGIVING

Why did it always rain on Thanksgiving? Maybe it didn't *always*, but Nora couldn't remember a single year when it hadn't since she'd begun to live "Down Here," as all the former New Yorkers she'd ever met there referred to the Washington area. Just think, though, she told herself, how depressed you'd be by now without Kleiny's company — whoops, Nora kept forgetting, she couldn't call Suzanne *that* anymore.

Bigger than the Fuji Film blimp these days, poor thing, and every bit as awkward, but a real sweetheart, and just as true-blue as ever, despite her little idiosyncracies, such as that pretense to a Clandestine Past, which Nora hadn't believed for a minute, and didn't really care about one way or the other. Kl—I'll just think of her as Suzie Q from now on, Nora decided—had always been that ordinarily self-effacing sort who, when they do attempt to make an impression, feel they've got to make it either a whopper or else something oh-so mysterious. That was an odd choice, though, Strolling Gut, or whatever, if you were out to forge yourself a fresh identity—could she've acquired it in the ordinary way, maybe, by getting hitched up with a man somewhere along the line? No, what *am* I thinking of, not Our Suzie Q—that really would be a whopper. . . .

In any case, it was nice to have someone else around who'd shared, and remembered, that Fine Old Feminist Fervor. But a shame Suzanne hadn't been any good, either, at keeping in touch with other members of their old CR group. ("Prob'ly all married by now," she'd grumped, "and 'having it all.'") The only child of alcoholics, Nora had no cherished family memories. The best holidays she'd ever known had been Hanukkahs, Christmasses, and Thanksgivings during the Seventies, spent in the tenderly exclusive companionship of newly self-styled "liberated women."

The turkey (organic capon, actually, thanks to Suzanne—and almost as much per pound as filet mignon!) was stuffed and in the oven, the candied yams and wild rice were awaiting their turns, and as they drove into Washington to pick up her guest, Nora gave her new/old roomie some background:

"Roosevelt Edwards used to play a very respectable tenor sax, I'm sure, but I wish you could've heard his son Kennedy on trumpet. Ken had the beginnings of greatness, if I've ever heard them. Play him any kind of music, things he'd never heard before, and he'd just grin and come right back with them, faking it perfectly and usually sounding twice as good as the original. Three bars into anything he did, I could never keep from making mental comparisons to, say, Wynton Marsalis. . . .

"Well, Ken died a year ago this past spring—liver and lung cancer both, it was horrible. He must've been pretty far advanced when I met him, but he hadn't even seen a doctor yet. I took him over to NIH—it's free to cancer patients, but not many inner-city blacks know that, they don't publicize it enough. I used to drive Roosevelt out there to visit. He was terribly uncomfortable at first about riding around Washington with a white woman—he's from small-town Alabama, and you still don't *do* that, down there. All the men in his family were coal miners, he lost his father and several brothers to emphysema. That's why he moved up here, he says, he didn't want that happening to Ken. So instead, to support his music studies, Ken found this job with some fly-by-night residential exterminators. They had whites to go inside people's houses and spray. Ken's job was to ride in the back of the truck, mix the stuff, load the equipment, and clean up afterward. The NIH said the levels of aldrin and dieldrin in his system were the highest they'd ever recorded. . . ."

Roosevelt Edwards was a stooped, bald, very black gentleman with Bassett eyes and wonderfully dignified manners, in a polka-dot bowtie, dazzling white shirt, and shiny but carefully pressed blue gabardine suit. He lived above a boarded-up storefront in a block so impressively rundown that Suzanne had to admit that her own in Toledo was almost middle-class by comparison. After considerable coaxing, he went back inside and fetched his "axe," as he called it, and as soon as they were at Nora's, he put some reeds to soak in a water glass. Later, while they all sat around the living room waiting for dinner to settle enough to provide room for the mince, key lime, and pumpkin pies Suzanne had discovered in a pricey little bakery on the way home the night before, he played some Dixielandish things, with very nice feeling and quite impressive skill, in spite of ill-fitting dentures and not having practiced at all since his son's funeral. Otherwise, he never made a sound unless spoken to directly.

Nora did her best to draw him out, though, and finally Edwards actually began to tell some sort of droll anecdote about himself. Suzanne wasn't paying much attention to anything but her digestive processes at that point, but it had to do with this librarian who had it in for him; it seemed he spent a good deal of his time at the public library, and he'd been trying to find some piece of scientific information, something about a pound of gas—but just then they all heard a key turn in the front door lock, and as the door banged open, Nora had to cut him off to call out, "Ruthellen, is that you? We're in here!"

— Student my ass, was Suzanne's first thought, just look at how both their faces glow when their eyes connect. If those two aren't making it together, I'm Amelia Earhart. They were equally stunning, too, in completely different ways, and Suzanne couldn't help rubbernecking back and forth, from slender, silvery Nora in her whispering white silk to this leggy young Eurasian beauty in an emerald velvet running suit with a crown of bright copper ringlets and the sort of body bikinis were invented for.

"Let's see, you two've met, haven't you—" Nora began as Edwards lurched to his feet, nodding, and the newcomer gushed, "Oh sure! I hope I'm not too late again to hear you play, am I?"

He glowed now, too, like anthracite. "Yes, indeed," he said, "you've been spared, again."

"Well," Nora persisted, "*you* two haven't met. Susan . . . Stroehlengutt?—Ruthellen Vliorishevski."

"Hi. You're almost as bad off as I am, aren't you," Ruthellen said with an antebellum accent and a laugh like tuned wine glasses, and when Suzanne still looked blank, "I meant our names—we should have wheelbarrows to cart those things around in, don't you think?"

Close up now, brushing palms, Suzanne could see that, gorgeously developed as she was, she really was still a child, sixteen at most. But having been that age herself once, Suzanne knew it didn't necessarily preclude anything.

"My great-grandaddy hailed from The Other Georgia," Ruthellen said, "what's your excuse?"

"Her folks met in Saigon, and she grew up in Savannah," Nora inserted, clearly doting.

"And you're teaching her all about the viola," Suzanne said, but her irony went blissfully unheard, so she hauled herself up out of her rocker and strode out into the kitchen to make the coffee and help herself to a full quarter of each pie.

Even with Suzanne to fetch and carry everything, it had been another very tiring day for Nora, and she didn't protest long when Suzanne volunteered to drive Ruthellen and Mr. Edwards home. Suzanne had always had a notoriously poor sense of direction, but she'd promised Gil she'd call tonight, and she was sure she could always manage to blunder back onto Massachussetts Avenue, which she now knew would take her back out to Glen Echo eventually.

Ruthellen's family lived in Georgetown, so she dropped her off first (Suzanne would've gone miles out of her way to do that, anyhow), cutting short the girl's effusions and the man's courtly adieu with a distinctly snappish "Yeah, all right, g'night!"

The rain had quit at last, and the nearly empty downtown streets gleamed under the streetlights as if they'd been scoured and polished. As she drove, Suzanne tried to think about what she was doing there in Washington, DC, and why, remembering only feeble, silly-sounding scraps of things Gil had told her over the past few days. Her mind's eye refused to focus for more than moments on anything but Nora's fluid face and long, expressive fingers, as she'd watched them in the candlelight, across the little drop-leaf table. . . .

Suzanne's couple hours of wandering through the Capitol three days before, and similar amounts of time spent at the Library of Congress the past two afternoons, had convinced her that penetrating the House of Representatives (for whatever purpose Gil purportedly had in mind) was something no pack of wisecracking potheads was ever going to accomplish—which, she increasingly suspected, was about all that Gil and his other colleagues actually amounted to. . . .

This, in fact, would explain his remaining uncaught and unsurfaced all this while as well as any other theory she'd come up with: he'd just stayed stoned for, lo, these many years, hanging out with a bunch of do-nothing old hippies, puffing their ancient revolutionary pipedreams. As in The Fabulous Furry Freak Brothers Wipe Out the Whole Damn Washinton Guvmint. . . .

She hadn't for an instant accepted that claim about Simon; she knew Gil had plucked his precise number ("seven indisputable geniuses" or whatever) out of nowhere, in a naïve attempt to take advantage of her presumed gullibility . . . he'd always been that way:

everybody Gil had any dealings with was "one of *the* greatest" at whatever it was they did . . . and as for Simon's unothodox drug-taking methods, if that was actually supposed to be an argument in his favor, well, she'd never heard anything more ridiculous . . . and she knew, if she were to confront Gil with her growing and increasingly basic doubts, the best she'd get out of him would be some ye-of-little-faith routine. He'd already actually said, two or three times, "Sooner or later, you'll see, *some*thing'll turn up. . . ."

Yeah, sure. In Suzanne's confirmed opinion, you didn't run a revolution (or commit an act of nihilist retribution, or whatever the hell it was they were supposedly up to here) by waiting around for miracles, large or small. Unless you were Joan of Arc, and just look what happened to her . . . which led Suzanne inexorably back to questioning her own motives, and since the best she could conceivably come up with in that department would be loneliness and pointlessness and boredom, she'd rather not get into any of that just now, if she could help it. . . .

She'd made very good time, she quite suddenly realized, when signs for Union Station appeared. She'd also totally forgotten Edwards' stiff presence there beside her until he cleared his throat surreptitiously. To break their silence, she asked him what he did for a living. He did have a job, she knew, because he'd mentioned back at Nora's that he had to be there at five o'clock the next morning.

"I have been called a 'mop jockey,'" he admitted, wryly, with what she guessed was an embarrassed smile.

"That's a janitor? Where do you work?"

"In the very bowels of *that* illustrious building," he said, pointing up Delaware Avenue as they went by, to where the Capitol dome loomed in its clustered floodlights like a grounded harvest moon. "And what is your profession, Miss Stroehlengutt, if I may be so bold as to inquire?"

"Huh? Oh! I—" But what Edwards had just divulged had driven the story Gil had coached her in completely out of her head. "— I do bodywork and teach martial arts to battered women," Suzanne heard herself saying.

❖

"Well, I agree with you on one thing," Simon said, once Gil had made sure that John had shut the bedroom door tightly behind him, "it's gotta be the vent system. But what you were groaning about last night—

what'd you call it, the Blackberry Syndrome?—is *not* the problem, it's your great hope: if there wasn't any overall design, if it just proliferated piecemeal, then there's a chance they don't know what all's in there, which means maybe there're some sections of it that haven't been secured yet."

"Oooh, do I like that notion!" Gil crooned.

"I said *maybe*. And even if there are, no way you'd be able to find and take advantage of 'em without some major sort of leg up. You'd need to know the basic layout, and what to be looking for. In other words, you'd want to see some plans first."

"Plans?" Gil asked, all innocence.

"You know, blueprints, wiring diagrams."

"And where d'you guess those would be?"

"Well, the Office of the Architect's a very good bet. I forget where it was—Christ, that place is big!—but we wandered by it three or four times, John and I." As with most New Yorkers and the Empire State Building or the World Trade Center, the majority of Washington-area residents with no business to conduct there never venture inside the Capitol Building, and Simon had been no exception, until yesterday.

"Just supposing we can get you in there, how much time would you need?" Gil asked him now.

"*Me?*"

"Who else is gonna know what to look for? C'mon, pal, just hypothetically—how long d'you think it'd take to learn what you need to know?"

"How the hell can I know that until I get in there and see what it's like? How well organized *they* are, for one thing. I dunno, I guess maybe a couple hours."

"But if I hold up my end—I mean, if I find a safe way to get you in and out of there some night, you'll do it, right?"

"Wait a friggin' minute!" Simon protested. "I very carefully did *not* say that."

"I know you didn't. But that's what I want you to say. So maybe you should tell me, what it'll take to get what I want. As of this minute I ain't got a glimmer, what such a way would be, I just know there's gotta be one, if we want it bad enough. But how's about this guarantee: you'd have the absolute final say-so when I do come up with some way in there, on whether it's feasible or not?"

"I should fucking hope so. That had better be thoroughly under-stood, from the beginning, by all concerned."

"Inside the building, then, and safely up to the door of the architect's office—if I get you that far, and a couple quiet hours, you think you can get in and find what you want?"

"I can certainly get in. There's nothing fancy anywhere near there, I did a little sweep with this—" Simon drew a tiny black disk out of his pocket "— and no locks a straightened paperclip wouldn't handle. I guess they still rely on the least reliable security system ever devised: a watchman on hourly rounds."

"Great! We'll say no more until I've got something."

"I don't like the way you say 'great!' Don't forget, Gil: I still haven't committed myself to a goddamn thing."

"Okay—is 'okay' okay? I'll let you know as soon as I get something set up, then."

"You do that. I won't hold my breath."

"Well! About time!" Mercy said. Which wasn't quite fair, John thought. True, he hadn't managed to call last night, either.

After spending most of Wednesday prowling the Capitol again, this time with Simon, he'd tried to dial as soon as he'd gotten back here to the apartment, only to learn there'd been an ice storm all across the western Catskills early that morning and the lines were still down in Meredith. He'd tried again today at noon, though, and spoken briefly to his mother-in-law (never a pleasant experience), who'd said Mercy and the kids had just driven into Delhi to get something or other still needed for the turkey.

"Are you enjoying yourself?" Mercy asked now.

"Ah, yeah, sort of."

"It must be better than 'sort of,' or you would've called before *this*, I should think." Mercy was even angrier at him than he'd expected. She never said 'I should think,' otherwise.

"Well . . . we've been pretty busy." There was nothing he hated worse than telling lies, to Mercy above all, but he didn't see any way around that one. "I've really missed you all, though."

"Good. When're you coming home?"

"Uh, I don't know exactly. Early next week, I hope."

"You 'hope.' Well, I certainly hope so, too. I suppose you'd like to say something to your children?"

— She 'supposed'? "Yes, I would."

"I'll see if Daddy's done telling them all their bedtime story, then. Daddy and Mommy and Faith and her whole brood have been here since yesterday afternoon, and we're all exhausted. Tell me something first, though: you're not *stoned* now, are you?"

"Huh? No, of course not."

She was gone a very long time. John sat staring at the discolored wallpaper in the tiny gold-and-maroon bedroom where Gil slept, where the phone usually was. *His* Thanksgiving had been Bass ale and tepid pizza-with-everything, and game after losing game of West Texas dominoes with Gil, until Simon had shown up a short while ago with six different flavors of Ben & Jerry ice cream. John felt as if he'd dwelt in this basement apartment forever, and Meredith, Mercy, Dierdre, Sean, and Colin all belonged to some former lifetime. In fact, he was beginning to feel about this place much as he always had about his parents' West Side Manhattan brownstone: he was afraid he was never, *ever*, going to get out of there. . . .

"— Hello? Sorry to take so long. Sean and Colin are fast asleep. And Dierdre says she's busy."

"She says *what*?"

"Just what I said. She told me to tell you she'd speak to you when you come home, and not before. I think I feel the same way. The whole house is a shambles and if Hope and I don't start to do something about it now I won't be able to sleep tonight for thinking about what it'll be like tomorrow. And now Faith's saying she *may* stay through the weekend! So goodbye."

"Just 'goodbye'?"

"Yes." Click.

Oh, boy. Then, as soon as he replaced the receiver, it rang— or rather, buzzed very softly. "For you—Suzanne," he told Gil, returning to the kitchen and glancing around desperately for the hash pipe. Simon took a parting toke and passed it over.

❖

"Oh, *wow*! And holy cow! *Get* him for us, sweetheart! Climb right into bed with him, if that's what it takes!"

"I'm sure he'd be shocked out of his blue-black skin if I made any move in that direction. Besides, I doubt I could make it with Robert Redford, anymore."

"Didn't know you ever did, congratulations."

"Fuck you, you *know* what I mean! Men just aren't built right for going to bed with. They smell bad and they're bony in all the wrong places."

"Couldn't agree with you more, m'dear—so how's it going with Our Ms. Sherman? I understand from Simon she's quite the fascinating article, swinging everywhichway. Are you getting any there yet?"

"Keep your filthy little mind to yourself!"

"No offense," Gil said quickly, aware that he'd just given plenty. "Tell you what: find out if this Kennedy cat was ever taped, bet he was, and talk like you know record companies. We'll see how far that gets us."

❖

The Gathering, in a bowl-shaped meadow of deep yellow grass surrounded by towering firs, was a feast and celebration of the onset of winter, some two hundred people of all ages joined in a common, timeless prayer of gratitude for the bounty and blessings in yet another year of dedicated living. There was feasting, too, all sorts of music, storytelling, dancing, flirting, and joking, and a great deal of enthusiastic swapping of gossip and useful information among friends and neighbors who seldom saw each other except at several get-togethers like this one spread out across each year.

Over everything, a special gentleness pervaded: plenty of drinking, but no drunks, no brawling, and no weapons in evidence. Jake was vividly reminded of New Mexico in the early Seventies, the heyday of homesteading and the back-to-the-land movement, so called. But it didn't feel at all like this out there anymore—it certainly hadn't, anyhow, at that ranch near Angel Peak. Or anywhere else that Jake was aware of, except for a very few tucked-away places like this one, almost all of them in northern California, Washington State, or Oregon. The most obvious change from those bygone days he noted was, if there were illegal drugs around, their users were behaving with exemplary discretion.

Elizabeth and Timmy had gone off with their guru Sarai and some other healer-types soon after the four of them arrived midafternoon in Sallyanne, so Jake and Eric strolled around the meadow, finding themselves welcome everywhere, sampling the food, drink, music, and conversation at each of the campfires strung out around the edge of the meadow. Eric hadn't wanted to come along at first, but Elizabeth had leaned on him a bit, and Jake silently rejoiced now to see him loosening up, drinking a little homebrew, playing some horseshoes, and even allowing himself to be persuaded to fill in as a partner in the figure-dancing after sunset, when an equally shy, berry-brown young woman summoned up her courage and asked him if he would, "pretty-please?"

Jake stayed away from the alcohol and managed to enjoy himself most of the time, despite the frequent sense of déjà-vu and one unfortunate, if inevitable, mishap: his already-in-need-of-mending bridgework snapped into three pieces while he was gnawing on a barbecued goat rib, leaving him with nothing but front teeth in his lower jaw.

He could get along for a few days like that, he'd done it before, but there was no choice now. He'd have to hunt up a dentist when they got back to civilization—and then he remembered, with a lurch like falling from a considerable height. He couldn't do that sort of thing unthinkingly anymore, not without making up a name and a story about why his dental records were unavailable—unless he wanted to risk spending all his remaining days, weeks, or months talking to the law. Which was probably why he hadn't phoned Gil when they stopped to gas up on the way here: he didn't want to be reminded of such risks again, or to hear Gil make that brainstorm of theirs seem within the realm of realizability, either. But none of that had left his mind entirely, and he'd given Simon's number a try while Eric was checking the oil and tire pressure. All he got, though, was the tape, since Simon had been on his way to Baltimore at that point in time. . . .

Once most of the fires had died down to coals and most kids were asleep or giggling and whispering under their blankets, a bright orange gibbous moon climbed above the treetops, and an all-night sweat began in an enormous lodge constructed that afternoon of green poles and fir boughs bent and lashed together, then covered with three-mil polyethylene film. Throughout the day Jake had heard some people objecting to the plastic, others calling its use a perfect "synergistic" symbol of their community, the wedding of old and new technologies. It was an argument that seemed to him to have gone on around him, nonstop, since the mid-Sixties. Even the individual voices sounded the same.

The sweat itself was first-rate, though, when he overcame the hesitation he'd always experienced on such occasions, peeled his clothes off quickly, and crept inside. There were at least forty other humans huddled in the ruddy darkness, and he wondered if those glowing rocks passed inside continually in battered buckets were really necessary. Their collective body-heat would probably have kept that space almost as hot. . . .

Somewhere long past midnight (the moon was down again already), feeling a little too much like a baked apple, Jake staggered out, sluiced himself with icy water from a 55-gallon drum, and took a steaming, naked ramble by starlight in search of a good place to take a leak— which was abruptly forgotten when he brushed aside some undergrowth to find himself ten feet away from Sarai Talks-to-Thunder leaning up against a tree-trunk, wrapped in a dark blanket.

Thin and wizened, in her sixties, with iron-gray hair in a schoolmarmish bun, she wasn't the silly witch he'd pretty much expected. No hocus-pocus, no dithering disciples at her elbows as she'd moved about the meadow earlier, or when she'd unobtrusively initiated the simple ceremony at the beginning of the sweat.

He stood still while she studied him for a long moment, then motioned him closer. Had she mistaken him for someone else, some lover, maybe? No, but she beckoned again, brusquely. Dubiously, he took another step, and she said, "Stop." He froze. She shut her large but shrewd eyes, rocked her head back against the rough bark, then shook it slowly, from side to side.

"Bad trouble," she said at last, in little more than a hoarse whisper.

". . . Yes," he admitted.

"I don't know if I can help you."

"I don't know if I'm asking you to."

She smiled slightly at that, eyes still closed, moistening thin lips with the tip of her tongue. "But you do need help."

"I guess I do."

"I need three days to decide whether or not I can do anything for you."

"I don't know where I'll be, after three days."

"No. Nor do I, or where I'll be, either. But if I can help you, you'll find me."

He saw no point in replying to that assertion. When she said nothing further and continued to stand motionless with her head thrown back and her eyes tightly closed, he moved quietly away, found a path that led him back to the sweat lodge, located his own clothes among all the indistinct little heaps outside the door, and put them on again, against the growing chill.

Eric was nowhere in evidence, and as Jake rolled into his bag in the even deeper darkness beside Sallyanne, he hoped that his son and that young woman had discovered a suitably secluded spot in which to overcome each other's reticence.

A week of seminars on natural medicine was scheduled to begin the Saturday after Thanksgiving, somewhere in the Bay Area. Elizabeth and Timmy were enrolled for all of it, and had a ride down leaving from Dunsmuir Friday afternoon. Elizabeth gave Jake the address in Berkeley where they'd be staying, but urged him and Eric to make themselves at home in the one-room cabin she and Timmy had use of, for as long they liked.

Jake was glad to be there, glad to be still. His wrestling match with death a week ago and the knowledge that he was being sought for questioning by the federal government both seemed long ago and far away whenever he was sprawled on that little porch, listening to one of Mahler's or Bruckner's symphonies and gazing out across a soaring silvery blue landscape that made him feel as if he were only one tiny brush stroke down in the bottom left-hand corner of some very large old Chinese watercolor. . . .

As soon as he was sure Elizabeth was definitely gone, Eric took his arsenal-away-from-home out from under Sallyanne's seat and went farther up the mountainside for some target practice in a place Timmy had shown him, but surely not with this purpose in mind. Eric hadn't wanted anyone to know he had guns with him; he knew his mother had always been afraid of them. He hadn't even told his father until Jake thought to ask, in Phoenix.

Aside from the Beretta .25, which no one but Claude had ever spotted and which practically lived against the small of his back, Eric had only brought the semi-auto .223 caliber rifle and two handguns: a Colt Woodsman he'd had since his teens, and a Ruger .357 that was really just along for the ride, since it was much too loud and too expensive to do any plinking with.

He always retrieved his brass, even the .22 casings he couldn't recycle. Fir cones left no foreign debris and made good targets, propped up against a big punky deadfall in a high hollow so densely wooded he'd bet no one could hear anything from more than a couple hundred yards away. Timmy had said it was over a mile to the nearest neighbors, around on the far side of the slope. Nobody ever hiked up here but Timmy, either, no other paths or sign around, aside from the deer's.

Shooting calmed him, he didn't care what anybody said to the contrary. Even when he was a little rusty, as now. That only added to the challenge, to relax and just keep at it until he got everything right again, smoother and easier with each fresh clip, faster, too.

Hunting didn't draw him much, though; he only did that for the meat or to protect his crops. But he'd loved pure shooting, target shooting, ever since Jake first handed him the old, single shot, bolt action .22 they'd traded a goat for to try to stop racoons and rabbits from doing in their first year's garden. Eric had soon taken that chore on entirely, over Elizabeth's vehement protests. After that, the only gifts he'd been interested in receiving for Christmas or his birthday were more guns, or books about them, or ammunition and reloading supplies. . . .

By Sunday afternoon, Jake still hadn't begun to be able to think for more than moments about that world he'd left out there somewhere, with all its sorrows, mysteries, and problems. He hadn't even thought about Nora very much, except to wonder just what degree of trouble, pain, and embarrassment knowing him had brought her to, and whether she now wished they'd never crossed paths. He couldn't even begin to speculate on what Gil might have in the works already, and he didn't especially want to travel those 8.7 miles again to learn more, either, but he knew they couldn't remain where they were for whatever scrap of time he had left—he certainly didn't want to drop dead on Elizabeth's doorstep, now they'd finally made peace between them.

At half-past three, reluctantly, he went inside, shed his sweatpants, pulled on his jeans and boots. If he hadn't kept his headphones on in order to finish the final movement of Mahler's third while he was doing that, he might've heard the car. Most likely not, though, because they stopped some two hundred yards up the driveway, as soon as they'd glimpsed the cabin through the trees, and completed their approach on foot. They were against either side of the doorway when he came out again.

They didn't have to tell him what they were, or what they wanted. But they did. He only half-heard them, and saw no point in protesting, or pretending he was somebody else. His first thoughts were of Eric, what Eric would feel when he returned and saw Sallyanne still there, but no Jake.

"Can I leave a note, just saying where I've gone, so no one'll worry?"

"All right," the one in the corduroy sportcoat said, "just be quick about it."

"Can you give me a phone number, where we'll be?"

"Just say the FBI office in Redding."

He scribbled that, and a crooked 'J,' with one of Timmy's charcoal drawing pencils on the back of a brochure about the seminars that was lying on the table. As soon as he'd finished, each man grasped one of his elbows and they all but carried him out the door and down the steps, then began to hustle him across the yard. He stumbled once, and felt his temper rising—after all, they'd said "wanted for questioning," not "under arrest."

He wasn't sure, later, what he heard that next moment: 'Put my father back where you got him,' it could've been, something that oddly phrased, in a small, pinched voice that somehow carried very clearly, without any echo, down the thirty yards from the path directly behind them—and as both men let go, leaped aside and whirled and crouched, drawing their weapons as they'd been trained, two shots, or short bursts, small-caliber, but deafening nonetheless—*Jesus, no, not this!*

If they'd only been a few minutes earlier, or Eric a few minutes later, or if he hadn't taken the time to leave a note. Infinitely better, to spend the remainder of his own life being grilled than for Eric to have *this* to run away from for the rest of his. Oh Jesus Christ, no, oh turn this back, *undo it!*

For half a minute, Eric couldn't believe it, either. All those years of patient practice, it was as automatic as any reflex now . . . he stumbled to the bottom of the slope, rifle dangling from his right hand, spare banana clip clutched in his left, the whole world around him flashing red and black with the pulse in his temples. They were dead all right, dead as anything could get. Eric wobbled as he stood there, gazing down, until Jake clutched his shoulders, pulled him to his chest, dry sobs racking them both.

Finally Jake found his voice again, and words: "We've gotta get out of here—get *this* out of here, too."

Eric nodded, gnawing at his lower lip exactly the way Jake remembered him doing whenever he'd done something wrong, from even before he'd learned to talk. And then they moved: like robots, but like efficient robots, going through pockets for keys, driving that anonymous new car down into the yard, dragging the bodies over to it, folding them into the trunk, packing and stowing their own gear, removing Jake's note, closing up the cabin, scuffing away all traces in the loose cinnamon dirt.

Eric drove the car and Jake, on straight adrenalin, led the way in Sallyanne. Halfway down the dirt road to the pay phone, he pulled over and walked back to say, "We don't know this country, we can't go driving all over it looking for somewhere to ditch this. I promised I'd call Gil at about this time, anyway. I'm gonna tell him what's happened, maybe he'll have some idea."

Eric shrugged and nodded, still chewing on his lip.

"Another thing: we're trading vehicles, you and me, right here. And if anything happens, I mean if you should see me get pulled over, I want you to promise me that you and Sallyanne'll keep right on going."

Eric took two deep breaths, and climbed out of the car.

"Promise?"

". . . Okay. Yeah, I will."

❖

Nora had a concert she couldn't miss that Sunday evening. She dropped Suzanne on the corner near Sherrill's, where Gil appeared, barely five minutes late, in an elderly but lovingly maintained Lincoln green MG.

"Where's your auntie's Plymouth?"

"Out in Baltimore, waiting for you," he said, handing her registration and insurance papers, a letter informing whomever-it-might-concern that Ms. S. J. Stroehlengutt had current use of the car, and the key ring. "You need your own wheels in this burg, and gray goes better with your wig than mine, dearie."

"Who's Orville Webster?" she asked, reading.

"Me, on occasion. If anyone wonders, your film company made it available. It's wearing Maryland plates these days, much less noteworthy around here than those Kansas ones. And now I'm gonna show you *how* you drive, whenever you go anywhere, but especially everytime you come out to Baltimore, okay?"

Gil circled three different blocks and cut abruptly through that many parking lots before getting onto the Beltway, then switched back and forth from I-95 to I-295 twice on narrow back roads, from Laurel to Maryland City, then over again to Dorsey from Waterloo and up I-695 through Dundalk and Essex to Fullerton, checking his rear-view mirror constantly and suddenly pulling over several times just beyond blind curves to let any cars behind them go past. "You get the idea, I'm sure," he said as he finally parked the MG, across the street from the Plymouth but five long blocks from the basement apartment. "There's lots of those little connecting roads, no reason why you'd ever need to take any route more'n once. Oh, by the way—any late-breaking news to report on our Custodial Connection?"

"You were right, Nora's got a bunch of Kennedy Edwards on tape. She played me an earful last night. I'm no judge, but I'm sure he was as good as she thinks. I told her what you said, about my boss having a record company as well. She gave me a number at Roosevelt's house and said I should speak to him myself. I tried this afternoon, but he's working the weekend."

"That's progress," Gil said cheerfully. "Rome wasn't torn down in a day."

The apartment seemed even darker, damper, and more forlorn than her dismal recollection. "Where's Nebby?" Suzanne wanted to know as soon as they were inside.

"It took some doing, but I got Simon to dog- and John-sit for the weekend—don't look so crestfallen, I'll do my best to keep you entertained." At that moment the phone buzzed, from a jack in the living room this time.

Gil grabbed it and said, "Howdy, pal, how you doing, just wait'll you hear what we've got hold of—huh?" Then he listened intently for a minute or more, while Suzanne watched his face go through a number of vivid transformations. ". . . Mm-hmm. Tell you what—keep heading south on I-Five with both vehicles and call me back in an hour or so, in any case before wherever-that-is where you've gotta choose between Frisco and Sacramento . . . yeah, Christ, I know. Just keep it all together somehow, man, take it one mile at a time, I'll come up with something, I promise."

It required considerable will power for Suzanne not to ask Gil what he'd just been told. His face was immobile now, but excitement radiated from every pore as he stared off into the middle distance. Without moving anything but his right arm, and even without blinking, he pulled out his flannel shirttail, reached into what Suzanne guessed was a money-belt, produced a small address book and tossed it at her. "End of the W's, halfway down the page, J S, a seven-one-eight number—dial it for me. And then in the bookcase beside my bed there's a road atlas, see if you can find me a Sacramento street map."

"... It's ringing," she said, rising and passing it over on her way out of the room. He hadn't said to close the door, or not to come back out to the couch to look up California. But there wasn't anything especially edifying to be overheard:

"Joe? Me again. Yeah. Hey, lemme ask you something: those guys you were telling me about, where do they hang out? No, I mean out in Sacramento ... no kidding? Where d'you dagos come up with those names, anyhow? Yeah ... that's off El Camino, but you're not sure what street? Okay, just wondered. Everything copacetic with you? Naw, nothing special. Give Arlene my best. . . ."

Suzanne had the page ready, her index finger pointing out El Camino Avenue. Gil glanced at it as he stood to go out to the refrigerator to study the ice-cream collection. When he returned and flopped down with the remains of a pint of Cherry Garcia, she told him, "If your brainstorm's over, I want to say something."

"Oh? Shoot."

"I don't mind being helpful, but I didn't come along to be your secretary. Or your maid, or your butler. Or your faithful Archie, or your Watson, either, so don't start telling me 'the game's afoot.'" After the genius-at-work routine she'd just witnessed, she wouldn't've put that line past him.

"Ah, yes! But the game's on *our* foot now!"

"I meant what I said, Gil. I don't expect to be told every blessed thing, but I don't want to be treated as if I wouldn't understand if you did tell me something once in a while."

"Uh-huh. You've got executive ambitions, maybe, you'd like a role in the decision-making process? Here's a good one for you to mull over, then—what d'*you* do with two dead feds? 'Cause that's what Our Jake just handed me. Any bright ideas?"

"... This is for real?"

"You're goddamned right it is, very much so at this moment for Jake and Jake Junior, I imagine. And for us, too, of course. We're all in this together now, my friend."

"How—what happened?"

"They tried to take Jake, and young Eric didn't let 'em. I didn't guess he had it in him. I tend to underrate those quiet types. I should know better by now."

"What're you going to tell them to do about it?"

"Well, since we don't have a nationwide stiff-disposal service of our own to draw on, I figured we'd borrow the best private one available. So I'm gonna have 'em deposit the parcel at—so help me—the Maroon Lagoon Saloon, where the local mob slobs reputedly polish their elbows. Whether they'll disappear it completely for us or not, that should at least cause a fair amount of delay and confusion all around, and we can use any breathing space we can get. Now, would you— please—see if you can cajole that address out of Information, or have I gotta do it for myself?"

It was past midnight in Baltimore when Jake called back from a truck-stop. No further problems—I-5 was full of weekenders returning to the Bay Area, that was all. Gil read off the directions, then said, "You get rid of all their ID? Well, do that first, okay? Leave their guns, take the cannoli."

"Take *what*?" Jake asked. "I can't hear very well here."

"Never mind, it wasn't important. Have Eric wait not too far off, but somewhere that pretty truck of yours won't stand out any more'n can be helped. Park the car toward the back of the lot if you can, put the keys in the ashtray, and walk away. Then you guys head for the coast. Got anywhere of your own to stay just for tonight? If not I'll—"

"Yeah," Jake said. The address Elizabeth had given him was in his wallet; he'd already checked.

"Okay. Park that sweetheart as far away from there as you can manage, take whatever you're gonna want—for godsakes, take the piece that did it—and kiss her goodbye. Call as early as you can tomor- row, I'll have somewhere really secure to put you by then, pal, until we can get you back here. G'night."

Eric dropped Jake and their baggage at the multi-colored Victorian monstrosity on Deakin Street, then drove out into Oakland to abandon Sallyanne and hike back. It was past midnight in Berkeley, too, by that time. A woman in a knee-length teeshirt answered Jake's tap at the frosted glass door and let him in without hesitation, whispered that he should find his own sleeping-space, then returned to hers. Every room he peered into seemed almost wall-to-wall with recumbent human forms already, so he spread out their bags in an alcove near the front door, where Eric would have the least trouble locating him. The only lighted room he saw was at the back of the house, and turned out to be the kitchen. The only person in it, seated at the table, sipping tea, was Sarai Talks-to-Thunder.

"You've found me," she said with neither preamble nor sign of surprise, "and I just decided this evening that I can help you. Tell me if I'm wrong: you don't expect to recover from your sickness, do you? You're only asking for a certain amount of time."

Jake tried to think about that. He was so exhausted by now that nothing registered in his mind quite as it should, but he nodded. All he really wanted out of life at this moment was a steaming mug of tea like Sarai's. He didn't think he'd said that aloud, but she pointed at the pot on the counter, then at cups hanging from pegs on the wall behind him.

"How much time?"

It was lemon-grass tea, weak but warming. Laboriously, he figured out today's date, then counted slowly, until the end of January. "Eight . . . no, nine weeks."

She shut her eyes tightly, lowered her head for some seconds, and then said, "Yes. I think I can take your sickness on myself for that long, but not any longer . . . and I'll do whatever I can about those who would stop you."

Jake stared, but he had never felt so weary, or so dull. "Does it matter to you," he asked finally, "whether I believe what you've just told me?"

That smile came again, open-eyed this time, and certainly amused. "No, it shouldn't matter. What matters is that *I* believe it. Hoard your faith for what *you* must do."

17: BERKELEY TO BALTIMORE

For the first time since they'd left Phoenix, Jake awoke craving a cigarette . . . and then he understood why. Impossible to believe, the killing of two fellow human beings yesterday, by his son and for his sake. Yet here he lay, on a strange floor that his memory told him was in the strange city of Berkeley, and his first conscious thought had been: *Gotta call Gil, our freedom and our lives are in his hands now. . . .* Then Jake remembered that Elizabeth was here in this house some-where; he should say goodbye and give her some explanation—but how could he explain why there'd be law swarming over the peaceful region she now called home, probably for months to come? How do you say, Our only surviving child's a cop-killer and it's my fault, I'm sorry?

Jake drew himself up on an elbow to find there was just one pair of eyes open to meet his among all the prone bodies around him, Eric's, and they looked as though they hadn't closed once all night. Silently, the two men dressed, shouldered their dufflebags, and let themselves out the front door.

They found Telegraph Avenue without a problem, but turned right onto it instead of left as they should've done and wound up trudging all the way to Oakland before they found anywhere to get breakfast. By then Jake had acquired a pack of Luckies, smoked two, and more or less managed to shake the conviction that every passerby was looking at them a little too intently. But he could see that Eric still felt very much that way.

Gil answered on the first ring: "Where are you? Telegraph and Fortieth? Oh, yeah, Uhuru Bakery, right? Great place, I love their scones! Okay, just stay put, Howie'll pick you up shortly. He may not look like much, but believe me, Howie's the best there is, anywhere. Anything you want, just ask him."

An omelette apiece and three cappuccinos later, a skinny little straw-colored guy in greasy overalls with thick whiz-kid glasses and a rampant cowlick came in, gulped a double espresso at the counter, then wobbled blindly back out past their table muttering, "I'm Howie, I paid your bill, follow me."

They did, at a cautious distance, to a decrepit-looking once-red International delivery van three blocks away. He shut them into the totally dark and empty rear of it, where they sat on their duffles for what seemed like at least half an eternity, careening around corners at what felt like eighty miles an hour. Finally the van stopped, and the doors swung open to a vast dim space smelling like both a tar pit and a pickle barrel, full of inverted boat hulls up on sawhorses in various states of reconstruction.

With a welcoming shrug, Howie led the way up a ladder to a dusty, ceilingless loft with a single bleary window overlooking an unlimited expanse of gray-green water. "You're in Sausalito, in case you wondered. I've gotta leave you up here for now, but I'll be back after dark to take you out to a houseboat, yonder. You'll be there three or four days, depending on how long it takes me to get everything together. Anything in particular you want to pass the time—newspapers, magazines, videos? There's three thirty-inch TVs and two VCRs out there. And playing cards, dominoes, Scrabble, and a chess set. A bunch of paperbacks, too, mostly mysteries and science fiction."

"Music," Jake said. He'd stuffed his Walkman in his bag, but no tapes, except for the version of Mahler's third symphony he'd been listening to yesterday. He knew he couldn't ever listen to that work again.

"Sure. Just write me a list."

"And double-A batteries. And a carton of Luckies."

"You got it. What about eats? Steak? Chicken? Seafood?"

"I've got a problem there," Jake said. "Broke my bridgework last week."

"Show me." Jake did. "Hell, that's no problem. I've fixed a lot worse'n that. What can I do for you, kid?"

"Nothing," Eric said.

"You'll think of something, I betcha. Just tell me tonight, I'll bring it out tomorrow. But hey, I almost forgot—gimme all your ID, travelers' checks, anything with your names on it. And I was told there's some hardware to dispose of." Slowly, Eric produced the rifle from the middle of his dufflebag.

"Any others?"

Nodding glumly, Eric handed over the Woodsman and the .357.

Howie stuffed them all and the ID into a boxful of junk in the back of his truck. "Well cared for," he said sympathetically.

"What'll you do with 'em?"

"You really wanna know? They go over the side of a trawler tonight, at least ten miles out there. Okay, any other requests? See you around nine, then. There's beer, bread, cheese, and cold-cuts in the fridge behind that door."

The houseboat, weatherbeaten and nondescript outside but with an interior as well appointed as any first-class hotel suite, (with a sunken tub, a jacuzzi, and two king-sized waterbeds), was the last of a dozen anchored off the end of a hundred yards of private dock. Howie took them out there in a fiberglass dinghy with an almost silent electric outboard motor.

After he'd shown them around and cautioned them against raising the blinds or appearing out on deck, he opened an inlaid wooden box filled with jeweler's tools and quickly put Jake's dentures back together with epoxy and a bit of silver solder, then smoothed the rough spots with a tiny grinding wheel.

"Here, try this. All right? You develop any sore spots, be sure to let me know. You've got baked potatoes in the warming oven, two T-bones ready for the broiler, and a tomato and avocado salad on the counter. There's a case of very decent Beaujoulais in the lower right-hand cupboard, and a bunch of other vino if that's not your choice, and there's also assorted beer and ale in the fridge, plus apricots in brandy and Black Forest layer cake if you go in for dessert. How's about abalone for tomorrow night, huh? You both like artichokes? Okay, sleep tight. . . ."

Jake did sleep well, to his surprise, not only that night but the two following. They left the television alone, and Eric kept his nose buried in one suspense novel after another, except for mealtimes and the couple of chess games Jake consented to play (and quickly lost, as he always had, ever since Eric first learned the game at the age of nine). Jake, however, didn't feel like reading—he'd read hardly anything, he realized, since he'd first learned of his sentence at Sloan-Kettering. The printed word had been central to much of his life, but whatever time he had remaining, he didn't want to spend it with books, especially not novels: that didn't feel like living, more like haunting, like spying on somebody else's life, invisibly.

Music was another matter, though, and Howie had returned with almost everything on that list Jake had expected him to select just a few from—not only Mozart's Requiem, but Berlioz', Verdi's, and Brahms' as well, and other titles suggested by Jake's requests, including Bach's B minor Mass and Beethoven's *Missa Solemnis*. Music was life to Jake now, the pure essence. As long as he was listening to something he loved, he could almost believe that nothing else could ever touch them. . . .

On the third evening, Howie brought clippers, strop, and straight razor, shaved them both clean to the tops of their ears, and gave them severe middle-American haircuts. "Don't squawk," he said when Eric protested, "I was told to put *you* in drag. I convinced him that never works with anybody your size."

Then he issued Fruit of the Loom underwear, Wranglers, Keds, hooded sweatshirts, baseball caps, and red nylon jackets that said 'Volunteer Fire Dept./Eddyville, Iowa' across the back. "Your own mothers wouldn't know ya now," he told them, admiring his handiwork. Then he handed Jake a roll of bills. "You gave me twenty-four-eighty in travelers' checks—an even grand was the best deal I could make. And here's your new ID, and the keys and papers for a two-year-old Dodge pickup with a brand-new Six-Pac camper shell, which awaits you back in the boat shed. These insurance numbers are dummies, so drive defensively. Otherwise, you're good for any make that might be run on you, short of fingerprints. You're uncle and nephew now, by the way, James and David Metzner. You've got a True Value franchise together back in Eddyville—here're your business cards.

"Okay: rots-a-ruck, as they say on the other side of this puddle. Tell ol' Gillie it was all my pleasure."

"Howie said to tell you it was all his pleasure."

"He did, huh? What that means is, he owed me a big one, and now he's free to soak me good next time around. Hey, look, there's blizzards due along both I-Seventy and I-Eighty through this coming week, so if I were you I'd head for LA and take I-Forty straight across. I'm leaving here tonight myself, gotta take John home, then spend some more time in Funk City, padding the old bankroll. Simon tells me we're gonna need something like a hundred G's for this little 'low-tech' operation—"

"Did you tell Simon what happened in Shasta?"

"Uh, not in detail, no, I figured *you* should do that, in person. Look, I'll probably be back before you get here, but in case I'm not, there's a spare key taped inside the light fixture over the door. C'mon in and make yourselves at home, call Simon if you want but pretty-please, don't call or try to see your Miz Sherman, she's still being watched and listened in on, we can be absolutely certain of that much—hey, I never did get to tell you our good news, did I? We've come up with the most beautiful route into that place, you'd never, in a million years . . ."

Standing at a roadside phone east of Altamont, looking back toward hundreds of gawky wind generators revolving idly in the soft mid-morning breeze along the tawny, rolling ridge they'd just crossed, Jake found himself increasingly irritated by Gil's alternating bossi-ness and carefree chitchat—even more so by the growing realization that this was for-real, Operation Remission or whatever the hell it was going to be called was actually going forward, and if it really did take place, *he* was going to make it happen—but other wills beside his own were already involved in every aspect, and plans were already evolv-ing into irreversible shapes without his knowledge or consent. . . .

"— Hello? You still there? Hey, friend, can I presume to tell you something for your own good? You stare back over your shoulder at the past too much, Jake. Don't let what can't be helped get *to* you like that, huh? What's done is *done,* and won't happen again. Look, man, everything's gonna be A-okay when you get here, and you *will* get here. They may be powerful, but they are *not* invincible, or all-knowing. They're fuckups, by the very nature of everything they stand for. They get lucky sometimes, they did there for a while, but they're just too gigantic, too tight-assed, too simple-minded for anything like flexibility or real imagination. If it were otherwise, there wouldn't *be* all this deep shit the world's drowning in today, right? Look, sorry, didn't mean to preach, you guys just have yourselves a nice uneventful trip, hey? And don't forget to stay in character: truckstops, Stuckeys', KOAs, or Motel Sixes all the way. . . ."

To hear Gil talk, Simon was wholeheartedly involved in this scheme already. In actuality, while Simon had spent several long stoned nights at the Baltimore basement discussing it with Gil and had even gone so far as to take one tour of the Capitol Building with John and two later by himself, if asked he would've been quick to explain that the inter-est he'd shown was mainly due to enforced leisure and the intrinsically fascinating nature of problems presented by what Gil said Jake was determined to do. The totally impossible had never drawn Simon, but the nearly so had always held tremendous attraction, and he was pretty sure this endeavor belonged in the latter category—if only because almost anything imaginable does, if you bring enough ingenuity, luck, and persistence to it. He'd rather have been scaling a cliff or exploring a cave or scuba diving along some coral reef, but this little project had similar aspects, on the face of it.

And the fact that it was Jake who wanted to do this made a good deal of difference in how seriously Simon took the basic idea. So did his own well-nurtured conviction that no government on earth—certainly not any recent one down at the other end of Massachusetts Avenue—was ever going to halt the galloping destruction of the global environment being carried out in the holy names of Progress and Free Trade, unless it was brought home to our so-called leaders that—as Lenny Bruce used to put it—*their* asses would be up for grabs, too, if they didn't.

Now that he was home again, though, Simon reset his sights on his fast-approaching three-week vacation in the Andes, buried himself in his back orders, and did his best not to think about any of that other stuff again, except for a single move: having mentioned to Gil that a former flame of his was a librarian at the National Bureau of Standards in Gaithersburg, Simon got to thinking fondly of the lady in question, called, and drove out there to see her one night, describing incidentally a few of the questions he was curious about. And she promptly photocopied quite a stack of material, so as to have a ready reason for him to drop by again. Which he did soon enough, and afterward, having tossed the limp bundle on top of the pile of reading matter nearest his bed, he began to spend an hour or two each night with such classics in the field as Seaborg and Loveland's *The Elements Beyond Uranium*, Hodge, Stannard, and Hursh's *Uranium/Plutonium/Transplutonic Elements*, Cleveland's *Chemistry of Plutonium*, Wick's *Plutonium Handbook*, as well as variously classified reports on the effects of ionizing radiation.

He read on with increasing curiosity, which soon turned to distinct uneasiness tinged with horror: he'd long known they were assholes for the most part, but he'd always assumed nuclear scientists would be fairly *competent* assholes. The further into the subject he went, though, the more apparent it became to him that *these creeps not only didn't know but didn't even care that they didn't know what the fuck they were talking about*! Their terminology was incredibly sloppy, and the harder Simon tried to pin anything down, the less he could find that they had really established for certain.

This problem was partly inherent in the elements themselves, as D. M. Taylor pointed out in passing: "Serious difficulties in chemical studies with Pu-239 are posed by the intense alpha radiation, 1.36×10^{11} disintegrations per minute per gram. . . ." Struggling to comprehend so vast a number, Simon found himself reflecting that this was only *alpha* rays; there were also beta, gamma, and X-rays to calculate, not to mention all those other anonymous particles banging away on their own.

But aside from the problems posed by an element that refused to stand still and let you scrutinize it, that was forever transmuting into other "unstable" elements, there was one glaring instability of human origin involved here, and every time Simon's eye alighted upon further references to it, his righteous indignation climbed another notch: except for isolated atoms, Pu-239 didn't even exist on this planet until August 1942. But since then, without the slightest hesitation to consider possible consequences, without admitting that they didn't understand the first goddamned thing about it, these bastards—Americans most of all but the Russians, French, and British as well, and just about everybody else with a nuclear generator—had been producing it and spreading it around everywhere, by the frigging *ton*!

"Hi, Mercy!"

"Oh. Hello again. Now what?"

— Now what? "I'm coming *home*, that's what!"

"Good. When?"

"Uh, tonight, I guess. That is, we're leaving tonight, we'll probably get there for breakfast."

"Who's *we*? And why can't you drive up in the daytime, like normal people?"

"Gil and me, that's all—and Nebby. And . . . I don't really know why, that's just when Gil said he wanted to leave—"

"Why can't you ever do what *I* want—and *who*? Look, John, I can't take any more company, I just finally got shut of Faith and her brats yesterday!"

"No company—Gil's just dropping me off, that's all. And Nebby's just a dog I . . . acquired down here."

"Oh, you did? Seems to me we might've discussed this first. As a matter of fact, I thought we did discuss pets a long time ago, and decided against having any. A puppy, I suppose. Who's going to train it and feed it and clean up after it?"

"Not a puppy—but no bigger than one, never will be. He's . . . very mature. And lovable. You'll see."

"I suppose I will. Hope's calling me. Goodbye."

Gil anyhow was his old, laid-back, down-to-earth self again, and they got most pleasantly stoned on the trip back to Meredith in the old MG, arriving precisely as Mercy departed for her job. While John introduced Nebby to the kids, Gil drove into the barn, shut the doors, stuffed two stainless-steel canisters into canvas duffle bags with his laundry for padding, wedged one in upright between the passenger's seat and the door, and strapped the other down with the safety belt. After devouring two bowls of blueberry granola, he said his goodbyes quickly and headed for Manhattan.

❖

Studying the current Rand McNally road atlas Howie had thoughtfully provided, Jake realized he didn't want to go anywhere near Banning again if they could help it—and a phone call soon informed him, yes, they could. The route through Yosemite was still open; they could go that way and as far east into Nevada as Tonapah, then head south along the western edge of the Nuclear Testing Site to Las Vegas, over the Hoover Dam, and on to Kingman, where they'd pick up I-40 East.

He'd never seen Yosemite before, or anything comparable. That's dumb of me, Jake thought: there isn't anything comparable, anywhere, there couldn't be. "Almost as pretty as home, ain't it?" he quipped without thinking, when they stopped at a scenic turnout to stretch their legs and gaze toward Half Dome.

Eric didn't so much as grunt in response, and Jake felt immediately how cruel it had been to remind him of his valley. Eric wasn't stupid; he certainly understood by now that he could never go back there to live again. . . .

They stayed in a Motel 6 at Mammoth Lakes, hitting the road again at 4:15 the next morning. Even so, by the time they reached Tonapah— where all the kids they saw were wearing teeshirts proclaiming "*I* ♥ *the Stealth Bomber!*"—they were glad the Dodge had come equipped with air conditioning. Beatty, Nevada, just a few miles east of Death

Valley, was like an oven, too. So was the endless drive south to Las Vegas along Route 95—which, they discovered, had a name as well as a number: Veterans' Memorial Highway. That wouldn't be for him and all the other GIs deliberately irradiated out here, Jake decided, but according to the map, Yucca Flat lay somewhere just beyond those low, dead-gray, naked mountains on their left. . . .

❖

"You're gonna have Mr. Roosevelt Edwards all signed up when I get back, right?" Those had been Gil's next-to-last words to Suzanne before he left for Meredith. "Tell ya what: if y'do, the MG's all yours, for keeps, and I'll take the Plymouth back." That last because she'd complained yesterday that the damn thing rode like a dumptruck, and only to switch subjects and mollify her somehow, after he'd let her know that John was taking Nebby home with him, "unless *you* take care of him from now on—at Nora's."

"I *can't* take him to Nora's!"

"Why not?"

"I can't, that's all. It'd be too much for her, having him underfoot, or she'd think it would be."

"Well, he can't stay here. You're not around enough to look after him and I don't expect to be either, from now on. And we are *not* running the risk of Jake or Eric getting popped accidentally, just because they were waltzing a goddamned dog around the block at an unlucky moment."

She couldn't really argue, not when he'd put it that way. As far as the Plymouth was concerned, a service-station guy suggested letting a few pounds of air out of the tires all around, but that hadn't helped much.

Nothing helped with Edwards, either. She'd been so excited when she'd first learned where he worked: here was her chance to show Gil that she was at least as good at this stuff as he was, maybe even that he'd made a big mistake in leaving her behind all those years ago in Chicago, they could've made a great team . . . but where the hell to begin? Edwards just stood there in her mind's eye, like a thin, twisted splinter of obsidian. Sure, he liked the idea of Kennedy's music being released commercially, but it never seemed to occur to him that any sort of quid pro quo might be called for, and all her hints in that direction simply caused him to blink nervously and look puzzled.

She knew where she'd *like* to begin. If she'd ever seen a candidate for radical, head-to-toe bodywork, he was it. 'You can't think properly, or avoid depression and self-doubt, unless you're standing correctly,' she'd love to tell him. 'Don't tip your pelvis out like that, don't lock your knees! Let your arms hang freely, but without dragging your shoulders forward!'

She knew what Edwards' response would be, though: 'Ma'am, I would if I could but I can't. Please, let us say no more about it.' She knew, too, that people *that* messed up needed more than being told. You had to grab hold and *show* them just what they'd been doing wrong all their lives—but he'd absolutely drop dead, she was sure, if she ever attempted any such thing. . . .

Grabbing hold of anyone, for any reason, had never worked out very well for Suzanne, anyhow. Maybe it was because she was so big— maybe she simply scared most people. That hadn't been the reason with Nora, though—at least, it hadn't stopped her once upon a time, back there on East 83rd Street in Manhattan. But something had certainly stopped her the other evening.

And it wasn't Ruthellen Vliorishevski. Suzanne could almost wish it was, but beyond the fact that Nora had a snapshot of the pair of them sawing away at their violas tucked into a corner of her dresser mirror, Suzanne had found no evidence of anything going on there besides lengthy Saturday morning lessons and a sometimes absolutely nauseating amount of mutual admiration. They weren't meeting elsewhere, either; Nora clearly had no time or energy left over from her job and her music for assignations. Ruthellen was just as clearly a juicy Georgia peach ripe for the plucking, but the kid was also—hard as it was to believe at first glance—much too naïve to comprehend, without extensive coaching, what those intense but delicious feelings all revolving around Nora really added up to. . . .

Anyhow, the other evening—it still hurt like whiplash to remember: Nora coming out of the bathroom on one crutch but quite nimbly, relaxed and aglow from a long hot soak in the tub, and Suzanne squeezing past, pajamas in hand. It was only going to be an impulsive little peck on the cheek, but then Nora's robe slid off her nearer shoulder, and she smelled so sweet. . . .

"No!" she'd said quickly, drawing back, dropping her crutch in her hurry to pull the terrycloth together again at her throat. "Please, don't!" Suzanne was far too needy, she'd realized. "I could certainly use some physical affection right now. But I'm afraid . . . we couldn't keep it simply that."

— She means *I* couldn't, Suzanne knew, forcing face and body to convey nonchalance. "Okay! Entirely up to you."

". . . We'd better not. I'm sorry—but recently I . . . got into something with someone, and it—well, it went too far, that's all. And I need time to . . . get used to being who I really am again. Look, please, I truly *am* sorry, it's just bad timing—I mean, it's a bad time, that's all. . . ."

❖

It had definitely been both of those things, from Nora's point of view. She *was* grateful, extremely, for all Suzanne's help around the house and her more than generous contributions toward the rent and every other expenditure. But Nora had learned a very long time ago that sex was never a safe way to show one's gratitude. . . .

Now the holidays were fast approaching, and that meant nineteen separate events for which she had to make most if not all arrangements. There was also a recital of her own to prepare for, her first in a year and a half. It was scheduled for the twenty-first of January, more than seven weeks away, but she knew how fast they'd go, and already there weren't nearly enough hours in the day or days in the week for everything else she had to attend to, let alone to practice!

She didn't even have the question of which crowd-pleaser to do totally resolved yet, in spite of the fact that the program and poster copy had been promised to the printer no later than next week. She'd really had her heart set on tackling the second Brahms opus 120 sonata this time, but her accompanist was arguing for Schubert's *Arpeggione* as a piece they were both sure they could handle: "I'm not saying *you're* not good enough, Noralove," Greg would say, "or that *I* can't play *my* notes—but can we put it all together yet, the way Herr Brahms intended? And if not, when, pray tell, will we find occasion to figure out how to do it at least as well as Kroyt and Balsam, between now and then?"

Greg was right, it couldn't be done. The way things were going, she'd be lucky to have her own works, the Schubert, and the Rebecca Clarke in presentable shape by that time. She dragged herself out of bed an hour earlier these days, come hell or high water, so as to get in at least two hours' practice, but she was usually too exhausted when she got home at night to do more than nibble at the pricey ready-made suppers Suzanne picked up someplace in Georgetown, before she crawled into the tub and then into bed. That was always when that peculiar, hard-to-locate little pain would start up in earnest, and she'd lie there wondering: Is it just that I'm pushing myself too hard . . . or is another tumor forming somewhere? Finally, she'd choke down the pills that allowed her to sleep, and sometimes, waiting for them to take effect, avoiding the specter of yet another operation, she'd catch herself thinking about Jake, where he might be by now, what he could've done, or be doing.

One night, in a dream, she found herself riding with Eric again, up the valley—but at full gallop, passing Eric's horse, leaving him far behind, the wind whipping her hair about her face, a glorious freedom at first, but then she lost hold of both reins, her horse stumbled, and she was pitched headfirst—awake, with a pounding heart, and another long day to face.

❖

I-40 again, Kingman to Gallup to Grants, twin gray ribbons spooling out endlessly eastward across the raw red, tan, or yellow earth, beneath an even emptier teal-to-turquoise sky. Another endless day, with Eric driving all of it and very little to break it up except for gloriously mournful music and, from a truckstop outside Holbrook, finally catching Simon at home for once and not too busy to answer. But a dozen video games flanked the unboothed pay phone, and nine of them were put to frenetic use as soon as Jake began to dial. All he could gather was that Simon was furious over an item he'd heard on the news an hour ago: the State Department had just issued travel advisories covering most of western South America.

"And there goes my trip, goddamnit—three of the four guys I was gonna be climbing with've already chickened out."

"What's going on? I haven't been following the news."

"Same old shit, just more of it—that jerk in the White House doesn't like the noises they're making down there about actually trying to negotiate with the insurgents. So he's beating his chest and swinging from the crystal chandeliers, while some goldplated asshole at the Pentagon's being quoted as predicting 'This won't be another Iraq, just another Panama.' Sonsofbitches are probably getting ready to napalm the last mountains on Earth where you don't have to wade through tons of previous climbers' garbage with a thousand juppies treading on your heels."

"A thousand *what*?"

"Juppies, Japanese yuppies, what else. They might as well *own* the Himalayas, and Christ, last time I went up Whitney—this was years ago, I'm sure it's even worse now—they were so thick on the trail, if I hadn't been freezing my nuts off I would've sworn I was strolling up Mount Fuji on the Emperor's birthday. . . ."

None of which was any part of what he'd meant to say or ask, Simon realized, or of what Jake had called to learn or tell, but he was so pissed off he couldn't stop himself, until Jake finally shouted, "This is hopeless, I can't hear one word in three! We ought to be there day after tomorrow, talk to you then, okay?" Once they'd yelled goodbye and disconnected, each man was left unsatisfied, uneasy, and as ignorant of the other's actual state of mind as before the call went through.

Jake began to doze off as they approached Albuquerque's glittering sprawl against the dusty fuchsia twilight. When he woke again, at ten to midnight by the dashboard clock, they'd left the Interstate somewhere behind them and were rocking along a potholed, shoulderless macadam road that was vaguely familiar. One particularly tight hairpin with jagged pink sandstone closely overhanging the bend made identification undeniable: they were northeast of Eric's valley, climbing to the mesa above the cliffs.

"I've gotta see it one more time," Eric said, when he noticed that Jake was conscious again and fumbling for his Luckies. "My friend Ernesto's herding sheep up here, he'll lend us some horses and never say anything to anybody, and it's only a couple miles from his shack to the top of the trail."

Jake didn't argue. Wrapped in his unzipped sleeping bag, looking almost straight down at the beaver ponds reflecting icy moonlight, remembering that afternoon six weeks ago when he'd tried to tell himself he'd never see this place again, he waited on the rimrock with both mounts while Eric ran down the path and along the creek to tap on Jerry and Judith's bedroom window and tell them they could do as they pleased with his livestock and everything else because, "I don't believe I'm ever coming back."

"Oh, wow, man, don't say that—this is your *home*, you're one of us. Don't you understand what that means?"

It took Eric quite a while to nod and say, "Yeah, I understand. Just you always be here, okay? Both of you—all of you. Be here a little extra, for me, too."

The rest of their trip was as uneventful as Gil could've wished, except for an ice storm that delayed them for a day and a half in Conway, Arkansas, where there was nothing to do but watch politicians on the motel TV yammering on about the nation's pressing need for more nuclear power plants, lower business taxes, and yet another multibillion-dollar satellite system to police the rest of the world with . . . or a pair of grim-visaged journalists in Banana Republic outfits interviewing a plump young Andean guerrilla in designer shades, Reeboks, a Mickey Mouse sweatshirt, and a beatific grin, while his comrades led daintily stepping llamas loaded with SAMs and mortar shells up a rock-strewn stretch of near-vertical trail behind them . . . or a semicircle of pundits in tailored tweeds and Grecian Formula on overstuffed sofas wittily debating whether the wholesale collapse of medical insurance and severe degradation of hospital care throughout the United States, taken together with the Surgeon General's recent announcement that AIDS was now the official Number One Killer, nationwide, of men—and Number Two of women—between the ages of nineteen and thirty-nine, were sufficient cause for serious concern in and of themselves, or "merely symptomatic of a more insidious societal malaise."

They arrived in Baltimore early in the murky evening of December fourth to find the entire city immobilized by three inches of slushy, sooty snow, the key to the basement apartment exactly where Gil had said it would be, and Simon not answering his phone because he was out in Gaithersburg again.

III: CHAOS

(1 2 / 5 – 1 / 2 4)

The law of chaos is the law of ideas,
of improvisations and seasons of belief.

— Wallace Stevens

18 : CATAFALQUE

When Jake opened one eye the next morning and saw that square-jawed, crewcut silhouette looming over him in the dim gray light, he was instantly convinced that whatever time he might have left was going to be spent entirely in courtrooms and jail cells. He only hoped they'd get to Eric in the next room before he woke up and reached for that .25 Beretta, which, as Jake had silently noted, had not been turned over to Howie with the rest of Eric's traveling arsenal.

"Good morning, Jake," Suzanne said. She'd scarcely whispered it, but as quickly as those other thoughts had flashed by, he'd identified her voice as the one that had answered Simon's phone two and a half weeks ago, and he could breathe again. "How was your trip? Want some coffee?"

"Very long. And yes, absolutely."

Jake pulled on his jeans and sweater and joined her at the kitchen table where she'd tossed her purse and wig on arrival. Even before the beans were ground or the water boiled, Suzanne began to fill him in, about Edwards first of all.

"Could you take *me* to see him?"

"Guess so. I've got to go back there anyhow, to return some tapes he had that Nora didn't. They're too rough acoustically."

"How is Nora?"

'Working herself sick,' Suzanne wanted to tell him, 'and scared to death another tumor's growing. Missing you fiercely, and gnawed to the backbone by worry about what you might be up to. But she won't admit to any of those things. . . .'

"Oh, fine," Suzanne heard herself saying.

"Good. But she's still being watched?"

"Uh, yeah, we're pretty sure," Suzanne said, because Gil had insisted on that point: as far as everyone else in this operation was concerned, Nora was definitely still under surveillance, even though

Suzanne had consistently reported that there'd been no indication of anything of the sort since the plumbers' truck she'd seen the first morning—and she had doubts now about that because she'd spotted what she was positive was the same truck several times since in different locations around Glen Echo, once with the back doors wide open and a couple of very plumber-looking guys expertly bending copper tubing behind it.

"I don't give a good goddamn," Gil had said. "I don't want any of us but *you* anywhere near that lady, and especially not Jake. And every blessed time you call or come near here, I want you taking every precaution I've taught you, and any others you can dream up. I just can't believe they're not hanging on tight as ticks there, somehow."

But nobody had ever tailed Suzanne anywhere, or Nora either, at least not when Suzanne was with her, and no one had tried to find out from Nora who Suzanne was and what she was doing there, she was positive on those scores. It was inconceivable to her—if not to Gil—that Nora would conceal such a thing, and Suzanne had been checking her rear-view mirror so often she'd nearly run into vehicles in front of her half a dozen times.

And, as she'd continued to get absolutely nowhere with Roosevelt Edwards—especially since Gil had gone off to New York—everything felt less and less substantial. She'd even begun to wonder about those two other cars with two more feds apiece that Gil had claimed he'd spotted staking out Nora's place that first night—had she actually seen them with her own eyes, or had Gil convinced her of their presence afterward? Could all of this be simply his paranoia and her imagination?

No. Nora had definitely been interrogated, and her phones must be tapped because as soon as Jake called her, he'd been pinpointed, then traced from one end of California to the other. Or was that just a coincidence? Or one of Gil's inventions? And what about those two agents Eric took out? Suzanne only had Gil's word for that, too. There was a novel called *The Magus* she'd read years ago, by a Britisher named Fowles, and she couldn't remember much more about it than a dizzying sensation of reality twisting away into illusion whenever the main character tried to grab hold of it, but . . . could *this* whole thing be nothing more than an elaborate leg-pull like that, with herself elected chief pullee?

Here was her chance to find out: Jake was certainly real enough, so was Eric when he appeared moments later, shrugging himself into a hooded sweatshirt. Both reminded her of somebody, she couldn't decide who, but probably the same somebody, at different ages . . . not anyone she'd known personally, she decided, someone she'd only seen in photos or on TV . . . maybe it'd come to her later. Neither was very impressive, physically—and Jake, now she'd noticed, really did look like a man with one foot in the grave—but there was something mutually distinctive about them, a special intensity, a sharper focus, a greater solidity somehow, than anything else in their present surroundings seemed to possess.

In fact—or so Suzanne was quickly persuading herself—she'd felt something different in this squalid hole as soon as she'd come in the door this morning, before either one had said a word, before she'd even seen them, just their shoes abandoned in the living room and jackets draped over the backs of two kitchen chairs. She couldn't begin to say what that difference was, any more than she could guess who it was they'd reminded her of momentarily, but she could recognize it as a significant part of what she'd been missing ever since Gil had met her plane at LaGuardia, and she could also feel it already making a difference in *her*, in how she felt about everything—

"When do you want to do that?" Jake was asking.

"Do what?"

"Return those tapes to Edwards."

"Today, if you like. He gets home from work about three."

They climbed the steep staircase to Roosevelt Edwards' room at 3:23; Suzanne knew that because she glanced at her watch to make sure they weren't too early before she knocked. The outside of the door was convincing evidence of the need for the multiple locks Edwards spent at least a minute undoing after he'd called out "Who is it?" and she'd identified herself. The door, and for that matter the rest of the building, looked as if repeatedly assaulted with every tool common to criminals or firemen, and she was sure it had been.

Jake was thinking much the same thing, or so she judged from the expression on his face as he looked around. It was only the two of them, Eric having volunteered to stay in Baltimore in case Simon called or came by; they hadn't reached more than his answering machine since Arizona.

"Hello, Miss Stroehlengutt, please come in," Edwards said, as politely as ever, but she'd noticed how he'd flinched at first moment of awareness that another, unknown figure stood in the dimness behind her, and that quick pulse of insight into what daily life must be like in this house, in this whole section of Washington, made her feel even more awkward with him than usual.

Suzanne held out the tapes and did the minimum by way of introduction while Jake glanced around the small, square room, scarcely big enough to contain the narrow bed, chest of drawers, and dropleaf table piled high with books—and then, at his first solid meeting of eyes with Edwards and to Suzanne's slack-jawed amazement, Jake decided on the instant to trust his impulse and simply tell it all, flat-out: what they hoped to do, and why, what they hoped it would accomplish, what they needed *him* for.

Edwards sat on the edge of his neatly made bed the whole ten or twelve minutes without speaking or moving, or even blinking, until he was certain that Jake was quite finished. Then he coughed behind his fist politely and said, "I had a nephew who got squirted with that Agent Orange stuff over there in Viet-Nam. He was a fine, upstanding young man before then—but he came home meaner'n a weasel and crazier'n a corkscrew, and now he's dead. Went for some peckerwood with an axe handle, right there on Main Street, on a Saturday afternoon. All the witnesses said the man didn't know him, didn't do more than look sideways at him."

"I've heard a lot of stories like that," Jake said. "Too many. That's part of what I was trying to say—part of why somebody's got to do something." And then he waited, hands on knees, on the wired-together kitchen chair that was the only other place to sit, while Suzanne remained standing like some bewigged caryatid against the door frame.

Finally Edwards coughed again and said levelly, "Well, I think you've got a pretty good idea there, Mr. Jacobsen. Whether you can accomplish everything you wish that way, however, is something no one can know until you attempt it. I can take you almost anywhere you want inside the building, but there is something I would like very much in return. Miss Stroehlengutt already knows what it is."

". . . I do?" Suzanne asked, when at last she realized that both men were looking her way.

"I want a record cut of my boy's music. A real record, mind you, none of those cass-it doo-dads. I want at least a thousand copies pressed, and one mailed to every radio station in the country. I hope you don't think me mercenary, Mr. Jacobsen, but every man does have his price, I guess, and this is mine. I wouldn't ask it of you if I hadn't been led to believe that you people can get it done without going to a great deal of trouble. It would fulfill my only remaining personal ambition, and then I wouldn't care, come what may."

"I think we can promise that—Suzanne?"

"Uh, sure!"

"It was *your* word I wanted, Mr. Jacobsen."

"You've got it, Mr. Edwards."

They rose to their feet together, stretched out their arms at the same time, and shook hands.

"You just let me know when you're ready, then," Edwards said as he closed and began to relock the door behind them.

❖

When Jake and Suzanne got back to Baltimore, Simon and Eric were seated across from each other at the kitchen table like a pair of George Segal's statues. Jake didn't need to ask, he could tell from their faces that Eric had told Simon about the FBI men; but even that memory couldn't detract from the euphoria he felt at what had just been accomplished. Draining the cold coffeepot into the cup he'd used earlier and torching up another Lucky, he straddled a chair and described his exchange with Edwards.

They listened to him as impassively at first as Edwards had, but by the time Jake was done, both faces had undergone several transformations, Simon's ending up in a ferocious grin.

"Great! Now I know where I'll be spending most of the next three weeks."

"You're sure you want to get into this?" Jake asked him.

"The way I see it, I never had a lot of choice about that. But even if I did—those crazy bastards've gone too far this time, that's all. They fucked up my vacation, the first real one I would've had in more than fourteen months! The least I can do in return is to see whether or not I can set this up for you."

"Look, Simon, I don't know what Gil's told you, but this isn't about settling scores with anybody—"

"Knowing you, I never thought it was."

"— and whether it succeeds or not, *they*'re certainly not going to view it as anything but a low-down, dirty trick—"

"Look, the way I see it, you won't actually hurt anybody if you do this properly, but in any case you've got an absolute right to use any means necessary to get those scumbags to listen up. Nixon gave us all that right, whether we wanted it or not: dirty tricks're an established part of what they love to call 'the political process,' at least since Watergate. Anyhow, I meant what I said, Jake, I really wanna find out if it's do-able."

"You think it is?"

"I wouldn't go anywhere near that far out on the limb yet. Suppose we put it like this: I think there's a slim but real possibility that there's a way that it could conceivably be done. How much of a possibility, I'll be in a better position to guess if and after this guy gets me into the Architect's office. Why I think so is something I'd rather save for later, too—but are *you* completely sure you want to do it, Jake?"

"If it can be done, yes, I do."

All four of them appeared to listen inwardly for a moment as that statement echoed again within each mind. Then Eric asked, "What made you decide to trust this fella Edwards?"

"*He* did, everything about him. When you meet him you'll see what I mean. But the first thing my eyes fell on was the book he'd been reading when we showed up: John Gribbin's latest on climate change. I guess that's what tipped the scale and made me decide to try. Then— I don't really know what I said, it just came out, without my having to think about how to put it to him."

"Hey, when can *I* talk to this guy?" Simon wanted to know. "I need to find out, and figure out, a bunch of stuff before I can start getting my gear together."

"He said whenever we're ready. Things like what?"

"Well, for starters, I think I'll want to establish a base camp in there somewhere."

"— Base camp?" Suzanne asked from the counter, where she was brewing tea to wash down the plastic bags full of Chinese takeout she'd picked up on their way back and scrubbing away with a rusty Brillo pad at the four least-encrusted plates and forks she'd been able to fish out of the sink. It was almost the first time she'd said anything at all since a little over an hour ago back in DC, when Jake had taken her breath away and set the world racing, and she'd spoken now with nothing in mind beyond her need to latch onto this scheme somehow, to become an essential part of it before it got away from her entirely. She didn't know yet what she might have to offer, but there had to be something.

Simon turned all the way around in his chair to look at her before he said, "That's right. I figure it could take several days' exploration to find what I think I might perhaps be looking for in there. And if it does, I'll need a safe, fairly cozy place where I can catch a couple hours' rest now and then and store my gear and food and water. I'm betting those vent shafts won't be very pleasant places to hang out in."

"— *Catafalque!*" Suzanne yelped, so suddenly she nearly frightened herself into dropping the cardboard container of hot-and-sour soup she'd just opened.

"Come again? Or should I say *Gesundheit?*"

"Washington's tomb—wait, it's in my notes. . . ."

For once in her life, Suzanne missed out entirely on the fried dumplings: the three men finished them off, and most of the spare ribs as well, while she was searching through her attaché case and then reading bits aloud. She didn't care; the look on all their faces when she was through was worth all the fried dumplings in Baltimore.

". . . Sub-basement: small vaulted tomb, wrought-iron gate (kept locked), intended for the body of George Washington. . . ."

"I thought he was buried in Mount Vernon."

"He was. And still is. There were plans, though, to enshrine him at the Capitol, and they went ahead and built in this tomb, but George's family wasn't having any of it. So it stayed empty for forty years, until Lincoln's assassination."

"Lincoln isn't in there, either, is he?"

"No, but he was the first person ever to lie in state up in the Rotunda. On a catafalque—which is just a big empty wooden box draped with black velvet that they set the coffin on top of. And ever since then, they've kept this catafalque in what was supposed to be George's tomb, inside a glass case. There's a plaque on one side of the gate that tells you about the tomb, and on the other side there's a list of all the Great Americans they've used the catafalque for, including Hubert Humphrey, Claude Pepper, and J. Edgar Hoover."

"Where'd you say this thing's located?" Simon asked. "I'll go by and take a look at it tomorrow. Sounds like just the ticket. In more ways than one."

❖

Simon had headed back to Glen Echo, Jake and Eric had gone off to bed, and Suzanne was just getting ready to leave, too, when Gil called. That made her day.

"Oooooh-*ooh*!" he crowed, when she'd finished relating all the news. "What'd I tell ya, kid? Sooner'r later things'd come together, I said, and now I ask you, is this coming together, or is this *coming together*!"

"You're a genius, all right," she said, but like everybody else, Gil never seemed to hear her irony, even when she thought she was shoveling it on. "When're you coming back?"

"Soon's I can get there, which means soon's I'm finished fund raising. But now I'm truly inspired, so you might just see me day after tomorrow. Meanwhile, keep up the terrific work, pal! And don't forget to—"

"*I* won't forget anything, pal," she snapped, and was about to click off before he could begin his eternal quarterbacking when she heard him say, contritely:

"I'm sorry, Suzanne. You really are doing a wonderful job, all around, and I don't mean to badger you—it's just that when things actually start going the way we want 'em to, I always start getting extra nervous. I wish to hell and back we knew what the fuck's going on with the govs! Still all negatives, I take it, on the Miz Sherman front? Has Jake said anything about her?"

"He asked how she was. I said 'fine.' He said 'good.'"

"That's *it*?"

"Practically. The only other thing was, he asked if she's still being watched."

"And you said she *is*, I hope."

"Naturally."

"Naturally. It *would* be natural, wouldn't it? And its *not* being the case is the most *un*natural state of affairs we could have, right? But apparently that's what we've got—and it's making me nuts! You never really do know exactly what the other side is up to in this business, you can't, unless they're so close to your ass you're goners anyhow. So you need to develop an ultra-fine-tuned hunch system—and this is one of the strongest hunches I've ever felt. But all I *know* is, if it was *me*, I'd be watching and listening in on that lady all the fucking time and everyfuckingwhere, including on the potty. They almost grabbed 'im once through her, they haven't got any other rabbit holes to hunker down beside, so where in God's Green Acres *are* they?"

"I don't know, Gil. I've gotta go. It's been a long day."

"Yeah, me too. Sorry again, kid, to chew on your ear like this. Didn't mean to bring you down. G'night."

That catafalque was just what the doctor ordered, plenty big enough for the purpose, Simon enthused the next afternoon when Suzanne, Jake, and Eric picked him up near Union Station. The lock on that wrought-iron gate was laughable, and he was sure there was some way to rig the glass case (which had to have at least one hinged side if they still used that box up in the Rotunda on occasion, as obviously they did) so that you could close it easily and rearrange the velvet drapery from inside. But the best thing about making that the base camp was the two-by-three-foot horizontal vent shaft crossing the vaulted hallway outside the tomb, coming out of one solid brick wall and going into the other but exposed on all four sheet-metal sides for a full ten feet, eighteen inches below midpoint in the arched ceiling and a mere eight feet away from the gate. What's more, there was nothing electronic anywhere: there'd been no one else in sight for ten minutes, and he'd swept the entire area thoroughly. . . .

"Sounds terrific," Suzanne told him, although she hadn't even tried to follow most of Simon's rambling analysis, "but let's decide what we're gonna do right now. We can't just go trooping in on Roosevelt. Not only would all these white faces attract too much attention in that building, but we could only fit into that closet he lives in two at a time."

"I'll go up alone and ask him if he'll come out and meet us some-place," Jake said. "I'll leave it up to him where."

But Edwards couldn't think of anyplace where either they or he wouldn't be too conspicuous for his comfort, so in the end they simply drove to one of the visitors' parking lots at the Smithsonian and did their talking in the Plymouth. Simon had calmed down by that time and had his questions pretty much in order, and Edwards was all business, so it didn't take long. By the time the windows had steamed up to the point where Suzanne decided to restart the motor and turn on the defroster, they'd covered everything necessary for the time being.

The sub-basement was where he was regularly assigned, Edwards said, so access to the catafalque would be a simple matter. Getting Simon upstairs to the Office of the Architect could be more difficult, though, especially with the beard.

"The beard?"

"Lots of the white fellows I work with have mustaches and sideburns, and hair even longer than yours, but you don't see any full sets of whiskers. If you'd consider shaving, Mr. Blake, and wear a set of gray or tan chinos, I could probably pass you off as a new man I'm breaking in, if we should run into anybody on our way up there. They do have me do that sometimes because I've been there so long, and I can get you a temporary identification badge, where you can write in any name. It's not likely anybody would stop us no matter what you looked like, but I do believe we should try to minimize risks wherever possible."

"I'm in total agreement there. So all right, the beard goes. It's time to start over anyhow, this one's beyond trimming."

He'd been scheduled to work days, from 6:00 a.m. to 2:30 p.m., for two more weeks, Edwards said, but there was seldom any problem finding someone on the graveyard shift who'd be happy to switch with him. "How soon would you care to do this, Mr. Blake?"

"The sooner the better, Mr. Edwards."

"Perhaps you and I could meet when I get off work tomorrow afternoon, then? I'll show you which outside door we'll use, and tell you what I've been able to arrange about my schedule."

"What about getting onto the grounds and up to that door, though? Isn't there a patrol?"

"Just a watchman who goes around once an hour. You'll be walking up the same way as everybody who works there does, and if you should bump into him, you'll just show him your temporary pass and say you were told to report to me. But chances are you won't, or if you do, he'll just nod and keep going."

"Aren't they worried about terrorists?"

"Well, they are, and they aren't. I mean, the higher-ups who get paid to worry about things like that are, I suppose, but they mostly depend on their gadgetry, not on the watchmen. Anyone who sneaked up at night and tried opening a door from outside would set off alarms and turn on floodlights all over, and guards would go running out and probably catch them. But for most of us it's just a job like any other, and when we see somebody who looks and acts like one of us, we don't tend to think about the possibility of him being anything else. Especially when he's with someone familiar, like me. Everybody in maintenance and security knows who *I* am. Or maybe I should say, they believe they do."

"You've done some thinking before now about doing something like this, haven't you, Mr. Edwards?" Jake asked.

"Oh, yes." Roosevelt Edwards' face abruptly crumpled into that same wide, warm, grandfatherly smile Suzanne had seen him bestow upon Nora and Ruthellen at Thanksgiving. "Many times. Not with any particular plan or reason in mind, you understand. But with as undemanding a job as mine is, and all the years I've been there, I've had lots of time to think, long and hard, about all sorts of things."

Edwards smuggled Simon into the Office of the Architect just before midnight on the night of December ninth / tenth. They encountered no one, either going in or coming out again, and Simon was able to spend a completely undisturbed three and a half hours rummaging through everything from database files to battered old wooden drawers crammed full of tightly rolled-up, very faded blueprints, copying whatever might be of use with a special camera he'd bought for caving but had only gotten around to using once before, to photograph sleeping bats in several limestone caverns in the Blue Ridge. None of those shots had turned out very well, but as Simon almost always did whenever something failed to meet his expectations, he'd taken the trouble later to learn exactly what he'd been doing wrong.

He arrived at the Baltimore apartment at 4:40 a.m., beyond exhaustion but exultant, to find that Gil was back and the only one awake, sprawled on the couch in the living room in an emerald and royal blue après-ski outfit and a droopy black mustache, thumbing through his ragged copy of *Gödel, Escher, Bach* and twirling a brandy snifter.

"'Mornin', Elvis." When Simon looked blank, Gil set down his glass and pointed. "The 'burns and the DA, pardner."

"You should talk. For the first couple seconds there, I thought you were Meier Baba Returned to Earth."

Gil stroked his upper lip uncertainly. "That bad, huh? Off it comes then, before Suzanne shows up and kills herself laughing. Meanwhile, why don't you get yourself a glass and try some of this cognac? It's Czech, but it's remarkably good."

"You know me and alcohol," Simon told him. "One slug of that stuff and I'd think I'd died and gone to Disneyland. But, hey—didn't anyone tell you where I've just been?"

"Yep."

"Aren't you gonna ask me how it went?"

"Figured I wouldn't have to ask," Gil said, standing up and heading for the bathroom, as Simon trailed after him with rising indignation.

"That's a hell of a thankyou."

"Excuse me all to pieces, and please, do, tell me all about it," Gil said, studying his visage in the mirror over the rust-streaked sink, then patiently tracking down a pair of scissors on the crowded, dusty shelf above the mirror and beginning to snip away at the mustache.

"I'm not sure I should bother, the way you're acting," Simon grumbled from the doorway, "but as a matter of fact, it could not've gone much better. For one thing, perfect timing: turns out they're still struggling up out of the eighteen-hundreds in there. They've had 'em for twenty years to judge by the models, but they've just finished feeding a lot of basic stuff into computers. Which means they've finally had to do a bunch of organizing, without which it would've taken me weeks to find everything I was hoping for. As it turns out, I've already got what there is—and I wanna look a lot longer and closer at all of it, but I saw enough while I was still in there to be able to say it seems like plenty, and—pounding hard on wood, of course—this little operation could just possibly be do-able!"

"Stop! You're breaking my heart!"

"Huh?"

"It's *off*, my friend." Gil had the glossy black hair under his nose trimmed down to nearly Hitlerian dimensions now, as their eyes locked comically in the splattered mirror.

"*What's* off?"

"The whole show, that's what. It ain't gonna happen."

"*Why?*"

"Because Jake says now he won't do it, that's why. I know you haven't had much chance to boob the tube in the past few hours, but it looks like it's Yellow Ribbon time again. A whole chopperful of US military 'observers' got SAM'd late yesterday afternoon somewhere in the northern Andes. There's a White House press conference scheduled for ten o'clock this morning, and the smart money's saying that plastic dildo who boards there these days is committed to out-johnwayning both George and Ron, and he plans to announce that he's formally committing US troops to save South America from the South Americans. Which means that ninety-nine out of every hundred of our benighted fellow citizens'll leap to the assumption that we're acting on behalf of either the heirs of Pablo Escobar or the *Sendero Luminoso*—or who knows, maybe both—if we carry out our little project. Anyhow, that's what Jake's decided. Maybe you can talk him out of it. *I couldn't.*"

1 9 :   T W E L V E   B E L L S

Simon went home to Glen Echo, broiled himself an organically raised sirloin out of the freezer, tossed a salad he'd run up three flights of stairs and picked from the tiny greenhouse he'd rigged up beneath a skylight in the attic, washed both down with the juice of eight carrots he'd grown last summer out in the back yard, took a solar-heated shower, and went to bed—but he found he couldn't even begin to think about sleep, so he was back at the Baltimore apartment in time to watch the presidential press conference with everyone else, on a huge, like-new color console Gil said he'd bought for eighty bucks out of the back of a rusted-out stationwagon down by the waterfront.

Two minutes behind Simon, Suzanne appeared as well. A clean-shaven Gil waved her over to the couch, made a generous amount of room for her there, and pressed two familiarly shaped bits of metal into the palm of her hand. "What's this?" she asked, peeking at a pair of keys.

"The MG," Gil stage-whispered. "For recruiting Roosevelt Edwards. Remember?"

"But I didn't make that happen, it was all Jake's doing."

"Save your modesty for the Oscars—shhh, looks like they're finally about to get their show on the road." But it turned out to be only some deputy press secretary sidling up to the podium, mouthing something about "matters still under deliberation" and refusing to take any questions. Then the networks returned to their regular programming, with solemn promises to interrupt instantly with any further developments, while CNN filled in with reruns of last night's items on the downed helicopter and lengthy snips from recent overviews of the Andean Crisis, as they were all calling it by this time.

"Hmm. Looks like there could be a glitch somewhere, huh? A Spaniard in the Works, maybe? Turn the sound down, would you, somebody? Who else is hungry?"

Only Suzanne expressed interest, so she and Gil set out on a brunch expedition, while Simon and Eric began a chess game on the living room rug, and Jake sat staring at the muted screen.

". . . Care to tell us what you're thinking?" Simon asked, tapping the nearer of Eric's extended fists, winning white, and quickly setting up his pieces, opening with his queen's pawn. Eric mirrored the move with the black.

"I wouldn't dignify what I was doing with that verb," Jake finally answered, with a self-disgusted toss of his head. "'Feeling sorry for myself' would pretty much cover it, I guess. I must've been beginning to believe that I might actually do something meaningful for once in my life."

"Jake—your life's already had a helluva lot more meaning in it than most. If nothing else, there's dozens if not hundreds of your former students—like myself—who see the world and everything in it—especially themselves—more clearly because *you* opened their eyes to how it really is, in ways no other teacher ever did, or could. I *mean* that, Jake, goddamnit! And don't forget, we still don't know what's going on down there. Also, even if those coprocephalics do drag us into another jolly little massacre, it could be argued—I will, if you'll let me—that what you had in mind would only be that much more appropriate."

"No. We can't, or anyhow I *won't*, take a chance of it being misunderstood—it would've been hard enough, anyhow, to make it clear beyond all question that this wasn't some sort of crazed act of revenge, or anything like that."

"How'd you figure to do that? To make it clear, I mean?"

"I don't know—I hadn't gotten that far. I wasn't going to let myself start thinking as if it was really going to happen until you found out whether anything *could* happen . . . did you?"

"Well, let's put it this way: I haven't found out anything yet that says it can't, and I've come up with quite a bunch of stuff to support my theory of how it might be workable . . . can I tell you a little bit about it?"

"Why not?" Jake grunted, punching out a cigarette, hauling himself to his feet, hobbling out to the kitchen on legs gone numb from inactivity, and pouring out another cup of coffee, adding a splash of Gil's brandy to it this time. "We don't have anything better to talk about."

"Okay, to be—shit, I didn't see that coming!" Simon said, taking one of Eric's pawns, losing a knight in return. ". . . To begin with, did you ever consider how difficult it would be to defend any old building that big and that complicated against turn-of-the-twenty-first-century technology, even if you've got an unlimited amount of such hardware at your own disposal? Those places—and I mean just about everything over a hundred years old—were built by people who saw the world very differently, and there's no way anyone today is going to be able to consider, and forestall, each and every one of the various possible ways huge, labyrinthine structures like that one could be vulnerable to penetration by state-of-the-art methods—which, of course, are constantly being improved upon by guys like me, anyhow, so there's never any guarantee that the system you install today will still be impenetrable tomorrow. Ideally, what you'd do is level the structure and rebuild it completely—but even that doesn't always work, as for instance that brand-new embassy they put up in Moscow back in the Eighties, which wound up with at least twice as many bugs in it as the one it replaced.

"So anyhow, what I figure they've done in the Capitol Building— what they've pretty much gotta do whenever they can't start over from scratch—is to designate specific surveillance perimeters around whatever they consider key regions, the two main ones obviously being the House and Senate chambers. And they've thrown an elaborate electronic cordon around each of these regions, creating distinct but largely invisible islands of tight security within the overall unsecurability. In the case we're concerned with, this would most probably encompass the entire south wing. Now, what you'd want to figure out how to do is to come up from below *inside* that cordon somehow."

"And how d'you plan to do that?"

"Well, that's where the hard work comes in—hey, wait a diddly minute here, what's going on?"

"I think that's mate," Eric said without expression, rocking back on his heels and folding his arms across his chest.

"Now how in hell did *that* happen?"

"He must've come up inside your cordon," Jake said. "Eric's pretty good at that."

❖

"Let's take the MG," Gil said. "*Your* MG, kid, here's the papers on it. Why don't you drive, and I'll point out its salient peculiarities. First off, how's about we put the top down. . . ."

Suzanne couldn't understand how he could be so goddamned cool about it. Here everything had been finally coming together so beautifully, and now this! Her disappointment was all the more crushing for her having lost all faith in this endeavor, only to regain it so swiftly five days ago, with Jake's and Eric's arrival. But learning (surprisingly quickly) how to maneuver that gorgeous old antique with some verve and grace did lift her spirits considerably. So did the odors emanating from the big white paper sack full of straight-from-the-oven onion, garlic, plain, and sesame bagels; the tub of fresh farmer's cheese with chives; and the huge slab of nova when Gil came out of the mall on Loch Raven Boulevard. And so, most of all, did this wonderfully summery weather.

But: "Courtesy the Greenhouse Effect," Gil had to go and croak, reading her thoughts even more easily than usual, as he settled back into the velvety, tobacco-colored leather. And that sardonic crack brought all her gloom crashing down upon her again. Twelve hours ago, there had seemed to be some real chance that the five of them— no, she kept forgetting him, but counting Edwards it was *six*—might have something vital to do with reversing that effect and saving whatever was left of the ozone layer, among other achievements. . . .

"Look, pal, don't give up so easily. This is *not* the end of our little story, whatever those jerks think they might be up to in the Andes."

"But you said yourself, without Jake—"

"We aren't without him yet, though. Maybe there're ways to finesse him past his scruples. And if not, maybe Simon can be goaded into doing it on his own, just to see if it can actually be done. But one way or another, we're going forward here because . . . well, I was going to have to tell you sooner or later: there're more irons in this fire than Jake and Simon are—or should be—aware of."

"Oh, yeah?"

"C'mon Suzanne, don't look so disapproving. You know as well as I do how these things ought to work, with everything kept on a strict need-to-know basis, because we're *all* safer that way. Fact of the matter is, there'll be something else going on in New York that needs to be coordinated with this State of the Union action, and for a lot of reasons, it can't be gotten underway until our enterprise here is up and running."

"What's the target up there, the UN? And is that why you had me and the orangutan in the monkey suit who came into the bar that day take a look at each other?"

"Hey, what'd I just get done saying about need-to-know? As my trusted lieutenant you're gonna hafta learn it all before it's over, but hold your horses for now, kid, and we'll just take it as it—hey, I damn near forgot, let's find out if anything's been percolating downtown," Gil said, switching on the radio.

❖

It would be another six hours before the unprecedented role played by almost the entire Latin American membership in the Organization of American States became public knowledge, but when Gil and Suzanne came back in the door, they were greeted by Simon's shout:

"Guess what, folks! Ecuador, Peru, Colombia, and Venezuela all threw us the finger! They said fuck *off,* Uncle Sam! How 'bout that? If I knew any of their national anthems, I might even sing a verse or two!"

"Smile when you call *them* 'us,' okay?" Gil deadpanned.

"That's all you've got to say?"

"Nope, but we caught some reports already, en route. A most intriguing development, all-righty-right. What d'*you* think, Jake? Are we back in business?"

"If Simon's willing to go ahead with his part—"

"And I am!"

"— I don't know why we couldn't take it that far, anyhow. You said it might take several days to see what can be done, right, Simon? By then we should know if these countries are going to be able to make their 'thanks but no thanks' stick."

"How soon can you get going in there?" Gil asked Simon.

"That mainly depends on how fast you guys can locate everything on this little shopping list I'm gonna give you in a minute," Simon told him, already scribbling furiously.

Simon was smuggled into the Capitol Building for the second time on the night of December thirteenth, planning to use the catafalque as a base for his exploration of the vent system, and warning that he might stay in for as long as four or five days. The OAS was still in around-the-clock session, but the Pentagon had already alleged that preliminary investigations assigned "highest probability" to the theory that "metal fatigue leading to rotor failure" was what actually caused the helicopter to crash, not a hand-held surface-to-air missile.

The night before, with Edwards, Simon had smuggled in two hand-truck loads' worth of lightweight ropes, climbing harness, and cavers' route markers, plus a hundred special little pitons he'd improvised in his Glen Echo shop, with self-tapping sheet-metal screws in place of the regular spike-ends for hammering into rock or ice. There was also an impressive amount of very compact electronic detection equipment, as well as an air mattress, space blankets, nylon coveralls, knee pads, a miner's lamp, goggles, the very best dust mask money could buy, bottled water, survival rations, and a folding portable toilet that used Ziploc baggies, all packed deep inside five big cardboard cartons labeled either 'Paper Towels' or 'Hand Soap.'

The next morning saw the Peruvian situation slide from the front page of both the *Washington Post* and the *New York Times* to make room for the House debate on the insurance crisis, as White House spokespersons downplayed what they termed "temporarily faulty communications" among OAS members, and news programs quit reporting on independent inquiries into either the story behind the downed helicopter or the question of who might be supplying Andean guerrillas with US-made Stinger missiles.

Three mornings later, after he'd alerted the Baltimore contingent with a 5:15 a.m. call from Union Station and they'd all gathered for a breakfast conference at ten o'clock, Simon was red-eyed and hollow-cheeked but practically dancing as he pinned up floorplans and elevations on the kitchen cabinet doors.

"Guess you must've gotten lucky, huh?" Gil asked.

"I wouldn't call it luck, exactly. I'm sure there's only been electricians and plumbers in those vents before now, just doing whatever they were told to and getting the hell out as soon as they could. No one ever thought of sending in a spelunker to see what he could find . . . is everybody ready?

"Okay then. The first thing I realized, after studying their blueprints, is that there are these huge vertical shafts in all the main interior walls—you see, there, there, and there?" Simon said, pointing with a wooden spoon. "Obviously they were built right in from the original plans, no doubt with some clever late-eighteenth-century mechanism in mind to force all that cool lower air upward somehow. But either whatever they were counting on to do that didn't work or the project got tabled somewhere along the line and eventually forgotten.

"Anyhow, it seemed reasonable that these mother-shafts would be laid out symmetrically—but if so, then two were missing right here and here in this southernmost row, which runs up through the wall between the Speaker's Lobby and the House Chamber itself. But there wasn't any easy way to get near where I figured they'd be, if they ever actually existed, on any level except the sub-basement, because all the ducts feeding off 'em were done away with on every other floor.

"So the first one I reached—that one—was bricked in solid down there, but I figured I'd check out the other one anyhow, even though it was a bitch and a half getting there—and whaddaya know, it's still there, wide open behind a little lath and plaster. That was a real experience, cutting into that space. I don't think anybody's realized it's there since it was sealed up, probably not long after the Civil War. It still feels like the eighteen-sixties in there."

"And what, pray tell," Gil wanted to know, "do the eighteen-sixties feel like?"

"I can't describe it any better than that, but you know what I mean—it feels the way a Matthew Brady photo looks, okay? So anyhow, get this, now: that long-lost shaft goes straight up to gallery level, 'way inside their surveillance perimeters, giving us direct access not only to the vents right over the Speaker's platform, but to all the main sound system cables on that side as well. I could cut in from that point right there, I'm pretty sure, and splice in a switch that could kill the mikes at the podium and replace 'em with a recorded message. Which should solve that problem you mentioned last week, Jake, of how to make it clear just what you're doing, and why."

"That all sounds very good," Jake said, "but am *I* capable of negotiating those shafts the way you did?"

"I think so. You're not especially claustrophobic, are you?"

"Not especially, no. But I'm not very happy in dark, tight places, either."

"Nobody is, not even the craziest of cavers. But we're not talking *very* tight here—the smallest it gets is nearly two feet square. Dark I can't deny, or dusty. But not noticeably buggy, and any rats there will probably get the hell out of your way. Also, you've only gotta do a total distance of maybe a hundred yards horizontally and seventy feet vertically. Of course, there's a bunch of zigging and zagging and some ups and downs to get from the catafalque to the foot of the shaft, and then you've got that whole vertical distance to do at once. But the route to it'll be clearly marked, and I'll put in a real rope ladder instead of the single line I went up, with two or three slings where you can rest on the way up . . . and I'll tell you what: I'll go in with you once beforehand, too, and lead you all the way through it."

Gil wagged his index finger. "Could we back up a little? Tell the rest of us about this recorded message, okay?"

"The mike goes dead somewhere in the middle of the prez's address, that's all, and they'll get Jake's voice instead, telling 'em exactly what he's just done, and why."

"I see some problems with that," Jake said. "There'll be a great deal of confusion. We need some way to get their complete attention, if I'm going to have time to say anything that might have any chance of getting through."

"— How about *twelve bells*?" Suzanne asked, her first words since Simon had begun his report. To everyone's blank looks, she went on to explain: "There's an elaborate bell code throughout the building. Even if you didn't notice the little cards stuck up everywhere explaining what they mean, if you've been in there at all during the daytime, you've certainly heard 'em, they're going most of the time. Two bells— two rings—tells you a vote's about to be taken on the House floor, and so forth, on up to twelve bells, which is actually listed as 'Nuclear Attack.' I don't know if anybody'd be calm enough at that point to be counting, but it *would* get everyone's attention, and *then* Jake could come on."

"That's perfect," Simon said.

"Not bad," Gil admitted, "but I was thinking maybe we could get Roosevelt to come strolling down the aisle at that moment with a banjo, singing, 'You All Caught De Plague Today, Doo-Da, Doo-Da!'" He looked around the table, at their uniformly disgusted stares. "That was supposed to be 'Camptown Races,'" he said, "in case you didn't recognize the tune."

"I'm afraid we did," Simon told him.

From then until New Year's Eve, most of what Jake found he could remember afterward was long nights at the kitchen table, shuffling through towering stacks of photocopies supplied by the indefatigable Gaithersburg librarian, drinking too much coffee, smoking too many Luckies, and bearing passive witness to Simon's towering indignation as he uncovered each fresh layer of official sloppiness and stupidity: "Those flaming ASSholes!" he'd roar, slapping the tabletop, kicking the wastebasket.

And endless dreary hours of compiling data on the fates of several thousand beagles exposed to plutonium during the Fifties by government researchers in Utah, or on the incidence of various cancers among victims of countless "nuclear mishaps," in order to establish just how much Pu 239 it would take within an enclosed space the size of the House Chamber to effect, not what the Nuclear Regulatory Commission considered a "safe exposure," but one that would be literally safe, and still detectable:

"A real but essentially homeopathic dose, you might say," Simon muttered. Then, after mulling it over for several days, he pared that amount down by two-thirds, just in case the distribution wouldn't actually be as even as he'd calculated: "We're gonna call it a twentieth of a gram," he'd finally decided.

"That's all?"

"Look, Jake, *any* of this shit is too goddamned much."

"Yeah. Tell me about it."

"Hey, I'm sorry—I just meant—anyhow, the next step's to establish proper glove box specifications."

"Glove box?"

"It's exactly what it sounds like," Simon said. "There are these protective gloves built right into this lead-lined box. You put your hands in 'em to work with your hot stuff inside, and you watch whatever you're doing to it through the window on top. I've actually got one already, a real relic I picked up at some agency auction when I first moved here—at least, I think it's still somewhere out in the garage. I was selling a few radium-powered gizmos for a while and thought I could cut costs, but it turned out I could buy that component ready-made for less money, not to mention monkey business and worry. Anyhow—as Gil would surely say if he were here—going out and buying ourselves a new glove box right now might not be too clever, it's an item they probably keep pretty close track of. So I should see if I do still have that one, and whether it can be beefed up enough."

He checked next day, and yes, it was out there, knocked flat and recartoned. "Might do the trick, too, if we can only figure out how to make sure it's sufficiently well shielded."

"Sufficient for what?"

"For the future health and welfare of whoever uses it."

"But if whoever that was didn't have any future, it wouldn't matter, right?"

"I guess not, if you could put the whole show inside somewhere that's heavily built and thoroughly insulated—like maybe a walk-in freezer. You'd contaminate that area to some extent, but there shouldn't be so much leakage from the box that it would cause anyone immediate impairment, and you could seal up the place afterward and label it plainly so nobody'd wander in there accidentally. It'd just be another hot spot, that's all—the world's full of 'em already, thanks to those assholes."

"Is this work I could learn to do?"

"A chimpanzee could learn it—all you've gotta do is to pulverize this stuff and load it into aerosol canisters. Well, I guess it may be a little more complicated because everything'll have to be done in an inert medium, since P-U-two-three-nine is 'pyrophoric when finely divided,' according to some texts."

"Meaning?"

"It might spontaneously combust when exposed to air, which in turn might be enough to set off whatever hasn't been ground up yet. Not a risk to be taken."

"And what'll we use for a medium?"

"That I couldn't say yet—we'll have to wait and see what form it's in, when Gil hands it over."

Gil had vanished again the day after Simon's vent shaft report, before Suzanne found the right moment to tell him what Edwards wanted in exchange for his help. She'd meant to do that as soon as they were face-to-face, but the Andean episode had bulldozed it straight out of her mind, and then events had moved too swiftly for her to remember anything. So she made a point of telling him the first time Gil called when she was at the apartment and able to take it unlistened-in-on, with the phone plugged into the bedroom jack—and he'd yelped:

"A *thousand* copies? No way! A hundred maybe, and a master, I think I can get that much done for around a grand by one of those vanity outfits."

"Why've you gotta be such a cheapskate?" Suzanne demanded. "How much more would it cost to give him what he asked for?"

"Including mailing it out to radio stations? Five Gs at least, I'll bet."

"That's such a big deal? Where would we be without Edwards?"

"My resources may be nefarious but they are not unlimited!" Gil protested. "But all right, what the fuck, I guess I should consider myself lucky he's not up-to-date enough to demand compact discs. Fed-X me those tapes; I think I can attend to that tomorrow or next day. It looks like I've gotta wait around here awhile longer for everybody's new ID, anyhow—am I correct in assuming Edwards has never applied for a passport? And by the way, I forgot to ask him, but Jake doesn't want anything along these lines, does he?"

"No, nothing for himself, just for Eric and the rest of us to be in the clear before it happens. His own disappearance afterward would negate everything he wants the action to mean, he told me. And I did ask Edwards, but he wouldn't even discuss it. 'The only essential change from my life now that prison would bring about,' he said, 'is that I will no longer be required to support this corrupt government by paying taxes to it.'"

"Christ, ain't principles wonderful? Well, great, that's a couple grand saved, right there. By the way: nobody's mentioned *me* to this guy, have they?"

"Not that I'm aware of. *I* certainly haven't."

"And he's never heard any name for you but Stroehlengutt?"

"Nobody has," Suzanne realized, as she said it.

"Good, keep it that way."

"Except, of course, for Nora."

"Ah, yes. And still no change on that front, right?"

"Not as far as I can tell."

"I hate to say this, I mean I'm superstitious as hell about believing it, let alone acting on it—and I sure as shit don't want *you* doing either—but it begins to look as if we might've gotten very, very lucky, and Our Miz Sherman's somehow fallen through the cracks. And who knows, maybe Jake did, too."

"How d'you figure that could've happened?"

"Well, to begin with, he was only one name in probably fifty or more that might just possibly lead 'em to *me*. When he wasn't tracked down and crossed off, he got more interesting, but hardly top priority. Maybe those two dudes who went looking for him had a whole laundry list to attend to that day around Shasta. And maybe those West Coast wiseguys vanished those stiffs but good, and the govs haven't even figured out yet who their boys got to on that list and who they didn't.

Maybe they've even leaped to the conclusion that it wasn't Jake who did 'em in, it was somebody else they haven't caught up with yet, either—and they're busy barking up another tree in a whole different part of the woods. It's been my distinct impression over the years that they do a bunch of that."

"That was a very tall stack of maybe's, though."

"I know, but here's something we keep forgetting: they've gotta function within a bloated bureaucracy forever threatened by budget cuts, hassled by civil libertarians, and strangled with red tape, and who knows what else they're up against. The guys in the field probably get the same sort of hunches as I do, but unless they can produce overwhelming arguments to back 'em up, they're liable to get ordered to do something totally different and completely irrelevant."

"Gil? What've you been smoking?"

"Nothing! Swear-to-god! Listen, pal, it can certainly be fatal to *under*estimate those dudes, but *over*estimating 'em can do you in, too. You cover your ass as best you can, that's all—you can't let yourself get so careful you're not gonna get anything accomplished *but* watching your ass."

"Uh-huh. Hey, it's late. I've gotta get back to Glen Echo."

"Okay—but wait, before you go, I keep meaning to ask: just when the hell *is* this State of the Onion, anyway?"

"Tuesday, January twenty-third," Suzanne said, shocked in spite of herself and how well she thought she knew him already, to learn that Gil hadn't bothered to find that out by this time.

"Four and a half more weeks, then. How're we coming along, has Simon said?"

"Just that they'll be needing that walk-in freezer setup by the first of the year."

"Wonderful. And where are you with that?"

"I'm plowing through two states' worth of yellow pages and calling a bunch of commercial real estate offices to see what's available, and I'm waiting for you to come up with the cover story and documentation you promised, that's where I am."

"What kind of money are they talking?"

"At least three or four times as much as *you* were. Plus two months' security. And all of it in certified checks."

"Ouch! You tried Delaware, the Eastern Shore? Lotta chicken ranchers over that way, I hear they're hard hit these days."

"You said to keep it within two hours of Washington."

"Yeah, but that was before I was fully apprised of the economic realities. Even if I *can* come up with it, it *hurts*, forking over that kind of real money for something we'll only be needing for a couple weeks."

"Okay, I'll see what I can find over there. G'night!"

❖

When he came back to Baltimore, Gil was still mostly absent, and whenever he did turn up at the apartment, he held himself to meekly phrased questions: "Look, while we're at it, wouldn't it be just as easy to knock out a few dozen more of these aerosols? And what about that brainstorm of yours the other night, Simon, how you could create a narrow-target weapon by encapsulating a smidgen of plutonium oxide in . . . what was it, I forget?"

"Cellulose nitrate. What movie film used to be made of."

"Oh, right—and this could be concealed in something as small as a cigarette or a ballpoint pen, you said, and left on somebody's desk, and ignited electronically later from a safe distance? What exactly's involved in turning out something like that? They ain't gonna capitulate, you know, unless they're convinced we can hit 'em again, even harder next time."

"No," Jake and Simon said at once.

"No what?"

"No to everything you just suggested."

"But why the hell not?"

"Because we're doing this *our* way, and strictly as a one-shot deal," Jake told him, and Simon quickly added:

"Because, while what you said is true enough—yeah, sure, it wouldn't hurt to let 'em think there's a lot more where that came from—the notion of any more of these toys in anybody's hands but our own is just as scary as the current state of military and industrial nuclear capabilities, that's why. And by the way, Gil: when do I get to see just what the hell it is you've got? And where is it, anyhow?"

"It's safe, and it's handy, that's where. You tell me when you're ready for it, you've got it in two hours."

"Well, there are steps we can't take, or plan for, until we know what form it's in."

"You want me to lug it in here tonight and dump it on the kitchen table? Is that what you want?"

"You could tell me what it's *in.* That might give me a hint."

"A stainless-steel can," Gil cupped his hands, a foot or so apart, "about yea big around, and oh, maybe thirty inches long."

"What sort of seals and markings?"

"I dunno, I never looked that close."

"How d'you know there's anything inside?"

"That'd be a scream, wouldn't it? All we find's a wadded-up fortune-cookie paper on the bottom, huh, and when we smooth it out, it says: 'Perseverance doesn't *always* further.'"

"And if there is what you think there is in it," Simon asked, "how d'you know it's not leaking?"

"If you're trying to make me nervous, pal, you're doing just great. If it *is* leaking, I'm wearing radioactive BVDs right now."

"Want me to bring a Geiger counter with me tomorrow?"

"I won't be here tomorrow," Gil said, "but I'm not sure I'd wanna know—it's sort of like testing HIV positive, ain't it?"

"There wouldn't be one whole helluva lot you could do about it at this point, no."

"Time enough when we get that far, then. Any idea yet, when that might be?"

"You'll have to ask Suzanne that—I've told her what we need, and she's looking."

"So what're you guys up to, meantime?"

"Why, does our apparent idleness distress you? Should we try to look busy whenever you put in an appearance?"

"Come on," Gil said, "you know I didn't mean it like that. I just wanna know where we stand, that's all, and what else you might be needing from me, besides money." He hadn't meant those last two words to come out sounding the way they did, and quickly added: "Speaking of which, you don't need any yet, do you, Jake?"

"No, I've still got most of the thousand Howie gave me." And nothing to spend it on, besides cigarettes and pizza orders. Jake and Eric hadn't left that basement once since the meetings with Edwards. There was no need for Gil to point it out (but he did, repeatedly): all unnecessary risks had better be avoided. The weather had turned back to slush and freezing drizzle, anyhow.

"And how's your health?"

That had been Gil's first question for Jake, and he asked it again every time he saw him. "There's a safe doctor near here if you need one," Gil said. But Jake had had enough doctors.

"Holding steady."

"When're you getting your tour of the vents?"

"Don't know that yet."

"Uh, as a matter of fact, we do—New Year's Eve," Simon said. "Is that okay?" he asked Jake. "I talked it over yesterday with Roosevelt, and we both think it makes most sense. He said either then or Christmas is when the maintenance and security staff on duty's the lowest in both numbers and seniority, and New Year's is best because most of 'em just hole up somewhere that night and get blotto together. I figure we want everything going for us we can get. You and I won't both fit in that box, so we'll have to suit up in a mop closet, go straight into the shaft, and when we come back out of it, go straight out the door again. I was gonna tell you all this last night, but—"

— But the longer you put off telling me, the less time I'd have to get worked up about it, Jake thought. "That's all right. New Year's Eve is fine with me."

20: SALISBURY

Christmas came, and Christmas went, unnoticed by the Baltimore contingent except for Simon's absence (he always spent the day with his parents in Florida) and the scarcely whittled-on goose and cardboard container of cranberry sauce that Suzanne squeezed into the refrigerator at some point during the evening. Nora's was too full of other leftovers, she explained. It made a change, anyhow, from pizza, fish and chips, or Chinese takeout.

Jake had discovered that he didn't want to hear any more requiems, and he left his Walkman and the tapes Howie had gotten for him stowed away in his dufflebag. What he missed was his Mahler collection, but while he knew Suzanne would be happy to get him anything he asked for, something at the back of his mind kept him from making that request—a vague sort of superstition that he preferred to leave unexamined, but he knew it was due to the fact that he'd been listening to Mahler's third when those FBI men appeared out of nowhere up at Mt. Shasta. . . .

There was a state-of-the-art sound system in the apartment, though, and a hundred-odd recordings, mostly CDs and mostly good jazz. Of the couple dozen albums that were classical, two-thirds were Bach or Mozart, which would only remind him of Nora, and knowing he was scarcely an hour away from Glen Echo was already hard enough to handle. There was, however, an old subscription club bonus set, not even unshrinkwrapped, of Toscanini doing all nine Beethoven symphonies; not Jake's first choice for that task, but he found they wore well, especially the third and the seventh. Soon, though, he'd turned to Lady Day, Armstrong, Coltrane, and Parker, staying longest with Bird, finding the most there to help him through the hours when Simon wasn't around.

Eric was ever-attentive to Jake's state of health and had taken what housework there was to be done upon himself, not only washing dishes whenever the sink filled up but even learning to use the vacuum cleaner, washer, and dryer. Eric wasn't much by way of company, though, spending most of his other waking hours buried in one after another of what appeared to be a complete set of Travis McGees he'd discovered on a shelf in the hallway closet.

Jake found it hard to sleep these nights, and harder still to think in any concentrated way about what he was going to be doing in a month's time. He knew he should be working on the last and shortest and most important public statement of his life, but he couldn't bring himself to think about that, either. Finally he decided to make it happen, to stay at that kitchen table after Simon went home until he got a draft at least started, somehow—but instead he'd quickly gotten very drunk, then violently sick, swilling down at least half of a scarcely broached quart of Jameson's Gil had left standing on top of the refrigerator.

The following day, while Eric watched but said nothing, Jake lurched through the apartment, gathering up all the other bottles that Gil was in the habit of leaving around like knicknacks and lining them all up on the bureau in Gil's bedroom, where he never had occasion to go, so he wouldn't be tempted to repeat that mistake. Giving in to another sudden impulse like that one could easily prove fatal. But there wasn't going to be another—the next day was New Year's Eve.

❖

Simon and Jake, both in gray chinos under the dark-blue ponchos they shed and stuffed away as soon as they were inside, met Edwards at a small black windowless door beneath broad stone stairs at the rear of the Capitol Building at 10:15 p.m. He shook hands wordlessly as he let them in, then led them at almost a lope along what Jake experienced as endless, empty, and totally aimless hallways, with once-rough brick walls slicked over by countless coats of thick white paint, and waxed slate floors where the rubber wheels on the handtruck loaded with their gear in a toiletpaper carton went on thumping, steadily off-beat to their footfalls, in the cracks between the unevenly worn slabs. Everything else was hushed and tomblike in the dim, fuzzy yellow light cast by big oldfashioned bulbs inside wire cages, sparsely dotting the middle of each corridor ceiling alongside an antique sprinkler system. Nothing, except for the distance they were required to travel, seemed real; otherwise it felt like being on the set for a movie by Lang, or Welles, or Demme. . . .

Then suddenly they'd turned into an even narrower and lower-ceilinged passageway, climbed four steep steps, and directly up ahead Jake saw the white-painted, spear-tipped wrought-iron gate, the glass case gleaming in the relative obscurity of the niche beyond it. But before he could really register what he was looking at, Simon had pushed him into a mop closet and handed him a stuff-bag containing nylon coveralls, a chest pack, moleskin gloves, knee pads, and what looked like a World War II aviator's cap. By the time Jake came out again with all those on, Edwards had set up a stepladder beneath the vent shaft, and Simon had already removed the panel in the top of it that he'd had to cut out in order to make his first trip inside, then replaced with six small metal clips.

"Climb in quick, facing right," Simon whispered, "but back up to the left so I can be in front, and take the stuff he hands you while I suit up."

The ropes and other gear were packed in two long sausage-shaped, padded nylon bags that could be dragged behind them. Jake shoved the first of these back between his legs, attaching the drawstring to his pack, leaving the heavier bag for Simon. Next came his dust mask and goggles, then Simon himself, while Jake was fitting those things tightly onto his face, the way Simon had taught him that afternoon. Then, abruptly, total darkness, as Edwards clipped the panel back in place.

It wasn't easy to breathe. It would be impossible to talk, except where their shaft made a junction with another, so Simon could back into that one, wait until Jake came abreast, then pull down his mask (taking in a mouthful of acrid, century-old dust), cup his hands, and whisper directly into Jake's ear. Or vice-versa. But speech was for emergencies only; they would mainly depend on a simple set of finger-on-palm signals Simon had given Jake to memorize beforehand.

He hadn't really believed any of it; it was only an idea to him until this minute, Jake realized. He still didn't, couldn't, believe it was actually happening, except in terrifying flashes. Most of the time he functioned automatically, shuffling forward blindly on his hands and knees as fast as he could manage, until he bumped into the bag Simon was dragging. Then he rested, with one hand on that bag, until it moved away again. Simon had told him to keep count of how many times he brought his right knee forward between the junctions they turned at and to try to memorize which way they went at each one, left or right or up or down, but he never managed to get beyond thirty in any attempt at a tally before his mind went elsewhere—make that nowhere. . . .

It took them an hour and twelve minutes by Jake's watch to reach the foot of the vertical shaft. That area was infinitely better: considerably less dust, and space enough to crouch side by side, or even to stand upright.

"Try to rest," Simon whispered. "I'll set up the ladders and slings, and come back down for you. Are you okay?"

Jake nodded, then remembered to lower his mask and feel for Simon's ear. But he found he couldn't whisper back, his tongue was a baked potato in his mouth, so he signed with finger-taps. Then Simon was gone, and the waiting began. Jake unzipped a pouch on his chest pack, felt for the straw in the cycler's bottle there, and took several long sucks of apple juice. For a while he leaned back, squinting up into the blackness, watching for the dazzle when Simon used his penlight to check a knot or set an extra piton, but soon his head drooped forward. When Simon returned some twenty minutes later, Jake was dreaming that they'd just popped the cork on the bottle of champagne that was waiting for them in the blue Dodge, eight blocks away.

"Coffee break," Simon whispered, offering a pull on another straw, lukewarm cappucino this time. "Ready? You go first, slow and easy. You've got three slings, they're every eighteen feet or so, use 'em all to take a breather in, if you need to."

Inchworm-like in his mind's eye, invisible rung by rung, Jake made it halfway up the shaft without pausing to catch his breath and without thinking of what would happen if he lost both grips on those quarter-inch nylon cords at once. Shifting his weight from the ladder to the tripled loops of that middle sling was a tricky, near-traumatic business, though, so was finding the rope rungs again with his sneakered feet some minutes later. He couldn't see his gloved hand in front of his goggles, let alone the bottom of the shaft almost forty feet down, but from that point on up he was constantly aware of how far he'd fall if he did fall, and he decided to make this whole ascent nonstop next time if possible. Next time: last time: the real time. . . .

— *Turn left*, Simon signaled from behind, tapping on Jake's ankle. It was a lot tighter up here, only twenty-two inches wide and high, he'd been told, but less completely dark somehow than where they'd been before . . . and then Jake saw why this was so: an oblong checkerboard of pale bluish light ahead, the squares in it getting bigger but not much brighter as he approached. He hadn't expected to see one of these, but he knew what it had to be.

— *Look but don't touch,* Simon signaled. Holding his breath, Jake craned forward on his elbows toward the grillwork until two square holes matched his goggles, and he could sense the vastness out there. He peered downward, at a row of dimmed wall sconces, as indistinct as far-off galaxies; then gradually, in the furry distance straight across, double ranks of faint brown dots came into focus: the backs and up-turned bottoms of seats in the visitors' gallery along the opposite side of the House Chamber.

— *Back up,* Simon tapped. It was only ten yards back to where Simon had cut a hatchway in the vertical shaft, but there wasn't room to turn around up here, and creeping in reverse was a lot more work and worry than creeping forward, Jake discovered. Simon went past the hole and motioned for Jake to enter it, then found his ear and whispered: "There's another grill thirty feet farther that way, two more about the same distances behind me. You'll use all four. But go on down now, and take your time. I'm just gonna grab a look at what's involved in splicing into those cables."

Descending that ladder was ten times more terrifying than the climb up had been, but maybe it was only that he was so tired and awkward by now, Jake told himself. It was 1:22 a.m. when he reached the bottom. Until Edwards went off duty at six-thirty, he'd be waiting by the catafalque from ten minutes until a quarter past each hour, beginning at 2:10 a.m. They couldn't make that first rendezvous, but maybe the next one. . . .

Jake made himself as comfortable as possible, drank more apple juice, ate some chocolate. When he sat still and stopped chewing, he thought he could hear the enormous volumes of air circulating through the whole network of shafts, like vast ensembles of strings and wood-winds very far away, eternally tuning up for some titanic concert. . . . He told himself he should try for a nap, even though he was wide awake now—or so he thought, but when he looked at his watch again, it said 2:58.

It took him several minutes more to pull himself together enough to understand that something must've happened to Simon, and that there was no avoiding it: he'd have to find the strength and courage somewhere to get himself up to the top of that ladder again and find out the worst.

❖

Suzanne and Eric were playing honeymoon canasta on the coffeetable in the living room and working in a desultory way on the warm final third of the second bottle in a full dozen of Tattinger's that Gil had considerately dropped off when he'd last stopped by. There were four more bottles thoroughly chilled in the fridge, but neither of them felt like opening another. Or anyhow not yet. More than once tonight as she'd refilled her broken-handled teacup, Suzanne had caught herself anxiously, half-consciously hoping that this being New Year's made it all right for them to be into the champagne already, that they weren't jeopardizing Jake's and Simon's expedition by celebrating its success prematurely.

She didn't much like to admit, even to herself, to being superstitious, but Suzanne was well aware of a persistent tendency—especially when she was as anxious and despondent as she was right now—to convert everything in view into omens. Spilled salt, black cats, ladders in her path, and so forth always forecast disaster, of course, but at times like this, nothing seemed simply what it was, and talismanic properties loomed within the most trivial events and objects, in spite of her stolidly atheistic upbringing.

Her anxiety was uncalled-for, the logical portion of her mind insisted. Even if it *was* going on five o'clock already, that portion iterated, as she sneaked another glance at her watch. If Simon could do this once, he could do it again, and Jake would be okay; he was looking better, if anything, than when he'd arrived almost a month ago. It was the despondent part of how she was feeling that Suzanne couldn't argue with: that was because she'd been counting on spending tonight in Glen Echo with Nora, just the two of them. Not that she had ever dreamed it would lead to anything more intimate than clicking wineglasses and chastely pecking each other's cheek as the clock struck twelve, but she *had* been counting on it.

They'd spent Christmas that way. True, it had happened only because Edwards begged off, saying he might have to work, and Ruthellen went home to Georgia with her family, while the retired cello teacher Nora had also invited this time was hospitalized on

Christmas Eve following a stroke. Even so, it had been wonderful, an experience Suzanne would've given almost anything to repeat: five whole hours of Nora's presence, all to herself. And Nora must've enjoyed it, too, or she wouldn't've asked so cheerily, while Suzanne washed the dishes later, "You don't have any plans for New Year's, do you? Me neither. Guess we'll just have to be two old maids again next week then, won't we?"

But yesterday, as soon as Ruthellen got back to town, the bitch called up Nora and invited her to join the Vliorishevskis for this evening—they had this soppy tradition of always spending New Year's Eve together, just the nuclear family plus one dearest-of-all friend apiece, Ruthellen had explained—and without a single second's hesitation, Nora had accepted. Not only that: when she'd told Suzanne this afterward (without apology), she'd gone on to ask if Suzanne knew for sure yet about her job, and if so, had she begun to look for a place of her own? "No hurry of course," Nora did hasten to add, "I just wondered. . . ."

The job was still very much up in the air, Suzanne had managed to mutter through her sudden desolation, conditional on what the would-be producers thought of the thirty-page treatment she was cooking up, but she'd been promised a decision by the end of January. ". . . Feel like playing another?" she asked Eric now, reshuffling the cards.

He had to be at least as anxious as she was, but he'd just nodded off for a moment. He jerked upright guiltily, glanced quickly at the clock on the wall above Suzanne's head, caught a series of yawns in his fist, and shrugged. "Sure, why not."

He certainly wasn't much of a talker. She still had no idea what sort of life he'd led before all this began, other than looking after his dying father. But she found him comfortable to be alone with, unlike most young straight males, and Eric seemed easy enough with her, too, apparently unruffled by whatever threats she might be considered, by many men, to represent. She'd never managed to figure out who it had been that both Eric and Jake almost reminded her of that first morning, but whoever it was had long since been erased by a vivid sense of each of them as a unique individual. She'd met a number of women, but only a couple of men in her entire life until now, who'd impressed her as being entirely genuine and complete in themselves. Eric and Jake were both definitely that, for Suzanne, and then some.

The card game had been her idea, but she barely remembered the rules well enough to teach it to him, and although she was winning handily, even she was bored with it by this time. Eric had counter-proposed chess, but she'd heard Simon bewailing how badly he'd been done in, and besides, she'd never liked chess, primarily because when you've lost at that game, you didn't simply lose, you weren't just unlucky—you were *beaten* by somebody. Skill and ruthlessness were what counted (plus, those qualities being equal, whether you happened to be white and privileged to lead or black and doomed to follow, for godsakes!) and in her opinion, all this was too much like real life under corporate capitalism to qualify as harmless amusement. Eric definitely didn't seem the type to excel at chess, he seemed far too selfless and gentle. . . .

The phone began to shrill, off in Gil's bedroom, as Eric cut the deck for luck. She knew he wouldn't race her to it, he feared and hated phones, always deferring to whomever else was present. So she refilled her cup nearly to the brim first, took a little sip, carried it in there, and set it down on the dresser, all very carefully. She was sure she knew who it was, who it always was—but as she lifted the receiver it suddenly occurred to her that it might be Jake and Simon with word that they were safe and on their way back to Baltimore. And then Suzanne passionately wished she could unthink that thought—because now it *wouldn't* be them, it never worked that way, it *would* be Gil.

"Did I wake you up?" Gil asked. "Are they back yet?"

"No. And no."

"Doesn't sound like you're having a happy, either."

"Not very—are you?"

"That lang syne routine gets aulder every goddamn year, if you ask me. You got *anything* good to report?"

"Matter of fact, yes. I think I've found our freezer. Well, actually it's a cooler, but I checked with Simon, and he said it should serve our purposes just as well. Near Salisbury, out where you suggested. A whole poultry processing plant in the middle of its own eighty-acre lot, for half what you said was the limit, and I'll bet we can knock 'em down even further. They must be desperate, to be fielding calls about it past five o'clock on New Year's Eve. Only one month's deposit, and they didn't say boo about certified checks. They do want references, though—when do I get 'em? And what kind of business are we, anyhow? They wanted to know, and so do I. I don't enjoy acting ignorant."

"I'm truly sorry, I humbly apologize, you'll have everything you need by tomorrow noon, I swear it by Bakunin's beard."

"Whoever the hell that is."

"You Marxists, you lead such sheltered lives, intellectually speaking. Mikail Aleksandrovich Bakunin, one of the two pillars of Russian anarchism, that's who. But come to think of it, Petr Alekseevich Kropotkin had an even better beard to swear by."

"I really don't need a lecture on old Russian anarchists, or their beards, at five o'clock in the morning, Gil. And we ought to be keeping this line open, just in case."

"You're so right, as always, but before I hang up lemme mention one little detail while I've got it in mind: next time you go shopping for those guys, buy yourself a foldup luggage carrier, will you? Make it a pretty good one, sturdy enough to handle as much as a hundred pounds. And plenty of bungie cords."

"These things're for me? What'll I do with 'em, when I've got 'em?"

"Just keep 'em handy, okay? I'll let you go now."

"— Wait, hold on a minute, I think I just heard the front door open . . . yeah, they're back, here's—"

She'd seen him so stoned on hashish he couldn't do more than giggle, and so livid over bureaucratic stupidity that she'd moved away instinctively, out of his reach. But she'd never seen Simon like this before: as bug-eyed and boiled-looking as a thirty-minute lobster, and unmistakably sozzled.

"Izzat who I think it is? Wish we coulda sent *him* in there, *he's* the right size—lemme give 'im a piece a my mind, okay, while there's still some left—" Grabbing at the phone, Simon turned a near cartwheel, somehow managing to keep the Tattinger's bottle he was hugging upright all the while. With equal aplomb and improbability, he himself landed right-side-up on the edge of the bed beside her, the bottle clutched in one fist, the receiver in the other. "What ho, you sawed-off little sonofabitch! Happy Fucking New Year! I wanted you t'know this—I just spent the *scaredest* couple hours in my everlovin' life!"

"Apparently you lived to tell the tale, though."

"Yeah, but y'know what? I don't think I'm gonna! Think I'd rather go pop another bottle of bubbly—thanks for which, by the way, it's pretty decent gargle, all right—'n' see how fast I can pass out. Here, I'll give you Jake—"

"Hello? Hello?"

". . . Yeah," Jake finally answered. "Look, I'm ready to pass out myself. As far as I can make out, we had a very close call. But everything turned out okay."

"Not only okay, we're a humungous step ahead of the game!" Simon roared from the hallway, where he'd collided with a closet door and slowly slid into a sitting position, his back ramrod straight, the now-empty bottle still perpendicular. "I made the splice! The rest is frigging child's play!"

". . . He went back up to check out the sound system cable, and I guess he accidentally snapped some hair-thin wire that would've set off sirens all over the place, but he caught both ends right at the break and kept 'em together somehow—for more than two hours—until he managed to tie in a loop on both sides that reconnected it."

"With nothing but a pair of tweezers—in my left hand, yet—'n' my teeth! How 'bout that? Bring on your walk-in cooler 'n' your canful of ploot *now*, Buddy-O, we're ready for 'em!"

❖

— Macrobiotic TV dinners, yet, she'd groaned, when Gil's packet was delivered on the morning of January second. With references out of the *Vegetarian Times* and the *Eastern Shore Organic Directory*! Suzanne felt like a total fool repeating that cover-story, but she had to admit that it worked well enough. By the afternoon of the fourth, she'd already received her copy of the lease—in exchange for a check clearly postdated February first, no less. Those poor unlucky chicken pluckers must've been so hard up she could've fed them any story at all, she thought later, maybe even including why she *really* wanted the place.

The plant itself, some ten miles northwest of Salisbury, Maryland, was not inspiring. A rambling shell of mildew-mottled cinderblock with three-quarters of its windows replaced by rotten plywood and most of its flat felt roof sagging and puddled, it swam alone in a sea of greasy black mud. The interior was dark and drafty and not just damp, it was sodden in most areas, and reeked throughout from its former use, but it did contain a big, sufficiently solid walk-in cooler, and the nearest neighbor was a deserted-looking junkyard half a mile farther down the dead-end asphalt road. There were no other buildings in view, and the only trees were on the dead-level horizon, strung along a die-straight county highway like a row of arthritic fists raised in help-less protest against a bruised and sullen sky.

They began shifting tools and materials over there from Simon's shop the next day in a U-Haul van. Eric did most of the transporting and the setting-up as well, with Simon's guidance. Jake stayed back in Baltimore as long as possible, husbanding his energy for the work ahead that no one else could safely do, and Simon could only manage to get over there for an hour or two each evening; his business was fast falling apart without him, he said. Suzanne was kept zipping back and forth over the Chesapeake Bay Bridge in the MG, chasing down all those little last-minute essentials no one had been able to think of until the various pieces actually began to fit together. All in all, the move and the readying of the cooler, including reinforcement and reassembly of the glove box, took four very long days.

Then they waited for Gil and his canister.

When he finally appeared, past eleven o'clock on the night of the ninth, Simon went over the thing thoroughly with a Geiger counter (which scarcely clicked) while it still lay in the trunk of the Plymouth. Then Gil and Eric lugged it between them through the building, into the cooler, and placed it in the glove box. While Jake donned coveralls and a ponderous lead apron, Simon made quick sketches of the like-liest ways to coax it open. "I wish to Christ we had closed-circuit TV," he grumbled, while Gil rolled his eyes at that imagined expenditure.

There was, at least, the intercom Simon and Eric had hooked up from the cooler to an office at the opposite end of the plant. Simon gave Jake's shoulder a quick squeeze—"If you see anything I haven't antic-ipated, just stop wherever you are and tell me all about it, okay?"— then herded Eric and Gil before him, past the shielded changing chamber they'd constructed and on outside. Painstakingly, Simon latched the reinforced doors.

They'd gone through two pots of coffee before the intercom buzzed. "It's open," Jake said, "I'm looking at it now, and the counter's not going too crazy, so this rig works, I guess. It's all in one big piece, and not like anything you described. I'll draw a picture, then I'll close it up again for now. . . ."

It was nearly another hour, and the windows were beginning to reveal how dirty they were, before Jake was ready to come out. Simon swept him and the paper in his hand with a second Geiger counter:

pretty damn clean. Their jerry-built system was functioning better than they had any right to expect—but as soon as he'd glanced at Jake's sketch, Simon wheeled on Gil: "MUF, you said! They may be godawful careless, but they *don't* go around mislaying plutonium triggers!"

"Is that what it is?" Gil wondered, round-eyed. "Really?"

"Yeah, *really*! That canister sure as shit did not fall off the back of any truck!"

"Like I told you, I had no idea, I wasn't there."

— Where were you, then? And where was there? And what did happen to Claude and Rafael? You promised you'd tell me about it when I came East. . . . Jake tried to think these things coherently, and would've said them aloud if he hadn't been so far-gone groggy and bone-weary. He'd been stiff with fear for most of the night, convinced that something was going to go terribly wrong inside that cooler, and he'd end up like the Los Alamos physicist back in the Forties that Simon had told him about, whose single little slip with a screwdriver consigned him to a horrible death after days of hideous agony, which must've been all the harder to bear for the knowledge that it was due to his own clumsiness. . . .

As for Gil, he'd had six weeks by this time to concoct a plausible story. That was precisely his problem: he'd rehearsed so many versions in anticipation of this moment that he was afraid he'd gotten several contradictory tales inextricably entangled in his mind. It was always best to wing it all the way, he knew, but no fresh inspiration struck him as he waited to be called to account by one of these guys scowling at him now.

Eric was in the best shape of all four by this time (past seven o'clock in the mucus-gray morning), and these questions had crossed his mind, too; but until this minute, Eric hadn't considered it his place to ask. He still wasn't entirely sure it was, and finally, like Simon, he told himself: *Not now—if it looks like nobody else is gonna do it next time Gil shows up, though, I damnsure will. . . .*

". . . Well, all right," Simon muttered, as the right moment for any questions passed them all by. He was fuzzily aware that Gil wasn't telling everything, and he did intend to find out just where and how that trigger had come into Gil's possession . . . but next time would do . . . it also seemed pretty academic at this stage; Simon wasn't sure there was much point to inspecting this gift horse's molars when they were

already perched on its back and galloping into the home stretch . . .
he'd be lucky to get home by noon today as it was, and he knew he
wouldn't get to shut his eyes before nine o'clock tonight at the earliest . . . he'd slept around the clock New Year's Day and that night, but
hadn't had more than three hours' sleep any night since, what with
running back and forth to this soggy hellhole, facing up to the fact
that his days in Glen Echo were definitely numbered, and beating his
brains out trying to put his business into less idiosyncratic, hence
more saleable, order. "At least now we know what we're dealing with:
enough of this shit to depopulate the entire District of Columbia. And
all we need to shave off is just one-twentieth of a gram. We'll manage
that somehow—I mean *you* will, Jake—but I don't know what the fuck
we'll do with the rest of it."

"Hm. I don't s'pose there's any way of getting it back in the can
afterward, is there, so it looks just like it did before?" Gil inquired,
cautiously.

"Like the jinni back in the bottle? Nope, no way. I didn't mean what
I just said, I'm so beat I don't know what I'm saying. I *do*, however,
know what we've gotta do here when we're done: seal up that thing,
plus anything we might've contaminated, inside that cooler, and hope
to hell somebody'll come along someday who can deal with it properly.
But hey, I better hit that road while I can still keep it in focus, more
or less. . . ."

As it turned out, no one got another chance to question Gil because
he vanished again that morning, and never called or returned to
Salisbury after the tenth of January.

21: JANUARY TWENTY-FIRST

Glen Echo, foggy Sunday. Nora woke at dawn—if you could call it that, on such a dungeon-like day as this was—with an exquisitely sweet-sad-cozy feeling at first, carried over from dreams; then awareness of a scratchy throat and, most probably, a fever. Shit and double shit, wouldn't you just know—but she wasn't going to let any bug get the better of her, not with her long-awaited recital scheduled for eight o'clock tonight. She hated to let go of those last few wisps of dreaming, though, and spent the next few minutes trying to weave them back together:

One part at least had involved meeting Ruthellen's family on New Year's Eve, which in real life was a wholly pleasant memory. Nora had found Congressman and Mrs. Vliorishevski openly and unaffectedly loving toward each other, interesting in themselves *and* genuinely interested in her, as well as fairly literate, not small or hypocritical about anything that came up in conversation, and not only devoted to but respectful of both their children, as persons in their own right; in other words, not the shallow, conniving politicos she'd half-expected. Of course they couldn't have been like that, not and raise a daughter like Ruthellen. Their son was quite charming, too, even if a West Point grad and engaged to a stick of a Mt. Holyoke senior. . . .

In her dreaming, though, now that she'd recalled more of it, she and Ruthellen had been desperately anxious over something, and Nora's gaining Ruthellen's parents' approval had been extremely important, almost as if the two of them had something to be guilty about . . . well, they didn't, and they wouldn't. Nora assured herself that she couldn't help it if her dreamlife made other claims occasionally. "In dreams begin responsibilities"—that was Yeats by way of Delmore Schwartz if she remembered rightly, and maybe true; but a lot of nonsense begins—and properly ends—there, also. . . .

She lay still for a few more long, lonely minutes, summoning courage, finally groping in the gloom for her robe and crutches, and swinging down the hall, banging the medicine cabinet open, swallowing a fistful of vitamin C tabs one after another, with a silent prayer to Linus Pauling and only disgustingly lukewarm tap water from her tooth glass to wash them down, then a decongestant and—after some hesitation—half a pain-killer for good measure.

It would've been heaven to be able to crawl back into bed and wait, as on most other mornings lately, for Suzie Q to brew and bring her a cup of strong black coffee. But Suzie Q wasn't there to do that or anything else for her today because Suzanne had gone up to New York last night, to be on time for a working brunch with those would-be producers, and while she was about it, to pick up the first pressings of the Kennedy Edwards album. (It was incredibly sweet of her to go to all this trouble; but odd, too, come to think of it, that she'd be able to do that on a Sunday.) She planned to be back in time for Nora's recital, though, and Roosevelt had said he'd be there, too. That was why Suzanne was running all the way out to Flushing today instead of waiting for the mails, so she could surprise him with it. . . .

Wearily, Nora hobbled into the kitchen, put the kettle on to boil, ground the beans (*Mmm!* that smell produced the first good reason for being alive since she'd wakened—she'd been missing out on that little daily treat, with Suzanne here), and readied her cup, cone, and filter, then sat herself down, tucked her robe around her legs against the damp, and patiently began to tune her viola for a long morning's practice.

❖

Salisbury, and another slimy-wet, malodorous day, just as depressing as all the others they'd spent here in this former bird-butchering factory. Inside the walk-in cooler, Jake welded the glove box shut around the canister and the remains of the nuclear trigger, then welded together a plate-steel box around that. Then he dragged the tanks and torches out and shed his coveralls and lead apron for the final time, while Eric welded the cooler doors shut as well. Eric had already stenciled a row of international radiation symbols and the words "DANGER!—¡PELIGROSO!—HAZARDOUS WASTE!" in Day-Glo orange paint across both doors.

The shaving and pulverizing had taken a matter of minutes, but readying everything necessary to perform those acts safely had required six twelve-hour days, while assembling the aerosol canisters had occupied another four. It had been tedious but nerve-twisting work, and the Eastern Shore, in midwinter, was the dankest, dreariest, foulest-smelling place Jake had ever experienced or imagined. Eric had stayed down there the whole time, too, doing whatever he could to ease Jake's labors—whatever Jake would allow him to approach— and seeing to it that there was hot food ready whenever Jake found time to eat, and that he stayed as warm and dry as possible.

Jake kept at it until his eyes refused to focus, but the hardest work came after he'd quit in the cooler each night, when he huddled beside an electric heater with a blanket draped over his head, Simon's pocket tape recorder running, a stopwatch in one hand and a Lucky burning in the other, trying to compress all his urgency and anguish into one simple, coherent, and convincing twenty-five-second explanation of what he was going to do with those aerosols, and why he felt he had to do it. Twenty to thirty seconds was as much time as there would be, they'd decided after much debate, before all hell broke loose inside the House Chamber or some technician simply cut him off. . . .

The four aerosol cans—astonishingly heavy inside all that lead foil—were already wrapped individually in black poly and packed away in the back of the Dodge, now stripped of its Six-Pac and equipped with a less conspicuous, more secure steel lockbox. While Eric loaded what little else they were taking back with them, Simon finally quit fiddling with the circuitry for splicing in the tapedeck, groaned his weary satisfaction, test-ran the final version of Jake's message over his headphones, then wrapped up everything in the same manner as the aerosols.

"Ready!" he called. "How about you guys, haven't you had enough of this place?" He looked at his watch: 11:41 a.m. Tight, but he should make it: he'd told two of his erstwhile competitors he'd show them around the shop at two-thirty and four o'clock respectively this after- noon, with intent to sell either of them the whole goddamned show— patents, client list, house and lot, the works. What he hadn't made clear, because he didn't dare, was that he had to close any deal tomor- row at the latest, and be paid in cash or something equally untraceable. If he could only take his own good time about it, he was sure that he could get five hundred thousand; the business was really worth twice that, just as it was. In just one more year, it could very well be worth four times that. It definitely *would* be, by god, if—

Yeah, well, okay; there wouldn't *be* one more year, thanks to . . . no, he had to be honest with himself, he couldn't blame Gil. And certainly not Jake. He'd made his own decision. Or failed to make one when he could've, which came down to the same thing in the end, didn't it? He could almost recall that precise instant of transition, from advising in impersonal second- to advocating in conspiratorial first-person-plural, with corresponding shifts from conditional to definite future tense: a slight dislocation in syntax, a momentary loss of linguistic balance, like not quite tripping over a low curbstone . . . so all right, he'd take a quarter-mil—the house and lot alone were worth more than that now. . . .

"Ready," Jake said. ". . . What'd you think of my message?"

"It's really good . . . but . . ."

"But what?"

". . . I mean—Christ, I wish I knew how to say this right . . . but you know, Jake, there's no real reason for both of us to go back in there. I could just as well set the aerosols in place when I cut in the tapedeck and timer."

"Just what the fuck are you trying to do to me, Simon? Can't you see how that'd make this whole thing meaningless as far as I'm concerned? It'd make *me* meaningless, to be more precise. Now come on, you've gotta tell me—what *did* you think of that message?"

"It's good, Jake. Good as anyone could do in half a minute."

"Yeah, but will it *work*? Will they understand?"

Jake looked godawful, Simon thought, as if he hadn't slept the whole time he'd been here. And maybe he hadn't. "I can't tell you that—we can only hope to hell they do. Where's Eric?"

"I'm right here. You're sure we've got everything?"

Simon double-checked, and nodded. "My place by seven-thirty tonight?" he asked Jake. "I told Edwards ten-oh-five, so it can't be much later. And you'd better get some rest before then."

"Exactly what I had in mind. See you at seven-thirty."

All three glanced back repeatedly as the Dodge and Simon's Saab rolled out across the flat black land beneath the leaden, low-hanging sky. Each was glad to be seeing the last of that spot. But leaving here, for Simon and Eric, meant they'd be taking permanent leave of Jake tonight. And for Jake himself, it meant all final goodbyes were only a matter of hours down the road. Edwards had informed them that there'd be the standard special-security measures in effect from tomorrow noon onward, and the very latest anyone could be smuggled in or out was five o'clock tomorrow morning. That left Jake with more than thirty-six hours to wait inside the catafalque, but it couldn't be helped. . . .

This wasn't what he was preoccupied with, though, on the drive back to Baltimore. He had another copy of his message in his shirt pocket, and a risky resolve in mind. Risky not only for himself and this whole project, but for Nora as well, he knew—but he couldn't force himself to factor in such considerations anymore. He hadn't seen or spoken with her since that spur-of-the-moment phone call from Banning. Tonight was his only chance, and he'd enlisted both Eric's and Simon's aid. Suzanne had also given him at least tacit approval. On one of her last trips out to the plant, Jake had questioned her again about surveillance at Nora's house—what did it consist of?—and Suzanne had confessed that there didn't appear to be any watch on the place; probably there was nothing but bugs installed on that day when they'd questioned Nora. "— So why're you asking?"

"I'm just curious," he'd said.

"And I'm just stupid, if I take that for an answer." But Suzanne had been grinning as she said it, so he'd told her what he had in mind, and that Simon would sweep the house beforehand. Gil would have three-colored kittens, she'd thought—but Gil didn't have to know, and he wouldn't learn about it from her.

Eric had arranged to meet Suzanne's return train and go with her to the recital, where he'd slip Nora a note saying that Jake would be waiting at her house tonight. Simon meanwhile would get Jake inside undetected and debug the place before meeting Edwards to be smuggled into the Capitol Building so he could go back into the vents this one last time, to set up the tapedeck and timer; he'd come out again when Jake went in at 4:50 a.m.

Jake couldn't and didn't want to guess what Nora's reaction to seeing him again would be. It was definitely too late now to worry about that, or anything else. . . .

❖

Downtown Philadelphia, bleak and vacant Sunday noon, with distant electronic church chimes dull as spoons on dinner plates in the sodden, motionless air. In an otherwise completely empty office cubicle—not so much as an old calendar on the puke-green walls—Gil and a thin man about as old as Jake in a purple silk turtleneck and double-breasted charcoal pinstripe sat facing each other on cheap foldup chairs, passing an old-fashioned dial phone back and forth across a foldup plywood table. Aside from his duds, age and intensity (fellow closet cokehead, or just another nutcase?), Gil hadn't paid the dude much heed; he was giving more of his attention to his peripheral vision, especially in respect to the only window, on his left, and only door, on his right.

Then the man swung one of his skinny arms around behind him, producing a navy-blue nylon two-suiter from underneath the black trenchcoat draped over the back of his chair. He hoisted it with a loud grunt, slapped it down on the tabletop, and unzipped it. Gil matched those motions with a brassbound, brown metal case, like a miniature footlocker, that he'd been holding ready between his knees. ". . . I'm giving it to him," the other man said into the phone. "He's opened it, he's counting. . . ."

Standing now, Gil took his time shifting the contents of the nylon bag into his case, licking his thumb, breaking open and riffling through packs of fifties and hundreds as if he had all afternoon. And why not? He didn't get to count a million bucks every day. Or even every other. And there were several things to think about beyond simple addition. As for instance: these serial numbers weren't in any order he could detect—and he knew he couldn't hope to spot any professional marking job—but that didn't mean these bills hadn't been marked, or selected from several series, then well shuffled. You controlled whatever you could, that's all, like bringing your own suitcase and replacing the bank wrappers with your own rubber bands, because either that two-suiter or those strips of paper could easily conceal a bug that could be followed clear to Timbuktu. . . .

Anything of the sort, of course, would mean these were govs he'd managed to connect with—but just supposing that's what they were, why had they taken so goddamn long to agree to any deal, and why hadn't they gone for the whole nine canisters at once instead of insisting on seeing a sample first? They'd *know* what they'd be getting, wouldn't they?

But then, Gil himself hadn't felt like coming on too strong, either, until Jake cracked open that first one. Triggers were what he'd figured all along he had to peddle, but hunches and suppositions weren't good enough at this end of the business because you couldn't just grin and say *caveat emptor*. There were *caveats* every which way, always, and it definitely wouldn't do to disappoint the sort of customer you were most likely to come up with for this sort of product.

And the initial arrangements for this little transaction had taken forfuckingever. They'd absolutely insisted on their sample, and Gil in turn had insisted on cash on the barrelhead—a cool million apiece, no doubt a tremendous bargain, but he'd always liked that quaint phrase. So here he was, and here it went, and what came next was anybody's guess. . . .

Finally Gil reached across for the phone, said "Okay," and asked to speak to his colleague. "So how we doin', pal? It's all hunkydory here, are they satisfied? Fine. So take it real easy, just remember what I've told you, and I'll see you real soon."

Hanging up, he grinned, snapped the suitcase shut, hefted it as he stood, grinned again, and went out the door with his cool million swinging from his left hand, jauntily. Ignoring the elevator, he ran down four flights of stairs, then outside and around the corner, where he jumped into a black Corvette and drove it three fast blocks, ducking into a parking garage that he left on foot by a side door scarcely two minutes later.

A little less than two hours and half a dozen other means of transport after that, he was leaning against a pay phone outside the men's room in a truckstop near the Francis Scott Key Bridge in southeast Baltimore, picking chicken-fried steak fibers out of his teeth and placidly listening to an answering service. He no longer possessed any suitcase.

At the back of a closed coffee shop in Manhattan's garment district, Suzanne replaced the flyspecked receiver on a yellow wall phone above a sinkful of soaking pots and skillets. Gorgeous George, in a black and gold jogging outfit that went better with that name—if not with his ponderous gut—than that elevator starter's uniform, saluted her quite gallantly, she thought, as she threaded her way among tables loaded with inverted chairs to let herself out the front door, which locked again with a sharp *snick!* behind her.

Perched back there on the steam table, that shiny steel canister had looked right at home, as if it were standard equipment in any restaurant kitchen.

Out on the deserted sidewalk again, she glanced both ways, then up at inscrutable rows of tall dusty windows, before heading east along

West 27th Street. Striding along, she made a conscious effort to center her weight properly above her pelvis, breathe from her diaphragm, keep her shoulders from rolling forward, reminding herself of the principles she'd extracted from years of bodywork: If you stand and walk as if you're frightened, you *will* be frightened, and you'll convey that message to any potential assailant. . . .

Overhead, wan sunlight struggled through clouds that reminded her of the greasy soapsuds in that sink she'd been staring down into while listening to Gil. Glancing over her shoulder frequently and spotting nothing that moved back there but pigeons, she walked almost to Seventh Avenue before she encountered another human being: a panhandler reclining against a hydrant with his bony legs in four pairs of pants stretched out halfway across the sidewalk, and so dejected he didn't try for eye-contact or even bother to raise his gritty palm as he croaked, "Spare change?"

She almost swept on past him, like any true New Yorker, before it occurred to her that she had no further use for that luggage carrier, and plenty to haul around as it was, with her satchel-sized shoulder bag full of assorted disguises. "How about some spare wheels?" she said, and laid it across his lap. He still didn't look up, but he did begin to pluck at the bungie cords, as if they were guitar strings.

Just as well she ditched that extra few pounds, she thought, as she hiked all the way up to Herald Square before seeing a single cab. She wished she could jump into that sweet little MG right now and zip straight out of town, but as Gil had cautioned when he gave it to her, "That baby turns heads, and people'll look a lot closer at you, too— they'll wanna know who they're envying," so she'd left it in a lot in downtown Washington.

When cabs did at last appear, they came in packs, naturally, and the first six or eight had their Off-Duty signs lit. Finally a wild-eyed Pakistani screeched to a stop. She had him take her to Broadway and 55th Street, where she ran into the black marble arcade of an office building, emerging three minutes later on 56th minus wig and makeup, the tan side of her windbreaker out now instead of the green plaid, in pink aviator glasses and chocolate-brown sweatpants with Reeboks instead of loafers and wrap-around red skirt. A second cab dropped her at the Ninth Avenue end of Port Authority, where she made another quick change in the ladies'—back to her wig with a blue suit and heels—and a ten-second phone call before catching the shuttle bus to

LaGuardia. Out there she made another fast call, then elbowed her way across several lines of people waiting to check their luggage, doubling back just in time for the shuttle's return trip to Manhattan.

She was positive she hadn't seen the same face twice, or met anyone, anywhere, who'd taken the slightest notice of her, so she caught another cab downtown, which got her to Penn Station in plenty of time to retrieve her other things from the locker where she'd left them when she'd returned from Flushing that morning, and even to find a deli two blocks away where she bought a Diet Pepsi and a crabmeat-salad-on-kaiser roll for the long, boring trip ahead. A paperback would be a good idea, she thought, but the terminal bookstore wasn't open, and the newsstand had nothing but romances and mysteries, so she reluctantly bought a Sunday *Times* and stripped it down to the Arts & Entertainment, Book Review, Travel, and Magazine sections at the nearest trashcan.

As soon as her train showed "Arrival" up on the schedule boards, she circled through dim, confusing, deserted-for-the-weekend passageways in search of a working phone that wasn't already in use, finally locating a whole long row she could take her pick from, down on the lower level. She rang the same number and left the same sort of message as before: "Just say Watson called again. I'm getting on now, and I'll see him real soon."

And when she did see Gil again, she'd have an earful for him because that cheap bastard had gone to some hole-in-the-wall recording company after all. And the smarmy Israeli who'd reluctantly handed over those two naked twelve-inch LPs now wrapped in tissue paper inside her overnight case had sworn up and down that fifty copies was all the order called for, and nobody had ever said anything to *him* about mailing any to radio stations or getting a jacket designed and printed, either. She'd given the creep Edwards' address and forty bucks to cover express-mailing the remaining forty-eight, but she was goddamned if this was going to be the end of the matter. . . .

She had her accumulated parcels and baggage stacked up precariously between her knees as she reached out to hang up the receiver, and she was wishing now that she'd hung onto that luggage carrier; it was going to be awkward boarding and finding a seat with all this loose stuff—when the pressure of what she instantly recognized as the business end of a pistol in the small of her back drove every other concern straight out of mind.

❖

At Union Station, Eric waited in vain for Suzanne to get off the 6:48 Amtrak from New York. He stayed around for the next two trains as well, but then had to leave or he'd miss Nora entirely. He had the address and knew how to get there, but wasn't easy about going alone—there was very little on earth Eric feared quite as much as a roomful of strangers. He had to deliver Jake's note, though, there was no way out of that. . . .

He arrived at the small recital hall near DuPont Circle just in time to hear the applause following the final encore, then stood pressed against the wall beside the lobby doorway watching the audience stand up, stretch, grin, struggle into coats, search for missing scarves, umbrellas, and companions, spill slowly past him down the steps, regroup in little clusters out in front of the building, then gradually disperse.

Nora, he could see, was still on stage in her wheelchair, surrounded by admiring friends, beaming up at their compliments. After another quarter-hour, two young women began to fold up chairs and turn off lights. Eric took the hint and retreated to the sidewalk, where the fog had turned to icy mist.

At last Nora came out, too, rolling down a ramp at the side of the building but still surrounded, then quickly whisked away in a caravan of cars, to celebrate. "Tune Inn!" he heard someone shout, but he didn't understand what they meant by that. Gate-crashing was something else that Eric had never in his whole life dreamed of doing, but he begged directions from the occupants of one of the last cars to pull away, and followed to find Nora in the back room of the big, dark, noisy bar, the enraptured focus of two dozen people's loving attention.

Reaching her was agony—but he resolutely returned to the bar, gulped a boilermaker for courage, then went back in there and started sidling closer. She looked his way a few times but didn't recognize him in that half-grown-out haircut Howie had given him along with those farmer-on-vacation sports clothes.

Finally he was near enough, and eventually she turned aside, toward him, to catch a sneeze in a wad of Kleenex. Eric grabbed her free hand, folded it over Jake's note, whispered "New Mexico!" without meaning to or knowing why, and then fought his way back out through the crowd to wait across the street in the Dodge for what seemed like hours more, until she appeared, still trading kisses, hugs, goodnights, and thank-yous, and was over-helped into her rusty blue Chevette.

He hadn't been at all sure what she'd do, but she drove away alone and went straight home, and he followed to make sure that no one else was following. It took more patience than he had left by now to squeeze that full-sized, long-bed pickup in between a maroon BMW and a little blue Toyota down by the turnaround, but it was the only possible space left on that one-block street, so he did it, finally—with his headlights off, in the slender hope that this would make him less conspicuous— and without bumping either car hard enough to set off its alarm. Then he waited some more, until all Nora's lights went out but the one in the rear in what he guessed was her bedroom.

And then he drove back to Union Station, to meet the last train of the night from New York. Still no Suzanne, and no answer (not that he expected any) at the Baltimore apartment. Speeding back to Glen Echo, he finally spotted Jake's rental car as he drove past it now for the third time, parked near the corner of Massachusetts Avenue.

As he was about to turn into Nora's street again, Eric saw that there was another car already in that spot where he'd been before— another car he recognized. Now he was twanging with apprehension. He drove on by, left the Dodge two blocks away, and crept back to where he could crouch behind a neighbor's bamboo hedge and watch both Nora's house and the car in the turn-around—which was empty, or else its occupant was lying down.

After ten or fifteen minutes, Eric saw a figure in a dark poncho approach the car nonchalantly, unlock the driver's door, climb in, and slouch down behind the wheel as if for an all-night vigil. That mist was trying very hard by this time to become a full-fledged rain. Eric wished he'd worn something waterproof, and warmer, but he wasn't leaving now for any reason, not until he learned what Gil and his Plymouth were doing there.

22: ANDANTE

Her ears were so plugged, her head was so stuffed up, that Nora truly couldn't say what she'd actually sounded like, but everyone seemed to think the whole recital had gone splendidly, even that self-important young critic from the *Washington Post* whose name she never caught —third or fourth string, most likely, but still. . . . And her own work, both short pieces, had received every bit as much applause as the Boccherini, the Rebecca Clarke, or even the Schubert. Really: she'd found a moment afterward to ask her accompanist, and he'd said he thought so, too—and Greg would certainly never say that if he didn't mean it. . . .

The hall was completely sold out, or so Ruthellen told her afterward, and ten or twelve people actually stood at the rear until intermission, when someone—bless them!—scared up more chairs from somewhere. Mrs V. (Denise, as she'd urged Nora to call her, but Nora somehow couldn't quite) had come as well, with a dozen gorgeous white roses and the Congressman's apologies. It was wonderful, too, how so many dear old friends had managed to make it, some of whom Nora hadn't seen in absolutely years, including five who'd driven down together from as far away as Maine! All in all, it had been so overwhelming that she hadn't even noticed Suzanne's absence until Roosevelt Edwards stepped out of the shadows as she was being wheeled up the aisle at long last, to thank her gravely for the great pleasure she had given him and to say goodnight. Of course, there was no telling what he really thought of her sort of music. . . .

By the time they'd reached the Tune Inn, she knew very well just how desperately tired she was. And no wonder, the way this bug just went on getting worse, seemingly by the minute. Such a beautiful feeling, to be so loved and fêted and appreciated, but . . . exhausting, too—turning aside to sneeze again, to find that distinctly odd young man at her elbow—*what?*—closing her hand around a wadded-up piece of paper so hard her knuckles crackled, whispering something mysterious: could that be some arcane equivalent of God-Bless-You? Only when his back was turned as he made swiftly for the door did she know him, remembering that back, on a horse and she was on another horse behind him . . . the note grew hot and soggy in her fist before she could get away to the ladies' to read it. By then she knew almost exactly what it was going to say.

She noticed the Dodge pickup following her before she was past the Mall, knew for sure it was Eric when he stopped two vehicles behind her at the red light on Independence and Third. Her mind was beginning to function somewhat again by then, but there was so little in there to work with: what in God's Name had they done, and why were they here, now? That whole episode, that often lovely but painful and sometimes scary week she'd spent out there in New Mexico, had seemed so long ago and far away, finally behind her—until she'd recognized Eric's retreating back. . . .

So Jake was waiting for her at her house. And he was "sorry to break in on you like this, especially tonight." But he needed to see her, he needed to "explain." He needed to say goodbye—again! Dear God, hadn't they said it, or agreed not to, already? And hadn't she gone through enough hell, afterward?

Oh God, oh God, oh God, Jake! *Don't do this to me anymore!*

He was sitting in the dark in her living room, in the only chair he'd ever used in there. He switched on the small lamp on the end table beside him as she swung herself in across the threshold from the entranceway. If Eric had been a shock—and he *had* been—Jake was ten times more so, even though she knew who it was this time: ages older, wearier, tense, and crazy—but still Jake, with all his aching, unwanted need and love for her. Still Jake, and immediately reviving, entirely against her will, all of hers for him.

"Don't speak, and don't touch me—not here."

Silently, he followed, into her bedroom, into her arms, into her bed. It was too quick, too urgent, not satisfying physically—it could've been any cock in any cunt, any mouths and hands seeking and grabbing—and she was glad of that. Afterward he lay still beside her like some ancient, worn-down stone carving of himself, flat on his back, looking straight up into the empty darkness there against the high, now invisible, vaulted ceiling.

"... I want to play you a tape I made," he said after what seemed like a very long while. "It's very short." This struck her as a laughably, incongruously inconsequential thing for him to want to do, at this moment.

"The tapedeck's on your side of the bed," she reminded him.

"I know. It's already in there."

"Play it for me, then."

DRING-DRING-DRING-DRING-DRING . . . that bell—it was exactly like the one in her high school's corridors between classes, it was too harsh, too loud, it was horrible, and it went on ringing, she'd lost count, but at least ten times. And then Jake's voice:

"Hiroshima, Nagasaki—and Minamata, Japan. Bikini, Johnson, Enewetak, and Rongelap Atolls. Bhopal, India. Chernobyl, Ukraine. Servezo, Italy. Yucca Flat, Nevada. Hanford, Washington. Rocky Flats, Colorado. St. George, Utah. Weldon Spring and Times Beach, Missouri. The whole Savannah River region of South Carolina and Georgia. Oak Ridge, Tennessee. Love Canal and West Valley, New York. Three Mile Island, Pennsylvania. Fernald, Ohio. You know these names, and you know this list could be a hundred times as long. Different places, different specific causes, but they all had this in common: nobody told those people anything, until it was too late. I'm telling *you* right now: everyone inside this Chamber has just been exposed to atomic radiation—"

"*No!*" she screamed, or whispered, she had no idea which. He'd clicked the thing off now, though, enabling her to say, in an almost normal voice, but as if to a child: "No, Jake, you can't do that."

"I'm going to. The night after tomorrow. Wait, it's tomorrow already—the night after tonight, then, I guess I mean. It'll be on TV. Which you don't even own, so maybe it won't matter."

"How can you make jokes? This *isn't* any joke, is it?"

"I don't know, call it gallows humor. There really is such a thing, I'm finding. But you've got to be right up there on that scaffold to appreciate it . . . but no, it isn't any joke. Unless it doesn't work, doesn't do anything to help the situation. Then it *will* be a joke, a bitter one, and not just on me."

She was silent. After another short while, he asked, "Can I—will you let me try to play the rest of it and to tell you about it? I don't have much time left." Not in any sense. "I've got to leave no later than three-thirty."

She let him try—and then was sorry, as she'd known she would be. Ignorant, she could see it so clearly. Filled with his words and ideas, she grew confused.

"You can't do that—I mean, you can't think about remission in that way. It doesn't translate."

"How do you know that?"

She just knew, that's all. She couldn't begin to say how. But she had to try. "It doesn't work like that, it's not the same. You can't treat human beings like cancerous cells!"

"That's not what I'm doing. I'm trying to wake them up."

"You're acting out of *anger*—you don't want anyone else to go on living, if *you* can't."

"That isn't true, you know it isn't. I want *you* to—I want the human race to keep on running, I want this poor poisoned planet to grow whole and well again. And I'll die content, I know I will, if I can only find some reason to believe that I've done something toward making that happen."

"You want to save humanity from itself. That's even worse than honest anger. You're acting out of an insane desire to live forever in people's gratitude."

". . . Why is that insane?"

— Got him there, she thought. Made him falter, made him doubt himself for a moment. Got to keep my eyes open, my brain working, I can talk him out of this yet. "Because you'll stop at nothing to accomplish it. You're forgetting basic principles, you're. . . ." She was running out of rhetoric, or was it simply out of energy? What time was it now? Past three, it had to be. . . .

"What am I forgetting?" he asked.

"That two wrongs, or a million, can't make a right!"

"That's neat logic, but reality's never that simple, you know it isn't, you're only trying to stop me any way you can because what I'm about to do offends some abstract moral sense you've never stopped to question since some sanctimonious Sunday School teacher drummed it into your head. You're not thinking at all about whether or not this *could* work, are you?"

"Jake, I just know it's *wrong*—and there's nothing abstract about it!" Hopping over there on her good leg, she plucked the snapshot out of the corner of the dresser mirror and hopped back, thrusting it out toward him, commanding him to look at it, but he wouldn't do it. "You see this young woman? I want to tell you something: I love her! And she's one of hundreds of completely innocent people who'll be in that place Tuesday night! You have no way of knowing how you might affect her life! She could die of leukemia like you, or develop tumors like me, or—"

He wanted her to believe he wasn't, but he was hearing every word. He'd retrieved his cassette, he was putting his clothes on now. He had to leave. He looked so thin and pitiful in the night light's ivory glow. So weary and sick and . . . no, he wasn't angry anymore, he was beyond it, beyond her and all her powers to persuade him. He was off to keep his appointment with his tomb.

He didn't stoop to kiss her, he didn't say goodbye. He glanced back from the doorway momentarily, and was gone.

It seemed only minutes later, but thinking back afterward, Nora realized she must've slept then for at least a couple hours, until she was dragged back up out of her total exhaustion to find a man she'd never seen before leaning over her bed, whispering urgently, telling her that Suzanne was in terrible danger, and only she, Nora, could save her. It wasn't a dream, and he was extremely convincing. And overnight, her world had become a place filled with desperate summonses and terrible dangers.

She agreed to meet him in the Cathedral parking lot as soon as she could get there. Then he vanished.

No, it wasn't any dream. She sat up, shook her head—hard—to try and clear it, hauled herself down to the foot of the bed where she could reach into her bureau, and methodically but quite quickly began to get dressed.

❖

It was the longest and most miserable night Eric could recall in his entire life, even with the black plastic tarp he'd finally remembered and taken a chance to run and get around two-thirty from behind the pickup seat.

He saw Jake leave by Nora's kitchen door at 3:45, saw that Gil had seen Jake, too. But Gil didn't leave then, so Eric didn't either; he stayed where he was, shivering and dripping. After another two hours, Gil got out of his car again, strolled around the block (but didn't stray from the sidewalks, so he didn't discover Eric behind the neighbor's bamboo), then walked straight up Nora's driveway, around to the back of her house, and slipped in through the same door.

Only minutes later, while Eric was still debating with himself whether or not to follow him inside, Gil came out again and resumed his waiting pose behind the wheel of the Plymouth. A quarter-hour after that, Nora's front door opened and she came swinging across the lawn on her crutches, climbed into her Chevette, and tried to drive away immediately, without letting it warm up, stalling it twice before she got it down the driveway. Chevette owners would know better, Eric realized, unless something very urgent crowded that knowledge out of mind. . . .

As soon as Nora was out of sight, Gil took off, in the same direction. Eric ran the two blocks back to the Dodge and did the same, but there was no one in sight when he reached the corner where he had to choose, right or left. Downtown, he decided, by the shortest route. Just when he'd become convinced that he'd guessed wrong—he should've headed for Canal Road—he sighted the Plymouth again, two blocks ahead on Massachusetts Avenue.

At Wisconsin, Gil signaled and turned sedately into the National Cathedral grounds. Eric didn't dare to make the turn so soon after him, he'd be much too noticeable. So he drove on past—then missed the next possible right at 36th Street, and discovered he couldn't turn again until he'd gone all the way to the Naval Observatory. Racing back out Massachusetts, he came abreast of the Cathedral once more just in time to spot the Plymouth turning back into the quickly increasing flow of work-bound traffic, and to catch a glimpse of Nora's pale gold head there behind the windshield now, beside Gil's black wig.

Determined not to lose them again, Eric made a U-turn at the next red light against a barrage of furious horns. But he knew he couldn't stay close behind for very long, or Gil would certainly recognize the Dodge. Gil was poking along in the slower lane now, not trying to make time, so Eric attempted to stay hidden behind a bakery van. That was a mistake: he got caught in a tangle of trucks near Third Street, and by the time he was moving again, the Plymouth was nowhere to be seen.

Five minutes later, waiting impatiently for the light at North Capitol and wondering just what the hell to do next, he glanced up ahead and there went Gil, in a hooded red nylon windbreaker now but definitely him, jaywalking across the avenue toward Union Station, two blocks away. Time for another quick decision: Eric cut across in front of two thru-traffic lanes just as the light was changing and turned left, left again on New York Avenue, and roared up Sixth Street to "M." The rented Corsica was in the middle of the block where Jake said he'd leave it for Eric to return sometime today, and the keys were on top of the left front tire, hidden by the fender. There weren't any empty parking spaces in sight, though, so he had to double-park the Dodge, pull the Corsica out, then squeeze the truck into that space somehow, while other drivers yelled and shook their fists at him.

Even so, he was back at Union Station in less than ten minutes— but now what? The Plymouth ought to be parked somewhere over there at the base of Capitol Hill, he figured, that's where Gil must've been coming from. But a quick cruise through that area didn't reveal it, and Eric's next move would've been to swing around the oval pickup area in front of the terminal, out of pure desperation. It was a good thing someone cut in front of him before he could do that because this was precisely when Gil reappeared, in horn-rimmed glasses, knit cap, and a different jacket—a garish green-and-yellow thing—lugging a brass-bound brown metal suitcase. He used the crosswalk this time, then rubbernecked his way like some tourist who'd just hit town to the corner of Louisiana and New Jersey, with Eric in the Corsica dawdling along a cautious block and a half behind him.

And there was the Plymouth, in plain sight, at a parking meter, with Nora still sitting in it: Eric realized he must've driven blindly right past her a couple of minutes before. There was an empty slot three cars behind it, and he backed into that space now to be less noticeable.

Gil opened the trunk, tossed the suitcase inside, shut the lid again and locked it, then climbed back into the driver's seat and turned to face Nora, whose door swung open a few inches as she appeared to be giving him some kind of argument. But that didn't last very long; soon she leaned back into her corner of the front seat, and Gil reached across, closed her door again, then started his motor, looked up at his rear-view mirror—while Eric quickly ducked down behind the Corisca's dashboard—and swung back out into traffic at first opportunity, headed for Rhode Island Avenue.

The rain had stopped, of course, as soon as they left Glen Echo, and enough bleary sunlight was leaking through the cloud cover to cast weak shadows now. Thanks to the heater, Eric's clothes were almost dry by this time, and he'd finally stopped shivering. But he couldn't remember the last time he'd eaten anything, and his bladder felt ready to explode. Something very strange and ominous was going on, though, that wasn't going to wait while he dealt with those little personal problems. And until he learned a good deal more about it than he knew now, he'd just have to grit his teeth and hang on, somehow. . . .

❖

Suzanne, at that moment, was as uncomfortable as Eric, in all those various ways, and then some. At least he was warm now, and he knew where he was, if not where he was headed or what was going on. All she knew was that she was in this room somewhere.

It was a perfectly normal room, except that it was as tall as it was square—about ten feet—and had only one door, heavy steel but painted chalk-white like all four walls, with nothing but a keyhole where the knob should've been. And no windows, just a little vent slot up at the ceiling in one corner. And the floor was white, too, but rubber-tiled, sloping slightly to a small drain in the middle with a perforated chromed-brass cover. And the only light was the cold glare of eight long fluorescent tubes set into the middle of the also white, acoustic-tiled ceiling. And there seemed to be no source of heat—it was forty degrees, at most. And until five minutes ago there had been nothing whatsoever in there beside Suzanne herself, crouched on her bare heels in the corner farthest from the door, hugging her bare knees and shivering in her leotard.

— Come to think of it, *nothing* about this room was normal, was it? She must be losing her marbles already. . . .

She had no notion of what had become of the rest of her clothes or of anything else—including where this room might be—because they'd crammed those tight-fitting sunglasses with black tape inside the lenses over her face as soon as the guy with the gun shoved her into the back of the limo. At least her fleeting impression was *this-is-a-limo*, but she wasn't even really sure of that much: he'd twisted her left wrist around into the small of her back and pushed her at a quick trot down a long dark echoing corridor and through a fire exit, and suddenly there was dazzling daylight and this car door swung open right in front of her, and in she went, headfirst onto the floor, then yanked around, slammed back against the seat, and those blinders jammed on. She never even glimpsed a face; all she knew was that there were at least three of them by then, counting whoever drove that thing, and that the two guys flanking her were at least as big and twice as strong as she was.

She had no idea of how long a trip it had been to wherever she now was, either, because when she'd recovered enough of her senses to suspect that they weren't feds (then immediately to wish they *were* feds, because if they weren't, what were they, what was going on, and what was going to happen to her?) and then noticed that they were avoiding talking in front of her (and immediately clutched at the straw of hope implicit in that: it might mean they didn't plan to kill her when they were done doing whatever they were going to do)—as soon as she'd gotten that far, she'd felt her jacket sleeve slit open, something twisted tight around that arm above the elbow, then the needle going straight into a vein . . . and about twenty minutes ago, she guessed, she'd wakened here, stripped to her underwear, shivering, thirsty and hungry, with this jackhammering headache.

If it weren't for the headache, she could be trying to figure out what it was all about. She still wasn't totally sure that she wasn't in the hands of some sort of government agency . . . however inexplicable its purpose, there was an unmistakably institutional quality about that room . . . doping her out instead of reading her rights to her didn't signify anything, she was sure; when it came to the sort of action she and Jake and the rest of them were attempting, those career fascists would feel justified in boiling her in oil if they thought it could prevent such a heinous desecration of what they held so holy . . . and who or what else could it—*damn* this headache! Pursuing any idea anywhere was like benchpressing hundreds of pounds!

Abruptly, Suzanne almost remembered something Gil had said a while back about getting nabbed: *It's like crossing that great divide, you're gone, and the rest of us will see you no more, but we'll fear your ghost forever. . . .* Almost: Gil's words flashed through her mind, through her misery, but as if they were spelled out in flickering lights, running around the top of that stupid building in Times Square, and they were gone before she could begin to recall what they meant, or how they fit with what had been there just before. . . .

— I've *gotta* do some thinking, I've got to make a plan, she'd tried to tell herself, but all that automatic admonition produced was another uninvited memory-flash, this time a Shel Silverstein cartoon she'd cracked up over, years ago: two ragged, wretched prisoners spread-eagled high up on a dungeon wall by heavy chains on wrist and ankle irons, one whispering to the other, "Now here's my plan. . . ."

Yeah, funny, ha-ha. Look, I haven't *gotta* do anything right now but try to stay alive and sane, and to empty my bladder very, very soon—over that drain, if there's no alternative. . . .

But then, five minutes ago, just as she was finally going to haul herself up and go out to the middle of the floor and do what she had to do, a slit in the door at about eye-level that she hadn't noticed until then clacked open and shut. Moments later, the whole door swung slowly inward and a hairless monster of a man in baggy gray sweats clumped into the room. He must've been close to seven feet tall, closer still to three hundred pounds—but he looked even bigger than that from down there on the floor—with a long, lumpy skull and a boulder-jawed face almost the same gray as his clothing and just as expressionless.

It took her several seconds to notice what he was carrying: a roll of masking tape in one bowling-ball-sized fist and a manila folder stuffed full of photographs in the other. He ignored her presence completely as he went about his business; she had to scoot out of his way when he got that far or he would've stepped on her, or so she believed. His business consisted of sticking up fifteen-by-twenty glossies side by side, a yard or so above the floor, all the way around the walls, doing it as fast as if he were getting paid piecework, not paying much attention to how even or level they were. From where she was, she couldn't make out a single picture through the reflected glare, and she'd be damned before she'd give him the satisfaction of seeing her show curiosity. When he got all the way around to the door again, he did finally turn and squint at her—with eyes as beady as an iguana's—before grunting, in a voice like the lowest playable notes on a tuba, "Better not tear 'em down," and while she was still telling herself, That can't be all he's going to do, he silently let himself out again.

Ever since then, that slit had stayed open. So she still felt ready to explode, as well as frozen, starved, and dangerously dehydrated. And her headache was, if anything, worse. But her rage and righteous indignation were fast overshadowing all of those discomforts: what in hell was this about, when were they going to tell her what they wanted from her?

Eventually Suzanne realized she couldn't *not* look at those photographs forever, even if that monster was watching her through that slit. And she definitely couldn't hold her bladder in check for much longer. So she drew herself up, gradually, until the lights no longer totally blocked out the three nearest photos on her left. That first glance nearly cost her whatever still remained in her stomach, but it couldn't keep her from looking at more and more of them, and finally at every single one. They weren't predominantly pictures of women; it only seemed that way to her because those were the ones that struck with the greatest velocity and impact.

They were grainy, black-and-white, high-contrast, distinctly unlovely close-ups of naked human beings. Most showed segments only: bowed or bent-back head and pinioned shoulders, or slack belly and swatch of pubic hair, or flabby, pimpled buttocks, or skinny legs with varicose veins and pale misshapen feet with ingrown toenails—portion after portion of exposed, defenseless, pathetically anonymous human bodies in the course of being subjected to cruelties the likes of which Suzanne might have vaguely heard, or seen briefly mentioned somewhere, but had never really thought about, and certainly never wanted to *see.*

As with her headache, there was no conceivable way it could get worse, the next horror couldn't possibly be more horrible than the last one, but it always was. She lost track, they seemed to repeat, or else she was going around the room more than once. She never made it to the drain and scarcely noticed the trickle down both legs, even when it became a scalding gush. She'd also forgotten how cold, hungry, and thirsty she was. There was no room in her mind any longer for anything but fear.

23 : TURNPIKE

"Nice nap?" Gil asked, smiling into their reflections on the windshield, not taking his eyes off the road.

Nora had been conscious for some time now, but trying not to let on. They were on I-95 North, she knew that much; they'd just passed an on-ramp and the usual cluster of signs. Blah-gray sky out there, a very nothing sort of weather, but she'd guessed it was about noon. Cars all around them like fish swimming smoothly along in a school, speedometer showing a safe, steady 65 MPH—should she roll down her window and scream for help?

A glance at all those zombies in the neighboring lanes told her that was hopeless. Maybe at the next toll booths, then: jump out (fall out, she meant—let's be realistic about this), create a ruckus? It was an idea . . . what if he went to one of those exact-change lanes, though, so there wouldn't be any tolltakers handy? She'd have to create an even bigger ruckus then, that's all . . . but for now at least, she thought she might as well behave herself, try to be civil, talk to this person, see if she couldn't learn something useful. "What did you drug me with?"

"The very nicest thing you can put in a needle: top-grade morphine."

"Morphine doesn't work instantaneously like that. And I didn't feel any needle." And she wasn't bruised or sore anywhere. But now that she was looking for one, she saw there *was* a neat little mark on the inside of her forearm. She'd had plenty of RNs make a worse job of it.

"Nope, that was my thumbs first. Properly applied, there's nothing quicker. A little trick I learned in G-Man school."

"You're not FBI."

He looked across at her, smiled again, apparently decided to abandon that gambit. "'Fraid not, lady. Though I've been accused of same, more'n once, and nobody's ever proved I wasn't." An even broader smile this time, but nothing menacing about it. Under different circumstances, she'd have to call it cheeky but quite charming. "So

• 262 •

who am I, then? And where d'you suppose we're going? D'you wanna play that game?"

"No," she said. "You'll only tell me more lies."

"Nope, I won't, honest-injun. I'm Suzanne's Good Friend Gil, just as you're her Good Friend Nora, and we're on our way to New York to try and figure out what happened to her yesterday. That much is gospel, cross my heart and hope to turn Republican."

"Supposing it is, I don't see how I can help you find her in New York."

"Ah, that's the part I *did* fib a little bit about. True enough, you won't be a lot of assistance up there. But at least I won't be distracted from the search by worry that you just might decide to tell that little bed-time story our other mutual friend told you last night to those nice men you spent the whole day with a couple months ago."

". . . I don't know what you're talking about."

"Oh-ho, now whose nose is growing longer? Yes, indeedy, you do too know! I *knew* you knew, the moment you opened those lovely Willow-ware-blue orbs and gazed up at me this morning. Before then, even. When I first stepped inside your house, I could *smell* everything you and Jake said to each other. No kidding, I can really do that. Not all the time, maybe, but when it's something important that got said, I can. It's a survival mechanism: one of the ways I manage to stay alive and free and usually at least one step ahead of everybody else."

— What was he driving at, anyhow? She couldn't begin to guess yet, but he didn't seem to be outright lying to her anymore. Was he simply trying to impress her? If so, he certainly had a strange way of going about it.

"Then when you agreed right off the bat to help me save Suzanne, that was the clincher. If Jake didn't come right out and tell you that part, you figured out for yourself that she's mixed up in this little caper, too, didn't you? Otherwise, you certainly would've asked a whole bunch of questions before racing off with a complete stranger who'd just walked into your bedroom and tickled you awake. Isn't that right?"

"I must've trusted you because your voice was familiar. You've called and asked for her a few times, haven't you? So I knew you had something to do with Suzanne. Of course, I didn't stop to think it through, I was still half asleep."

Gil's look now was wholly admiring. "Great try, kid, but no ceegar. I've never talked to her on your phone—the govs've got enough prints of my voice already, thanks very much. But look, there's a couple of things we've gotta get straight before this next toll plaza, or you're gonna find yourself taking yet another nap. So listen closely, please.

"First thing to be understood: I don't go around hurting people I like if I can help it, and I like *you,* I really do. Secondly, you should understand that if you blow the whistle on Jake, Suzanne's going to get dead in a nastier way than either of us would care to imagine. I know you don't think very much of *me* at the moment, but if you could meet the folks who've almost certainly got *her,* you'd think I was Mohandas K. Gandhi.

"There's more, but that covers the basics. So, to summarize: you try to get loose and stop Jake, no way that's not gonna be screaming news at this point, and the minute those guys hear it, they'll turn Suzanne into salami and split. Is that perfectly clear? Another thing: if *any*body's gonna save Suzanne's ass, it's yours truly. Now think hard about all this, then think up some way to prove to me that I can trust you, okay?"

Gil's sincerity throughout that speech was quite convincing in itself, but while he was talking, Nora had found another good reason for cooperating with him, at least for the moment. Leaning forward for an all-out blow into the last of her clean tissues, she'd discovered that she could see the cars behind them in the outside mirror on her door, and there was a cinnamon-brown Ford Corsica switching lanes just then, half a dozen cars back—and that was what Eric had been driving the second time she'd seen him this morning, when the Plymouth was parked on New Jersey and Gil was inside Union Station checking, he said, in case Suzanne had somehow made a morning train or left a message.

Actually, she'd seen Eric only that once. The other occasion had been earlier, on Massachusetts, when she'd noticed the Dodge pickup behind them in traffic and had wondered sleepily where she'd seen one exactly like it recently, royal blue with sky blue trim. The answer clicked into place later when she spotted Eric in the Ford, so intent, so clearly searching for someone or something. She might've called out—*Here I am, it's me you're looking for, isn't it?*—but she still hadn't quite made up her mind yet how she felt about Gil. . . .

If that *was* Eric again back there, she didn't want to be rendered unconscious now, whatever it took to convince Gil she wouldn't try to escape. Even if it wasn't, Nora loathed needles, hated the very idea of them poking through her skin. In her mind at least, it was almost as bad as being raped. Nothing for it then but to go on talking to this man. But she knew it wouldn't work if she were suddenly to become all agreeable and acquiescent.

"Tell me something. Why are you wearing that ridiculous wig? Don't you realize how unreal you look in it?"

He definitely blushed as he took the silly thing off and tossed it into the back seat. "I've always loved disguises, I guess that's the only honest reply. But one of life's bitterest lessons is that even what's most fun can become a stupid habit. I was better at it out West. Wish you could've seen me in my small-rancher-in-town-for-shopping-day outfit: Tony Lama lizards ever-so-slightly worn down at the heel, aging but creaseless pearl-gray Stetson, Levis with a Copenhagen circle worn almost through the right hip pocket, pigskin vest, and—here's the brilliant part—a *madras* shirt just to make me a little bit different, for that real authentic touch . . . would you hand me that big plastic bottle, pretty-please, that's in the glove compartment?"

She'd been right, he headed for an exact-change lane, steering with his left knee as he shook some copper-colored disks the size of quarters out, rolled his window down, and tossed them into the chute. The occupied booths looked practically soundproof anyhow, the attendants in them bored beyond the ability to notice anything short of the Second Coming.

". . . Why'd you get me to drive into Washington to meet you? Wasn't that taking quite a chance, that I'd wake up enough to think it over and decide not to go?"

"Didn't wanna leave your car sitting there in your driveway and you not at home, too suspicious. I was waiting up the street, and I'd fixed your phone before I woke you so you couldn't call out. Actually, it was just laziness. I could've put you out right there, moved your car myself, walked back, and collected you."

"You didn't do anything to my phone. I used it to call my office, to leave a message that I wouldn't be in—but the machine there was all messed up, as usual."—I didn't have to tell him that last part, she realized, a moment too late. He hadn't heard it, though; he was too embarrassed by the way she'd caught him out.

"Well, I meant to. Must've slipped my mind, somehow."

She'd bet the truth of the matter was he didn't know how to "fix" a phone, short of cutting the cord. But it wouldn't do to needle him; she should say something soothing. "That wasn't quite right about your being lazy, either. I'll bet you just love taking chances."

That brought back his grin. "Any way I did it, lady, there'd be chance involved. Chance is what life is all about. Now let me ask you one: what *do* you think of good ol' Jake's bright idea?"

He'd sprung that question too quickly for Nora to keep all the truth off her face. The best she could manage was: ". . . I'm afraid it won't work . . . it won't change anything."

"I'll go along with that first part, if by 'work' you mean 'make the government see reason.' But your second assertion doesn't necessarily follow, you know. It can't help but change things, it's bound to up the ante somehow."

"What's your part in this?"

"Who, me? How d'you know I've got any? Why can't I be just another innocent bystander, like you?"

"Because there's nothing innocent about you."

"Oh, come now, Miz Sherman, that's a bit unkind, don't you think? I'm just a catalyst."

"— A what?" She'd been blowing her nose again, and trying for another quick squint at the mirror; and yes, that brown Ford was still back there. "Did you say what I thought you said—you're 'just a capitalist'?"

"Ha! Okay, sure, that, too—I've never seen anything very wrong with 'unfettered competition,' there's always some cute way around it. But what I said was *catalyst*. I just help things to happen, that's all, just coax 'em along whenever and however I can, by providing little missing links. Good things, I mean, at least in my opinion—like Jake's show, now, I thought that was worth a tithe. In any case, it'll Further the Process."

"What 'process'?"

"Would you snicker if I said Perpetual Revolution? I know, it's not a very trendy political concept nowadays. But it was good enough for Tom Jefferson—that's where Leon Trotsky swiped it from—and it's good enough for me."

"I don't understand you . . . at all."

"You wanna know something? I don't always understand myself. I don't even try, most of the time. There's seldom any percentage in it. Most human motives don't bear thinking about—and when they can pass moral muster, they're still in a state of constant flux, and any attempt to nail 'em down is inevitably doomed. . . ."

He simply liked hearing himself talk, Nora decided; he didn't seem to care whether she made any response or not. Or no, that probably wasn't true, or he wouldn't be making so many outrageous statements. They'd gone through another couple of toll plazas, they were on the Jersey Turnpike already, and he was rambling on about his philosophy or modus operandi or whatever, which he called 'winging it':

". . . True, there's sometimes a lot of wasted motion in the Improvisation Biz, since you can't ever really tell where you're headed until you get there. But the sweet corollary to that is, no one *else* can tell, either. And if you ain't got no plan, nobody's gonna be able to thwart it. . . ."

"Could we please stop somewhere soon?" Nora asked. "I'm starving, and I've got to use a bathroom."

"Hm. I could eat, too, come to think of it, and it looks like we've got less'n a quarter-tank left."

"Oh, good!" Nora said, pointing to a sign flying by that promised a service area just two miles farther up the road.

"Nope, I don't think we'll do that. But tell ya what, I'll take the next exit, see if we can't find us a little village diner where it'll be easier for me to keep an eye on you."

"Why? I can't run away! I thought you said you were going to trust me."

"Oh, I'm trusting you, all right. I'm just not about to *tempt* you too much, that's all."

As they swooped down the off-ramp, Nora risked a look across Gil's line of vision as the cinnamon-colored Corsica passed by and yes, it *was* Eric; he'd swung over into the right-hand lane, too, but didn't follow them off the Turnpike. She wouldn't let that worry her, though, he must know what he's doing, and she was positive he'd seen where they'd gone. He'd come this far; he certainly wouldn't desert her now. . . .

Darkness. Silence. Jake's elbows lay against his ribs, but both hands touched wood, and wood again, just inches above his chest. A few seconds' panic, the fleeting preconscious notion that he'd been buried alive; then he recalled where he was, and why. Almost that bad, not quite: the catafalque, Papa George's rejected tomb . . . another middle-aged American, a clearly more successful one in most ways, but he'd had much worse troubles with *his* dentures . . . a most middle-class, middle-of-the-road, muddle-through-it-somehow sort of revolutionary, our George the First . . . can't help wondering what he'd think, though, of what this nation's become, and of what I'm trying to do about it. . . .

The darkness inside that box was total. The space wasn't a great deal more than there would be in a coffin, but there was sufficient ventilation, food, water, even Simon's collapsible bedpan gadget with self-sealing disposable containers: everything necessary to survive undetected in there for days . . . in theory, anyway . . . how long've I been inside this thing, so far? Jake lifted his left wrist to his face. *1:47:32p* and *1/22 Mo*, the glowing green dots said when he finally remembered how to punch the button. It took what seemed like several minutes more to compute the almost nine hours since—that's *all*? . . . then I'm not even a quarter of the way there . . . Jesus but it's gotten hot, I can't think, can't even breathe!

Because both my nostrils are completely plugged, that's why, and my whole throat's aflame. I've got a hell of a fever, too—Christ, I've caught another bug, *I need those antibiotics.* . . .

Then he remembered again where his antibiotics were: on the dashboard of that rented Corsica he'd driven in from Glen Echo twenty hours earlier and parked at Sixth and M Streets. Of all the incredible things to forget! He'd remembered them at the corner of Massachusetts Avenue, though; he'd turned around and started to run back there, when a prowl car out of nowhere blocked his path, and he was charged with crossing against the light—at 4:26 in the pitch-black, drizzly morning, not another waking human for miles around, he'd bet. Which was why those two cops had nothing better to do than deliver a ten-minute wisecrack-studded joint lecture on pedestrian-caused accidents before writing out, then tearing up, a ticket. "See, ain't we good guys?" And then there wasn't enough time to go back all that way; he'd promised to meet Edwards at precisely 4:50.

Shit!—if he's got a virus coming on now, it could easily kill him by tomorrow night, as quickly as that other one so very nearly did, before Eric got him to that hospital in Banning. And if he's got one, he knows exactly where he caught it. So maybe Nora *will* stop him, after all—but don't think about Nora or you'll bring it all back, everything she said . . . *No, Jake, you can't do that. It doesn't translate.* . . .

But it does! It's got to!

Don't begin again, for godsake—for your own sake. You haven't got the strength or the clarity to argue that or anything any further.

You've spent too much time already, trying to answer her objections and everybody else's, trying to get it down on paper, all of it that wouldn't fit into those twenty-five seconds of tape . . . and even more time wrestling with the ineluctable truth that this isn't really your own act, isn't much like what you'd imagined it ought to be—it's just the *available* act, the one that happened to cross your path in time, just the best you can do, that's all . . . and then with the fact that, left to your own initiative, without Gil's intervention, without his and Simon's, Edwards', Suzanne's, and Eric's help, you wouldn't be doing anything more significant right now than wandering around the country, searching for any shreds of evidence that you ever existed, until you're hauled into some other emergency ward somewhere, most likely a little too late, next time. . . .

But nobody ever gets anywhere without a lot of mostly gratuitous help from others—or ever gets exactly where they wanted to be, either, for precisely that reason. And there aren't, there never were, any ought-to-bes, you damn-sure ought to know *that* much about real life by this time—*Christ! Will you stop it!* Too late now, pal, for all this goddamn wheel-spinning! What you've gotta be focused on from here on out is simply how you're gonna hold yourself together without those antibiotics, just long enough—you absolutely cannot start playing will-I-won't-I now; too many people've put their own lives on the line to get you this far. The best you can hope to do anymore is just to keep it all on track. . . .

They'd left the Turnpike at Swedesboro, but Gil meandered on nearly to Mickleton before he happened on something that suited both his fancy and Nora's disability: an aluminum-clad diner with only a single three-inch step out front for her to negotiate, and an Exxon station right next door. "If you're gonna burn this stuff at all," he growled when the elderly attendant finished topping off the tank, "I figure you might as well buy it from the biggest pigs in the business."

The diner was otherwise empty, except for a sad-eyed man in a plaid mackinaw hunched over an empty coffee cup at the end of the counter and a peroxided, gum-chewing waitress doing crossword puzzles on the stool beside him. Gil ordered the dinner menu special— fresh ham steak with apple sauce, lima beans, and whipped potatoes— plus a chocolate malted and coffee. Nora had the Belgian waffles and was sorry; the "maple" syrup was nine-tenths corn. But she didn't complain, she was good as gold—except for the note she scrawled with her eyebrow pencil on a paper towel and left stuck to the mirror in the ladies' with a sliver of soap. That was on her second trip into the cramped and very difficult, one-at-a-time toilet, just before they left. "So you won't have to stop again anytime soon," she told Gil.

They'd sat in the booth nearest the door, practically underneath the old-fashioned wall pay phone. After he'd ordered, Gil stood up and reached around to make a call, and before he turned his back, she'd distinctly heard him say, "Hi, Mercy, Gil here, how's everybody, and is John handy, by any chance?"

She'd folded the note up like an envelope, and printed on the outside, in as sane and severe a hand as she could manage with her implement:

> *Please Give This To The Young Man*
> *Who'll Come Asking About Me*
> *His Name is ERIC*

The message inside wasn't much longer:

> *He says we're going to NYC to find Suzanne. He*
> *called Mercy and John—does that help? He*
> *doesn't know about you. Be careful.*

While Gil was calling Meredith from Mickleton, Nora's phone was ringing back in Glen Echo. And ringing. Ruthellen, at home in Georgetown, couldn't understand why the answering machine wasn't switched on. Nora was really good about always doing that before she left the house. And also why, if Nora wasn't there to answer it, she wasn't at the performing arts center, either, and hadn't called in sick. Or anyhow, Ruthellen had been told Nora hadn't—but such things didn't always get officially noted there, she knew, when Nora wasn't present to see to it that they were. And the phone company insisted there wasn't anything wrong with Nora's home line—Ruthellen had already called the number where they check that for you, over an hour ago. . . .

Well, maybe Nora was being sensible for a change, and she'd taken that terrible cold of hers to a doctor, and since she had no appointment she was spending most of the day parked in some waiting room, leafing through old *Vanity Fairs*. All Ruthellen could do was keep trying, even if that made it impossible to get anywhere with the four book reports she was supposed to turn in as soon as school began again next week, if she wanted as much as a C+ in English for the semester. But she *had to* get hold of Nora by this evening, or her mother was going to feel duty-bound to tell Heather—that Jell-O-head!—to go ahead and tell her roommate Tracy—who was even more of a Jell-O-head—that *she* could have Bruce's seat at the State of the Union, instead of Nora.

Freshman congressman that he was, Ruthellen's father said he'd had to do "some real old-fashioned old-boying," but he managed to get hold of four seats in the visitors' gallery. Bruce was Ruthellen's usually quite intelligent brother, and Heather was the stick he'd unaccountably gotten himself engaged to. Bruce was stationed at Fort Belvoir, just down the Potomac from Mount Vernon, so he'd been sure he could attend—but then yesterday, without warning, Bruce's special unit, whatever it was (he was always letting on it was *very* special), had been ordered to Ecuador. Bruce, of course, had been completely zipper-lipped to his kid sister about where they were going, but he never could tell credible fibs to their mother, and Ruthellen had just happened to be on the line last night when Mrs. Vliorishevski confided to her best friend back in Georgia how extremely worried she was. . . .

That made eighteen rings this time, she'd been counting as she prayed for an answer (pretending all the while that she wasn't really, just wishing hard—Ruthellen had long ago decided she'd outgrown Catholicism, after having had agnosticism and the big-bang theory explained to her by a former music teacher when she was thirteen and a half). Better hang up again, try to get back into *Middlemarch,* and do her best to keep those other vivid images from marching back and forth across the page: Nora cold and white and motionless against her ivory bathroom tiles, Nora sprawled across the terra-cotta linoleum on her kitchen floor. . . .

❖

— Wait, maybe Simon had something with him for colds; he said he'd leave his pocket medicine kit. Switching on the tiny lamp, Jake probed the bulging nylon bags along the splintery catafalque walls, until he located a plastic case the size and shape of a pack of Luckies . . . they definitely wouldn't help, but that, and music, were what he craved most right now: deep, long drags on a cigarette, and his ears full of a

Mahler symphony. Inverting Simon's case on his chest, Jake examined
everything in it, item by item: Motrin for muscle cramp, Valiums,
codeine, dental floss, cotton swabs ... wait, here's three antihistamines; they ought to help with the breathing, at least. . . .

No antibiotics.

Drink some juice, then, with one of these antihistamines right now,
hold off on the other two as long as I possibly can. Better eat something
now, too, try to relax. But his throat was too sore to swallow anything
bigger than that Spansule, or even to chew a piece of the nicotine gum
Suzanne had thoughtfully provided. Try to sleep some more, he told
himself, but he couldn't do that either, and he couldn't turn off the
monologue. Finally he switched the lamp back on and groped for his
spiral-bound notebook. He'd filled even more pages than he remembered, but most were already X'd out. He flipped through until he
found where he'd tried to deal with the issue that Simon had termed
"statistical murder":

> ... *taking at face value computations based on
> half a century of federally sponsored experiments
> and assuming an even distribution (as you'd be
> sure to say in our place, we've done 'everything
> humanly possible' to achieve that), this much
> Pu-239 constitutes a 'minimum dosage,' as cur-
> rently defined in US Nuclear Regulatory
> Commission documents. And even though the
> element is considered to be at least a quarter-
> million times more lethal by weight than
> cyanide, it should cause no apparent injury or
> discomfort to anyone within the Chamber at that
> moment. What this exposure will mean, though,
> is that as a group they'll begin to show slightly
> higher rates for various forms of cancer within
> ten years than would've been the case had they
> not received it. Collectively, they'll have had a
> couple thousand years, give or take a few hun-
> dred, lopped off the sum-total of all their life
> expectancies.*
>
> *'Statistical murder': all right, I'll agree to that
> label being applied to what I'm about to do, but
> only if we also apply it to what governments and*

> *industry go on doing, routinely, year after year,*
> *worldwide, with horrendous impunity. But what-*
> *ever we call it, I'm NOT here to commit retalia-*
> *tory terrorism; I don't believe what I'm doing*
> *qualifies as 'terrorist' in any sense, unless you've*
> *stretched that dirty little word to cover any*
> *means the powerless majority of humankind can*
> *possibly contrive to strike back in the face of*
> *near-certain annihilation. . . .*

No. Not good enough. Wiping his sore, gluey eyes with some toilet paper, uncapping his nylon-tipped pen, Jake turned to the next clean page and prepared to begin again, for what had to be the twentieth time, at least, from the beginning:

> *Consider these pages a footnote to what you'll*
> *have heard, if everything goes as planned before*
> *this notebook becomes public property. Now I've*
> *got to try to give you the rest of my case, or enough*
> *of it that you—I mean everybody in this poor old*
> *poisoned world of ours—will understand that I'm*
> *not acting out of motives of revenge, or even anger*
> *or despair. Desperation, yes, I can't deny that.*
> *But these are desperate times, surely we can all*
> *agree on that much. A hopeful act, as well. . . .*

And neither was that good enough, nowhere near it. Twenty-six hours before I'm out of this box, twenty-nine in all to hang on: and any bug coming on this strong, this fast, is sure to be a real sonofabitch. Nothing for it now but prayer. Jake sincerely wished he could attempt such a feat, in perfect faith, the way he remembered his grandfather doing, on his knees beside his rocking chair, aloud and earnest, head up, eyes open, sublimely confident that he was being listened to, somewhere. . . .

— Dear God, please don't let me die quite yet, not before I *do it*. . . .

Yeah, sure. If there *was* a God, of any sort that gave a good goddamn, I wouldn't have to be here now, would I?

❖

No other cars were leaving the Turnpike at the Swedenboro exit at that moment, and Eric was sure Gil would take a hard look at the Corsica if it followed him off that closely—there hadn't been time to slow down and allow enough space to grow between them. He thought momentarily about pulling over past the on-ramp and waiting there, but again, the risks involved all seemed too great: first, of their not getting back on here; second, of Gil spotting him as they drove past him, if they did; and third, of a cop stopping to find out what Eric was doing parked there. But it was thirteen miles to the Mickleton exit, another thirteen back, and there went half an hour. Only after he'd done that did he finally get to empty his bladder (Eric was sure he'd never leave that raspberry-scented restroom, he'd be pissing there until the end of time) and to grab some nourishment: two half-pints of milk from one vending machine, three Mounds bars from its neighbor.

He spent the next three-quarters of an hour questioning surly pump jockeys and suspicious waitresses: a light gray Plymouth, ten or twelve years old, a blonde woman on crutches, and a man with a mustache—*maybe* a mustache—about so tall? He was able to rattle it all off quite smoothly by the time he walked into the aluminum diner.

The gum-chewer didn't give him a chance to say very much of it, but she looked him up and down with obvious approval before she said, "You're Eric, I betcha," and handed him the paper towel from a shelf beneath the cash register.

"How long ago did they leave?" he asked, as soon as he'd glanced at the message.

"Oh, I dunno, it's been at least twenny minutes."

He guessed then that he'd lost them, but he got back on the Turnpike at Mickleton and drove as fast as he dared, as far as the approaches to the George Washington Bridge, before giving up. There wouldn't be much point to wandering around Manhattan, hoping to spot a gray Plymouth. . . .

The only person Eric could think of who might possibly be able to tell him who and where John and Mercy were was Simon, and Simon couldn't be reached by phone: he was spending his last day and night in the United States with a ladyfriend, he'd said, but not which one, or where. All Eric knew was that he was supposed to meet him tomorrow morning at eight at a grass field near Claggettsville, Maryland, where Simon's antique Beech Bonanza was hangared, and they were going to fly from there to Montreal together on the first leg of their escape.

Reluctantly, Eric headed south again and returned the Ford to the rental company in Washington. That was when he discovered Jake's antibiotics at the bottom of the deep crevice between the windshield and the dashboard, but there wasn't any label on that plastic tube, so he had no way of knowing it was Jake's or what was in it. Then he recovered the Dodge and spent a nervous, lonely night in a shabby motel near West Friendship, Maryland, with nothing but warm Pepsi, terrible take-out pizza, and the umpteenth rerun of *Batman* on the tube for company.

The only good thing Eric could've said at this point for all his efforts over the past thirty-odd hours was they'd left him so exhausted that when he finally fell into bed at 3:30—for the first time since Mt. Shasta—those two forever-falling FBI men weren't waiting there within his private piece of darkness to continue their silent, tireless tumbling act. . . .

24: SNOW

Snow fell as predicted across the Northeast all that night and the next morning:

Gigantic orange highway department trucks were creeping along I-70 West with their plow-blades down, spraying sand or salt behind them, as Eric and Simon converged on Claggettsville. Four pristine inches blanketed the field there already, with billions more big, picture-book flakes drifting down out of the breathless, pearly sky. . . .

Manhattan's avenues were merely slick and shiny-black with the melt-off, but less-traveled side streets wore a sooty-edged coating of white this morning, and enough of the powdery stuff had accumulated in Tompkins Square Park, across Tenth Street from the brownstone building where Gil and Nora still lay asleep, to glaze the scuffed gray earth and black arthritic tree limbs, outlining the broken benches, overturned trash baskets, and dozing derelicts with softly glowing haloes, as in some old silver-nitrate photograph. . . .

Most of the Catskills received between two and six inches overnight, but the hills around Meredith hadn't gotten any of it yet. After a lemony, near-zero sunrise, though, the air was now turning warmer and wetter there. A sharp breeze out of the northwest had freshened, and hard crystals like tiny hailstones were beginning to fill depressions in the shrunken, blackened roadside piles remaining from last week's blizzard. . . .

Snow was falling in the Washington area as well, so thickly that Denise Vliorishevski had to turn the heavy-duty wipers on her Bronco III up to high speed to see where she was going along Canal Road, at barely twenty miles an hour. Snow made her very nervous; driving in it was something you never learned how to do in either Saigon or Savannah. Luckily there wasn't much traffic headed out of town at this hour—she pitied those poor folks immobilized nose-to-tail across the guardrails, pointed the other way. At the far end of the seat, Ruthellen chewed on her lower lip (only the right side, the side Denise couldn't see) and rubbed her copies of Nora's keys between her thumb and fore-finger one after the other, almost like a rosary (as soon as she realized *that*, she stopped doing it), wishing very, very hard that everything would be explained, and just fine, when they got to Glen Echo. . . .

At the Capitol Building, janitors were rolling out long black Neo-prene mats at all the entrances, to take up the worst of the slop that thousands of feet would soon be tracking in across the polished marble floors. Down in the sub-basement, inside the catafalque, snow fell in Jake's swirling dreams, too: blinding white crests in the sun along the peaks of the Sangre de Cristos . . . and softer snows from his Penn-sylvania boyhood, the fluffy, friendlier stuff of snowmen and forts and snowball fights . . . mittens and the knees of his thick blue woolen suit soaked, red-and-white-striped scarf trailing behind him, and all the buckles on his black rubber arctics come undone—shoes inside them squishing with each step—he trudges across the orchard, up the porch stairs, into the steamy good smells of his grandmother's kitchen to announce, "I think I've caught a cold, Grammaw," then watches her soft round face disintegrate with deepest sorrow for him, as she waves both floury hands, *goodbye, goodbye.* . . .

The Beech Bonanza was only one-third Simon's. Two friends had put up most of the money several years before, and he'd done almost all the restoration. He hadn't told either partner, but his plan was to fly it to Quebec, put it in storage up there at a little field near Montreal, then direct the bill to them so they'd know where it was, before assuming his new identity and boarding a jet bound for Portugal with Eric. Simon was aware that there were simpler and quicker ways to get to Canada. What he didn't know was when, if ever, he'd acquire another plane of his own—or partly his own, but anyhow one that he could fly himself around in. There was very little he'd done in his life, except for sky-diving, that gave him such a sense of absolute freedom.

Simon devoted less than half an ear now to what Eric had to tell him about Gil and Nora. His mind was mainly on the weather: for most of the morning, he didn't know for sure if he could get clearance to take her up at all. If he did, he realized, it could be—probably would be—instrument-flying much of the way. The predictions were favorable, but even with satellites and all the other wonderful new technology, meteorology was still a long way from being an exact science. This storm system was apparently moving out in a due-northerly direction rather than northeastward as it should've been doing, and they'd be heading almost due north. So they might very well catch up with it again, or it could simply hunker down up there over central New York State or southern Quebec for the rest of the day.

Sure, Simon knew who John and Mercy were, and where they lived—but he couldn't buy the notion that the Meachams could be involved in anything at all nefarious. And the way it sounded to Simon, Gil's phoning them like that, within Nora's hearing, was strong evidence that *he* wasn't up to anything too terrible, either. When Eric produced the note on the paper towel, Simon was quick to point out that Nora hadn't claimed anywhere in it that she'd been kidnapped, or anything of the sort. As a matter of fact, what she'd actually written was: "*we're* going to NYC." And by Eric's own account, hadn't she driven herself into Washington yesterday morning?

Eric just knew what he'd felt then, and felt still. "So why leave me a note at all, or tell me to be careful? And what *did* happen to Suzanne?"

"Beats me. I've never understood what was going on with her, anyway. Maybe she just decided, since her part in this was over, she might as well go into her own vanishing act a few days early. Want me to call John up there in Meredith and ask him what he knows, if anything?"

No, Eric didn't want that. He didn't know what he wanted, exactly, but something was very wrong, or might be, and he didn't like running off like this, without finding out any more about whatever was going on, especially since it involved Nora. That seemed disloyal to Jake.

As Simon kept on pointing out, though, there wasn't any time left to do anything else, unless they wanted to cancel their carefully laid—and also very complicated, and expensive—travel arrangements. And while he didn't say so to Eric, Simon had his own loyalty to Jake to consider: the last chance they'd had to talk alone, at Nora's on Sunday evening, Jake had gotten Simon to promise that, whatever happened, he'd make certain that Eric got safely out of the country before the shit hit the fan. And that was going to be less than twelve hours from right now. Hard as that was to imagine. Simon found himself having trouble believing it was really going to happen, as he watched the sky and waited for it to open up enough to let them take off—and *he'd* set the timer. At precisely 9:28:05 p.m., for no good reason beyond the fact that it had to be precisely something. . . .

It was almost noon before the Bonanza was all checked out, fueled, and cleared for take-off. By then, Eric had something else occupying his mind: he'd never been aloft in any sort of aircraft before. He was aware that millions did it every day, and he knew it was supposed to be safer, statistically, than riding in a car. But he'd never trusted statistics much, and when Simon said Nope, no parachutes—the civil aeronautics board discouraged their use in private planes, understandably preferring that people guide their planes down rather than abandon them to crash into homes or schools or wherever—Eric stopped talking altogether and prepared himself to get through it, since there was no way out now. Once they finally got up there, though, he felt fine—there was no sense of height, or speed either, since you couldn't see a foot beyond the windows.

Simon, however, found it even scarier inside that cotton-wool ocean than he'd expected. He'd done hardly any intrument-flying beyond what was required for his license, and had never enjoyed it—no feeling of freedom then: you're the abject slave of those dials and gauges. But here he was now, more blind than any bat ever was (unless deprived of its sonar), entirely dependent on those quivering indicators, in an aircraft most pilots would say belonged in a museum. Everything still worked, more or less, but a lot of what was displayed there on that hand-rubbed mahogany panel was pretty damned primitive by contemporary standards. And as with any machinery that old (two years older than his Saab, come to think of it), there was no telling how much longer any given part would continue to function properly. As, for instance, the de-icers. That was what worried Simon most, the way the ice kept building up out there on the wingtips. . . .

By the time they were over Scranton, Simon was very nervous. The storm front *had* hung in, precisely as he'd feared, along the New York–Pennsylvania border. Much as he hated to do it, he decided to radio for permission to put down in Binghamton to see what could be done about the accumulating ice. If nothing, maybe they could catch a commercial flight from there to Montreal or else to New York or Newark, where they'd certainly find something that would get them up to Canada. . . .

Landing by instruments was the trickiest part of all, as he knew very well from nearly failing the exam that way, and there was scarcely any better visibility at ground level here than at ten thousand feet. But Simon did it perfectly the first try, by god—there wouldn't have been any difficulty whatsoever if the plow operator hadn't missed one small frozen heap of scrapings where the landing gear first touched the runway.

The Bonanza executed an elephantine pirouette straight out of *Fantasia* before it wobbled, bobbled, shuddered, very slowly tipped forward, then plunged nose-first into a snowbank.

❖

If it was snowing outside, wherever this room was, Suzanne had no intuition of it. Nothing had changed in there since the photos went up on the walls. Except that she'd learned not to look at anything but the floor, the ceiling, or the door. And that she and her leotard must smell ten times worse—she could no longer tell. They'd fed her once, though, if you could call it that: she'd managed to sleep for a while somehow (cried herself to sleep like an abandoned baby, that's how) and woke again when Big Stoop (that's who he reminded her of, the Dragon Lady's bodyguard in the old *Terry and the Pirates* comic strip) reopened the door just far enough to toss in a vaguely familiar white paper bag.

When Suzanne finally decided to creep over and investigate, she couldn't believe the contents: her very own crabmeat-salad-on-kaiser-roll, still neatly wrapped, and her sixteen-ounce Diet Pepsi, unpop-topped. Just looking at them brought it all back, what it felt like to be free, to walk into a deli somewhere and buy whatever you wanted. It took her several minutes to stop sobbing and gulp both down.

The warm Pepsi fizzed all over her face, immediately caused intense gas pains, and made her even more thirsty. And then the sandwich—she had no idea how old it was by this time; it seemed to her like weeks, at least, that she'd been shivering in here. Maybe she'd die of food poisoning. Maybe that was why they'd given it back to her now, so they could get their jollies by watching through that slit while she went into convulsions, or whatever you do with botulism. But she didn't really care anymore, what happened next. . . .

Nothing did happen, in fact, except that she began to sneeze as well as shiver, and to realize both how constipated she must be, and that this was the root cause of her headache. And then, at last, she remembered bodywork. Her thumbs were too cold and stiff to do it really well, but she began to massage the muscles at the base of her skull, across her shoulders and lower back, and it did dramatically ease all her pains—

only temporarily, but enough to reawaken some vague sense of herself, of who and what she'd been, long ago, before she was shut up in this place. And what else did she have to do? So she kept on kneading every muscle she could reach until her arms and hands were the sorest parts of her, and she could fall back into a kind of slumber. . . .

She was weak and giddy but not in quite so much agony when she awoke again. She seemed a little bit warmer, too; or maybe it was just that you can get used to anything, in time . . . and then she smelled the jasmine—olfactory hallucinations?—and saw that she was no longer alone in there. Wearing another super stylish jogging suit (burnt-orange with lime green trim this time), in need of a shave but with that tarnished-silver pompadour of his perfectly in place, Gorgeous George was leaning back against the door, staring straight at her, with a mug of tea clutched in one beringed hand and a key on a brass chain dangling from the other.

Suzanne wished she could claim that she'd already figured out that *he* was who it *would* be; but it was nearer the truth to say the whole question of *why* she was suffering here had receded into the realm of philosophical abstraction.

— Now I'm finally going to learn what it's all about, she did manage to think dimly, but the answer no longer really mattered to her. What *did* matter was that intoxicating scent of jasmine. She couldn't take her eyes off that brimming mug in his fist, except to try to follow the teasing wisps of steam rising from it.

"Just tell me where the rest of 'em are," he said, "and ya get a whole potful. And anything ya wanna eat. And a shower. And yer clothes back. And we letchya go."

". . . The rest of *who*?" she finally managed to whisper. That bit of breath coming out seemed to tear her throat wide open.

"Not who—*what*. And ya know goddamn well what."

"But I *don't*!"

"Ya delivered one of 'em tah *me*, fer fuck's sake!"

". . . Oh. But as far as I knew, that was all there was."

"Okay. Keep on playin' dumb, bitch, and ya'll wind up in our pitcher gallery." He swiftly turned his broad backside to her, stuck the key in the lock and twisted it. All Suzanne could think about was that now he was going to take that warm, wet, delicious-smelling tea away. . . .

❖

Damage to the Bonanza was minimal, considering, and Eric was only shaken up—he'd done worse to himself, any number of times, falling off a horse. But Simon's seat belt had let go somehow, and he came to several minutes later to discover that the goose egg on his forehead wasn't his only souvenir of the experience. He reached up to touch the swelling lump with his right hand and almost passed out again—*fuck!* A busted collarbone and at least a couple of cracked ribs on that side, he quickly realized: it wasn't his first experience with either type of fracture. . . .

Eric rode along in the ambulance to the hospital in downtown Binghamton and paced the emergency ward waiting room while they did their preliminary examination. Naturally enough, the doctors wanted to hold Simon overnight in case he'd suffered a concussion—but Simon wasn't having any of that.

Well, he wasn't going anywhere for several hours yet, a hulking black intern with a gold ankh dangling from one earlobe informed him. Certainly not until they'd done all their X-rays and then taped him up from neck to waist, however urgent his business elsewhere might be—and if he didn't quit cussing the staff out as if it was all *their* fault, they'd claim he'd gone into shock, put him in restraint, and hold him until tomorrow whether he liked it or not. "So just cool it, fella!"

But the intern did allow Eric and Simon to have five minutes of privacy before they put Simon under in order to pin his clavicle back together. "I've been looking at a map," Eric said, "and Meredith is only seventy miles from here. You ever been there, to John and Mercy's place?"

"Nope. All I know is it's got a humungous old barn that John never tires of rattling on about, and it's on Elk Creek Road. But hey, wait a minute—"

"I've gotta find out what's going on. I can rent a car two blocks from here, I've already asked, and it's only four o'clock now. The earliest they'll turn you loose is ten, the guy said—I'll be back long before that. And while I'm at it, I'll see what I can line up to get us out of here tonight. Everything's still grounded now. Buses aren't even running."

. . . So let 'im have his little wild-goose chase, Simon told himself as he ground his teeth and sweated, waiting for whatever they'd administered to do what it was supposed to do, and for the orthopedic surgeon to get his act together.

Eric was a chip off the old Jake block, all right. Once a question got inside that thick skull, it stayed in there until he'd answered it to his own satisfaction. Simon had never pictured himself as anybody's baby-sitter, anyhow . . . thinking about Jake next, though, wondering how *he* was holding up—maybe it was only the drug they'd just administered, but Simon found his eyes were wet, all of a sudden. Christ, but he was gonna miss that old bastard. He felt a big, raw hole looming there inside his mind already, like a freshly missing wisdom tooth. . . .

Step—step—step—step . . . a single leather sole, and in between (inaudible but Jake could easily imagine he was hearing them, too) the rubber tips of metal crutches striking the stone floor. It had to be Nora—she was searching for him, she was coming all the way down here to the sub-basement to thrust that snapshot in his face again, to tell him that he was just another dying human who'd swallow any lie he could tell himself, commit any sort of abomination, merely to inject some febrile illusion of purpose, some vain hope of immortality, into the final moments of his miserable, meaningless little life—

No! Stop it! Sip some more water, turn over for a while, try to clear your lungs, moisten the sponge again and wipe this greasy sweat off your face, take another look at the time: only 3:17 p.m. . . . Christ! I've gotta get *outta* here, gotta stand, gotta stretch out, gotta flex my arms and legs—at least sit up, if only for a second, oh Jesus God, *please!*

This was one problem neither he nor Simon had anticipated. What had that dolphin guy—Lilly?—called it? "Sensory" something . . . "sensory deprivation," that was it. Well, thirty-seven hours of it could turn out to be more than he was good for. . . .

His brand-new driver's license and American Express card—in his brand-new name—worked beautifully. But it was still past five o'clock, and black as midnight out there, by the time Eric was handed the keys to a new white Chevrolet compact. There was nothing four-wheel-drive obtainable anywhere in Binghamton at the moment, he'd called several other places. And no chains for that Chevy, but the rental company had left a flatful of sandbags by the gate, so Eric stopped and tossed half a dozen into the trunk for better traction. And I-88, as far as Oneonta, wasn't bad at all; the weather seemed to be clearing, and the plows had been through recently.

As soon as Eric got onto Route 28, though, and started the long steep climb up out of the Susquehanna Valley, it was an icy nightmare, with vehicles in the ditches every few hundred yards. Meredith was only twelve miles more according to his map, and there was nowhere he could turn around, anyhow, so he just kept going—until the last big hill, up out of Meridale.

He was making it just fine for three-quarters of the way up, until he came around a bend to find a car and a pickup kissing front bumpers, squarely across both lanes. Once he'd touched the brakes there was nothing to do but sit there hanging onto the wheel, sliding sideways, almost completely around, then backward, coming to rest eventually some fifty yards back downhill and at the bottom of a twenty-foot embankment.

It was 7:42 by the dashboard clock. But the map said Meredith was right up there on top of that ridge where he could see a few lights winking through the still thickly falling flakes, and he wasn't giving up this close to his objective. Anyhow, getting back to Binghamton when he'd said he would looked even less feasible. No telling when a wrecker would get here on a night like this, even if he had a phone to call one from.

So he started walking. He was wearing thermal pacs and glad of it; the fresh snow was considerably more than a foot deep here, with no signs of a let-up. He trudged through it alongside the highway wherever he could, just beyond the plow's throw, because the road surface itself was as slippery as any skating rink. He was glad he was wearing his hooded down jacket and thick woolen gloves, too: it was getting to be cold as hell, with a tricky wind that kept corkscrewing around to toss needle-sharp ice crystals straight at his eyes whenever he least expected it.

He was within sight of the top when a dumptruck spreading sand came up the hill and passed him. He tried to wave it down. The driver waved back but kept going. Eric didn't blame him, he wouldn't've tried to stop there, either, even in a rig like that—but he needed to know where Elk Creek Road was. A panel truck with chains on following close behind the sander did pull over, though, as soon as it got to the crossroads where Route 28 crested, and waited there until Eric caught up.

"That's Turnpike Road yonder," the driver said, nodding to his left. "Elk Creek's off t'yer right, two 'r three miles down it, but I'm pretty sure it don't say so—Miller Hill Road, I think i-tis. But it gits y'there." And nope, sorry, but he didn't know any Meachams, or which place might be theirs.

It was more like four miles to the fork, Eric thought, and even windier up there along the ridge. Luckily, a plow had been along Turnpike a while back, and so had a car within the past half-hour, so he could tightrope-walk for a while in one or the other of those twin tracks whenever he got tired of scuffling through the more than ankle-deep snow in the roadbed.

Miller Hill Road hadn't been plowed at all yet, by the looks of it, but that most recent car had turned down that way, too, scraping through the drifts collected in the low places but having no serious trouble anywhere, apparently. In any case, it had made walking a good deal easier than it would've been otherwise. And, deep as some of the drifts were, it was pretty much all downhill. It was warmer now, too, off the ridge, out of the wind. Within ten minutes, Eric had come to a T with what had to be Elk Creek Road. Now which way?

There was a row of five mailboxes on a post set into the little triangle formed by the two directions traffic could take at the T. He got his Mini-Maglite out of his back pocket to read the names on them but found none, just numbers. Then he thought to open one of them and found that each had a typed or handwritten list taped inside for the mailman's benefit. "*Meacham /John, Mercy, Dierdre, Sean, Colin/ Freewheelin' Cycle Repair*" was the big red one in the middle of the row.

Now, at last, for no particular reason, Eric became aware of the barn directly across the road, behind him. It was one of the biggest and fanciest he'd ever seen, outside of a lovely little book about barns by Eric Sloane that he'd been given for his tenth birthday. He'd always had a special feeling for barns. They brought back many of his earliest memories, of visits to his grandparents in Pennsylvania and Ohio, before Jake and Elizabeth left New York City for New Mexico. Barns had been as romantic and magical to him back then as castles are to most kids.

This one was built in what he recognized as the traditional Catskill farm arrangement: the house set back a hundred yards or so on a

knoll and surrounded by shade trees, the barn downhill from the road-
way and as close to it as the terrain would allow, with the shortest possible earthen wagon ramp straight up into the hayloft, and therefore
the least possible amount of plowing or shoveling for the farmer
himself to have to do in order to get on or off the county-plowed road.

There were lights on in the house up there, none in the barn, or
anyhow none that he could see from where he was standing—but those
fresh tracks he'd been following all the way in from Route 28 went
directly across Elk Creek Road and straight up into that hayloft. Eric
climbed up the ramp and squinted into the crack between the big
double doors. It was darker than the inside of a cow in there, as his
Grandad Jacobsen used to say, but when he'd cupped his temples with
his hands and waited for his eyes to adjust, he didn't need his flashlight
to recognize the rear silhouette of Gil's Plymouth just a couple yards
from his nose.

Before he started up the path toward the house, Eric took off his
gloves, stuffed them in a pocket, unzipped the bottom of his jacket
several inches upward and transferred the .25 Beretta from its cus-
tomary place at the small of his back to behind his belt buckle where
he could get at it more quickly.

25 : THRUWAY

Everybody's a maze of contradictions when you get to know them (she certainly couldn't deny that *she* was), but *he* had to be *the* most contradictory human being of either sex or any description that Nora had ever met. Last night (nearly four o'clock this morning, rather, when he'd finally stopped poking around all in five boroughs for traces of Suzanne) he'd gone to unbelievable lengths to demonstrate to her that any thoughts of escape she might still be entertaining were pointless.

First he'd shoved a huge sofa across the only door out of that yuppified studio apartment overlooking Tompkins Square Park. Then he'd made sure the grates on all three windows were locked as well, and the keys jammed down into one of the tight front pockets of his Levis. Then he'd unplugged the bedroom phone and taken it away. And then, apparently, he'd slept sitting up, propped against the sliding doors to the bedroom after he'd shut her in there—with her crutches across his lap, no doubt.

And yet this morning he seemed to trust her with his whole mind and all its contents. There was seemingly nothing he wouldn't willingly reveal, all she had to do was ask. But he spoke as if sharing humorous little incidents that had occurred long ago and far away, as if today wasn't Tuesday, January twenty-third, as if tonight wasn't the State of the Union Address—as Nora had remembered it was, as soon as she'd opened her eyes. Or else he spoke as if she couldn't help but agree with, approve of, even admire him if he could just tell her all the truth about everything, as he saw it. Or sometimes as if endeavoring by persistent trial and error to discover what would shock her most severely. Or in all those ways at once. . . .

As when, over her poached eggs in a noisy, steamy, greasy Ukranian restaurant on Avenue A (while Gil gobbled his pirogis, boiled cabbage, kielbasi, and beet borscht—how could anyone *do* that to himself, for breakfast?), she'd asked (but didn't really expect to be told) who these people were he seemed so sure had kidnapped Suzanne, and he'd straightaway told her about those plutonium triggers and the sale he'd been negotiating:

"... Now, I've got no idea what these gizmos actually look like. Simon showed me a diagram in a book, but it meant very little to my unscientific eye. I can tell you this much, though: without one, a hydrogen bomb couldn't hurt you unless it got dropped on your big toe. There's lots of governments that'd love to join the club, who've scrounged up pretty much everything else necessary, but don't have the technological sophistication or whatever to manufacture triggers. Yet these gadgets get schlepped all over the U.S. in unmarked, unescorted reefers like so many crates of lettuce, because once upon a time some dumbo in charge of security decided that the *real* threat was the anti-nukers, so the policy ever since's been to keep it all low-profile, so's not give 'em anything visible to demonstrate against."

"What's a 'reefer'?"

Gil blinked, as if everyone on earth should know the answer to that. "Well, I didn't mean a mari-ja-wanna cigarette, if that's what threw you. It's a refrigerated truck ... where was I? Oh yeah: so I'd heard this, see, and while I've never been known for overestimating the intelligence of government employees, I didn't know for a fact they could *be* that stupid—I just thought it was worth checking out. So we moseyed on up to Rocky Flats and did a little tailing, and I'll be a Dan Quayle, if a whole truckload of 'em didn't drop right in our laps."

"How'd that come about?"—And how many lives did it cost? Nora wondered, but didn't ask, for fear he'd tell her.

"How? Completely by chance. Remember what I said yesterday? Well, chance is what it's all about, the tiger you've gotta ride if you wanna go anywhere. And that's not just in our random little lives— chance plays a helluva lot bigger role throughout this whole reality of ours than anybody wants to give it credit for. It's simply the sort of universe we happened to wind up in: very sloppy, haphazard, half-assed. That's obviously why nothing *ever* works out quite as it ought to. Y'ever read *Wonderful Life* by Stephen Jay Gould, or *Chaos* by some geek named Gleick?"

No, Nora hadn't. And she didn't feel up to discussing books or the nature of the universe at the moment, thanks just the same. Her mind was focused on an imagining of her wristwatch as and where it must still be, lying on her nightstand back in Glen Echo. She'd rediscovered its absence from her wrist half a dozen times since yesterday morning, always with a swift pang of loss followed by this mostly reassuring image: it meant she actually did have some other existence, absolutely real and tangible, still waiting for her *back there*. But not entirely reassuring: that watch also reminded her of time's inexorable advance . . . and a glimpse now of the clock on the yellowed wall behind the cash register automatically included an instantaneous calculation of the ten and one-quarter hours remaining before Ruthellen and all those other people would begin to climb the steep marble steps, show their invitations, and take their seats in the visitors' gallery overlooking the House of Representatives. . . .

As Nora painstakingly pictured that black leather strap and plain round white face with old-fashioned gold hands and spidery roman numerals against that curly maple nightstand, Ruthellen twitched open the venetian blinds in that room—and as soon as she saw Nora's watch lying there, she felt her accumulated fears coagulate into a cold hard lump of certainty in her stomach.

The first wrong, or at least not-right things she'd noticed were Nora's viola case leaning against the coat rack behind the front door, with her best coat—the black velvet one she'd worn to her recital— flung carelessly over it. Nora always kept her instrument in the living room, where she practiced, and her coats in her closet, on hangers.

Next, there wasn't any morning coffee mug rinsed and soaking in the kitchen sink, no plastic cone inverted over the spoon that wasn't standing in it. Then, as Ruthellen had seen just before she twisted the wand on the bedroom blinds, the little red eye was glowing on the stereo. Nora always made sure she flicked that master switch before she left the house, just as she always turned on the answering machine. And she never went anywhere, not even to the bathroom, without her only watch on her wrist.

Ruthellen knew all these things as surely as she knew the sun rose in the East, knew them not from direct observation over a scientifically valid sampling of time spent here, but from an intensive and constant, if furtive and mostly unconscious, scrutiny of every available detail of Nora's daily life that she'd be hard-put to explain—and explanations were what her mother was preparing to ask for, she realized. She'd already been queried as to why she had her own set of Nora's house keys.

"Because I'm her best friend," Ruthellen had answered, but that hadn't gone down too well. Fortyish women and fifteen-year-old girls couldn't be best friends, not by Denise Vliorishevski's definition. They could become very close, as mother-and-daughter, or aunt-and-niece, or even teacher-and-student; but there'd still be great chasms between them because one would've already experienced (or missed out on) most of what life has to offer, while the other still had it all before her. Unless they were—but Denise wasn't going to think that thought, let alone pronounce it. Not even in French. And certainly not about her own daughter. She could be amazingly liberal-minded sometimes, for a convent-educated upper-class Eurasian woman; but not *that* liberal.

"Perhaps Nora did leave here in a bit of a rush, but I don't see any signs of anything really wrong." Denise meant signs of violence or coercion, but she avoided those words, too, aware that saying them aloud, even as negatives, would make Ruthellen's worries much more explicit. "Look, you don't know her whole life, Relly. Maybe one of her parents suddenly took sick and—"

"Nora's parents are both dead! She told me so! And she doesn't have any other close relatives!"

"Well, what do you want to do, then? Call the police, report her missing? She might not thank us, you know, if we did that. How can you be sure she's not with a . . . boyfriend?"

That was just it, Ruthellen *couldn't* be sure, of that or anything. She knew there'd been men in Nora's past life, not by direct information, but from various clues and allusions. Her mother could be right; her mother usually *was* right, no getting around that often infuriating fact . . . and then it ocurred to her: there were no signs of Suzanne's recent presence in the house, either. A quick hot flash of something very much like jealousy swept through her mind, in the wake of a crazy notion—the two women had run off somewhere together. But why would they do that, why would they want or need to? Ruthellen shook her head to clear it of such nonsense . . . but even when those feelings went away, her first impression stuck: *something* was very wrong here. . . .

❖

There was a heavy enough mixture of sleet and snow coming down now to make tempers short and headlights necessary, so that it seemed (even more than it usually did) to take forever and two coffeebreaks to get north of Manhattan and the Bronx. But the weather cleared briefly when they reached the pseudo-countryside of Westchester, where the seasonal lack of greenery made the imposture all the more transparent.

Gil hadn't said where they were headed, and Nora hadn't inquired. Questions about some of what he'd said back in the restaurant had begun to drift together, though, in her mind. ". . . Who was the rest of the 'we' you went 'moseying on up to Rocky Flats' with?" she wondered aloud, when he finally gave up on the fading 'KCR signal and clicked off the radio.

"Huh? Oh, just a couple of friends. Not Jake or Simon, if that was what you were wondering. Used-to-be friends, I should've said. They weren't quite as lucky as I was, I guess. We went our separate ways immediately thereafter, so I'm only surmising here, but a single'll get you a grand it was good ol' Claude who sicced the govs onto Jake, along with who-the-hell-knows how many other folks I'd been seeing lately, which brought the law all around Cock Robin's barn to *your* door at the same time as *I* was about to knock on it. Jesus, I still spin my wheels whenever I remember that one: talk about your wild, weird, and whacko long shots. . . ."

He'd already told her that part, from a couple of different approaches. In fact he'd told her too much, too fast, to digest all at once, and it wasn't until they'd crossed the Tappan Zee Bridge and were inching along through more flurries in the Nyacks that she'd sorted through enough more of what he'd said to ask, "What country is this George person you mentioned acting for?"

Gil threw up both hands from the wheel to convey total ignorance, and total unconcern.

"What if it were Iran . . . or Libya . . . or Syria . . . or Iraq?" Nora asked as dramatically as she could, with vague hopes of stirring any vestiges of conscience that might be hiding somewhere underneath that complacent cynicism.

"Hm. Now, those may be unpleasant ideas at first glance, but let's think about this for a minute: there'll never be a serious effort made to stop this nuclear nonsense until the jerks who've got these toys get the bejesus scared right out of 'em, and that's gonna take some bunch of idiots using some in anger. So, the more idiots who've got 'em, the sooner it's likely to happen, the sooner everybody sobers up. And it's much better all around if it's a newcomer with only a couple, instead of one of the Big Boys, since the tendency'll be to shoot off all you've got while you're at it, because *you*'re down the tubes then, in any case.

"So why *not* some Ay-rabs? Better them than almost anybody, maybe. Might even keep 'em from pumping that oil for a while. Besides, it's about as far from *us* as you can get, at least in this hemisphere. Tough on Asia of course, India especially, but they need any sort of help they can get in curbing their runaway population growth rate, don't they? Also on the plus side, that scenario'd be bound to bring about an end—I'd say it's the only possible permanent end—to the Israeli-Palestinian conflict. And that's gotta be a *mitzvah*. For the rest of us, anyhow."

— No, there weren't any vestiges, Nora decided, shrinking back into the seat, staring out her side window at the whiteness whirling by. ". . . I thought you were a revolutionary. You sound more like Herman Kahn."

"I do, huh? I'll tell you something, Miz Sherman: politics, radical politics in particular, is like what they say about gorgeous scenery— great stuff to have, but you can't eat it, smoke it, or pour it in your gas tank. Sooner or later you begin to realize that the Revolution is *not* gonna come along in time to save your butt, so all you've really got going for you is luck and the smarts you were born with."

This man believed in nothing, cared for nothing, but himself . . . he did keep speaking of friendship, though; maybe that still had meaning for him. "What about Suzanne?" Nora asked, after a few more minutes' silence.

"Huh? What about her?"

"You've given up on Suzanne, haven't you? You've written her off." Unless that whole story was a lie; Nora didn't know what to believe anymore. She felt as if there'd been a whole crowd of different Gils parading before her these past two days. That had been the Realpolitik Gil just now, but she'd also met Courteous Gil, Scary Gil, Silly Gil, and even Pious Gil, as when he'd said about what Jake intended to do, 'I thought it was worth a tithe.' It was like being held hostage by the Seven Dwarfs, Nora found herself thinking; but there were more Gils than that, and now here came Self-Righteous Gil:

"No, not so! I've done everything I could think of, goddamn it! And if I come up with anything else, I'll do that, too!"

And Wry Gil: "Suzanne's worth a pair of Emma Goldmans, in my book—and I don't mean just pound for pound."

And Humble Gil: "I really am doing my best. If it's not good enough, well, I'm not God, or Superman, or even President. This world happens to be full of things I can't help."

"You sent her there," Nora accused them all. "You said so yourself!"

"Sure I did, but I thought I was sending her on a milk run," Indignant Gil replied. "How was I to guess those yo-yos would be so stupid as to think I'd be green enough to give 'em anybody who could tell 'em what they wanna know?"

"And what's that?"

"Where the rest of those gadgets are, what else?"

"Suzanne didn't know?"

"Of *course* she didn't know! Otherwise I never would've used her!" Outraged and Disgusted Gil shouted, in unison. "Of all the dumb-ass luck—I had to run into a bunch of jerk-offs who don't even know Rule One about this business. . . ."

— And what about herself? Nora wondered, unable to keep that question at bay any longer. Where was he taking her now, what would become of her? Would she be used, mislaid, and abandoned, like Suzanne? She knew, if she asked, he'd say something reassuring, with complete conviction. That was why she didn't want to ask. But she no longer expected Eric to come galloping up alongside that Plymouth to rescue her. And she had no energy, not even sufficient resentment left, to fuel any further hopes. It had been a crushing disappointment, when she realized sometime late last night that she'd steered Eric astray with those names she'd overheard. If Eric had even gotten her note. They must've had to do with something else, she'd finally decided, when Gil hadn't mentioned any Mercy or John again—

"You haven't noticed anybody on our tail, have you?" Gil suddenly asked, biting into her thoughts like an axe-blow.

"What? No."

"Good. I kept seeing a blue Toyota back there yesterday, and again for a while today, but not since Suffern."

If it wasn't a cinnamon Ford, she couldn't care less what might be back there behind them. . . .

❖

Scratch. Twitch. Nibble. Grooming its whiskers, daintily. Up on its hind legs, perched there on his belt buckle, looking straight at Jake now, black pin-head eyes glittering. . . .

It couldn't be a dream this time, he was right here, where he should be, inside this goddamned box, he could reach out and touch it, on both sides, feel the fuzzy old unfinished lumber, and everything else was solid, too, was there, was absolutely real.

Except for that tiny gray mouse, and the certainty that it wasn't just a mouse, it was Sarai Talks-to-Thunder, come to tell him: *Time's up, Jake. Here's your sickness back again. I've kept my bargain. Now you'll have to keep yours, by yourself, as best you can. . . .*

— Oh, shit, unbelievable, it's not even half-past three yet! We can't go on like this, we'll never make it. Take that second antihistamine, eat some chocolate, or some cheese, or some of Simon's trail mix. Drink some more water, too, to wash it down—c'mon, swallow it, you fucker, swallow!

❖

Nora had fallen asleep, and woke abruptly to find it was totally dark and snowing much more heavily. They were creeping along at thirty miles per hour in a single line of cars behind a gigantic plow. But Gil, she sensed immediately, was back in his usual good spirits, whistling soundlessly, keeping time with his thumbs against the steering wheel.

She felt as if she'd spent half her life in this car, with this man, with all these different men. She felt almost married to him, to them— now, there was a truly horrible thought. After her first operation, one of the stuffiest and most doddering of the trustees at the performing arts center had said to her: "No matter how bad things get, my dear, I find that if I can imagine something even worse, it always makes me feel better." Nora had taken offense at first, then felt sad, at the notion of people getting through their lives by playing such tawdry tricks on themselves. But the recollection very nearly made her smile now, in spite of everything.

"— Where are we?" she asked, stretching, shifting her weight off her good leg for a few minutes. That buttock had gone numb.

"Almost to Kingston."

"Is that as far as we're going?"

"'Fraid not. But we'll be getting off the Thruway there and stopping for a while," Solicitous Gil said. "Y'hungry yet?"

"No." She glanced down at her wrist again, remembered where her watch was again . . . remembered Ruthellen and the State of the Union again . . . remembered Plosh, her Chevette, parked behind the National Cathedral on Massachusetts Avenue in DC, with her folded-up wheelchair still lying—at least she hoped so—in plain view in the back, along with the homemade goats' milk fudge from the friends up in Maine and the Vliorishevskis' long-stemmed white roses . . . good thing she'd lugged her viola into the house along with her velvet coat that night—it seemed so *long ago!*—when Jake was waiting there for her; at least she didn't need to worry now about tempting a thief with *that* . . . nobody would break in for a wheelchair, would they? . . . well, why not, if they know or can guess how much one costs? "— What time is it now?" she asked.

"Four : seventeen."

Her guess would've been more like midnight. . . .

When they reached Kingston he was still being Solicitous Gil, thoughtfully inquiring whether she'd like to use a ladies' before they went to the Sears mall, where he'd probably have to leave her shut up alone in the car for a while. Yes, thanks, and when they got to the Greek diner, a hot cup of tea and a bowl of tapioca pudding felt very good going down, too. And she believed him—as much as she could believe anything by this time—when he said quietly, there in a booth near the door:

"Look, I know you've been worried, and wondering. Well, you've cooperated, I've found that I can trust you, and it's almost over now, it really is. In just a few more hours you'll be on your way back to Glen Echo, the quickest and most comfortable means possible. That's a real promise. And by the way—I'm glad your cold's better." Her cold: it *was* much better; she'd nearly forgotten about it. He'd bought her a family-sized box of tissues in a Brooklyn *bodega* yesterday, and it still looked full. . . .

And it *was* a real promise, she felt, and he *was* trusting her—as much as he ever trusted anyone. But when they reached the mall, he parked at the far end of the lot, hundreds of snow-blown yards from everything but some dumpsters heaped with trash, and he locked her crutches into the trunk, as he'd done whenever he'd left her in the car the previous night for more than a minute or two. She watched him trot off among the tall gray plow heaps toward the Sears storefront, where most of the other cars in the lot—just six or eight of them—were congregated.

This would be her last, her only real opportunity, she knew, to . . . to do what? She wasn't sure yet, of what; but almost as far away as

Sears, in the other direction, she saw a row of three more storefronts, brightly lit, still open for business: doughnut shop, pharmacy, laundromat. One of them, surely, would have a working pay phone. She could take some of those quarter slugs out of Gil's bottle in the glove compartment and . . . what? crawl all that way? No: it was forty feet or more out of the direct route, and she *would* have to crawl that far, but she'd spotted a trash barrel with several of what looked like cardboard mailing tubes, four or five feet long, sticking up out of it. With one of those in each hand for props, she just might possibly be able to hobble all that distance, if *he*'d be gone long enough. First she'd have to get herself up and out of here, though, then down on her bare hands and one working knee. It wouldn't be easy or pleasant: the wind sliced through her warm-enough-for-Maryland anorak, sweater, and slacks the instant she shoved her door outward and began to haul herself upward by its sharp, freezing top edge—

"*You'd never make it,*" he said suddenly from close behind her, chuckling sympathetically at her small scream. "It's really slippery under these last few inches. Damn near gone ass-over-teacup myself, three or four times already."

Nora swung herself back on the inside of the open door and dropped like a sack of cement onto the seat again, catching her head in her hands. ". . . I wasn't going to call the police," she whispered through her despair.

"Oh, sure. You just remembered a hairdresser's appointment you had to cancel."

"I'm telling the truth! I couldn't *not* believe you, what you said would happen to Suzanne. But there's someone else I . . . care very much about . . . who plans to be in that place tonight. I had to try to stop her from going."

"Just that she'd better stay home, and never mind *why*, you'd tell her all about it later? That never works, you know. And if it did, somehow, you'd find yourself with a whole bunch of very awkward explaining to do, afterward. But hey, you should've told me exactly what was bugging you because you've been getting worked up over nothing. The most that's gonna happen in that dump tonight is a good old-fashioned media event. I did try to talk 'em into making it the real McCoy, but not awful hard because like I told you, all that really mattered to me was verification of what I assumed was in those canisters. Fact of the matter is, both Jake and Simon're so scared of bad press for their little show-and-tell that what's actually gonna be released in there probably doesn't amount to much more than the normal background radiation. Honest injun, and I'm quoting Simon himself here: your friend'd be facing greater risks if she got her molars X-rayed."

Nora didn't argue or question him further and didn't even consider trying again. In any event, as she saw when she finally sat up and looked out there, he'd plucked every cardboard tube out of that barrel as he passed it and carried them all clear across the lot before jamming them into another.

He was gone for what felt like the better part of an hour this time, and when he came back he drove her to the still-open but empty laundromat, where he waited with her on a bench while he had a pair of studded snow tires mounted on the rear wheels. He was Gil the Boy Scout now, proudly showing off all his other purchases: a high-boy jack, a come-along (he demonstrated that by dragging one of the washing machines out of line), a double-bitted axe, a shovel, a nine-volt battery lamp, a fold-up cooking kit, a collapsible Coleman stove, two sets of thermal underwear, two stocking caps, two pairs of down mittens, even a small portable TV.

"Are we going camping?" she asked.

"Well, in weather like this," he said, "it really does pay to Be Prepared." And, nodding toward the television set: "Not my vice ordinarily, but I figured tonight's special is Not To Be Missed, wherever we might happen to be."

Then he was Serious Gil again, for a moment: "Can I ask you something? If I hadn't happened by the other night, d'you think you would've tried to stop Jake? Or are you glad, in a way, that I've taken that decision out of your hands?"

Nora sighed, shut her eyes, and shook her head. She really didn't know the answer anymore—if she ever had. . . .

But it was old grinning Gil the middle-aged Dead End Kid who touched her arm a minute later, pointing out the window to where the Plymouth awaited them again. "Well, if he makes it, he's at minimum gonna serve notice on all those dingbats, they *are* vulnerable, and prove to the whole wide woolly world, you don't *need* to build a bomb." He'd already told Nora—more than once—about the MUF rate, Materials Unaccounted For. "There's gotta be a *lotta* folks out there with access, just wondering what the hell they can do with it. So, with any luck at all, Our Jake's gonna start a new radical fad: Save The Earth—Nuke A Politician! Which is a big part of why I was willing to do *my* bit for him, on the way to my retirement fund."

Route 28 West was nothing but windshield wipers slishing back and forth and snowflakes arcing in the headlights, whenever Nora managed to force her eyes open. She was remotely aware of their having stopped another time, at the Great American in Delhi, Gil dumping a sackful of groceries into the back seat, and the acrid scent of scalding black diner coffee in a cardboard cup. . . . The next thing she knew, the motor was off again, the rear doors were open, and Gil was grunting as he laid something heavy down on the floor behind her seat. No wind here, no snow. They were inside some vast, dark, enclosed space that smelled of many things at once: old wood and leather, ancient musty hay, rubber cement, and kerosene.

"Hi, how we doin'?" Gil asked, when he saw she was sitting up and looking around. "I think we're gonna hang out here for a while, at least until the plows come by again. D'you think you could negotiate a ladder?"

"I guess so, if you'll take my sticks."

"Certainly. Warm enough? It's less drafty downstairs, but maybe you'd better climb into these longjohns first. Go ahead, I won't peek. . . ."

Hobbling across to where a column of dim bluish light ascended from a square hole in the floor, she saw that this was a barn, or had been, but bicycle wheels and frames now festooned the walls and beams she passed. The ladder, so-called, was just a series of narrow boards nailed across between a pair of the posts supporting the splintery plank floor. With both hands free, though, she didn't have much trouble getting down it.

A milking parlor, that's what she guessed the floor below must've been, by the light of that little lamp Gil had bought: peeling white-washed walls, dusty stanchions, and only faint traces of cow odor remaining. It wasn't much if any warmer down below, but he'd put down a plastic tarp inside a calving box and spread his other purchases around. He'd made it almost cozy in there, in fact, with a kettleful of Dinty Moore beef stew warming on the stove, plastic bowls and spoons laid out, and at the back, the television screen flickering like a little hearth. There was something leaning against the old crate he'd put the set up on that wasn't so cozy, though: an automatic rifle, daubed dull green, tan, and black, with a webbed strap dangling from the barrel and a long banana clip. Gil helped her to sit down and make herself comfortable on one corner of the tarp, then leaned her crutches up against the other side of the TV where she could reach them easily.

"Hungry yet?" When she shook her head, he helped himself to stew and a chunk of pumpernickel, then squatted on his heels in front of the set and turned the sound up slightly. The screen showed the Capitol Dome, Nora saw now, with a pair of vaguely familiar heads muttering wisely to each other in the foreground. She couldn't recall either name, but they were two of the superannuated anchorpersons the networks trotted out year after year on such occasions.

"— Sanctimonious assholes!" Gil snorted to himself at one of their pronouncements, then turned toward her with an eager grin that told her he'd just thought of something too clever to keep to himself. "Y'know what? In a world full of sanctimonious assholes, the glibbest hypocrite is king."

26 : LARGO

Footsteps, and bristles on stone, swish-tap, swish-tap; continuing, and coming nearer. Then stopped. And after the right amount of time, key in the gate, turning, click of the latch, faint sighing squeak of the hinges. Squeak again, click again, steps again, to the back, just where they should be—glass panel lifting, and now the velvet drapery. . . .

Jake grasped the edges of the box on either side, the way Simon had told him to do—*hey, it's Time, c'mon, guy!*—and dragged himself outward, like a horizontal chin-up . . . then rolled his eyes back: and there were Edwards' anxious eyes straight above him, his whole long face looming, looking very strange like that, upside down, lips twisting now, beginning with the softest of whispers:

"Come on out now, Mr. Jacobsen. I've got some very good news for you."

Then suddenly Edwards' wide, warm smile and normally deep, strong voice:

"There's no need to do it anymore! Miss Sherman and I, we talked things over, you see, and decided to tell them all about it. They've postponed the President's address in order to convoke a special session of both Houses, and they want you to be present upstairs when they announce unilateral disarmament and immediate decommissioning of all nuclear power plants—"

— *No*, goddamnit! It really *is* Edwards, it really *is* Time!

"Here, let me help you, Mr. Jacobsen. Are you all right? Careful, now, just hang on to me. . . ."

— Jesus, this crypt is gigantic, it's bigger than Yankee Stadium, and all that enormous hallway stretching away across the universe out there, too much space, and all this *light*, it's so sharp and jagged—gotta get back inside, I can't take this—

"Your chest pack, Mr. Jacobsen. Here, I'll fasten it for you. Now the kneepads. Here're your cap, your goggles, and your gloves. Are you sure you're well enough? Easy there, just a few more steps, here's the ladder ready. . . ."

— Gonna be so good to get up there, inside that thing: dark and close and safe again, not like out here in the middle of all this blinding, sprawling, terrifying openness—wait, something to tell him, something I can't forget . . . got it now, but words, gotta remember how to get words out: "What I told you, notebook, give it to the *Post*?"

Edwards shushed him anxiously, nodding that he understood.

Jake tried again, managing to make it a hoarse whisper this time: "Couldn't do it, couldn't tell it right, just kept opening up more cans of worms. Wrote some stuff, you'll find it inside there, but I want it destroyed. It wouldn't help, believe me—or don't, read it for yourself, I'm sure you'll agree."

Nodding, Edwards gently helped him up the wooden stepladder borrowed from the electricians' storeroom. It was mercifully darker up there on top, kinder to Jake's seared, throbbing eyes. He found the panel and laboriously removed each clip, dropping only one (which Edwards silently retrieved), then slid the sheet of metal forward until he could ease himself down inside, on his knees—oh yeah, that's better, dark and safe . . . but hey, it's too goddamned dusty to breathe in here, where's my mask?

Edwards reached down into the duct and put it on for him, adjusted the straps, then did the same for his goggles. The four aerosols were in a long nylon bag lined with spongy plastic so it wouldn't clunk on anything as he dragged it behind him. Edwards passed that inside now, like a huge black sausage, one hefty link at a time.

"Are you ready now for me to close it? You have everything? And you're sure you're strong enough?"

Jake nodded, trying to speak, trying to keep it down to a whisper again, finally realizing that the dust mask covered his mouth now. He pulled it away with one gloved hand. "Yes. Thank you. Goodbye, Mr. Edwards."

"Goodbye, Mr. Jacobsen. Good luck."

One gentleman to another. Those corny old war movies that Jake had grown up on, though Edwards probably hadn't: Niven at the Spad's wing in the dawn mist to Flynn, up in the cockpit . . . von Stroheim to . . . not Gabin, who was that other Frenchman anyhow, never did know his name. . . .

Blackness again, and walls close round his shoulders, but not as reassuring as he'd thought they would be, with one endless void opening up before him and another trailing close behind. He could feel all that dizzymaking space out there in front, even if he couldn't see it, and he resolved not to use his light unless absolutely necessary. And not to let himself think about anything beyond what had to be done now. Thinking requires energy and attention, gotta conserve what little I've got left of both—and most of all, *no then-whats.* . . .

Eric had studiously avoided asking that question, just as he'd avoided saying any final goodbyes when they'd separated, by leaving the Baltimore apartment to go pick up Suzanne at the same time as Jake left, and offering to lead Jake around the Beltway to Glen Echo in order to remove any risk of his getting lost in those look-alike slurbs (Eric had never been wrong about the way back to anywhere he'd been once)—and then not stopping or even slowing down when they reached Simon's place, just wagging a curt sort of backward salute in the rear window of the Dodge as he headed on in toward Union Station. . . .

Simon hadn't been able to leave it unasked, though, after he'd swept Nora's whole house—finding nothing but a dead phone tap—and was packing his tools as fast he could to race downtown for his own rendezvous with Roosevelt.

"Then I'll just give myself up and they'll have me for as much longer as I've got left, which I don't expect will be very long," Jake could still hear himself saying, "but however much time's remaining, I'll just keep trying to get across why I did it, that's all, and how swift and decisive *they're* gonna have to be, to have any hopes of turning anything around."

Simon had nodded curtly, and tried to conceal the sudden fog on his glasses by grabbing Jake in a quick fierce bearhug before slipping out the door. . . .

—What'd I just get done telling myself, about unnecessary thought? Here I still am, I haven't moved ten feet yet, I'm falling asleep on my knees and elbows!

All right, this is it, here we go, Jake told himself, with all the resolve he could scrape together. Just the way we practiced, just the way we did it last time, Simon and I: hand, knee, hand, knee, don't forget to keep count, don't think about where you're going or anything else, too late for *any* reflections—*oh god*: that last antihistamine, the one he'd been saving!

Three hours to go, and it could make all the difference. It wasn't in his breast pocket, he was sure of that, it was still in Simon's kit, back there in the catafalque. Jake didn't have to stop, didn't have to tug his glove off, check every pocket, open the pack, and poke into every corner where it might possibly be.

But he did all that, anyway.

It wasn't there.

Three hours. Simon said it should take him two at most, to get up there and put it all together. Simon Said, that was a kid's game, wasn't it? So was this, something only kids would do. The last tunnel Jake remembered crawling through, except for basic training, he couldn't've been more than eleven . . . a storm drain under a highway, smooth brown ceramic, about a foot and a half in diameter, there were three of them doing it on a dare and he was in the middle and halfway through when Brucie Eggleston, in front, got scared and stuck and pissed his pants and started bawling like a sick calf, so Jake and Jimmy Pedersen behind him had to back up all the way, then run half a mile to the fire house, and it took the men over an hour to get a rope in there and drag Brucie out by the heels, bruised and scraped raw and really bawling by now . . . and all three of them got the worst lickings ever when their dads got home from work that night . . . but that flitting mental mention of basic training a moment ago inflicted further punishment now without transition as the three boys, instantly aged a decade, drafted, and multiplied into battalions, fell out as ordered, in full combat gear with those film badges pinned to their chests, and dog-trotted the whole way through the sagebrush by starlight to Ground Zero, to stand there at attention until the scalding flash, the roar beyond any powers of hearing, the tremendous wind that scattered them all across the scorched-bare land like khaki tumbleweeds. . . .

— *You're doing it again, Jake—getting tangled up inside your head, not keeping count!* But before he could become completely paralyzed by the notion that he'd lost his way in that inky labyrinth, he spotted the next marker, just six or eight feet farther along. Turn left here, it told him . . . but first we'd better rest a couple minutes, give this poor old heart a chance to stop hammering as if it wanted out . . . pull that mask down too and try to cough out that mucous, and then let's start all over again . . . but this time we'll do it by the book: *one* right hand and knee, left hand, left knee, *two* right hand, right knee. . . .

Recalling then something else Simon had said, but only in an effort to make what he had to do seem feasible: the horizontal distance from

Tomb to House Chamber was just a little more than three hundred feet, then seventy-odd straight up. That three hundred was of course as the crow flew—but as Simon had also noted, crows didn't fly around down here too much, inside these vents. As the mole burrowed then, as the rat ran in the maze. But this particular mole or rat or whatever Jake was now had a crib sheet imprinted in his memory, and dabs of phosphorescent paint at each point of intersection to tell him which twist or turn to take, thanks to the cleverer mole or rat who'd been through here before him . . . no, there I almost went again, can't let myself get started thinking anymore about Simon, can't wonder how it's going with them or where they might be by this time . . . because I wouldn't stop there, I'd go on to worrying about Eric, and what his future holds. . . . *Gone but with us always,* that'll be for me now, too, won't it, not just poor little Miriam . . . the *gone* part, anyhow . . . but Eric, he's got to go on *being there* somehow, somewhere, I can't afford to think of him otherwise. . . .

— *Can't afford to think at all, Christ, I've gone and mixed up the count again!* . . . and once more, up ahead, Jake thought he saw the next marker glowing . . . but as he approached he realized that wasn't any daub of paint, it was Miriam's, his daughter's face, retreating out there before him, beckoning him onward into the dark—no, wait, he was wrong about that, too, it was her gravestone, the big yellow boulder where he'd chiseled that inscription, on the first steep rise after the cornfield, at the edge of the arroyo, under the blasted juniper, where you could gaze back across the creek toward the house, the cottonwoods and locusts . . . *Was mir die Blumen auf der Wiese erzählen—* Jake didn't speak German, but he knew what those words meant: What the meadow flowers tell me. . . .

— Wake up, Jake, you almost went down that hole head first! But we've done it, this much of it anyhow, don't know how we got here but we've reached the foot of the shaft! And here are the ropes, the first rung. Catch your breath but don't stop now. If you let yourself sit down here even for a minute, you know you won't get up again —

. . . But whoa there, getting really steep now, and you also know you can't run your head full-throttle like this and your legs and lungs at the same time, not anymore you can't, not at this altitude . . . *Was mir die Tiere im Walde erzählen,* that's what the woodland creatures tell me. . . .

— Never mind the slings, just keep going, you inchworm, just keep on keeping on, rung by rung by rung—because this *isn't* the mesa you're climbing, this is *next time: last time: the* real *time*—and real time, according to those glowing dots on your left wrist, is 8:47 already, which means you've mislaid more than an hour somehow—but at least you didn't let go of both ropes at once while you were making that discovery, at least there should still be enough time, if you can only make it all that way up there —

. . . Well, right now where I'm going is the top of those cliffs . . . not even that far, if I don't get a move on . . . but everything was thinning out rapidly, opting for one quality—toughness—over quantity, as the limits of what could be endured by any living thing came steadily closer . . . and just listen to that music, those kettledrums, that's gotta be good ol' Gustav himself banging away up there on the ledge, how's about that for a welcome?

— *That's your own heart pounding, Jake*—just don't let it stop quite yet, and don't you slow down now, either; any slower you'll never make it—and you're almost at the top, you must be—must be—two or three more rungs at most—it'll be this next one, then, it's *gotta* be this next one—okay, then, *this* one—oh Jesus, finally! . . . but I can't quit yet, gotta get all of me out here onto this blessedly horizontal surface before I black out again, and haul that string of sausages up out of there, too —

At first he thought it was the ocean, giant waves smashing against sheer cliffs; then as the sound gradually faded, he understood it was applause . . . *Was mir der Mensch erzählt,* what The People tell me . . . it seemed to take minutes for his eyes to focus well enough to make sense of those red dots this time: *9:14*— you're losing it *again*, Jake, not doing what you're here for . . . but first he had to reach those grills, and before he did that, he'd better detach that last pair of links for the two grills behind him, no sense in dragging them any farther than he had to . . . but he couldn't find the fasteners in the inches-thick coat of dust the nylon bag had collected along the way . . . the dust of centuries, nearly two, anyhow . . . finally he managed to part the Velcro, tugged out an aerosol, tucked it in the crook of his arm like a football . . . okay, c'mon, then: hand, knee, knee, hand. . . .

Even louder applause reverberated through the metal ducts as he approached the nearest grill, where the checkerboard wasn't pallid blue anymore, it was now a much stronger, creamy yellow . . . Simon says *look but don't touch* . . . lights blazing everywhere down there now, no more rows of brown dots that had been upturned seats, strings of glittering beads instead, every color imaginable . . . Life at the Edge, where there's no room for surplus or sympathy . . . the oaks were still hanging in there, though, so were those garish gold and orange and mustard-yellow blotches of lichen . . . and listen, would you, here's the Mahler back again, loud and clear and triumphant . . . *Langsam* . . . *Ruhevoll enpfunden* . . . and oh yeah, *Was mir die Liebe erzählt*, that's what love tells me . . . tells me life on this old planet *never* gives up, does it? . . . but *I* do . . . says, Tell it all goodbye, Jake, you won't see this again . . . but deep inside his head, his own voice again, bellowing:

Hell yes I will!

Then, blasting through all other sound, one totally unlike any Gustav Mahler ever wrote:

DRING-DRING-DRING-DRING-DRING-DRING-DRING-DRING-DRING-DRING-DRING-DRING. . . .

27: SCHERZO

Eric approached the farmhouse cautiously, expecting a dog to bark, but none did, so he crept close enough to peer between snow-burdened bushes into the only lighted room downstairs. It had to be the living room, with a big tiled woodstove up on a dais of paving bricks in the middle of the floor. Books filled one of the two walls he could see and a couch covered with a fake Navajo blanket stood against the other, with framed posters and kids' drawings above it. Two rocking chairs facing the same way were both empty, but the nearer one was still rocking.

While Eric watched, a pudgy, balding man with an inch of reddish beard covering most of his face, in sheepskin slippers, baggy khakis, and red suspenders over a faded green sweatshirt, stepped back to stand directly in front of the window, having just switched on a TV. Eric couldn't see the screen, only the glow. The man bent forward again out of view to adjust the sound or picture, then shuffled backward slowly toward the rockers, squinting to see whatever the program was while he polished the lenses of his glasses with a blue bandanna. He had that peculiarly soft, unselfconscious look of someone who believes himself to be entirely alone and unobserved.

But there were other lights showing upstairs, and Gil had to be around here somewhere, if that Plymouth was. . . .

John put on his glasses and sank back into his chair, but just then they broke for a bunch of commercials, one of them a beer ad, and he suddenly remembered that there was, or should be, a single bottle of Bass ale remaining from the six-pak he'd splurged on last week . . . he'd crossed the darkened kitchen, flung open the refrigerator door, hunkered down to squint at the back of the bottom shelf, found what he was looking for, and stood erect again, all before he became aware of that tall young stranger standing there at his elbow, pointing a tiny but extremely real-looking gun straight at his heart.

Somehow he didn't drop the bottle before the young man took it away with his left hand and set it down gently on the counter beside them. Through the register directly overhead, John could clearly hear Mercy's voice in the room above them, reading their nightly installment of Tolkien to the kids. Of course, the young man could hear her, too, and when he motioned emphatically toward the back door, John decided it would be unwise to argue.

He wished he had his parka and rubber boots on, though, as he was herded straight past them through the mud room and some thirty yards down the unshoveled path toward the barn before being told to stop. His teeth were chattering already. The snow seemed to have quit falling for the time being, but the wind was stronger now and blowing so much of it around that he could scarcely see the house from where he stood. He could *die* on this spot, John couldn't help thinking. He could lie bleeding to death right down there, where his feet and ankles must be turning blue by now. The drifting snow would cover him in a matter of minutes, and he was sure that no one would find him until morning, when all of him would be blue. . . .

"Look, I don't wanna hurt anybody," Eric said, looming tall and black with the blurry yellow oblongs of the living room windows behind him. "Just tell me where Gil is."

"I don't know!—I mean, sure, I know who you mean," John added quickly, realizing that it might be fatal to pretend otherwise, "and he did call yesterday, he said he might be coming up soon, but honestly, he's not here now."

"Then why's his car in the hayloft?"

"It *is*? I didn't know that, honestly, and he's nowhere in the house, I swear—"

"I know, I just looked, upstairs and down. Guess he's gotta be in the barn somewhere, then. C'mon, let's get a move on."

". . . If he's not in the bike shop—I mean the hayloft," John gasped, slipping and sliding on ahead, "then I don't know where he could be, that place is enormous and honestly, I haven't even explored it all myself yet!" He was talking too much, he knew, repeating 'honestly' too often, revealing how terrified he was.

Eric seemed to think so, too. "Shut up," he said, "and just keep going."

Entered from below, at the back, the barn was a warren of horse stalls, calf pens, tack rooms, feed bins, a century's worth of collected odds and ends of all things agricultural. Everything was festooned with cobwebs that glittered in the beam of Eric's little flashlight as they tiptoed along through a forest of rotting posts and ominously sagging ceiling beams.

"You see," John eventually turned back to whisper, "there's no one—" just as Eric cut the light off and poked the gun into his ribs, hissing for silence. At the end of this rubble-strewn passageway there *was* something now, a softly flickering source of bluish light. . . .

Eric wished to Christ he could just garrote this jerk soundlessly, painlessly, the way commandos did it in old movies, or at any rate, quickly and securely truss him up, gag him, and stow him somewhere. Eric couldn't let John go now; he might be even more afraid of Gil and try to warn him, wherever Gil was. So the only thing to be done was to keep that fierce grip on John's arm, the Beretta's muzzle pointed at the small of his back, and keep nudging him along, inch by inch . . . the light grew gradually brighter, and soon Eric was able to make out a row of stanchions, then the small screen with two figures in matching knit caps hunched in front of it, their backs toward him, less than twenty feet away now—

But just then John tripped over something and went sprawling, loudly, nearly taking Eric down with him.

Gil leaped up, grabbed his M16, and swung around as Eric ducked behind the nearest post. The rifle fired one wild round as Nora's crutch sent it flying. Both Gil and Eric leaped for it, but Eric was closer and faster. And now he crouched with it at the ready, between Gil and the ladder up to the loft.

Knowing exactly what Eric could do with a weapon like that, Gil didn't hesitate for a nano-second: whirling, he dashed for the far wall and dove straight through the small square window in the middle of it, knit cap and elbows first. He was out of sight in the swirling snow before Eric could get over there, but Eric didn't have to reflect for long to understand that Gil must be figuring to scramble up somewhere along the steep bank not much more than an arm's length beyond that wall, in order to run up the road and get to the loft and the Plymouth by means of the wagon ramp.

But the big double doors were still closed when Eric peeked over the edge of the hole in the loft floor at the top of the ladder, and they stayed that way as he quickly but carefully approached them, from post to post, along the outside wall. Through the crack between them, he could see why:

Gil was standing in front of the headlights of a new black four-wheel-drive Isuzu Trooper in the middle of Elk Creek Road with his hands on top of his head, as a man in a velvet-collared topcoat and canary-yellow earmuffs frisked him, while another—very large—man in a down vest and a bearskin shako held both of Gil's wrists clamped behind his back with one huge paw and the stubby barrel of a machine pistol pressed against the base of his skull with the other. It looked to Eric like a new Uzi, and they didn't look like any kind of law. What else they might be, there wasn't time to speculate about: the big man quick-marched Gil back down the road now to where he'd clambered up the bank just two or three minutes ago—and as they passed the Isuzu, the one in the topcoat tugged the passenger door open and jerked somebody else out of there by the wrist.

The cab domelight was on her only for a second, but Eric recognized the slope of Suzanne's shoulders and her combed-forward brush-cut. He ran back to the ladder and slid more than climbed back down to the milking parlor, where Nora and John both crouched, transfixed, in front of the television set.

"C'mon, quick, *out* of here!" Eric said, hauling Nora upright, grabbing her crutches for her, boosting her up with his shoulder into the hayloft. "— C'mon!" he called again urgently to John, but John was as if spiked to the floor in his amazement: the President's speech had just been cut off by the shrilling of bells and now the entire Chamber was going berserk, as Jake's voice boomed out. . . .

Then a shotgun barrel was poked through the shattered window, just as a huge foot kicked down the rotten plank door at the end of the row of stanchions, and Gil and Suzanne plunged in over it with their hands clasped together behind their necks, followed by the man in the yellow earmuffs and the big guy. Both of them carried Uzis now.

The man with the shotgun snapped the remaining shards of glass out of the bottom of the window, climbed in through the empty frame, kicked over the TV, grabbed John by his suspenders, and threw him against the wall between Gil and Suzanne. From the ladder hole, Eric could only see some lower legs and feet now, but he heard everything that was said:

"George wants the rest of 'em."

"Okay," Gil answered. "Sure. Absolutely. Nothing's worth getting killed over."

"So where are they?"

"They're here—but you'd look for a year and never find 'em. Whoa, take it easy! You'll get 'em, but first I want some guarantee that you'll—"

"First you want this twelve-gauge rammed down yer throat, cock-sucker! Where *are* they?"

"In the smoke shed! But—"

"Where the fuck is that?"

"I'll show you. . . ."

The man carrying the shotgun—he had a peacoat and a Greek fisherman's cap on, Eric could see now—stepped over the smashed door first, and after looking both ways, proceeded on outside, followed by the three prisoners, prodded onward by the pair with the Uzis.

Eric checked the ignition switch first and sighed his gratitude—yeah, the key was in it—and helped Nora into the front seat, then followed the group's progress outside through cracks and knot holes in the loft walls . . . god*damn* it!—the shotgun man fell out of line at the foot of the ramp. He was staying with the Isuzu.

❖

Up at the house, Nebby was driving Mercy absolutely nuts, running in circles around the kitchen floor, tugging at her sweatpants, whimpering, and clawing at the back door. He'd been perfectly fine upstairs just a minute ago, lying calmly by the foot of Colin's crib as Mercy finished reading and distributed goodnight pecks on all three foreheads. The moment he'd come out into the hallway to follow her downstairs, though, he'd started carrying on like this. It was John's job to take him out so he could do his business, not hers; she'd made that very clear to both of them from Day One.

"John? Nebby wants out."

He'd turned the sound up too high as usual; he couldn't hear her over it.

"*John!* Are you too busy to kiss your children goodnight?" She went to the living room doorway. Wouldn't you know, he wasn't even in there, he'd just walked off and left the thing blaring like—and then she looked at the picture tube and listened to what they were saying, catching enough in a matter of seconds to be dumbstruck: oh my God, the whole government's been *irradiated by terrorists*!

"— John!" She pushed the bathroom door inward, it wasn't locked, he wasn't in there. At last she paid attention to Nebby, followed him out the kitchen door, through the mud room, and from the porch she could see a light bobbing around behind the barn, on the path leading down toward the creek. Scuffing off her slippers, struggling into her rubber boots, throwing an old coat over her shoulders, and grabbing the big flashlight, she began to run in that direction, calling "John! John!"

But Nebby was nearly down there already. The moment she'd opened the outer door, he'd left the porch like a bolt from a crossbow.

They were almost exactly to where Gil had in mind. Close enough, he decided, and instantly acted: the same second those two motherfuckers turned around to see what all that commotion was coming down the hill behind them—and precisely as that furry little guided missile struck the big guy's nearer ankle—Gil hit them both across the knees with everything he had, so hard he nearly went over the edge with them, down into the snow-filled foundation hole where one of the largest outbuildings had stood when this farm was a working dairy. Then he gripped Suzanne's wrist and streaked for the smoke shed, where the Meachams kept their garden tools—and hanging beside the door, their two pairs of snowshoes, which Gil snatched up in passing.

At the same time, John was shouting "Go back!" at Mercy, and running as fast as he could toward the house, after her, in his stocking feet—he'd lost both slippers by then. As if to speed him on, one of his former captors fired off a burst, straight up, while they were thrashing around down there, in eight feet of feathery snow.

Eric, who'd been able to watch most of this from between the loose boards at the back of the loft, ran back to the double doors now and saw his chance: the shotgun man, who'd pulled the Isuzu over to the side of the road a few yards uphill from the ramp and lit a cigarette, had heard the Uzi go off and was wading down through the drifts around the side of the barn toward his colleagues. "Hang on!" Eric told Nora, turning the key hard. The Plymouth caught at first crank; he threw it into reverse and floored it, shooting back straight through the punky old doors, down the ramp, slewing hard around. Then he slammed it straight into second gear and roared on up Elk Creek Road toward where it joined Turnpike Road at an acute angle, about a mile away.

But Eric didn't know that's what he'd done until the two roads parted company again another mile or so farther along, where he followed the compass in his head and kept left on Elk Creek Road, eventually arriving at the four corners in East Meredith. At that first crossroads, he'd only turned the way the plow seemed to have gone most recently, and had narrowly avoided going almost straight there, on up Ehlermann Hill Road.

Which was precisely what the Isuzu driver did, less than a minute later, trying to catch up with what he assumed to be Gil and Suzanne making a getaway somehow, because he was going too fast at that point to notice which way Eric's tracks had gone.

He soon discovered that this part of the world was criss-crossed by an amazing number of little roads that didn't go much of anywhere: Ehlermann Hill Road led him to Davis Road, across Jersey Road, into Dickman Road and on to Meridale, where he finally blundered out onto Route 28. So it was forty minutes before he'd found his way back to the Meachams' place.

By then, both sides of Elk Creek and Miller Hill Roads were lined with vehicles for at least a hundred yards each way. They were mostly Chevrolets, Plymouths, and Fords from the State Police and the Delaware County Sheriff's Department, but also included a dozen or more assorted pickups and vans with little magnetized lights stuck to their roofs, belonging to members of the local volunteer fire department, and (he noticed because it was the only import there) a small blue Toyota. Tucking his shotgun away under his seat, he cruised straight on past, but much more sedately now, until his shivering associates stepped out of a clump of evergreens and flagged him down about three-quarters of a mile farther along toward Delhi.

Eric, meanwhile, had followed his instinct again and gone straight at the crossroads in East Meredith. He'd guessed correctly this time, as well—that was the most direct route to Oneonta—but it got him into what could've been serious trouble because the plow had turned left there, swinging around back to Meridale. Soon the snow was more than bumper-deep, with patches of ice underneath, and the Plymouth couldn't quite make it up over Dutch Hill to Davenport Center.

Looking for anything that might help, Eric opened the trunk and found not only the shovel, axe, and jack Gil had bought in Kingston, but two bags of sand, a set of chains, a brass-bound case crammed full of bundles of fifty- and hundred-dollar bills, and four stainless steel canisters exactly like the one he'd helped lug into the cooler in Salisbury.

With those chains on, they reached Oneonta in another fifteen minutes. I-88 was scraped clean, and by 11:20 they made it to Binghamton, where Simon had insisted on signing himself out of the hospital as soon as they allowed him to, and was pacing the emergency waiting room—as poker-spined now as a graduating West Point cadet, with all that tape they'd wound him up in—while doing his best to keep up with nonstop contradictory reports from Washington on both the wall-mounted television and a transistor radio belonging to one of the orderlies.

28: FRACTALS

There was one feature of their farm that John had never mentioned to Gil, or to hardly anyone else since they'd bought the place, because its presence there—even though no fault of his own—embarrassed him somehow. A previous owner, in the Fifties apparently, had constructed a bomb shelter in a corner of the basement, with foot-thick poured-concrete walls, floor, and ceiling, and a door that looked as if it had come off some old bank vault. Prison-cell bunkbeds, shelves full of rusty tin cans, and demijohns of murky water lined the mildew-stained walls, together with a padlocked first aid kit, a hand-crank generator, and many less identifiable survival tools. There was even a phone extension in there, which still had a dial tone; but how anyone, even back then, could've expected Ma Bell to survive World War III was more than John could guess at.

This was where he and Mercy had scurried now, hustling somnambulant Dierdre before them, with blanket-wrapped Sean and Colin in their arms. The kids were very good. Colin never woke up at all, and both Sean and Dierdre kept their voices down to excited whispers without very many reminders. This was the best adventure they'd had in a long time.

The door only locked from inside, and since there was no telling how long they might be in there or how long the air supply would last—and because he couldn't've heard a cannon ten feet away with it closed—John left it ajar, but remained beside it listening for sounds of pursuit upstairs, while Mercy pulled her coat up over her head, called the operator, and whispered for the police. "— Close that for a minute, will you," she finally said. "They keep telling me to speak up!"

John did so, but asked quietly, "D'you think that's wise?"

"What? Now they want to know which do we want, the State Police or the Sheriff's Department—*Both! Hurry!*"

"What'll we tell them?"

"What d'you mean? That men with guns're running around here

trying to kill us, that's what!—Hello? Yes! This is Mercy Meacham on Elk Creek Road, where Miller Hill—what? We're being attacked! With *machine guns!* . . ."

"Where's Nebby?" Sean suddenly wanted to know. "Daddy, they won't shoot Nebby, will they? Will they?"

"No, of course not," John said automatically, but feeling as he said it that it was a totally incomprehensible world out there beyond that door, where the horrendous and the inexplicable could and often did happen: where strangers strolled into your kitchen and pointed guns straight at your heart . . . and people you thought you knew, people you admired and believed were friends of yours, not only involved *themselves* in unthinkable acts but callously tricked *you* into getting entangled in them, too. . . . John was beginning to realize also, with a surge of despair that flung him light-years beyond any previous understanding of existentialism, that this whole bleak, hideous, inscrutable reality he'd suddenly plunged into bore no relation whatsoever to the ideals he'd been chasing for most of his life . . . that those sweet Sixties notions of the unlimited powers of love and freedom, of the essential simplicity and goodness of his fellow human beings, had application only on some magical floating island somewhere, or in some octopus's garden at the bottom of the becalmed blue sea of middle-class niceness he and most other babyboomers had been raised in. . . .

After what seemed like another hour but was more likely five minutes, John did hear heavy feet clumping around up in the kitchen, doors banging, a chair crashing over. But nobody opened the cellar door up there, and soon the throbbing silence returned. It was only then, as he flopped down, exhausted, on the bunk beside her, that Mercy noticed the oval bloodstain on John's back and screamed: "You've been shot!" But when he pulled up his sweatshirt, all she found was a splinter, probably from the barn wall he'd been slammed against, and it hadn't gone very deep. He scarcely felt anything when she pulled it out, and the wound didn't even bleed anymore. No matter, Mercy was off again:

"Just look what that precious Gil of yours got us into—and he almost got you killed! I'm telling the police everything, so are you, I hope! Believe me, John, you'd better!"

John tried to think about what he was going to tell them, but he was just too tired to think. There didn't seem to be anything he could tell anyone that would make any sense at all, or that wouldn't make him seem very foolish—if not criminal. Until tonight, he'd never looked into the barrel of a gun. Now it seemed to him as if there were all manner of deep, dark holes confronting him . . . for the moment, though, he simply wished that who or whatever Mercy had summoned would get here, and then leave very quickly, so that he could just curl up and. . . .

"— John? *John!* Wake up! Can't you hear those sirens?"

Neither one of them had been thinking very clearly by then, Simon intermittently realized, or they wouldn't've let Nora go on sleeping on the back seat; they would've found a place for her to stay in Binghamton and transportation back to Washington in the morning. As it was, he didn't envy her the quizzing she would probably have to endure —she didn't need crossing into Canada with two unexplained men added to the list of questions she might have to come up with answers for. Too late now, though, at least until they reached Watertown— Jesus, it was as bleak and empty as Nebraska up here north of the Thomas E. Dewey Thruway. . . .

Meanwhile there was something else to get clear about—but what the hell was it, anyhow? Simon hadn't taken any of the pain pills they'd given him, but whatever it was they'd shot him up with in order to set his collarbone was taking forever to wear off, and he kept fading in and out . . . he was sure there was something, though, besides Nora, that had to be dealt with . . . oh yeah:

"Eric? Those canisters—we gotta get rid of 'em. It'll be scary enough otherwise, crossing the border in a car registered in a name we don't have ID for, with a trunkful of money."

Which maybe they should get rid of, too, in case they got searched— but the best (the *only*) offer for Simon's business had been a pathetic forty-seven grand, supposedly awaiting him up in Montreal . . . so that cash back there was Pennies from Heaven. . . .

"Tell me what to do, I'll do it," Eric said. He'd been at the wheel of one vehicle or another for so long now, it seemed, he could scarcely recall what it felt like to do anything else. He wasn't sleepy, but every now and then he'd blink and catch himself thinking that it was Jake snoring there on the seat beside him instead of Simon, and the two of them were still driving across the West somewhere, in Sallyanne or the blue Dodge, through the moonless night.

. . . A goddamned good question, what to do with 'em . . . finally they left I-81 at Adams Center, and after ten or fifteen minutes of crunching deafeningly along freshly plowed back roads with head-high snow-banks on either side that sparkled in the headlights like the palace of the Ice Queen, Eric found a big pond with no houses in view that was both near the road and swept clean of all but a few inches of snow by the wind, where he used that brand-new axe to chop a hole out in the middle, not much bigger than you'd want for fishing, through the ten-inch-thick clear green ice. Then he slid all eight of the canisters down the bank one after another, skidded them out to the hole like so many stainless-steel toboggans, and eased them into the black water: first the four in the trunk, then the ones they'd discovered on the floor in the rear seat when Nora shifted back there in Binghamton. She was still sleeping so soundly she didn't stir when the dome light went on, as Eric opened the back doors to get at those.

He switched on his pocket flash for a few seconds as soon as he was done to watch long bluish needles of ice begin to knit the hole back together, even before the bubbles stirred up by the last can had completely trailed away. He hefted the axe as he stood erect again and turned toward shore—then he swung back around, tugged off his right glove with his teeth, reached under his parka and inside his jeans at the small of his back, yanked out the Beretta and quickly tossed that down the hole, too. He knew he was going to feel pretty naked for a while, but he'd feel a lot worse if it caused their arrest at the border; having never crossed one before, he had no idea how closely they could expect to be scrutinized. He would've had to ditch it somewhere before he went through the airport detectors anyhow, or else tell Simon of its existence, and without having to think about why, Eric knew he'd rather not do that. Simon was into a lot of things, but guns weren't among them. . . .

Those canisters had to be good for at least a century in fresh water, Simon figured. He told Eric to be sure to write down exactly where they were located, though; he'd figure out later how best to make the local citizenry aware of their presence. Soon after mumbling that much, Simon drifted out again, before he could re-remember about dropping Nora off in Watertown . . . while Eric drove steadily northward.

❖

The media outdid themselves that night. There was scarcely a television or radio station anywhere in the United States that failed to round up a skeleton crew and at least a couple of recognizable pundits to interrogate. NPR researchers set to work immediately and had a dramatic ten-minute segment supplying background on all the place names in Jake's message ready to run in time for *Morning Edition*. . . .

Those sudden deafening bells, and then that list of names, most of them places she'd never heard of, were all that Ruthellen really took in before Denise Vliorishevski, on the aisle beside her, seized her wrist in a grip as irremovable as handcuffs, went white as milk and stiff as a plank with only her neck touching the back of her own seat and her ankles wedged under the one in front of her, and then began to scream, on one endlessly quivering, unearthly note like Tibetan singing bowls, so piercing that it drowned out all the other noise around them—although it seemed as if everyone else in the visitors' gallery was either screaming, too, or else shouting their lungs out for quiet, so that they could listen to whatever was being bellowed over the public address system.

Ruthellen had never known her mother to scream at *anything* before, and that part of the experience alone would've been completely unnerving. Just seconds ago, she'd been not so much worrying anymore as simply woolgathering, imagining for one thing the funny faces Nora would probably be making by this time at those resounding clichés making up the president's speech, and how easy it would've been for either of them to start the other off giggling when he proclaimed that "Ever Greater Growth is what America has always been about!" and maybe it was just as well that Nora wasn't present—and then *this*: as if the entire fabric of that safe, sane, fair, kind, and logical world she'd lived in now for nearly sixteen years had been ripped wide open and exposed as literally that: a taut, concealing fabrication merely, a cloth-thin artifice like a painted backdrop in a theater, with nothing behind it but howling black emptiness. . . .

She was vaguely aware that Heather, her brother's fiancée, was bending over her, competently kneading Denise's face and neck and shoulders, trying to find the combination that would unlock her rictus; and also that Heather's roommate Tracy was coolly engaged in performing the same sort of service for a gray-haired, red-faced man gasping and flapping his rubbery arms, farther along the row. "We took a first aid course together last year," Heather yelped proudly in Ruthellen's ear. "They showed us just what to do for hysteria!"

"*Please stay in your seats! There is no danger!*" somebody was roaring over and over, through a loudhailer. "*You can't get out now, anyway! The doors have all been temporarily secured, for everyone's protection!"*

Then Congressman Vliorishevski himself was there, clambering over seats and people to get to them, sweeping his womenfolk up in his long arms, crushing the three he recognized as such all at once against his starched white shirtfront, and gradually his wife's scream subsided, until Ruthellen could make out what her father kept repeating under his breath, a whispered litany of outrage: ". . . dirty sonsabitches, goddamn dirty sonsabitches! . . ." Which disturbed her almost as much as her mother's condition because it wasn't at *all* like him; he'd even once been called, in print, "the most amiable emerging figure in Georgia politics."

His Army and antiwar arrest records, plus the fact that Wendell AKA Jake Jacobsen had been on an FBI priority list since the disappearance of two of their agents in November (and yet no extraordinary measures had been initiated at any level to secure his apprehension) were leaked from somewhere before midnight, giving everyone stiff springboards for launching all kinds of theories, with a clear majority of commentators employing the latter item as text for sermons on the ineptitude of law enforcement in general, the FBI in particular. "We cluck our tongues over governmental impotence in places such as India or Colombia," one said sternly. "What about here at home, if events like the World Trade Center bombing or this latest outrage are even conceivable?" Another called Jake "an appropriate John Wilkes Booth for this age of mass disaster," while two more, on KPFA and WBAI, compared him to John Brown. . . .

Word that a body "presumed to be Jacobsen's" had been recovered from the ventilation ducts wasn't released until 1:35 a.m. Asked if there was any evidence yet to prove whether Jake acutally did what he'd claimed to have done, the presidential press secretary's least senior assistant (upon whom the delivery of this announcement had devolved because she'd been watching it at home with her kids and husband, unlike all her bosses) smiled apologetically and said: "Sorry, I'm unable to comment on that, or anything else, at this time."

But by then so many conflicting statements had been issued by, denied, or attributed to various federal agencies that no one knew what to believe, least of all those who'd been inside the House Chamber at 9:28:05 p.m.—and *they*, after all, included everyone in whose name any such statement would necessarily have been made. Everything was further complicated by the fact that there was no consensus among available experts as to whether existing instruments for measuring recent exposure to low-level radiation were reliable in any degree.

❖

As an official line began to solidify overnight (Yes, he had possessed the capability but No, he hadn't actually released any radioactive material within the House or anywhere else because he had died first of pneumonia and "other natural causes") scarcely anybody, in government or out, could be found who would accept it at face value. To virtually everyone, Jake's death seemed entirely too convenient. Even as early as 3:20 a.m., when Gil quit twisting the dial, the word 'cover-up' had already been aired so many times as to become historically indelible. . . .

"Now there's an angle I never even thought of!" Gil said, switching off the car radio as they approached the Rhinecliff Amtrak station. "It's the Oswald Syndrome, in spades —beautiful! C'mon, pal, don't you think that's beautiful?"

Nothing on earth seemed beautiful to Suzanne that night, least of all this grinning cockroach squeezed against her, inside this tiny hot-wired Subaru, and there were only three sources of comfort. One was that railroad depot coming into view, where she would finally see the absolute last of this absolute asshole. Another lay curled nose-to-tail in her lap, snoring serenely. The third was an idea revolving langorously in her mind. She knew she wouldn't do it, but it was the sweetest possible thought to think, and she'd been savoring it all the way from Delhi, where Gil had swiped this Subaru, to the Kingston-Rhinebeck Bridge:

Turn this bastard in—let them lock him up forever! She couldn't do it: there *is* no good-enough reason to fink, ever, ever, *ever*—that was what she'd heard and believed all her life. But this smug little fucker had to be the most convincing argument to the contrary that anybody could dream up in a million years. The next-best move would be the lethal edge of her hand—*Ya!*— just below his ear when he wasn't looking (she'd learned how, but had never executed the blow on anything other than an overgrown zucchini). She wasn't going to do that, either, she realized, but she'd come dizzyingly close to it, more than once, a couple of hours ago. The first time was when they'd had to stop to put on the Meachams' snowshoes, and he'd told her to leave Nebby behind—after Nebby had just saved their lives!

"That was *me*, kiddo," Gil had snapped, "not this yapping dustmop. I guess you weren't paying attention."

Another nearly deadly moment was when they'd reached the ridge east of Elk Creek and stopped to listen (to nothing—nobody was going to get through those drifts without either snowshoes or a snowmobile), and he'd had the incredible gall to tell her that everything that had gone wrong was *her* fault! She must not've followed all of his instructions or she wouldn't've been nabbed, and how'd she ever guess where his stash was—and what happened to the venerable rule against squealing?

"That didn't take any genius, the way you're always throwing those cute little hints around. And I was following the oldest rule of all: Stay Alive."

"There's really only *one* way to do *that* right, pal, and everybody but *you* knows it, from the angleworm on up: *Don't get caught*." But since she had been, just out of curiosity, had she come up with any guesses as to who it might be that George and his buddies were working for?

She wasn't telling Gil anything, ever again, but it could've been Serbs or Croats or Armenians or North Koreans for all she knew, or the Shining Path or the Khmer Rouge, for that matter, if any of those outfits had that kind of money. That creep in the dopey Greek cap had actually been singing Pol Pot's praises on the drive upstate.

"There's the sort of leader Asia needs a whole lot more of," he'd said. "*He*'s got the answer to their population problem." That was what they'd talked about most of the way, to Suzanne's amazement: "the population problem." Earmuff's answer was AIDS—a "blessing in disguise," he called it. "It's gonna kill off all the dumbos on the planet, and leave the species with twice the present average IQ."

Big Stoop, in his down vest and bearskin hat, never said one word the whole time, but the way he kept looking at her out of the pink corners of his lashless, colorless eyes was harder to take than all the disgusting remarks the other two came up with, put together. . . .

Suzanne was sure of one thing only: she hadn't been the first captive held there, in that white room. Wherever it was—she still didn't know exactly because they'd made her wear those glasses again until they were rolling along on the Palisades Parkway. But her first guess would've been the Upper East Side of Manhattan—maybe in one of the embassies up there—because the bathroom Big Stoop led her to, as soon as she'd told George she could guide them to what they wanted, was the kind she'd never seen anywhere else: antique but clean and warm and spacious, well tiled and well toweled, with massive, ornate brass plumbing, a huge marble-topped mahogany commode, and one of those big scales clinics have, with sliding weights (she'd felt absolutely emaciated, until she learned she'd only lost seven pounds). It was when she looked at the array of soaps, shampoos, and lotions on top of the commode that Suzanne knew for certain that they were thoroughly experienced at what they'd done to her. Right up front where she couldn't miss it was precisely what she needed most and hadn't expected to find: a big blue plastic jar full of glycerin suppositories. . . .

"In any case, *not* nice folks," Gil had said then, as Suzanne maintained her stony silence, "and I'm not inviting 'em to any more of *my* parties."

"— But hey, c'mon, cheer up!" he said now, gliding smoothly to a stop beside the curb at the Amtrak entrance. "It's over, it's history, which as we know, is bunk. Look at me—I'm not whining over my lost millions, am I? Not to mention picking up the whole tab for Jake's little experiment which, as you must be aware, was hardly inconsiderable. Figure it this way: I got out alive, with all limbs and faculties intact, so did you, and that makes us both winners. You're only a loser in *this* game when you can't walk away from the table . . . well, okay, then, sulk if you must—but you're really sure now, this is what you want, you're just gonna call it quits and go on back to Detroit?"

"— *Toledo!*" Suzanne couldn't keep from bellowing, as she scrambled out. And she could hardly wait to get there—where life might be depressing, but was at least generally predictable and held real pleasures, however small and shabby. Her second-place preoccupation for the past hour had been how to smuggle Nebby onto the train and plane, but she'd just solved that with the discovery of a capacious plastic shopping bag neatly folded on the rear window ledge of the Subaru, and a fairly clean piece of blanket under her seat to wrap him in. Lillian's last remaining Siamese (the three Suzanne hadn't been able to give away) weren't going to be overjoyed to see him, but that was *their* problem. . . .

"Right. I was only checking to see if *you* remembered which wasteland it was. So hang in there, kid, give my best to the ex-working class and—"

Whatever else he'd had to tell her was sealed into the Subaru as she slammed the door and stalked away.

Gil waited until Suzanne was well inside the depot, then headed for the pay phone by the door, digging his little book out of his belt and change out of his pockets . . . no slugs, more's the pity, so he'd have to give 'em real coin of the realm this once, since his bottle was still in the Plymouth's glove compartment, along with Suzanne's new ID . . . a pity, too, that she'd never get to see the name he'd chosen for her this time . . . the first number he punched had been disconnected, he was told by a recording . . . the second rang seven times, he'd looked up a third and was about to click off when he heard a sleepy "Yes, hello?"

"Hi, Eugenia—you'll never guess who this is."

"There's only one man in *my* life, Bert, who calls me at . . . what ungodly hour is it, anyway?"

"Later than you think."

"Isn't it always? Where're you calling from this time?"

"Twenty minutes away, Sweetie—would I perchance be welcome?"

"Since when do you have to ask? Would you like me to fire up the sauna?"

"Yes, indeed. I can't think of anything much nicer."

"Well, *I* certainly can. But we'll discuss *that* when you get here. Drive defensively, now, I'm sure the roads are very icy. . . ."

❖

". . . I'll bet he spells his name with two els," Nora was saying around a voracious bite of freshly fried doughnut in the Calico Coffee Shop just outside Gananoque, Ontario. "That's what he's going to grow, whenever necessary. That man is a survivor. . . ."

Eric had just finished retelling what he'd seen from the back of the hayloft before their sudden departure.

"Well, I hope Suzanne got away—even if she was dishonest with me, and I can't help feeling just a bit *used*. . . ."

Nora looked anything but *used*, Simon thought; he'd never seen her quite so radiant as she'd been ever since she'd caught a brief snatch of commentary as she finally woke up—some jerk quoting the government version with full approval and conviction, that Jake hadn't actually managed to do anything. She'd immediately begun to smile, and quit paying attention to the nonstop news coming out of the Plymouth's radio. Eric also appeared not to have a care in the world this morning. Both were chattering away now as if it had been a simply wonderful little adventure—starring the two of them, of course. Whenever Nora remembered another instance of *his* derring-do, he praised her fancy crutch-work again, in knocking that M16 out of Gil's grasp. . . .

Well, okay, some people get the giggles at funerals, too—and I *am* viewing everything and everybody through piss-colored glasses this morning, Simon admitted to himself. They actually were yellow-tinted, since he'd cracked his clear pair in the Bonanza yesterday. He'd taken a triple dose of painkillers forty minutes ago, but his ribs and clavicle were still throbbing like he couldn't believe, and he itched like crazy everywhere under all that adhesive tape—which he wasn't supposed to peel off for at least another week. His head was still humming, too, from the shock of waking to find they were already *at* the border, and a beefy Canadian customs man was glancing through the fistful of ID that Eric had handed him, and in at each disheveled one of them in turn—then grinning and passing everything back and waving them on through without so much as a glance in the trunk, just some jolly crack about it being "too cold for smuggling."

Simon had long since given up trying to catch what was coming out of the radio on the counter behind him. He couldn't make any sense out of the gobbledy-gook they'd been spouting about Jake, and he couldn't make up his mind whether Jake had managed to pull it off or not—or whether it really mattered, if he had or hadn't. And Jake himself already seemed . . . so dead and gone, so long ago. . . .

They hadn't any of them known what the hell they were really doing, as it turned out. As a matter of fact, they'd fucked up all over the place, just like the you-know-who—but they'd certainly shook 'em up, and that couldn't be bad. It'd have to be done again, though, again and again, other times and places. Not what Jake did, no more ploot, thanks, and no more Gils, for sure—nothing violent at all, necessarily. Just keep letting 'em know: we're still out here, we're *not* gonna go away. We're down here behind the footlights, and *you're* up there on the stage. We can always get at you when you least expect it, but you can't spot us so well. So you'd better listen up, and listen good!

And either it'd work or it wouldn't. And sure, it was almost certainly too damn late already; but it *was* something to do with the time remaining, a hell of a lot better than sitting on his hands, feeling guilty as well as hopeless. In any case, as he'd always known deep down, he wasn't cut out to be a businessman. . . .

This had been Simon's basic attitude before the event as well, but there'd been a much brighter cast to it all until yesterday. It wasn't as if he hadn't expected there'd be days like this in the life of a . . . what was he now, anyway? He knew what *they*'d call him, what they were calling Jake already—"Eco-Terrorist!"—and he objected strenuously. *Not* terror, goddamn it, we don't even wanna hurt anybody. We just wanna put the fear of God—of Gaia, rather—into 'em . . . eco-boogie-man, maybe? No, wait, that's racist, unfortunately, sexist as well . . . what was that James Whitcomb Riley line he'd loved so much as a kid?

"The gobble-uns'll get *you*, if you——don't——watch——out!"

That didn't get it, either . . . well, he'd known there'd be bad times ahead, when nothing would look feasible, endurable, or even worthwhile. Mountains were like that, too. He hadn't expected to hit one of those days so early on, that's all. . . .

In any case, time to be on the road again. He'd called from Binghamton last night while he was waiting and had managed (at a stiff additional charge) to get their Air Portugal reservations changed to this evening, and he didn't want them to miss this one, as well. And before they boarded, they had to arrange some safe way to send all that cash on ahead to the next place they'd be for a while, and put Nora on a Dulles-bound flight.

If she could use the passport Eric had found in the glove compartment again, that they figured Gil must've obtained for Suzanne ("Sondrella Lipschitz," it said, and the photo didn't look in the least like either of them), then there'd be no record of Nora Sherman being anywhere on earth since Sunday night. And maybe she could give 'em the old amnesia routine—if anyone could hope to get away with a hoary chestnut like that one, it was Nora . . . Simon signaled for the check, paid it, tucked the locally correct tip under his saucer, a-hemmed, looked at his watch, drummed with three fingers on the tabletop, and still neither of them paid him any attention. They'd come back around to Gil, it sounded like:

". . . I know who he is, really," Nora said, clearly believing herself the first ever to make this identification: "He's the Gingerbread Man! 'Yah, yah, yah, you can't catch me!'"

"— And who am I?" Eric asked—not slyly, exactly, but unlike any Eric Simon had heard before.

"You?" Nora pursed her lips and knit her brow, thought hard for a moment, then flashed her famous grin. "You're the Playboy of the Western Wor-r-rld, you are," she brogued, "'for you've turned a likely gaffer at the end of all, the way you'll go romancing through a romping lifetime from this hour to the dawning of the judgment day.'"

Eric had no idea where that speech came from, but it sounded good. He figured that "judgment day" could very well be tomorrow, for himself if not the whole ballgame, but he fully intended to romp while he could. He had only a vague notion of the plans Simon had made for them both and little preference so far as their immediate itinerary was concerned, but he'd begun to feel some excitement at the general idea of more travel. He figured there must be a lot more world out there worth looking at and living in, while it lasted. . . .

❖

Mr. Roosevelt Edwards had not gone to work this morning. He hadn't called in with an excuse, either; he was not about to tell anyone any lies. He understood that his absence without notice might very well direct suspicion his way. All the better, he felt; let events take their course, he was ready. He'd eaten his immutable breakfast of cornflakes with condensed milk and whole-wheat toast with peanut butter, he'd drunk his single daily cup of coffee, he'd washed the dishes and put them back up on the closet shelf.

He was wearing his suit pants and one of his two stiff white shirts. No tie yet; it and his suitcoat were both draped carefully over a wire hanger on the nail in the back of his door where he could don them on his way out. He assumed they would allow him that much time. He'd also (though he wasn't sure he'd be able to take it with him) gone downstairs and gotten his saxophone from its usual place of safe-keeping with his landlady, who never left her apartment and was noted throughout the neighborhood for owning a double-barreled shotgun and not hesitating to use it. And he'd put some reeds to soak when he'd come home from work last night.

He sat on his chair beside his kitchen table and gazed around his room. It looked even neater than usual, due in part to the half-hour he'd spent straightening it up this morning, but primarily because he'd returned every library book he'd had out on loan—including one that had been due before Halloween, but had slipped unaccountably down behind a row of his own books on the shelf above his bed. It was the slimmest of the half-dozen he'd been told might contain the answer to the question of how much space a pound of greenhouse gases would occupy; but none had held a clue ... so he'd asked Mr. Blake, the second time they met, if *he* could say, since he seemed very knowledgeable about scientific matters. And Simon had replied, Well, as with so many things, there isn't any straightforward answer: it depends on the temperature and the air pressure, or the altitude, when and where you measured it. That seemed reasonable; but when Roosevelt had gone on to ask, "From how little to how big, though? How many bushels or pecks?" Simon had looked uncomfortable, finally saying that he'd want to check back over some article he'd read a while ago before making any guesses, however rough ... but then neither of them had brought up the subject again.

Actually, Roosevelt wasn't *quite* ready for them yet. There was someone else he very much hoped would arrive first. He'd found an Attempt To Deliver notice in his mailbox yesterday, and he'd phoned the number printed on it and told the recording, after the beep, that he would definitely be home this morning. It could, of course, be something other than what he expected, something he didn't even want, but he doubted that. He received very little mail, as a rule.

As soon as he'd finished cleaning his room, he'd taken a quick shower down at the end of the hall before getting into his Sunday clothes. While shaving in the communal bathroom there afterward, he'd overheard fragments of news from somebody's TV in the room next door. (He didn't own one of those things, not even a radio anymore—his son Kennedy had given him a very nice radio/tapedeck for his fiftieth birthday, but of course it had been stolen the next time his room was broken into.)

He'd felt sorry for Mr. Jacobsen at first, but then he'd thought, perhaps that was the way Mr. Jacobsen had wanted it. But it was a good thing that he'd happened to hear some of what they were saying about what Mr. Jacobsen had done: otherwise he might have burnt the entire notebook, as he'd been asked to do.

He'd read everything in it last night, and then very carefully, over his enamel washbasin, reduced each page to ash with one of the Bic lighters he was always finding in the course of his janitorial duties— all but the entry now lying over there beside his homburg and his saxophone case on top of his bureau. Yes, he'd agreed about the rest of the notebook; there had been very little in there that would've helped the general public to understand. Many entries were simply illegible, others were full of four-letter words, and the rest of it was, well, simply . . . too personal, in Mr. Edwards' opinion.

That passage, though—he would have liked it a lot better with one word deleted and proper spelling and punctuation throughout, but it had a sincere tone, he felt, and possibly it might correct some of the misapprehensions apparently becoming accepted as the truth, if only he could get it into the right hands. He still had the stamped envelope addressed to the news desk at the *Post* that Mr. Jacobsen had given him last week. Yes, perhaps he should—but before he tucked the two small pages in there, he read them through once more:

> I want to try to say a few words directly to those people who are going to be in that Chamber tomorrow night. I'd like to tell them I'm sorry— it's true, I am, I've stood in those shoes, after all. Many, I'm sure, are decent people at heart, who mean as well as I do. Some are as innocent as anybody in this day and age can be: there'll be wives and kids, and all those young pages . . . I wish to God I could be more selective, some- how—but I *am* being as selective as I *can* be; there is *no* other gathering, anywhere, of so many of those who *could* turn things around, if they can only be made to see how crucial it is that things *be* turned around, beginning *right now. . . .*
>
> It's not as if they're unaware of what's been going down, these people who could. They couldn't help but know, if they read newspapers or watch TV. The problem must be that none of it's happened to *them* yet. Somebody, somehow, has got to make them understand: You live on the same damn planet as all the rest of us victims. You *can't* be allowed to continue deluding your- selves that it won't happen to you and yours, as well, sooner or later. Otherwise, you'll *never* do

anything that might curtail anybody's almighty
right to turn a quick dollar. You've *gotta* realize,
we're *all* at risk here . . . and if this deliberate,
restrained shortening of those relatively few
human lives tomorrow night has any chance at
all of accomplishing this awakening, then I can
only believe that I am fully justified—

As he was licking the flap, Mr. Edwards heard footsteps downstairs on the front porch. He looked out his window, saw the mail truck at the curb, and ran down there as quickly as he could, knowing that the door-bell didn't work. The parcel was larger and heavier than he'd expected, and in his excitement he almost didn't remember Jake's envelope. The self-important young Asian postwoman didn't accept it with a very good grace, but accept it she finally did, as he returned her pen and the slip she made him sign.

He went back up the stairs two at time, laid the package on his bed, and cut away all the tape with his penknife, to find forty-eight copies of "The Golden Trumpet of Kennedy Edwards" in plain white sleeves— that's what was scribbled with a green felt tip on the slip of pink paper that fell out when he picked them up, one at a time, looking for covers. There weren't any covers, no labels either, on any of the discs, and there was no other message anywhere. Even so, he was very pleased. But he wished he had a phonograph, he'd love to hear what it actually sounded like . . . and he hoped they'd take good care of the photo he'd lent to Miss Stroehlengutt for the cover design—it was Kennedy's high school graduation picture, the only copy he had.

Very well, then. Roosevelt went over to the bureau, selected a reed from the glass, and snapped open his saxophone case. Since he couldn't listen to Kennedy, he'd just have to blow a little himself while he was waiting for them.

He hoped it wouldn't disturb any of his neighbors unduly—but he had to celebrate somehow!

— THE END —

A 1960s political activist, 1970s homesteader, founding editor of *Win Magazine*, and recipient of the War Resisters League's 1993 Peace Award, **PAUL JOHNSON** now lives with his wife, Frances, in Brooklyn, New York, where he supports his writing habit with freelance carpentry and copyediting. A previous novel, *Killing the Blues*, was published in 1987. His articles, shorter fiction, and reviews have appeared in such places as *The New York Times*, *The Chicago Herald-Tribune*, *Evergreen Review*, *Saturday Review*, *Upriver/Downriver*, *Zero*, *Small Press Review*, *Athanor*, *Place*, *Natural Lifestyles*, *The Nonviolent Activist*, *In These Times*, and *New Mexico Review*.